WELCOME TO
THE WORLD OF UNICORNS

Julie's Unicorn (Peter S. Beagle) * *Sea Dreams* (Kevin J. Anderson & Rebecca Moesta) * *The Same But Different* (Janet Berliner) * *Seven for a Secret* (Charles de Lint) * *The Brew* (Karen Joy Fowler) * *Mirror of Lop Nor* (George Guthridge) * *The Hunt of the Unicorn* (Ellen Kushner) * *Winter Requiem* (Michael Marano) * *A Rare Breed* (Elizabeth Ann Scarborough) * *A Plague of Unicorns* (Robert Sheckley) * *Survivor* (Dave Smeds) * *A Thief in the Night* (S. P. Somtow) * *Half-Grandma* (Melanie Tem) * *Three Duets for Virgin and Nosehorn* (Tad Williams) * *We Blazed* (Dave Wolverton)

Peter S. Beagle's

IMMORTAL UNICORN

VOLUME TWO

Edited by

Peter S. Beagle

and

Janet Berliner

HarperPrism

A Division of HarperCollinsPublishers

HarperPrism
A Division of HarperCollins*Publishers*
10 East 53rd Street, New York, NY 10022-5299

This is a work of fiction. The characters, incidents, and dialogues are
products of the authors' imagination and are not to be construed as
real. Any resemblance to actual events or persons, living or dead, is
entirely coincidental.

Individual story copyrights appear on pages 443–444.

ISBN 0-06-105929-3

HarperCollins®, ☷®, and HarperPrism® are trademarks of
HarperCollins Publishers Inc.

Cover design © 1999 by Richard Rossiter
Cover illustration © 1999 by Michael Sabanosh

A hardcover edition of this book was published
in 1995 by HarperPrism.

First paperback printing: May 1999

Printed in the United States of America

Visit HarperPrism on the World Wide Web at
http://www.harperprism.com

❖ 10 9 8 7 6 5 4 3 2 1

Acknowledgments

The editors wish to thank both Harpers—Laurie Harper of Sebastian Agency and HarperPrism—for their support and enthusiasm, and Martin H. Greenberg, arguably the world's most renowned anthologist, for his advice and confidence. And, as always, there's the (mostly) unflappable "Cowboy Bob," Robert L. Fleck, without whose assistance this volume would probably still be in the pipelines. They wish to thank each other for keeping every promise made, the most important one being: "We're going to have fun, stay friends, and create something unique."

Peter sends his special love and gratitude to his wife, Padma Hejmadi.

Yet one more time, Janet Berliner extends unending love, affection, and gratitude to Laurie Harper for all of the long hours she put in, the countless conversations, and her invaluable input; to Bob Fleck, her personal assistant; her feisty mother, Thea Cowan; her daughter, Stefanie Gluckman; and her mentor and friend, Dr. Samuel Draper. You'll love *these* stories, Sam. To paraphrase, methinks that, "Age shall not wither them, nor custom stale their infinite variety."

CONTENTS

Preface

As Peter has written in his foreword to this volume, the range and literacy of the stories we collected is nothing short of mind-boggling. Clearly, the theme of immortality, together with the symbol of the unicorn, tapped a vein in the writers we approached. For that I am extremely grateful.

More clearly, and this is something which Peter-the-modest would never say himself, they would not dare to have given us anything but their very best, their unique efforts. Some of them know him well and are old friends; all of them stand in awe of his modesty and his talent.

I first met Peter more than fifteen years ago, at a writers conference in Los Altos Hills, California. Of course I didn't know it was Peter, as I stood near the campus swimming pool on that hot summer's day, eaveswatching a man who looked like a bearded Jewish magician converse with a shaggy mongrel.

"I talk to dogs, you know," the magician said, when he noticed my presence. "And they answer me." Addressing, I suspect, the skepticism on my face, he said, "Look, I'll prove it. I'll tell the dog to jump in the pool, swim across, get out at the other side, and then walk around the pool back here." He turned to the dog. "What's your name?"

"So you've trained your dog," I said. "Terrific."

"This isn't my dog. I've never seen it before in my life."

The dog obeyed, I became a believer, and Peter S. Beagle—converser with dogs—and I have been friends ever since.

Before I left the campus that Sunday, I had purchased copies of two of Peter's books, *A Fine and Private Place* and *The Last Unicorn*. Those dog-eared, well-read copies have gone with me on every journey. I have long wanted to find a project that would enchant us both. It is my particular joy to have been the instrument that has reunited Peter with the unicorn.

As for the theme of immortality, it too comes directly from Peter's soul. One of the many things I have admired in him over the years is his insistence upon keeping in touch with old, "forgotten" writers. Those who perhaps wrote one opus, and then hid away, thinking themselves unloved and unremembered. It is he who consistently reminds them that, though they may not be immortal in the physical sense, the words they have created are.

I can't tell which I love most, the heart of the man or his incredible talent; I can tell you that it's been a true joy putting this book together with him.

Thank you, Peter.

—Janet Berliner
Las Vegas, Nevada
April 1, 1995

FOREWORD

—◦◦◦◦◦—

. . . and great numbers of unicorns, hardly
smaller than an elephant in size. Their hair is like
that of a buffalo, and their feet like those of an
elephant. In the middle of their forehead is a very
large black horn. Their head is like that of a wild
boar, and is always carried bent to the ground.
They delight in living in mire and mud. It is a
hideous beast to look at, and in no way like what
we think and say in our countries, namely a beast
that lets itself be taken in the lap of a virgin.
Indeed, I assure you that it is altogether different
from what we fancied . . .

—Marco Polo

In the first place, I blame Janet Berliner for everything. This book was her idea from the beginning: she did
the vast bulk of the editing, the telephoning, and all the
other grunt work; and if you like *Immortal Unicorn*, it's
mostly Janet's doing. If you don't like it, I'm covered.

In the second place, I could happily live out the rest
of my time on the planet without ever having another
thing to do with unicorns. Through what I persist in
regarding as no fault of my own—my children were
enjoying the chapters as I read them aloud, so I just kept
going—I've been stuck with the beasts for some twenty-

seven years now. First begun in 1962, published in 1968 (worlds and worlds ago, in a culture that measures time by elections and Super Bowls), *The Last Unicorn* is the book people know who don't know that I ever wrote anything else. Never a best-seller, never so much as a reliable annuity, it's been translated into fourteen languages, made into an animated film, and dramatized in half a dozen versions. People have written wonderfully kind and moving letters to me about it over the last twenty-seven years. I ran out of shyly spontaneous replies around 1980, I think it was.

But what amazed me as these stories began to come in is the eternal command the unicorn retains over the human imagination. Whether they turn up in the classic tapestry guises of Susan Shwartz's Arthurian tale, "The Tenth Worthy," or Nancy Willard's poignant variation, "The Trouble with Unicorns"; as dangerously attainable passions, in such works as P. D. Cacek's "Gilgamesh Recidivus" or Michael Armstrong's "Old One-Antler"; or as a source of karmic aggravation and cranky wonder to a rural community in Annie Scarborough's delightful "A Rare Breed," the damn things continue somehow to evoke astonishingly varied visions of soul-restoring beauty, indomitable freedom, and a strange, wild compassion, as well as the uncompromised mystery and elusiveness without which no legend can ever survive. Bigfoot, Nessie, Butch and Sundance, the unicorn . . . they leave footprints and dreams, but never their bones.

The title of this book has far less to do with physical immortality than with the unicorn's wondrously enduring presence in some twilight corner of our human DNA. From the European horned horse or dainty goat/deer hybrid to the ferocious, rhinoceros-like *karkadann* of Persia, India, and North Africa, to the Chinese *k'i-lin,* whose rare appearances either celebrated a just reign or portended the death of a great personage, there are surprisingly few mythologies in which the unicorn, or something very like it, does not turn up. India was the great medieval source of unicorn sightings; but over the centuries there have been accounts out of Japan, Tibet, Siberia, Ethiopia (Pliny the Elder and his contemporaries had a distinct tendency to stash any slightly questionable marvel in Ethiopia), Scandinavia, South Africa, and even Canada and Maine. Entirely regardless of whether they exist or not, something in us, as human beings, seems always to have needed them to be.

(It's worth mentioning that men have for centuries been manipulating the horn buds of cattle, sheep, and goats to produce a one-horned animal—with evident success, if that's your idea of success. Judith Tarr's story, "Dame à la Licorne," deals movingly and realistically with an eminently believable version of this ancient practice. But horns don't make the unicorn; it's the other way around.)

The possibility that unicorns might need humans just as much, in their own way, is well worth a moment's consideration. In *Through The Looking Glass,* after all, Lewis Carroll's unicorn says to Alice, ". . . Now we have seen each other, if you'll believe in me, I'll believe in you. Is that a bargain?" And there is a very old fable which holds that the unicorn was the first animal named by Adam and Eve, and that when they were barred from Paradise the unicorn chose to follow them into the bitter mortal world, to share their suffering there, and their joys as well. You might think about that legend when reading Robert Devereaux's story "What the Eye Sees, What the Heart Feels."

I've indicated earlier that I find the diversity of these stories as exceptional as their quality. What I expected (and after twenty-seven years of being sent cuddly stuffed unicorns, so would you) was an embarrassment of wistfulness, a plethora of dreamy elegies to metaphoric innocence betrayed, and a whole lot of rip-offs equally of *The Glass Menagerie* and the unicorn hunt scene in T. H. White's *The Once and Future King*. I couldn't have been more wrong.

The bulk of the tales in this book focus more on the power, and at times the genuine ferocity and aggressiveness of the unicorn—which is far more in keeping with the mythological record—than on its vulnerability. They range in setting from Lisa Mason's turn-of-the-century San Francisco to Eric Lustbader's all too contemporary Bedford-Stuyvesant district, to Cacek's Siberia, George Guthridge's linked Mongolia and Arctic Circle, Karen Joy Fowler's 1950s Indiana, Will Shetterly's nineteenth century American Southwest, Janet's own South Africa, and Dave Smeds's scarifying wartime Vietnam. Their tone cuts across a remarkable spectrum of action, style, and emotion, at one end of which we may with confidence place Robert Sheckley's quietly and profoundly flaky "A Plague of Unicorns." Somewhere in the middle we find Melanie Tem's tender and haunting "Half-Grandma," Fowler's "The Brew," Marina Fitch's lovely "Stampede of Light," Kevin Anderson and Rebecca Moesta's "Sea Dreams," Shetterly's "Taken He Cannot Be" (which swept away my grim resistance to reading one more flipping word about Wyatt, Doc, and the O.K.

Corral), and Lucy Taylor's "Convergence"—stories less about unicorns *per se* than about generosity, courage, loneliness, love, and letting go: all immortal realities embodied by those aggravating creatures I appear to be stuck with. A little way along, a splendidly unique fantasy like Mason's "Daughter of the Tao" shades into "Dame à la Licorne," science fiction in the best sense of the term. (Incidentally, no man would have been likely to produce that one, by the way—I speak as the father of two daughters.)

Tad Williams' elegantly original "Three Duets for Virgin and Nosehorn" fits comfortably on the near side of "Daughter of the Tao," as does my own "Professor Gottesman and the Indian Rhinoceros." I'm honored to be in such company, and pleased that we've done our bit to restore the glamour (in the old Celtic sense of enchantment) of a noble beast, maligned and derided from Marco Polo through Hemingway and Ionesco. (Ionesco, by the way, had never seen a rhinoceros when he wrote the play that made the word a synonym for insane conformity. Introduced to two at the Zurich Zoo, I was once told he studied the creatures for a long while, and finally bowed formally, saying, "I have been deceived, and I apologize." Then he shook his walking stick at them and shouted, "But you are not real rhinoceroses!")

At the furthest end of the book's reach stalk Lustbader's "The Devil on Myrtle Ave.," Smeds's "Survivor," Michael Marano's "Winter Requiem," George Guthridge's "Mirror of Lop Nor," and S. P. Somtow's astonishing "A Thief in the Night." These are violent stories, as much or more in tone and vision as in action; and in these, too, unicorns as unicorns are less crucial than the central characters. The unicorn of "Winter Requiem" is a demon, plain and simple; the one literally depicted in "Survivor" is nothing more than a tattoo on a soldier's chest; while Somtow's unicorn is a shadow, a hoofprint, only seen fully for a moonlit moment at the end of this encounter between the Messiah and a strangely sympathetic Antichrist on the boardwalk at California's Venice Beach. For that matter, the unicorns of "Sea Dreams" are narwhals, the steeds of undersea princes in a young girl's fairy tale; in Dave Wolverton's "We Blazed," there is no immortal beast at all, but a rock singer searching for his wife through the universe of her dreams. You won't find these unicorns up at the Cloisters museum, but you may very well recognize them all the same.

Strangers still ask me whether I believe in unicorns, really. I don't, not at all, not in the way they usually mean. But I do believe—still, knowing so much better—in everything the unicorn has always represented to human beings: the vision of deep strength allied to deep wisdom, of pride dwelling side by side with patience and humility, of unspeakable beauty inseparable from the "pity beyond all telling" that Yeats said was hidden at the heart of love. Even in my worst moments, when I am most sickened by the truly limitless bone-bred cruelty and stupidity of the species I belong to, I know these things exist. I have seen them, and once or twice they have laid their heads in my lap. In their very different manners, the stories in this book—altogether different indeed from what we fancied—express this old, foolish, lovely dream of the unicorn.

As I said at the beginning, any praise for *Immortal Unicorn* rightfully belongs to Janet Berliner. Me, I'm happy to be what used to be called, in the New York City garment trade, the "puller-in"—the guy who stood right outside the store and literally yanked people off the sidewalk, you absolutely got to see what we got here for you, fit you like custom-made. Not all of these tales may fit the unicorn of your imagining; but come inside anyway, come in out of the flat, painful sunlight of our time, blink around you for a bit, and see what might almost be moving and shining in the cool shadows.

—Peter S. Beagle
Davis, California
March 25, 1995

PETER S. BEAGLE

JULIE'S UNICORN

Janet: There comes a time in all of our lives when we feel
the urge to look up old friends and see what they've been
doing. Sometimes, it's a dreadful bore; our old friends
seem much less interesting than we remember them. Other
times, it's as if no time at all has passed.

When you're a writer, those old friends can be your
characters. Peter told me when we talked about what he
should do as his story for this paperback edition, "I had
fun going back and revisiting the people and the world
from *The Innkeeper's Song* for *Giant Bones*. Maybe I can
do something like that again." The friends he visits this
time are from one book further back, Julie and Farrell
from *Folk of the Air*.

Recently, someone asked me to name my favorite
Peter Beagle story. "The last one I read," I answered without hesitation. "Julie's Unicorn" is now the last one I
read. My answer remains true. "Julie's Unicorn" is a
charming tale, just sentimental enough, just thoughtful
enough, just contemporary enough. This man, this col-
league, this buddy of mine, keeps getting better. Enjoy. I
know that you will.

Julie's Unicorn

THE NOTE CAME WITH THE ENTREE, TUCKED NEATLY under the zucchini slices but carefully out of range of the seafood crepes. It said, in the unmistakable handwriting that any graphologist would have ascribed to a serial killer, "Tanikawa, ditch the dork and get in here." Julie took her time over the crepes and the spinach salad, finished her wine, sampled a second glass, and then excused herself to her dinner partner, who smiled and propped his chin on his fingertips, prepared to wait graciously, as assistant professors know how to do. She turned right at the telephones, instead of left, looked back once and walked through a pair of swinging half-doors into the restaurant kitchen.

The heat thumped like a fist between her shoulder blades, and her glasses fogged up immediately. She took them off, put them in her purse, and focused on a slender, graying man standing with his back to her as he instructed an earnest young woman about shiitake mushroom stew. Julie said loudly, "Make it quick, Farrell. The dork thinks I'm in the can."

The slender man said to the young woman, "Gracie, tell Luis the basil's losing its marbles, he can put in more oregano if he wants. Tell him to use his own judgment about the lemongrass—I like it myself." Then he turned, held out his arms and said, "Jewel. Think you strung it out long enough?"

"My dessert's melting," Julie said into his apron. The arms around her felt as comfortably usual as an old sofa, and she lifted her head quickly to demand, "God damn it, where have you been? I have had very strange phone conversations with some very strange people in the last five years, trying to track you down. What the hell happened to you, Farrell?"

"What happened to me? Two addresses and a fax number I gave you, and nothing. Not a letter, not so much as a postcard from East Tarpit-on-the-Orinoco, hi, marrying tribal chieftain tomorrow, wish you were here. But just as glad you're not. The story of this relationship."

Julie stepped back, her round, long-eyed face gone as pale as it ever got. Almost in a whisper, she asked, "How did you know? Farrell, how did you know?" The young cook was staring at them both in fascination bordering on religious rapture.

"What?" Farrell said, and now he was gaping like the cook, his own voice snagging in his throat. "You did? You got married?"

"It didn't last. Eight months. He's in Boston."

"That explains it." Farrell's sudden bark of laughter made Gracie the cook jump slightly. "By God, that explains it."

"Boston? Boston explains what?"

"You didn't want me to know," Farrell said. "You really didn't want me to know. Tanikawa, I'm ashamed of you. I am."

Julie started to answer him, then nodded toward the

entranced young cook. Farrell said, "Gracie, about the curried peas. Tell Suzanne absolutely not to add the mango pickle until just before the peas are done, she always puts it in too early. If she's busy, you do it—go, go." Gracie, enchanted even more by the notion of getting her hands into actual food, fled, and Farrell turned back to face Julie. "Eight months. I've known you to take longer over a lithograph."

"He's a very nice man," she answered him. "No, damn it, that sounds terrible, insulting. But he is."

Farrell nodded. "I believe it. You always did have this deadly weakness for nice men. I was an aberration."

"No, you're my friend," Julie said. "You're my friend, and I'm sorry, I should have told you I was getting married." A waiter's loaded tray caught her between the shoulderblades just as a busboy stepped on her foot, and she was properly furious this time. "I didn't tell you because I knew you'd do exactly what you're doing now, which is look at me like that and imply that you know me better than anyone else ever possibly could, which is not true, Farrell. There are all kinds of people you don't even know who know things about me you'll never know, so just knock it off." She ran out of breath and anger more or less simultaneously. She said, "But somehow you've gotten to be my oldest friend, just by goddamn attrition. I missed you, Joe."

Farrell put his arms around her again. "I missed you. I worried about you. A whole lot. The rest can wait." There came a crash and a mad bellow from the steamy depths of the kitchen, and Farrell said, "Your dork's probably missing you too. That was the Table Fourteen dessert, sure as hell. Where can I call you? Are you actually back in Avicenna?"

"For now. It's always for now in this town." She wrote the address and telephone number on the back of the Tonight's Specials menu, kissed him hurriedly and left the kitchen. Behind her she heard another bellow, and then Farrell's grimly placid voice saying, "Stay cool, stay cool, big Luis, it's not the end of the world. Change your apron, we'll just add some more brandy. All is well."

It took more time than they were used to, even after more than twenty years of picking up, letting go and picking up again. The period of edginess and uncertainty about what questions to ask, what to leave alone, what might or might not be safe to assume, lasted until the autumn afternoon they went to the museum. It was Farrell's day off, and he drove Madame Schumann-Heink, his prehistoric Volkswagen van, over the hill from the bald suburb where he was condo-sitting for a friend and parked under a sycamore across from Julie's studio apartment. The building was a converted Victorian, miraculously spared from becoming a nest of suites for accountants and attorneys and allowed to decay in a decently tropical fashion, held together by jasmine and wisteria. He said to Julie, "You find trees, every time, shady places with big old trees. I've never figured how you manage it."

"Old houses," she said. "I always need work space and a lot of light, and only the old houses have it. It's a trade-off—plumbing for elbow room. Wait till I feed NMC." NMC was an undistinguished black and white cat who slept with six new kittens in a box underneath the tiny sink set into a curtained alcove. ("She likes to keep an eye on the refrigerator," Julie explained. "Just in case it tries to make a break for freedom.") She had shown up pregnant, climbing the stairs to scratch only at Julie's door, and sauntering in with an air of being specifically expected. The initials of her name stood for Not My Cat. Julie opened a can, set it down beside the box, checked to make sure that each kitten was securely attached to a nipple, briefly fondled a softly thrumming throat and told her, "The litter tray is two feet to your left. As if you care."

At the curb, gazing for a long time at Madame Schumann-Heink, she said, "This thing has become absolutely transparent, Joe, you know that. I can see the Bay right through it."

"Wait till you see her by moonlight," Farrell said. "Gossamer and cobwebs. The Taj Mahal of rust. Tell me again where the Bigby Museum is."

"North. East. In the hills. It's hard to explain. Take the freeway, I'll tell you where to turn off."

The Bigby City Museum had been, until fairly recently, Avicenna's nearest approach to a Roman villa. Together with its long, narrow reflecting pool and its ornamental gardens, it occupied an entire truncated hilltop from which, morning and evening, its masters—copper-mining kinglets—had seen the Golden Gate Bridge rising through the Bay mist like a Chinese dragon's writhing back. With the death of the last primordial Bigby, the lone heir had quietly sold the mansion to the city, set up its contents (primarily lesser works of the lesser Impressionists, a scattering of the Spanish masters, and the entire oeuvre of a Bigby who painted train stations) as a joint trust, and sailed away to a tax haven in the Lesser Antilles. Julie said there were a few early Brueghel oils and drawings worth the visit. "He was doing Bosch then—maybe forgeries, maybe not—and mostly you can't tell them apart. But with these you start seeing the real Brueghel, sort of in spite of himself. There's a good little Raphael too, but you'll hate it. An Annunciation, with *putti*."

"I'll hate it," Farrell said. He eased Madame Schumann-Heink over into the right-hand lane, greatly irritating a BMW, who honked at him all the way to the freeway. "Practically as much as I hate old whoever, the guy you married."

"Brian." Julie punched his shoulder hard. "His name is Brian, and he's a lovely, wonderful man, and I really do love him. We just shouldn't have gotten married. We both agreed on that."

"A damn Brian," Farrell said. He put his head out of the window and yelled back at the BMW, "She went and married a Brian, I ask you!" The BMW driver gave him the finger. Farrell said, "The worst thing is, I'd probably like him, I've got a bad feeling about that. Let's talk about something else. Why'd you marry him?"

Julie sighed. "Maybe because he was as far away from you as I could get. He's sane, he's stable, he's— okay, he's ambitious, nothing wrong with that—"

Farrell's immediate indignation surprised him as much as it did Julie. "Hey, I'm sane. All things considered. Weird is not wacko, there's a fine but definite line. And I'm stable as a damn lighthouse, or we'd never have stayed friends this long. Ambitious—okay, no, never, not really. Still cooking here and there, still playing a bit of obsolete music on obsolete instruments after hours. Same way you're still drawing cross sections of lungs and livers for medical students. What does old ambitious Brian do?"

"He's a lawyer." Julie heard herself mumbling, saw

the corner of Farrell's mouth twitch, and promptly flared up again. "And I don't want to hear one bloody word out of you, Farrell! He's not a hired gun for corporations, he doesn't defend celebrity gangsters. He works for non-profits, environmental groups, refugees, gay rights—he takes on so many pro bono cases, half the time he can't pay his office rent. He's a better person than you'll ever be, Farrell. Or me either. That's the damn, damn trouble." Her eyes were aching heavily, and she looked away from him.

Farrell put his hand gently on the back of her neck. He said, "I'm sorry, Jewel." Neither of them spoke after that until they were grinding slowly up a narrow street lined with old sycamore and walnut trees and high, furry old houses drowsing in the late-summer sun. Julie said, "I do a little word-processing, temp stuff," and then, in the same flat voice, "You never married anybody."

"Too old," Farrell said. "I used to be too young, or somebody was, I remember that. Now it's plain too late— I'm me, finally, all the way down, and easy enough with it, but I damn sure wouldn't marry me." He braked to keep from running over two cackling adolescents on skate-boards, then resumed the lumbering climb, dropping Madame Schumann-Heink into second gear, which was one of her good ones. Looking sideways, he said, "One thing anyway, you're still the prettiest Eskimo anybody ever saw."

"Get out of here," she answered him scornfully. "You saw an Eskimo that wasn't in some National Geographic special." Now she looked back at him, fighting a smile, and he touched her neck again, very lightly. "Well, I'm getting like that myself," she said. "Too old and too cranky to suit anybody but me. Turn right at the light, Joe."

The Bigby City Museum came upon them suddenly, filling the windshield just after the last sharp curve, as they rolled slightly downward into a graveled parking lot which had once been an herb garden. Farrell parked facing the Bay, and the two of them got out and stood silently on either side of Madame Schumann-Heink, staring away at the water glittering in the western sun. Then they turned, each with an odd, unspoken near-reluctance, to face the Museum. It would have been a beautiful building, Julie thought, in another town. It was three stories high, cream white, with a flat tile roof the color of red wine. Shadowed on three sides by cypress trees, camellia bushes softening the rectitude of the corners, a dancing-dolphin fountain chuckling in the sunny courtyard, and the white and peach rose gardens sloping away from the reflecting pool, it was a beautiful house, but one that belonged in Santa Barbara, Santa Monica or Malibu, worlds and wars, generations and elections removed from silly, vain, vainly perverse Avicenna. Farrell finally sighed and said, "Power to the people, hey," and Julie said, "*A bas les aristos*," and they went inside. The ticketseller and the guest book were on the first floor, the Brueghels on the second. Julie and Farrell walked up a flowing mahogany stairway hung with watercolors from the Southwestern period of the train-station Bigby. On the landing Farrell looked around judiciously and announced, "Fine command of plastic values, I'll say that," to which Julie responded, "Oh, no question, but those spatio-temporal vortices, I don't know." They laughed together, joined hands and climbed the rest of the way.

There were ten or twelve other people upstairs in the huge main gallery. Most were younger than Farrell and Julie, with the distinct air of art students on assignment, their eyes flicking nervously from the Brueghels to their fellows to see whether anyone else had caught the trick, fathomed the koan, winkled out the grade points that must surely be hiding somewhere within those depictions of demon priests and creatures out of anchorite nightmares. When Julie took a small pad out of her purse, sat down on a couch and began copying certain corners and aspects of the paintings, the students were eddying silently toward her within minutes, just in case she knew. Farrell winked at her and wandered off toward a wall of train stations. Julie never looked up.

More quickly than she expected, he was back, leaning over her shoulder, his low voice in her hair. "Jewel. Something you ought to see. Right around the corner."

The corner was actually a temporary wall, just wide and high enough to hold three tapestries whose placard described them as "... mid-fifteenth century, artist unknown, probably from Bruges." The highest tapestry, done in the terrifyingly detailed millefleurs style, showed several women in a rich garden being serenaded by a lute-player, and Julie at first thought that Farrell—a lutanist himself—must have meant her to look at this one. Then she saw the one below.

It was in worse shape than the upper tapestry, badly frayed all around the edges and darkly stained in a kind of rosette close to the center, which showed a knight presenting a unicorn to his simpering lady. The unicorn was small and bluish-white, with the cloven hooves, long neck and slender quarters of a deer The knight was leading it on a silvery cord, and his squire behind him was prodding the unicorn forward with a short stabbing lance. There was a soapbubble castle in the background, floating up out of a stylized broccoli forest. Julie heard herself say in a child's voice, "I don't like this."

"I've seen better," Farrell agreed. "Wouldn't have picked it as Bruges work myself." The lance was pricking the unicorn hard enough that the flesh dimpled around the point, and the unicorn's one visible eye, purple-black, was rolled back toward the squire in fear or anger. The knight's lady held a wreath of scarlet flowers in her extended right hand. Whether it was meant for the knight or the unicorn Julie could not tell.

"I wish you hadn't shown me this," she said. She turned and returned to the Brueghels, trying to recapture her focus on the sliver of canvas, the precise brushstroke, where the young painter could be seen to step away from his master. But time after time she was drawn back, moving blindly through the growing crowd to stare one more time at the shabby old imagining of beauty and theft before she took up her sketchpad again. At last she gave up any notion of work, and simply stood still before the tapestry, waiting patiently to grow numb to the unicorn's endless woven pain. The lady looked directly out at her, the faded smirk saying clearly, "Five hundred years. Five hundred years, and it is still going on, this very minute, all to the greater glory of God and courtly love."

"That's what you think," Julie said aloud. She lifted her right hand and moved it slowly across the tapestry, barely brushing the protective glass. As she did so, she spoke several words in a language that might have been Japanese, and was not. With the last syllable came a curious muffled jolt, like an underwater explosion, that thudded distantly through her body, making her step back and stagger against Farrell. He gripped her shoulders, saying, "Jewel, what the hell are you up to? What did you just do right then?"

"I don't know what you're talking about," she said, and for that moment it was true. She was oddly dizzy, and she could feel a headache coiling in her temples. "I didn't do anything, what could I do? What do you think I was doing, Joe?"

Farrell turned her to face him, his hands light on her shoulders now, but his dark-blue eyes holding her with an intensity she had rarely seen in all the years they had known each other. He said, "I remember you telling me about your grandmother's Japanese magic. I remember a night really long ago, and a goddess who came when you called her. It all makes me the tiniest bit uneasy."

The strange soft shock did not come again; the art students and the tourists went on drifting as drowsily as aquarium fish among the Brueghels; the figures in the tapestry remained exactly where they had posed for five centuries. Julie said, "I haven't done a damn thing." Farrell's eyes did not leave her face. "Not anything that made any difference, anyway," she said. She turned away and walked quickly across the gallery to examine a very minor Zurbaran too closely.

In time the notepad came back out of her purse, and she again began to copy those scraps and splinters of the Brueghels that held lessons or uses for her. She did not return to the unicorn tapestry. More time passed than she had meant to spend in the museum, and when Farrell appeared beside her she was startled at the stained pallor of the sky outside the high windows. He said, "You better come take a look. That was one hell of a grandmother you had."

She asked no questions when he took hold of her arm and led her—she could feel the effort it cost him not to drag her—back to the wall of tapestries. She stared at the upper one for a long moment before she permitted herself to understand.

The unicorn was gone. The knight and his squire remained in their places, silver cord hauling nothing forward, lance jabbing cruelly into helpless nothing. The lady went on smiling milkily, offering her flowers to nothingness. There was no change in any of their faces, no indication that the absence of the reason for their existence had been noticed at all. Julie stared and stared and said nothing.

"Let you out of my sight for five minutes," Farrell said. He was not looking at her, but scanning the floor in every direction. "All right, main thing's to keep him from getting stepped on. Check the corners—you do that side, I'll do all this side." But he was shaking his head even before he finished. "No, the stairs, you hit the stairs. If he gets down those stairs, that's it, we've lost him. Jewel, go!" He had not raised his voice at all, but the last words cracked like pine sap in fire.

Julie gave one last glance at the tapestry, hoping that the unicorn would prove not to be lost after all, but only somehow absurdly overlooked. But not so much as a dangling thread suggested that there had ever been any other figure in the frame. She said vaguely, "I didn't think it would work, it was just to be doing something," and sprang for the stairway.

By now the art students had been mostly replaced by nuzzling couples and edgy family groups. Some of them grumbled as Julie pushed down past them without a word of apology; a few others turned to gape when she took up a position on the landing, midway between a lost-contact-lens stoop and a catcher's crouch, looking from side to side for some miniature scurry, something like a flittering dust-kitten with a tiny blink at its brow . . . But will it be flesh, or only dyed yarn? and will it grow to full size, now it's out of the frame? Does it know, does it know it's free, or is it hiding in my shadow, in a thousand times more danger than when there was a rope around its neck and a virgin grinning at it? Grandma, what have we done?

Closing time, nearly, and full dark outside, and still no trace of the unicorn. Julie's heart sank lower with each person who clattered past her down the stairs, and each time the lone guard glanced at her, then at Farrell, and then pointedly wiped his snuffly nose. Farrell commandeered her notepad and prowled the floor, ostentatiously scrutinizing the Brueghels when he felt himself being scrutinized, but studying nothing but dim corners and alcoves the rest of the time. The museum lights were flicking on and off, and the guard had actually begun to say, "Five minutes to closing," when Farrell stopped moving, so suddenly that one foot was actually in the air. Sideways-on to Julie, so that she could not see what he saw, he slowly lowered his foot to the floor; very slowly he turned toward the stair; with the delicacy of a parent maneuvering among Legos, he navigated silently back to her. He was smiling as carefully as though he feared the noise it might make.

"Found it," he muttered. "Way in behind the coat

rack, there's a water cooler on an open frame. It's down under there."

"So what are you doing down here?" Julie demanded. Farrell shushed her frantically with his face and hands. He muttered, "It's not going anywhere, it's too scared to move. I need you to distract the guard for a minute. Like in the movies."

"Like in the movies." She sized up the guard: an over-age rent-a-cop, soft and bored, interested only in getting them out of the Museum, locking up and heading for dinner. "Right. I could start taking my clothes off, there's that. Or I could tell him I've lost my little boy, or maybe ask him what he thinks about fifteenth-century Flemish woodcuts. What are you up to now, Joe?"

"Two minutes," Farrell said. "At the outside. I just don't want the guy to see me grabbing the thing up. Two minutes and gone."

"Hey," Julie said loudly. "Hey, it is not a thing, and you will not grab it." She did lower her voice then, because the guard was glancing at his watch, whistling fretfully. "Joe, I don't know if this has sunk in yet, but a unicorn, a real unicorn, has been trapped in that miserable medieval scene for five centuries, and it is now hiding under a damn water cooler in the Bigby Museum in Avicenna, California. Does that begin to register at all?"

"Trouble," Farrell said. "All that registers is me being in trouble again. Go talk to that man."

Julie settled on asking with breathy shyness about the Museum's legendary third floor, always closed off to the public and rumored variously to house the secret Masonic works of Rembrandt, Goya's blasphemous sketches of Black Masses, certain Beardsley illustrations of de Sade, or merely faded pornographic snapshots of assorted Bigby mistresses. The guard's money was on forgeries: counterfeits donated to the city in exchange for handsome tax exemptions. "Town like this, a town full of art experts, specialists—well, you wouldn't want anybody looking at that stuff too close. Stands to reason."

She did not dare look to see what Farrell was doing. The guard was checking his watch again when he appeared beside her, his ancient bomber jacket already on, her coat over his arm. "On our way," he announced cheerfully; and, to the guard, "Sorry for the delay, we're out of here." His free right hand rested, casually but unmoving, on the buttonless flap of his side pocket.

They did not speak on the stairs, nor immediately outside in the autumn twilight. Farrell walked fast, almost pulling her along, until they reached the van. He turned there, his face without expression for a very long moment before he took her hand and brought it to his right coat pocket. Through the cracked leather under her fingers she felt a stillness more vibrant than any struggle could have been: a waiting quiet, making her shiver with a kind of fear and a kind of wonder that she had never known and could not tell apart. She whispered, "Joe, can it—are you sure it can breathe in there?"

"Could it breathe in that damn tapestry?" Farrell's voice was rough and tense, but he touched Julie's hand gently. "It's all right, Jewel. It stood there and looked at me, and sort of watched me picking it up. Let's get on back to your place and figure out what we do now."

Julie sat close to him on the way home, her hand firmly on his coat-pocket flap. She could feel the startlingly intense heat of the unicorn against her palm as completely as though there were nothing between them; she could feel the equally astonishing sharpness of the minute horn, and the steady twitch of the five-century-old heart. As intensely as she could, she sent the thought down her arm and through her fingers: we're going to help you, we're your friends, we know you, don't be afraid. Whenever the van hit a bump or a pothole, she quickly pressed her hand under Farrell's pocket to cushion the legend inside.

Sitting on her bed, their coats still on and kittens meowling under the sink for their absent mother, she said, "All right, we have to think this through. We can't keep it, and we can't just turn it loose in millennial California. What other options do we have?"

"I love it when you talk like a CEO," Farrell said. Julie glared at him. Farrell said, "Well, I'll throw this out to the board meeting. Could you and your grandmother possibly put the poor creature back where you got it? That's what my mother always told me to do."

"Joe, we can't!" she cried out. "We can't put it back into that world, with people capturing it, sticking spears into it for the glory of Christian virginity. I'm not going to do that, I don't care if I have to take care of it for the rest of my life, I'm not going to do that."

"You know you can't take care of it." Farrell took her hands, turned them over, and placed his own hands lightly on them, palm to palm. "As somebody quite properly reminded me a bit back, it's a unicorn."

"Well, we can just set it free." Her throat felt dry, and she realized that her hands were trembling under his. "We'll take it to the wildest national park we can get to— national wilderness, better, no roads, people don't go there—and we'll turn it loose where it belongs. Unicorns live in the wilderness, it would get on fine. It would be happy."

"So would the mountain lions," Farrell said. "And the coyotes and the foxes, and God knows what else. A unicorn the size of a pork chop may be immortal, but that doesn't mean it's indigestible. We do have a problem here, Jewel."

They were silent for a long time, looking at each other. Julie said at last, very quietly, "I had to, Joe. I just never thought it would work, but I had to try."

Farrell nodded. Julie was looking, not at him now, but at his coat pocket. She said, "If you put it on the table. Maybe it'll know we don't mean it any harm. Maybe it won't run away."

She leaned forward as Farrell reached slowly into his pocket, unconsciously spreading her arms to left and right, along the table's edge. But the moment Farrell's expression changed she was up and whirling to look in every direction, as she had done on the museum stair. The unicorn was nowhere to be seen. Neither was the cat NMC. The six kittens squirmed and squeaked blindly in their box, trying to suck each other's paws and ears.

Farrell stammered, "I never felt it—I don't know how . . ." and Julie said, "Bathroom, bathroom," and fled there, leaving him forlornly prowling the studio, with its deep, murky fireplace and antique shadows. He was still at it when she returned, empty-handed as he, and her wide eyes fighting wildness.

Very quietly, she said, "I can't find the cat. Joe, I'm scared, I can't find her."

NMC—theatrical as all cats—chose that moment to

saunter grandly between them, purring in throaty hiccups, with the unicorn limp between her jaws. Julie's gasp of horror, about to become a scream, was choked off by her realization that the creature was completely unharmed. NMC had it by the back of the neck, exactly as she would have carried one of her kittens, and the purple eyes were open and curiously tranquil. The unicorn's dangling legs—disproportionately long, in the tapestry, for its deerlike body—now seemed to Julie as right as a peach, or the nautilus coil inside each human ear. There was a soft, curling tuft under its chin, less like hair than like feathers, matched by a larger one at the end of its tail. Its hooves and horn had a faint pearl shine, even in the dim light.

Magnificently indifferent to Farrell and Julie's gaping, NMC promenaded to her box, flowed over the side, and sprawled out facing the kittens, releasing her grip on the unicorn's scruff as she did so. It lay passively, legs folded under it, as the squalling mites scrimmaged across their mother's belly. But when Farrell reached cautiously to pick it up, the unicorn's head whipped around faster than any cat ever dreamed of striking, and the horn scored the side of his right hand. Farrell yelped, and Julie said wonderingly, "It wants to be there. It feels comforted with them."

"The sweet thing," Farrell muttered, licking the blood from his hand. The unicorn was shoving its way in among NMC's kittens now: as Julie and Farrell watched, it gently nudged a foster brother over to a nipple next down from the one it had chosen, took the furry tap daintily into its mouth, and let its eyes drift shut. Farrell said it was purring. Julie heard no sound at all from the thin

blue-white throat, but she sat by the box long after Farrell
had gone home, watching the unicorn's flanks rise and
fall in the same rhythm as the kittens' breathing.

Surprisingly, the unicorn appeared perfectly content
to remain indefinitely in Julie's studio apartment, living
in an increasingly crowded cardboard box among six
growing kittens, who chewed on it and slept on it by
turns, as they chewed and slept on one another. NMC, for
her part, washed it at least twice as much as she bathed
any of the others ("To get rid of that nasty old medieval
smell," Farrell said), and made a distinct point of sleeping
herself with one forepaw plopped heavily across its body.
The kittens were not yet capable of climbing out of the
box—though they spent most of their waking hours in
trying—but NMC plainly sensed that her foster child
could come and go as easily as she. Yet, unlike its litter-
mates, the unicorn showed no interest in going anywhere
at all.

"Something's wrong," Farrell said after nearly a
week. "It's not acting properly—it ought to be wild to get
out, wild to be off about its unicorn business. Christ, what
if I hurt it when I picked it up in the museum?" His face
was suddenly cold and pale. "Jewel, I was so careful, I
don't know how I could have hurt it. But I bet that's it. I
bet that's what's wrong."

"No," she said firmly. "Not you. That rope around its
neck, that man with the spear, the look on that idiot
woman's face—there, there's the hurt, five hundred years
of it, five hundred frozen years of capture. Christ, Joe, let
it sleep as long as it wants, let it heal." They were standing together, sometime in the night, looking down at the
cat box, and she gripped Farrell's wrist hard.

"I knew right away," she said. "As soon as I saw it, I knew it wasn't just a religious allegory, a piece of a composition. I mean, yes, it was that too, but it was real, I could tell. Grandma could tell." NMC, awakened by their voices, looked up at them, yawning blissfully, round orange eyes glowing with secrets and self-satisfaction. Julie said, "There's nothing wrong with it that being out of that damn tapestry won't cure. Trust me, I was an art major."

"Shouldn't it be having something beside cat milk?" Farrell wondered. "I always figured unicorns lived on honey and—I don't know. Lilies, morning dew. Tule fog."

Julie shook her head against his shoulder. "Serenity," she said. Her voice was very low. "I think they live on serenity, and you can't get much more serene than that cat. Let's go to bed."

"Us? Us old guys?" Farrell was playing absently with her black hair, fanning his fingers out through it, tugging very gently. "You think we'll remember how it's done?"

"Don't get cute," she said, harshly enough to surprise them both. "Don't get cute, Farrell, don't get all charming. Just come to bed and hold me, and keep me company, and keep your mouth shut for a little while. You think you can manage that?"

"Yes, Jewel," Farrell said. "It doesn't use the litter box, did you notice?"

Julie dreamed of the unicorn that night. It had grown to full size and was trying to come into her bedroom, but couldn't quite fit through the door. She was frightened at first, when the great creature began to heave its prisoned shoulders, making the old house shudder around her until the roof rained shingles, and the stars came through. But in time it grew quiet, and other dreams tumbled between her and it as she slept with Farrell's arm over her, just as the unicorn slept with NMC.

In the morning, both of them late for work, unscrambling tangled clothing and exhuming a fossilized toothbrush of Farrell's ("All right, so I forgot to throw it out, so big deal!"), they nearly overlooked the unicorn altogether. It was standing—tapestry-size once again—at the foot of Julie's bed, regarding her out of eyes more violet than purple in the early light. She noticed for the first time that the pupils were horizontal, like those of a goat. NMC crouched in the doorway, switching her tail and calling plaintively for her strange foundling, but the unicorn had no heed for anyone but Julie. It lowered its head and stamped a mini-forefoot, and for all that the foot came down in a bright puddle of underwear it still made a sound like a bell ringing under the sea. Farrell and Julie, flurried as they were, stood very still.

The unicorn stamped a second time. Its eyes were growing brighter, passing from deep lavender through lilac, to blazing amethyst. Julie could not meet them. She whispered, "What is it? What do you want?"

Her only answer was a barely audible silver cry and the glint of the fierce little horn as the unicorn's ears slanted back against its head. Behind her Farrell, socks in hand, undershirt on backwards, murmured, "Critter wants to tell you something. Like Lassie."

"Shut up, Farrell," she snapped at him; then, to the unicorn, "Please, I don't understand. Please."

The unicorn raised its forefoot, as though about to stamp again. Instead, it trotted past the bed to the rickety little dressing table that Farrell had helped Julie put together very long ago, in another country. Barely the height of the lowest drawer, it looked imperiously back at them over its white shoulder before it turned, reared and stretched up as far as it could, like NMC setting herself for a luxurious, scarifying scratch. Farrell said, "The mirror."

"Shut up!" Julie said again; and then, "What?"

"The Cluny tapestries. *La Dame à la Licorne*. Unicorns like to look at themselves. Your hand mirror's up there."

Julie stared at him for only a moment. She moved quickly to the dressing table, grabbed the mirror and crouched down close beside the unicorn. It shied briefly, but immediately after fell to gazing intently into the cracked, speckled glass with a curious air almost of puzzlement, as though it could not quite recognize itself. Julie wedged the mirror upright against the drawer-pull; then she rose and nudged Farrell, and the two of them hurriedly finished dressing, gulping boiled coffee while the unicorn remained where it was, seemingly oblivious of everything but its own image. When they left for work, Julie looked back anxiously, but Farrell said, "Let it be, don't worry, it'll stay where it is. I took Comparative Mythology, I know these things."

True to his prediction, the unicorn had not moved from the mirror when Julie came home late in the afternoon; and it was still in the same spot when Farrell arrived after the restaurant's closing. NMC was beside it, now pushing her head insistently against its side, now backing away to try one more forlorn mother-call, while the first kitten to make it into the wide world beyond the cat box was blissfully batting the tufted white tail back and forth. The tail's owner paid no slightest heed to either

of them; but when Julie, out of curiosity, knelt and began
to move the mirror away, the unicorn made a sound very
like a kitten's hiss and struck at her fingers, barely missing. She stood up calmly, saying, "Well, I'm for banana
cake, *Bringing Up Baby*, and having my feet rubbed.
Later for Joseph Campbell." The motion was carried by
acclamation.

The unicorn stayed by the mirror that night and all
the next day, and the day after that. On the second day
Julie came home to hear the sweet rubber-band sound of
a lute in her apartment, and found Farrell sitting on the
bed playing Dowland's "The Earl of Essex's Galliard."
He looked up as she entered and told her cheerfully, "Nice
acoustics you've got here. I've played halls that didn't
sound half as good."

"That thing of yours about locks is going to get you
busted one day," Julie said. The unicorn's eyes met hers in
the hand mirror, but the creature did not stir. She asked,
"Can you tell if it's listening at all?"

"Ears," Farrell said. "If the ears twitch even a bit, I try
some more stuff by the same composer, or anyway the
same century. Might not mean a thing, but it's all I've got
to go by."

"Try Bach. Everything twitches to Bach."

Farrell snorted. "Forget it. Bourrees and sarabandes
out the yingyang, and not a wiggle." Oddly, he sounded
almost triumphant. "See, it's a conservative little soul,
some ways—it won't respond to anything it wouldn't have
heard in its own time. Which means, as far as I can make
out, absolutely nothing past the fifteenth century. Binchois
gets you one ear. Dufay—okay, both ears, I'm pretty sure
it was both ears. Machaut—ears and a little tail action,

we're really onto something now. Des Pres, jackpot—it actually turned and looked at me. Not for more than a moment, but that was some look. That was a look."

He sighed and scratched his head. "Not that any of this is any help to anybody. It's just that I'll never have another chance to play this old stuff for an informed critic, as you might say. Somebody who knows my music in a way I never will. Never mind. Just a thought."

Julie sat down beside him and put her arm around his shoulders. "Well, the hell with unicorns," she said. "What do unicorns know? Play Bach for me."

Whether Farrell's music had anything to do with it or not, they never knew; but morning found the unicorn across the room, balancing quite like a cat atop a seagoing uncle's old steamer trunk, peering down into the quiet street below. Farrell, already up and making breakfast, said, "It's looking for someone."

Julie was trying to move close to the unicorn without alarming it. Without looking at Farrell, she murmured, "By Gad, Holmes, you've done it again. Five hundred years out of its time, stranded in a cat box in California, what else would it be doing but meeting a friend for lunch? You make it look so easy, and I always feel so silly once you explain—"

"Cheap sarcasm doesn't become you, Tanikawa. Here, grab your tofu scramble while it's hot." He put the plate into the hand she extended backwards toward him. "Maybe it's trolling for virgins, what can I tell you? All I'm sure of, it looked in your mirror until it remembered itself, and now it knows what it wants to do. And too bad for us if we can't figure it out. I'm making the coffee with a little cinnamon, all right?"

The unicorn turned its head at their voices; then resumed its patient scrutiny of the dawn joggers, the commuters and the shabby, ambling pilgrims to nowhere. Julie said, slowly and precisely, "It was woven into that tapestry. It began in the tapestry—it can't know anyone who's not in the tapestry. Who could it be waiting for on East Redondo Street?"

Farrell had coffee for her, but no answer. They ate their breakfast in silence, looking at nothing but the unicorn, which looked at nothing but the street; until, as Farrell prepared to leave the apartment, it bounded lightly down from the old trunk and was at the door before him, purposeful and impatient. Julie came quickly, attempting for the first time to pick it up, but the unicorn backed against a bookcase and made the hissing-kitten sound again. Farrell said, "I wouldn't."

"Oh, I definitely would," she answered him between her teeth. "Because if it gets out that door, you're going to be the one chasing after it through Friday-morning traffic." The unicorn offered no resistance when she picked it up, though its neck was arched back like a coiled snake's and for a moment Julie felt the brilliant eyes burning her skin. She held it up so that it could see her own eyes, and spoke to it directly.

"I don't know what you want," she said. "I don't know what we could do to help you if we did know, as lost as you are. But it's my doing that you're here at all, so if you'll just be patient until Joe gets back, we'll take you outside, and maybe you can sort of show us . . ." Her voice trailed away, and she simply stared back into the unicorn's eyes.

When Farrell cautiously opened the door, the unicorn

paid no attention; nevertheless, he closed it to a crack behind him before he turned to say, "I have to handle lunch, but I can get off dinner. Just don't get careless. It's got something on its mind, that one."

With Farrell gone, she felt curiously excited and apprehensive at once, as though she were meeting another lover. She brought a chair to the window, placing it close to the steamer trunk. As soon as she sat down, NMC plumped into her lap, kittens abandoned, and settled down for some serious purring and shedding. Julie petted her absently, carefully avoiding glancing at the unicorn, or even thinking about it; instead she bent all her regard on what the unicorn must have seen from her window. She recognized the UPS driver, half a dozen local joggers—each sporting a flat-lipped grin of agony suggesting that their Walkman headphones were too tight—a policewoman whom she had met on birdwatching expeditions, and the Frozen-Yogurt Man. The Frozen-Yogurt Man wore a grimy naval officer's cap the year around, along with a flapping tweed sport-jacket, sweat pants and calf-length rubber boots. He had a thin yellow-brown beard, like the stubble of a burned-over wheatfield, and had never been seen, as far as Julie knew, without a frozen-yogurt cone in at least one hand. Farrell said he favored plain vanilla in a sugar cone. "With M&Ms on top. Very California."

NMC raised an ear and opened an eye, and Julie turned her head to see the unicorn once again poised atop the steamer trunk, staring down at the Frozen-Yogurt Man with the soft hairs of its mane standing erect from nape to withers. (Did it pick that up from the cats? Julie wondered in some alarm.) "He's harmless," she said, feeling silly but needing to speak. "There must have been lots of people like him in your time. Only then there was a place for them, they had names, they fit the world somewhere. Mendicant friars, I guess. Hermits."

The unicorn leaped at the window. Julie had no more than a second's warning: the dainty head lowered only a trifle, the sleek miniature hindquarters seemed hardly to flex at all; but suddenly—so fast that she had no time even to register the explosion of the glass, the unicorn was nearly through. Blood raced down the white neck, tracing the curve of the straining belly.

Julie never remembered whether she cried out or not, never remembered moving. She was simply at the window with her hands surrounding the unicorn, pulling it back as gently as she possibly could, praying in silent desperation not to catch its throat on a fang of glass. Her hands were covered with blood—some of it hers—by the time the unicorn came free, but she saw quickly that its wounds were superficial, already coagulating and closing as she looked on. The unicorn's blood was as red as her own, but there was a strange golden shadow about it: a dark sparkling just under or beyond her eyes' understanding. She dabbed at it ineffectually with a paper towel, while the unicorn struggled in her grasp. Strangely, she could feel that it was not putting forth its entire strength; though whether from fear of hurting her or for some other reason, she could not say.

"All right," she said harshly. "All right. He's only the Frozen-Yogurt Man, for God's sake, but all right, I'll take you to him. I'll take you wherever you want—we won't wait for Joe, we'll just go out. Only you have to stay in my pocket. In my pocket, okay?"

The unicorn quieted slowly between her hands. She could not read the expression in the great, bruise-colored eyes, but it made no further attempt to escape when she set it down and began to patch the broken window with cardboard and packing tape. That done, she donned the St. Vincent de Paul duffel coat she wore all winter, and carefully deposited the unicorn in the wrist-deep right pocket. Then she pinned a note on the door for Farrell, pushed two kittens away from it with her foot, shut it, said aloud, "Okay, you got it," and went down into the street.

The sun was high and warm, but a chill breeze lurked in the shade of the old trees. Julie felt the unicorn move in her pocket, and looked down to see the narrow, delicate head out from under the flap. "Back in there," she said, amazed at her own firmness. "Five hundred, a thousand years—don't you know what happens by now? When people see you?" The unicorn retreated without protest.

She could see the Frozen-Yogurt Man's naval cap a block ahead, bobbing with his shuffling gait. There were a lot of bodies between them, and she increased her own pace, keeping a hand over her pocket as she slipped between strollers and dodged coffeehouse tables. Once, sidestepping a skateboarder, she tripped hard over a broken slab of sidewalk and stumbled to hands and knees, instinctively twisting her body to fall to the left. She was up in a moment, unhurt, hurrying on.

When she did catch up with the Frozen-Yogurt Man, and he turned his blindly benign gaze on her, she hesitated, completely uncertain of how to approach him. She had never spoken to him, nor even seen him close enough to notice that he was almost an albino, with coral eyes and pebbly skin literally the color of yogurt. She cupped her hand around the unicorn in her pocket, smiled and said, "Hi."

The Frozen-Yogurt Man said thoughtfully, as though they were picking up an interrupted conversation, "You think they know what they're doing?" His voice was loud and metallic, not quite connecting one word with another. It sounded to Julie like the synthesized voices that told her which buttons on her telephone to push.

"No," she answered without hesitation. "No, whatever you're talking about. I don't think anybody knows what they're doing anymore."

The Frozen-Yogurt Man interrupted her. "I think they do. I think they do. I think they do." Julie thought he might go on repeating the words forever; but she felt the stir against her side again, and the Frozen-Yogurt Man's flat pink eyes shifted and widened. "What's that?" he demanded shrilly. "What's that watching me?"

The unicorn was halfway out of her coat pocket, front legs flailing as it yearned toward the Frozen-Yogurt Man. Only the reluctance of passersby to make eye contact with either him or Julie spared the creature from notice. She grabbed it with both hands, forcing it back, telling it in a frantic hiss, "Stay there, you stay, he isn't the one! I don't know whom you're looking for, but it's not him." But the unicorn thrashed in the folds of cloth as though it were drowning.

The Frozen-Yogurt Man was backing away, his hands out, his face melting. Ever afterward, glimpsing him across the street, Julie felt chillingly guilty for having seen him so. In a phlegmy whisper he said, "Oh, no—oh, no, no, you don't put that thing on me. No, I been watching you all the time, you get away, you get away from me with that thing.

You people, you put that chip behind my ear, you put them radio mice in my stomach—you get away, you don't put nothing more on me, you done me enough." He was screaming now, and the officer's cap was tipping forward, revealing a scarred scalp the color of the sidewalk. "You done me enough! You done me enough!"

Julie fled. She managed at first to keep herself under control, easing away sedately enough through the scattering of mildly curious spectators; it was only when she was well down the block and could still hear the Frozen-Yogurt Man's terrified wailing that she began to run. Under the hand that she still kept in her pocket, the unicorn seemed to have grown calm again, but its heart was beating in tumultuous rhythm with her own. She ran on until she came to a bus stop and collapsed on the bench there, gasping for breath, rocking back and forth, weeping dryly for the Frozen-Yogurt Man.

She came back to herself only when she felt the touch of a cool, soft nose just under her right ear. Keeping her head turned away, she said hoarsely, "Just let me sit here a minute, all right? I did what you wanted. I'm sorry it didn't work out. You get back down before somebody sees you."

A warm breath stirred the hairs on Julie's arms, and she raised her head to meet the hopeful brown eyes and all-purpose grin of a young golden retriever. The dog was looking brightly back and forth between her and the unicorn, wagging its entire body from the ears on down, back feet dancing eagerly. The unicorn leaned precariously from Julie's pocket to touch noses with it.

"No one's ever going to believe you," Julie said to the dog. The golden retriever listened attentively, waited a moment to make certain she had no more to confide, and then gravely licked the unicorn's head, the great red tongue almost wrapping it round. NMC's incessant grooming had plainly not prepared the unicorn for anything like this; it sneezed and took refuge in the depths of the pocket. Julie said, "Not a living soul."

The dog's owner appeared then, apologizing and grabbing its dangling leash to lead it away. It looked back, whining, and its master had to drag it all the way to the corner. Julie still huddled and rocked on the bus stop bench, but when the unicorn put its head out again she was laughing thinly. She ran a forefinger down its mane, and then laid two fingers gently against the wary, pulsing neck. She said, "Burnouts. Is that it? You're looking for one of our famous Avicenna loonies, none with less than a master's, each with a direct line to Mars, Atlantis, Lemuria, Graceland or Mount Shasta? Is that it?" For the first time, the unicorn pushed its head hard into her hand, as NMC would do. The horn pricked her palm lightly.

For the next three hours, she made her way from the downtown streets to the university's red-tiled enclave, and back again, with small side excursions into doorways, subway stations, even parking lots. She developed a peculiar cramp in her neck from snapping frequent glances at her pocket to be sure that the unicorn was staying out of sight. Whenever it indicated interest in a wild red gaze, storks'-nest hair, a shopping cart crammed with green plastic bags, or a droning monologue concerning Jesus, AIDS, and the Kennedys, she trudged doggedly after one more street apostle to open one more conversation with the moon. Once the unicorn showed itself, the result was always the same.

"It likes beards," she told Farrell late that night, as he patiently massaged her feet. "Bushy beards—the wilder and filthier, the better. Hair, too, especially that pattern baldness tonsure look. Sandals, yes, definitely—it doesn't like boots or sneakers at all, and it can't make up its mind about Birkenstocks. Prefers blankets and serapes to coats, dark hair to light, older to younger, the silent ones to the walking sound trucks—men to women, absolutely. Won't even stick its head out for a woman."

"It's hard to blame the poor thing," Farrell mused. "For a unicorn, men would be a bunch of big, stupid guys with swords and whatnot. Women are betrayal, every time, simple as that. It wasn't Gloria Steinem who wove that tapestry." He squeezed toes gently with one hand, a bruised heel with the other. "What did they do when they actually saw it?"

The unicorn glanced at them over the edge of the cat box, where its visit had been cause for an orgy of squeaking, purring and teething. Julie said, "What do you think? It was bad. It got pretty damn awful. Some of them fell down on their knees and started laughing and crying and praying their heads off. There were a couple who just sort of crooned and moaned to it—and I told you about the poor Frozen-Yogurt Man—and then there was one guy who tried to grab it away and run off with it. But it wasn't having that, and it jabbed him really hard. Nobody noticed, thank God." She laughed wearily, presenting her other foot for treatment. "The rest—oh, I'd say they should be halfway to Portland by now. Screaming all the way."

Farrell grunted thoughtfully, but asked no more questions until Julie was in bed and he was sitting across the room playing her favorite Campion lute song. She was nearly asleep when his voice bumbled slowly against her half-dream like a fly at a window. "It can't know anyone who's not in the tapestry. There's the answer. There it is."

"There it is," she echoed him, barely hearing her own words. Farrell put down the lute and came to her, sitting on the bed to grip her shoulder.

"Jewel, listen, wake up and listen to me! It's trying to find someone who was in that tapestry with it—we even know what he looks like, more or less. An old guy, ragged and dirty, big beard, sandals—some kind of monk, most likely. Though what a unicorn would be doing anywhere near your average monk is more than I can figure. Are you awake, Jewel?"

"Yes," she mumbled. "No. Wasn't anybody else. Sleep."

Somewhere very far away Farrell said, "We didn't see anybody else." Julie felt the bed sway as he stood up. "Tomorrow night," he said. "Tomorrow's Saturday, they stay open later on Saturdays. You sleep, I'll call you." She drifted off in confidence that he would lock the door carefully behind him, even without a key.

A temporary word-processing job, in company with a deadline for a set of views of diseased kidneys, filled up most of the next day for her. She was still weary, vaguely depressed, and grateful when she returned home to find the unicorn thoroughly occupied in playing on the studio floor with three of NMC's kittens. The game appeared to involve a good deal of stiff-legged pouncing, an equal amount of spinning and side-slipping on the part of the unicorn, all leading to a grand climax in which the kittens tumbled furiously over one another while the unicorn looked on, forgotten until the next round. They never came close to laying a paw on their swift littermate, and the unicorn in turn treated them with effortless care. Julie watched for a long time, until the kittens abruptly fell asleep.

"I guess that's what being immortal is like," she said aloud. The unicorn looked back at her, its eyes gone almost black. Julie said, "One minute they're romping around with you—the next, they're sleeping. Right in the middle of the game. We're all kittens to you."

The unicorn did a strange thing then. It came to her and indicated with an imperious motion of its head that it wanted to be picked up. Julie bent down to lift it, and it stepped off her joined palms into her lap, where—after pawing gently for a moment, like a dog settling in for the night—it folded its long legs and put its head down. Julie's heart hiccuped absurdly in her breast.

"I'm not a virgin," she said. "But you know that." The unicorn closed its eyes.

Neither of them had moved when Farrell arrived, looking distinctly irritated and harassed. "I left Gracie to finish up," he said. "Gracie. If I still have my job tomorrow, it'll be more of a miracle than any mythical beast. Let's go."

In the van, with the unicorn once again curled deep in Julie's pocket, Farrell said, "What we have to do is, we have to take a look at the tapestry again. A good long look this time."

"It's not going back there. I told you that." She closed her hand lightly around the unicorn, barely touching it, more for her own heartening than its reassurance. "Joe, if that's what you're planning—"

Farrell grinned at her through the timeless fast-food

twilight of Madame Schumann-Heink. "No wonder
you're in such good shape, all that jumping to conclu-
sions. Listen, there has to be some other figure in that
smudgy thing, someone we didn't see before. Our little
friend has a friend."

Julie considered briefly, then shook her head. "No.
No way. There was the knight, the squire, and that
woman. That's all, I'm sure of it."

"Um," Farrell said. "Now, me, I'm never entirely sure
of anything. You've probably noticed, over the years.
Come on, Madame, you can do it." He dropped the van
into first gear and gunned it savagely up a steep, narrow
street. "We didn't see the fourth figure because we weren't
looking for it. But it's there, it has to be. This isn't Comparative Mythology, Jewel, this is me."

Madame Schumann-Heink actually gained the top of
the hill without stalling, and Farrell rewarded such valor
by letting the old van free-wheel down the other side.
Julie said slowly, "And if it is there? What happens
then?"

"No idea. The usual. Play it by ear and trust we'll
know the right thing to do. You will, anyway. You always
know the right thing to do, Tanikawa."

The casual words startled her so deeply that she actually covered her mouth for a moment: a classic Japanese
mannerism she had left behind in her Seattle childhood.
"You never told me that before. Twenty years, and you
never said anything like that to me." Farrell was crooning
placatingly to Madame Schumann-Heink's brake shoes,
and did not answer. Julie said, "Even if I did always
know, which I don't, I don't always do it. Not even usually. Hardly ever, the way I feel right now."

Farrell let the van coast to a stop under a traffic light before he turned to her. His voice was low enough that she had to bend close to hear him. "All I know," he said, "there are two of us girls in this heap, and one of us had a unicorn sleeping in her lap a little while back. You work it out." He cozened Madame Schumann-Heink back into gear, and they lurched on toward the Bigby Museum.

A different guard this time: trimmer, younger, far less inclined to speculative conversation, and even less likely to overlook dubious goings-on around the exhibits. Fortunately, there was also a university-sponsored lecture going on: it appeared to be the official word on the Brueghels, and had drawn a decent house for a Saturday night. Under his breath, Farrell said, "We split up. You go that way, I'll ease around by the Spanish stuff. Take your time."

Julie took him at his word, moving slowly through the crowd and pausing occasionally for brief murmured conversations with academic acquaintances. Once she plainly took exception to the speaker's comments regarding Brueghel's artistic debt to his father-in-law, and Farrell, watching from across the room, fully expected her to interrupt the lecture with a discourse of her own. But she resisted temptation; they met, as planned, by the three tapestries, out of the guard's line of sight, and with only a single bored-looking browser anywhere near them. Julie held Farrell's hand tightly as they turned to study the middle tapestry.

Nothing had changed. The knight and squire still prodded a void toward their pale lady, who went on leaning forward to drape her wreath around captive space. Julie imagined a bleak recognition in their eyes of knotted

thread that had not been there before, but she felt foolish
about that and said nothing to Farrell. Silently the two of
them divided the tapestry into fields of survey, as they had
done with the gallery itself when the unicorn first
escaped. Julie took the foreground, scanning the ornamental garden framing the three human figures for one
more face, likely dirty and bearded, perhaps by now so
faded as to merge completely with the faded leaves and
shadows. She was on her third futile sweep over the scene
when she heard Farrell's soft hiss beside her.

"Yes!" he whispered. "Got you, you godly little
recluse, you. I knew you had to be in there!" He grabbed
Julie's hand and drew it straight up to the vegetable-
looking forest surrounding the distant castle. "Right
there, peeping coyly out like Julia's feet, you can't miss
him."

But she could, and she did, for a maddening while;
until Farrell made her focus on a tiny shape, a gray-white
bulge at the base of one of the trees. Nose hard against the
glass, she began at last to see it clearly: all robe and beard,
mostly, but stitched with enough maniacal medieval
detail to suggest a bald head, intense black eyes and a
wondering expression. Farrell said proudly, "Your basic
resident hermit. Absolutely required, no self-respecting
feudal estate complete without one. There's our boy."

It seemed to Julie that the lady and the two men were
straining their embroidered necks to turn toward the castle and the solitary form they had forgotten for five centuries. "Him?" she said. "He's the one?"

"Hold our friend up to see him. Watch what happens."

For a while, afterward, she tried to forget how grudg-
ingly she had reached into her coat pocket and slowly

brought her cupped hand up again, into the light. Farrell shifted position, moving close on her right to block any possible glimpse of the unicorn. It posed on Julie's palm, head high, three legs splayed slightly for balance, and one forefoot proudly curled, exactly like every unicorn I ever drew when I was young. She looked around quickly— half afraid of being observed, half wishing it—and raised her hand to bring the unicorn level with the dim little figure of the hermit.

Three things happened then. The unicorn uttered a harsh, achingly plain cry of recognition and longing, momentarily silencing the Brueghel lecturer around the corner. At the same time, a different sound, low and disquieting, like a sleeper's teeth grinding together, seemed to come either from the frame enclosing the tapestry or the glass over it. The third occurrence was that something she could not see, nor ever after describe to Farrell, gripped Julie's right wrist so strongly that she cried out herself and almost dropped the unicorn to the gallery floor. She braced it with her free hand as it scrambled for purchase, the carpet-tack horn glowing like abalone shell.

"What is it, what's the matter?" Farrell demanded. He made clumsily to hold her, but she shook him away. Whatever had her wrist tightened its clamp, feeling nothing at all like a human hand, but rather as though the air itself were turning to stone—as though one part of her were being buried while the rest stood helplessly by. Her fingers could yet move, enough to hold the unicorn safe; but there was no resisting the force that was pushing her arm back down toward the tapestry foreground, back to the knight and the squire, the mincing damsel and the strangling garden. *They want it. It is theirs. Give it to them. They want it.*

"Fat fucking chance, buster," she said loudly. Her right hand was almost numb, but she felt the unicorn rearing in her palm, felt its rage shock through her stone arm, and watched from very far away as the bright horn touched the tapestry frame.

Almost silently, the glass shattered. There was only one small hole at first, popping into view just above the squire's lumpy face; then the cracks went spidering across the entire surface, making a tiny scratching sound, like mice in the walls. One by one, quite deliberately, the pieces of glass began to fall out of the frame, to splinter again on the hardwood floor.

With the first fragment, Julie's arm was her own once more, freezing cold and barely controllable, but free. She lurched forward, off-balance, and might easily have shoved the unicorn back into the garden after all. But Farrell caught her, steadying her hand as she raised it to the shelter of the forest and the face under the trees.

The unicorn turned its head. Julie caught the brilliant purple glance out of the air and tucked it away in herself, to keep for later. She could hear voices approaching now, and quick, officious footsteps that didn't sound like those of an art historian. As briskly as she might have shooed one of NMC's kittens from underfoot, she said, in the language that sounded like Japanese, "Go on, then, go. Go home."

She never actually saw the unicorn flow from her hand into the tapestry. Whenever she tried to make herself recall the moment, memory dutifully producing a rainbow flash or a melting movie–dissolve passage between worlds, irritable honesty told memory to put a sock in it. There was never anything more than herself standing in a lot of broken glass for the second time in two days, with a faint chill in her right arm, hearing Farrell's eloquently indignant voice denying to guards, docents and lecturers alike that either of them had laid a hand on this third-rate Belgian throw rug. He was still expounding a theory involving cool recycled air on the outside of the glass and warm condensation within as they were escorted all the way to the parking lot. When Julie praised his passionate inventiveness, he only growled, "Maybe that's the way it really was. How do I know?"

But she knew without asking that he had seen what she had seen: the pale shadow peering back at them from its sanctuary in the wood, and the opaline glimmer of a horn under the hermit's hand. Knight, lady and squire— one another's prisoners now, eternally—remained exactly where they were.

That night neither Farrell nor Julie slept at all. They lay silently close, peacefully wide-awake, companionably solitary, listening to her beloved Black-Forest-tourist-trash cuckoo clock strike the hours. In the morning Farrell said it was because NMC had carried on so, roaming the apartment endlessly in search of her lost nursling. But Julie answered, "We didn't need to sleep. We needed to be quiet and tell ourselves what happened to us. To hear the story."

Farrell was staring blankly into the open refrigerator, as he had been for some time. "I'm still not sure what happened. I get right up to the place where you lifted it up so it could see its little hermit buddy, and then your arm . . . I can't ever figure that part. What the hell was it that had hold of you?"

"I don't see how we'll ever know," she said. "It could have been them, those three—some force they were able to put out together that almost made me put the unicorn back with them, in the garden." She shivered briefly, then slipped past him to take out the eggs, milk and smoked salmon he had vaguely been seeking, and close the refrigerator door.

Farrell shook his head slowly. "They weren't real. Not like the unicorn. Even your grandmother couldn't have brought one of them to life on this side. Colored thread, that's all they were. The hermit, the monk, whatever—I don't know, Jewel."

"I don't know either," she said. "Listen. Listen, I'll tell you what I think I think. Maybe whoever wove that tapestry meant to trap a unicorn, meant to keep it penned up there forever. Not a wicked wizard, nothing like that, just the weaver, the artist. It's the way we are, we all want to paint or write or play something so for once it'll stay painted, stay played, stay put, so it'll still be alive for us tomorrow, next week, always. Mostly it dies in the night—but now and then, now and then, somebody gets it right. And when you get it right, then it's real. Even if it doesn't exist, like a unicorn, if you get it really right . . ."

She let the last words trail away. Farrell said, "Garlic. I bet you don't have any garlic, you never do." He opened the refrigerator again and rummaged, saying over his shoulder, "So you think it was the weaver himself, herself, grabbing you, from back there in the fifteenth century? Wanting you to put things back the way you found them, the way he had it—the right way?"

"Maybe." Julie rubbed her arm unconsciously, though the coldness was long since gone. "Maybe. Too bad for him. Right isn't absolutely everything."

"Garlic is," Farrell said from the depths of the vegetable bin. Emerging in triumph, brandishing a handful of withered-looking cloves, he added, "That's my Jewel. Priorities on straight, and a strong but highly negotiable sense of morality. The thing I've always loved about you, all these years."

Neither of them spoke for some while. Farrell peeled garlic and broke eggs into a bowl, and Julie fed NMC. The omelets were almost done before she said, "We might manage to put up with each other a bit longer than usual this time. Us old guys. I mean, I've signed a lease on this place, I can't go anywhere."

"Hand me the cayenne," Farrell said. "Madame Schumann-Heink can still manage the Bay Bridge these days, but I don't think I'd try her over the Golden Gate. Your house and the restaurant, that's about her limit."

"You'd probably have to go a bit light on the garlic. Only a bit, that's all. And I still don't like people around when I'm working. And I still read in the bathroom."

Farrell smiled at her then, brushing gray hair out of his eyes. "That's all right, there's always the litter box. Just don't you go marrying any Brians. Definitely no Brians."

"Fair enough," she said. "Think of it—you could have a real key, and not have to pick the lock every time. Hold still, there's egg on your forehead." The omelets got burned.

KEVIN J. ANDERSON
& REBECCA MOESTA

SEA DREAMS

Peter: **Kevin J. Anderson** and his wife **Rebecca Moesta** are best known for their work on various *Star Wars* projects, both separately and as a team, but their story "Sea Dreams" has absolutely nothing to do with George Lucas or Darth Vader. It's about friendship, about storytelling, and about the ineffable place where magic and madness sometimes become one.

Janet: Kevin and Rebecca are dear friends of mine. I have long had the sense that their combined writing voice would contain some of the charm of their unique relationship with one another . . . which is why I solicited this coauthorship. It's so nice to be right!

Sea Dreams

J ULIA CALLED ME TONIGHT AS SHE HAS SO MANY TIMES before. Not on the telephone, but in that eerie, undeniable way she used since we met as little girls, strangers and best friends at once. It usually meant she needed me, had something urgent or personal to say.

But this time I needed her, in a desperate, throw-common-sense-to-the-wind way . . . and she knew it. Julia always knew.

And she had something to tell me.

Alone in the tiny bedroom of my comfortably conservative Florida apartment, I felt it as surely as I felt the cool sheets beneath me, and the humid, moon-warm September air that flowed through my half-opened window. At such times, common sense goes completely to sleep, leaving imagination wide awake and open to possibilities. And she called out to me.

Julia had been gone for five years, gone to the sea. Others might have said "drowned," might have used "gone" as a euphemism for "dead." I never did. The only thing I knew—that anyone *could* know for certain—was this: Julia was gone.

It had begun when we were eleven. That year, my parents and I left our Wisconsin home behind to spend our vacation at my grandmother's oceanside cottage in Cocoa Beach, Florida.

I had grown up in the Midwest, familiar with green hills and sprawling fields, but nothing had prepared me for my first sight of the Atlantic: an infinite force of blue-green mystery, its churning waves a magnet for my sensibilities, a sleeping power I had never suspected might exist.

Excited by the journey and the strange place, I was unable to sleep that first night in Grandmother's cottage. The rumble of the waves, the insistent shushing whisper of the surf muttering a white noise of secrets, vibrated even through the glass . . . and grew louder still when I got up and nudged the window open further to smell the salt air.

There, in the moonlight, a young girl stood on the beach—someone other than Grandmother, her friends, and my parents, talking about grown-up things while I patiently played the role of well-behaved daughter. Another girl unable to sleep.

I put on a bikini (my first) and a pair of jeans, tiptoed down the stairs, and let myself out the sliding glass door onto the sand. As I walked toward the ocean, reprimanding myself for the foolhardiness of going out alone at night, I saw her still standing there, staring out into the waves.

She seemed statuesque in the moonlight, fragile, ethereal. She had waist-length hair the color of sun-washed sand, wide green eyes—I couldn't see them in the dark, but still I *knew* they were green—and a smile that matched the warmth and gentleness of the evening breeze.

"Thank you for coming," she said. She paused for a few moments, perhaps waiting for a response. As I carefully weighed the advisability of speaking to a stranger, even one who looked as delicate as a princess from a fairy tale, she added, "My name is Julia."

"I'm Elizabeth," I replied after another ten seconds of agonized deliberation. I shook her outstretched hand as gravely as she had extended it, thinking what an odd gesture this was for someone who had probably just completed the sixth grade. Which, I discovered once we started to talk, was exactly the case—as it was for me.

We spoke to each other as if I had been there all along and often came out for a chat, not like strangers who had just met on the beach after midnight. Within half an hour, we were sitting and talking like old friends, laughing at spontaneous jokes, sharing confidences, even finishing each other's sentences as though we somehow knew what the other meant to say.

"Do you like secrets? And stories?" Julia asked during a brief lull in our conversation. When I hastened to assure her that I did—though I had never given it much thought—she fell silent for a long moment and then began to weave me a tale as she looked out upon the waves, like an astronomer gazing toward a distant galaxy.

"I have seen the Princes of the Seven Seas," she said in a soft, dreamy voice, "and each of their kingdoms is filled with more magic and wonder than the next. . . . The two mightiest princes are the handsome twins, Ammeron and Ariston, who rule the kingdoms of the North."

She had found a large seashell on the beach and held it up to her ear, as if listening. "They tell me secrets. They tell me stories. Listen."

Julia half closed her green eyes and talked in a whispery, hypnotic voice, as if reciting from memory—or repeating words she somehow heard in the convolutions of the seashell.

"They have exquisite underwater homes, soaring castles made of coral, whose spires reach so close to the surface that they can climb to the topmost turrets when the waves are calm and catch a glimpse of the sky. . . ."

I giggled. Julia's voice was so earnest, so breathless. She frowned at me for my moment of disrespect, and I fell silent, listening with growing wonder as her story caught us both in a web of fantasy and carried us to a land of blues and greens, lights and shadows, beneath the shushing waves.

"Each kingdom is enchanted, filled with light and warmth, and the princes rarely stay long in their castles. They prefer instead to ride across the brilliant landscapes of the underwater world, watching over their realms.

"Their loyal steeds are sleek narwhals that carry Ammeron and Ariston to all—"

"What's a narwhal?" I asked, betraying my Midwestern ignorance of the sea and its mysteries.

Julia blinked at me. "They're a sort of whale—like unicorns of the sea—strong swimmers with a single horn. Ancient sailors used to think they were monsters capable of sinking ships. . . ."

She cocked her head, listening to the shell. Her face fell into deep sadness for the next part of her story, and I wondered how she could make it all up so fast.

"The sea princes enjoy a charmed existence, full of adventure—they live forever, you know. One of their favorite quests is to hunt the kraken, hideous creatures that ruled the oceans in the time before the Seven Princes, but the defeated monsters hide now, brooding over their lost empires. They hate Ammeron and Ariston most of all, and lurk in dark sea caves, dreaming of their chance to murder the princes and take back what they believe is rightfully theirs.

"On one such hunt, when Ammeron and Ariston rode their beloved narwhal steeds into a deep cavern, armed with abalone-tipped spears, they flushed out the king of the kraken, an enormous tentacled beast twice the size of any monster the two brothers had fought before.

"Their battle churned the waves for days—we called it a hurricane here above the surface—until finally, in one terrible moment, the kraken managed to capture Ammeron with a tentacle and drew the prince toward its sharp beak, to slice him to pieces!"

I let out an unwilling gasp, but Julia didn't seem to notice.

"But at the last moment, Ammeron's brave narwhal—seeing his beloved prince about to die—charged in without regard for his own safety, and gouged out the kraken's eye with his single long horn! In agony, the monster released Ammeron and, thrashing about in the throes of death, caught the faithful narwhal in its powerful tentacles and crushed the noble steed an instant before the kraken, too, died."

A single tear crept down Julia's cheek.

"And though the prince now rides a new steed, his loyal narwhal companion is lost forever. He realizes how lonely he is, despite the friendship of his brother. Very lonely. Ammeron longs for another companion to ease the pain, a princess he can love forever.

"Ariston also yearns for a mate—but the princes are wise and powerful. They will accept none other than the perfect partners . . . and they can wait. They live forever. They can wait."

We watched the moon disappear behind us and gradually the darkness over the ocean blossomed into petals of peach and pink and gold. I was awed by the swollen red sphere of the sun as it first bulged over the flat horizon, then rose higher, raining dawn across the waves like a firestorm. I had never seen a sunrise before, and I would never see one as beautiful again.

But with the dawn came the realization that I had been up all night, talking with Julia. My parents never got up early, especially not on vacation. Still, I was anxious to get back to my grandmother's house, partly to snatch an hour or two of sleep, but mostly to avoid any chance of being caught.

I knew exactly what my parents would say if they knew I had gone out alone, spent the quiet, dark hours of the night talking to a total stranger—and I wouldn't be able to argue with them. It *did* sound crazy, completely unlike anything I had ever done before. *Irresponsible*. Even thinking the terrible word brought a hot flush of embarrassment to my cheeks.

But I wouldn't have traded that night for anything. Though I resisted such silliness for most of my life, that was the first time I ever experienced magic.

The vacation to Cocoa Beach became an annual event. Even when I went back to Wisconsin, Julia and I were rarely out of touch. My parents taught me to be practical and realistic, to think of the future and set long-term goals. Julia, however, remained carefree and unconcerned, as comfortable with her fantasies as with her real life.

We wrote long letters filled with plans for the future, and the hopes and hurts of growing up. We weren't allowed to call each other often, but whenever something important happened to me, the phone would ring and I would know it was Julia. She knew, somehow. Julia always knew.

During our summer weeks together, Julia spent endless hours telling me her daydreams about life in the enchanted realms beneath the sea. She had taught herself to sketch, and she drew marvelous, sweeping pictures of the undersea kingdoms. After listening to her for so long, I gradually learned to tell a passable story, though never with the ring of truth that she could give to her imaginings.

From Julia, I learned about the color of sunlight shining down from above, filtered through layers of rippling water. In my mind, I saw plankton blooms that made a stained-glass effect, especially at sunset. I learned how storms churned the surface of the sea, while the depths remained calm though with a "mistiness" caused by the foamy wavetops above.

I learned about hidden canyons filled with huge mollusks—shells as big and as old as the giant redwood trees—which patiently collected all the information brought to them by the fish.

Julia told me about secret meeting places in kelp forests, where Ammeron and Ariston went to spend carefree hours in their unending lives, playing hide-and-seek with porpoises. But the lush green kelp groves now seemed empty to them, empty as the places in their hearts that waited for true love. . . .

One day we found a short chain of round metal links at the water's edge. What its original purpose was or who had left it there, I could not fathom. Julia picked it up with a look that was even more unfathomable. She touched each of the loops again and again, moving them through her fingers as if saying some magical rosary. We kept walking, splashing up to our ankles in the low waves, until Julia gave a small cry. One of the links had come loose in her hand. She stared at it for a moment in consternation, then gave a delighted laugh. She slid the circlet from one finger to the next until it came to rest on the ring finger of her right hand, a perfect fit.

"There. I always knew he'd ask." Julia sent me a sidelong glance, a twinkle lurking in the green of her irises. She loosened another link and slipped it quickly onto my hand.

"All right," I sighed, feeling suddenly apprehensive, but knowing that it was no use trying to ignore her once she got started. "Who is 'he,' and what did he ask?"

"I am betrothed to Ammeron, heir to the Kingdom of the Seventh Sea," she said proudly.

"Sure, and I'm betrothed to his brother Ariston." I held up the cheap metal ring on my finger. "Aren't we a bit young to get engaged, Jule?"

Julia was unruffled. "Time means nothing in the kingdoms beneath the sea. When a year passes here, it's no more than a day to them. Time is infinite there. Our princes will wait for us."

"You really think we're worth it? Besides, how do they know whether or not we accept?" I challenged, always adding a completely out-of-place practicality to Julia's fairy tales. But my sarcasm sailed as far over Julia's head as a shooting star.

"Wait," she said, grasping my arm as she swept the ocean with her intense gaze. Suddenly, she drew in a sharp breath. "Look!" Her eyes lit up as a dolphin leapt twice, not far from where we stood on the shore. "There," she sighed, "do we need any more proof than that?"

Even in the face of her excitement, I couldn't keep the slight edge out of my voice. "I'll admit that I've never seen dolphins leap so close to shore, but what does that have to do with—"

"Dolphins are the messengers of the royal families beneath the sea," she replied in her patient way. Always patient. "One leap is a greeting. Two leaps ask a question. Three leaps give an answer." She flashed a smile at me. There was certainty in her voice that sent a shiver down my back. "And now they're waiting for us to respond!"

I struggled for a moment with impatience but couldn't bring myself to answer with more of my cynicism. I tried my most soothing voice. "Well, I'm sure Ammeron will understand that you—"

But she wasn't listening. Before I could finish my thought, she was running at top speed along the damp, packed sand. I looked after her, and, as I watched in amazement, she executed three of the most graceful leaps I had ever seen, strong and clean and confident. I knew I would look foolish if I even tried something like that. I'd probably fall flat on my face in the sand.

By the time I caught up to her, Julia was looking seaward, ankle-deep in waves, with tears sparkling on her lashes—or perhaps it was only the sea spray.

In her hand she held two more of the metal links from the chain she had found. Silently she handed me one of the links, then closed her eyes and threw the remaining one as far into the water as she could. I did the same, imitating her gesture but without the same conviction.

"Elizabeth," Julia said after a long moment, startling me with her quiet voice, "you are a very sensible person." It sounded like an accusation—and coming from Julia, it probably was.

We moved to drier sand and sat for a long time watching the waves, letting the bright sun dazzle our eyes. Perhaps too long. But Julia's hand on my arm let me know that she saw it, too.

Far out in the water a dolphin leapt. Three times.

Our lives were divided each year into reality and imagination, north and south, school and vacation, rationality and magic, until we finished high school.

I planned my life as carefully and sensibly as I could. My parents had taught me that a woman had to be practical—and I believed it. I chose my college courses with an eye toward the job market, avoiding "frivolous" art and history classes (no matter how much fun they sounded). After all, what good would they do me later in life?

My one concession to the lifelong pull the ocean had exerted on me was that I chose to go to school at Florida State. Luckily, it was a perfectly acceptable school for the business management and accounting classes I intended to take, so I wasn't forced to define my reasons more precisely.

And it allowed me to see Julia more often.

Julia, on the other hand, always lived on the edge of reality. My parents disapproved of her, and I grew tired of defending her choices, so we came to the unspoken agreement that we would avoid the subject entirely . . . though even I couldn't help being a bit disappointed in my friend. To me, it seemed Julia was wasting her life at the seaside.

I tried to help her make some sensible choices as well. She wasn't interested in college, preferring to spend her days hanging out near the ocean, making sketches that she sold for a pittance in local gift shops, doing odd jobs.

I convinced her to learn scuba diving. With her love of the sea, I knew she would be a natural, and in less than a year she was a certified instructor with a small, steady business. I even took lessons from her, as did one of my boyfriends, though that relationship ended in disaster.

As for romance, I occasionally went out on dates with men I met in classes, since I felt that our mutual interests should form a solid basis for long-term partnership, but my dating resulted only in passionless short-term relationships that usually ended with an agreement to be "just friends." I never let on how much these breakups really hurt me, except to Julia.

After each one, I would call Julia and she would meet me at The Original Fat Boy's Bar-B-Que, waiting patiently while I drowned my sorrows in beer and barbecued beef. Then we would drive to the beach, where I'd cry for a while, tell her the whole miserable tale, and vow never to make the same mistake again. Sometimes she drew tiny caricatures of my stories, forming them into comical melodramas as I spoke, until I was forced to acknowledge how silly or inconsequential each romance seemed as I dissolved into laughter and tears.

Julia dated often, drifting through each relationship with little thought for the future, until the inevitable stormy end—usually (I suspected) sparked by Julia's spur-of-the-moment nature and consequent unreliability that frequently frustrated men. Somehow on those nights, she would call to me and, no matter where I was, I would feel the need to go walking on our beach. And she would be there.

Once, particularly burned at the end of a tempestuous relationship, she asked what she was doing wrong—a rhetorical question, perhaps, but I answered her (as if *I* had had a better track record in love than she). "You're spending too much time in a fairy tale, Jule. I used to really love your stories about the princes and the sea kingdoms, but we're not kids anymore. Be a little more practical."

The ocean breeze lifted her pale hair in waves about her face as her sea-green eyes widened. "Practical? I could say you're living in just as much of a fairy tale, Elizabeth. The American Dream . . . following all the rules, taking the right classes, expecting to find treasure in your career and a prince in some accountant or lawyer or doctor. Doesn't sound any more realistic to me."

I felt stung, but she just sighed and looked out to sea, getting that lost expression on her face again. "I'm sorry. I didn't mean to dump on you like that. Don't worry. I guess I shouldn't be so upset either. It doesn't really matter, you know. After all, I'm betrothed to the Prince of the Seventh Sea."

And I managed to laugh, which made me feel better. But Julia had a disturbing . . . *certainty* in her voice.

The last time I ever saw Julia, her call was very strong. I was studying late on campus preparing for a final exam when for no apparent reason I felt an overpowering need to get away from my books, to talk to Julia. It had been months since I'd seen her.

No—she needed to talk to *me*.

Even though there was a storm warning in effect, I ran out the door without even stopping to pick up a jacket, got into my car, and sped all the way to Cocoa Beach. As I sprinted down to the beach behind Julia's house, I saw her standing on the sand. Dimly silhouetted against the cloudy sky, wearing nothing but a white bathing suit, her long hair blew wildly in the wind as she stared out to sea. It reminded me of the first time I had seen Julia as a little girl, standing in the moonlight.

When I came to stand beside her and saw her startled expression, I abruptly realized that something was very wrong: Julia hadn't expected me.

"You called me, Jule," I said. "What's going on?"

"I . . . didn't mean to." She seemed to hesitate. "I'm going diving."

Then I noticed the pile of scuba gear close by, near the water. I understood Julia's subtle stubbornness enough to realize that she placed more weight on her feelings than on simple common sense, so I stifled the impulse to launch into an anxious safety lecture and kept my voice neutral. "I know you have plenty of night diving experience, but you shouldn't dive alone. Not tonight. The weather's not good. Look at the surf."

For a while, I thought she wouldn't answer. At last she said softly, "David's gone."

"The artist?" I asked, momentarily at a loss before

successfully placing the name of the current man in her life.

She nodded. "It doesn't really matter, you know. He fell head-over-heels for a pharmacist. It hit him so hard, I almost felt sorry for him. Don't worry; I don't feel hurt. After all . . ." Her voice trailed off. Her fingers toyed with the plain metal ring that hung from a silver chain around her neck. She had kept it all these years.

Her face was calm, but the storm in her sea-swept eyes rivaled the one brewing over the ocean. "After all," she finished with an enigmatic quirk of her lips, "I think tonight is my wedding night."

Uneasy, I tried for humor, hoping to stall her. "Don't you need a bridesmaid, then? I'll just go get my formal scuba tanks and my dress fins and meet you back here, okay?"

After a minute or so she looked straight at me, clear-eyed and smiling. "Thank you for coming. I really did need to see you again, but right now I think I need to be alone for a while."

"I'm not so sure I should leave," I said, stalling, reluctant to let her go, unable to force her to stay. "Friends don't let friends dive alone, you know?"

"Don't worry, Elizabeth," she said, barely above a whisper. "Remember, no matter what happens . . . I'll call you." She put on her diving gear, letting me help her adjust the tanks, kissed me on the cheek, and waded into the turbulent water. "I'll call you in a week—probably less. I promise."

As I left the beach I looked back every few seconds to watch her until I saw her head disappear beneath the waves.

Later, Julia's tanks and her buoyancy compensator vest were found in perfect condition on the shore a few miles away. And a plain silver neck chain. That was all.

That was five years ago. And tonight, when I needed her the most, I heard her call again.

Now, sitting on the damp sands, I listened to the hushed purr of the waves and stare at the Atlantic Ocean under the moonlight.

At times like this, here on the beach where Julia and I used to sit together, I wondered if I really was the sensible one. Yes, I made all the "right" choices, earned my degree, found a suitable job, got a comfortable apartment—though no dashing prince (accountant, lawyer, or otherwise) seemed to notice. I had been supremely confident that it would only be a matter of time.

But then, with a simple blood test, I ran out of time. Next came more tests, then a biopsy and a brief stay in the hospital. And behind it all loomed the specter of more and more time spent among the other hopeless cancer patients, walking cadavers, with the ticking of the death-watch growing louder and louder inside their heads.

I would rather listen to the ocean.

It wasn't fair!

I raged at the universe. Hadn't I done everything right? Then why I had fallen under a medical curse, with no prince to kiss my cold lips and dislodge the bit of poisoned apple from my throat?

I needed to hear Julia's stories again. I longed to

know more about the princes and their sea-unicorns, the defeated kraken, the tall spires of coral castles, in that enchanted undersea world where everyone lived forever.

I found a seashell on the shore, washed up by the tide, as if deposited there for me alone. I picked it up, brushing loose grains of sand from the edge, held it to my ear . . . and listened.

Far out in the water, I saw a dolphin make a double jump, two graceful silver arcs under the bright light of the moon.

My heart leapt with it, and I stood, blinking for a moment in disbelief. Then, feeling surprisingly restless and full of energy, I decided to go for a run along the beach.

And if I happened to leap once, twice, or three times . . . who was there to know?

JANET BERLINER

THE SAME BUT DIFFERENT

Peter: Anything I might say about **Janet Berliner**'s "The Same But Different" would be at best taken as seriously biased. We've been friends for a long time, and I'm very fond of her. Writer, teacher, superb editor, onetime agent, first-rate pool player, she hustles more determinedly, on more fronts, and in a tougher ballpark than anyone I know; and if she occasionally hustles me into gigs that I have no business taking on—such as this book—they tend to work out surprisingly well. Crazy as a jaybird, of course, but a real artist and one hell of a human being. I wouldn't have missed knowing her for anything. I wish she'd get some more sleep, is all.

The Same But Different

$$\sim\!\!\!\text{\small\ss}\!\!\!\sim$$

KNOW WHAT *I* WANT, LEGS-BABY? *YOU* WANT TO MAKE *me happy, get me ethnic. Ethnic's what's happening. . . .*

Alex "Legs" Cleveland tried not to feel irritation with his partner. *Ethnic,* he thought. Made sense to *him.* He had spent a lifetime letting go of the Reservation. Every time he believed he'd succeeded, the universe decreed otherwise.

Still, it had taken him no time at all, and embarrassed him only slightly, to nod, smile at his partner, and agree to find *ethnic* for the new showroom at the MGM. Something like Mirage's Cirque de Soleil. *The same but different.*

Find me ethnic, with some tits and ass on the side, and I'll love you, Legs-baby. Vegas'll love you.

Maury was so damned L.A. Even worse, so Holly-wood. He could look into the eyeballs of a full-blooded Navajo, say, "Ethnic's what's happening," and expect to be taken seriously.

Which, in this case, Legs thought, looking out of the window at the Christmas lights strung across Hollywood Boulevard, he was. Though what drove Alex to choose to go to South Africa on his search for *ethnic* was not entirely clear to either one of them. Whatever the reason, once he thought of South Africa, it felt like his only choice.

Next thing he knew, he was in Johannesburg, renting a car so that he could drive to Bophuthatswana and scour Sun City—the Las Vegas of South Africa, the brochure read—for *ethnic*.

Oh well, he thought, laughing at himself. This was no more or less foolish than last year's trip to Madagascar, a fruitless search for a Roc's egg inspired by the awesome success of *Jurassic Park;* or the year before, spending his vacation in the Grenadines searching for buried treasure at the bottom of the Caribbean. He had found neither the egg nor the treasure; he *had* discovered little Marsha McDonald belting out "Going Under" in a Calypso tent in Grenada. At fifteen, she was the youngest Calypso Queen ever. Cute little thing. If only he'd gotten to her in time, before she signed on with that funny little German, Wolfie, and his Tobago Cabaret.

The good part was that, inevitably, he found something in each place to rationalize the journey. Mostly after the fact. So although what he thought he might find in Bophuthatswana was right now anybody's guess, he knew from experience that he would find something.

Which, he reminded himself, was how he had come to be driving on the left side of a road somewhere near Bechuanaland, in a rental car which put-putted like an old camel and whose air-conditioning was, to be kind, substandard.

So, apparently, were other things. He got as far as the outskirts of Krugersdorp before steam started pouring out of the hood and into the low desert.

After a suitable amount of time devoted to expletives, and the doffing of a layer of clothing, he decided that sitting around and humidifying the desert was not the way to go. He studied the map the car rental company had given him, and the touring guide next to the name of the town: Three hotels, a couple of gold mines, and daily tours of Sterkfontein Caves.

Not knowing what else to do, he stuffed his camcorder into his overnight bag—all the luggage he'd brought—and left the car.

He stood outside in the hot sun, sweat trickling down his neck, thumb in the air. After ten minutes, the driver of a small truck picked him up.

The driver, a tall, extremely black man, was a man of few words. He answered the questions put to him, but volunteered nothing.

"What's your name?"

"Sam Mtshali."

"Where are you headed?"

Thus prodded, Sam explained that he was a Zulu, a mine worker, and the sometime lead dancer of a troupe of dancers who called themselves The Zulu Warriors, and that yes—with what was almost a smile—he *had* finished school, *had* matriculated. He had even, he admitted, spent four years at the University, getting a degree in "something useful." And no, he knew nothing about cars.

"What do you suggest I do?" Legs asked.

"Might as well take it easy," Sam said. "It will take the rental car company a day, two maybe, to find another car and send it from Pretoria."

One phone call, made at the side of the road, proved the Zulu right. "Meanwhile, Mr. Cleveland, why not relax." Rolling her *rr*s. "See a little of our beautiful country. Go to the Caves, it's cool in there. Take a bus to the Voortrekker Monument."

Turned out that The Zulu Warriors were about to give a performance. With little much else to do, Legs was fairly easily persuaded to go and watch.

He was sitting half-asleep in rudely constructed bleachers, exposed to the midsummer African sun and daydreaming about a clean room, a soft mattress, and a very cold shower, when a simple drumroll echoed the distant thunder of an electrical storm.

At once the dusty arena was filled with bodies— jumping, arching, twisting, shaking the dusty earth with the pounding of feet and drums. Lunging, retreating, thrusting their marquise-shaped, cowhide shields forward and waving their clubs. Their beaded headbands catching the sun. Red and white goatskin bands on their legs and arms, copper bangles to the elbows, moving forward in unison, crouching, standing, bowing.

Enchanted, Legs imagined them in a showroom. Mine dumps in the background, dust rising from their feet, a backdrop of steel and glass high-rises on the horizon. What a set it would make. Wait till America gets a load of these guys, he thought, happy again at life's synchronicity. He'd pick up a couple of acts from the local shebeen, some women dancers to satisfy the tits and ass requirement, and a canary—not necessarily Miriam Makeba, but good enough. Afro was in. Caribbean was in: the Caribbean Allstars, with their reggae and calypso; Zulu Spear, with their steel drums; the West African Highlife Band, O. J. Ekemode and the Nigerian Allstars, with their Afrobeat. But no one, *no one,* had anything like this.

When they'd wanted legs, he and Maury had given them legs. When they'd wanted tits, he and Maury found them tits. Now they wanted African-authentic, *the same but different*. Well, they would get the same but different: The Zulu Warriors. The real thing. Just what "they" were looking for. Radio City would be calling him after The Zulu Warriors had made a couple of Vegas appearances. After that, a world tour, Hollywood. . . . One thing was certain, this wasn't the same old thing. They could stop telling him that. This wasn't leggy showgirls, cross-dressers, comics on the way up, the way down. This would bring in the Afro-American audience.

Legs wasted no time finding Sam when the dances were over.

"Who's your manager?" he asked.

"I am." A lithe African of indiscernible age stepped out of the shadows. "Nkolosi, also head of AFI, Africans for Independence." He put out his hand European fashion. "What do you think of my boys?"

He stared at Legs, his eyes expressionless. "Think you can do something for them?"

"Can I do something for them?" Legs grinned at Nkolosi, buying himself time while he tried to dredge up what he knew about the AFI and about this man.

"Can I do something for them?" Legs repeated. "Does a dog piss on fire hydrants?"

"Don't struggle so hard, Mr. Cleveland," Nkolosi said. "You have read of me. I am called revolutionary. Witchdoctor. Keeper of Ngwenya, the Mother of all Lightning Birds." His accent was cultured, Anglicized. It was that which reminded Legs of what he had read. This man was educated in the halls of Oxford—or was it Cambridge? No matter. He was dangerous, or so the *Time* article had said. Educated in the ways of the white man and in the lore of his father and his father's father. Unsatisfied with Mandela and the coalition . . . there was more, but Legs couldn't quite remember what. Politics wasn't his bag, nor was voodoo. No more than spirit magic. Bunch of crap. Far as he was concerned, Nick—or however you pronounced it—was the manager of The Zulu Warriors. Still, it was a good pitch, he thought. Nice and *ethnic*. Meeting Nkolosi was a quirk of fate, one he intended to use for his own aggrandizement.

"Very well, then, Mr. Cleveland," Nkolosi said. "In that case we'll meet later. Sam will tell you where and when."

"Right." Legs waved his hand. "Later, Nick."

Overhead, a cloud obscured the sun. Legs looked up. Shook his head. Took off his sunglasses and cleaned them. This African sun was a pisser. Did strange things to a man, worse than when he was a kid out in the middle of the Mojave. He could have sworn he'd seen a dragon up there, belly on fire, wings jagged.

He looked at his wristwatch. Four o'clock in the afternoon in Johannesburg. Subtract ten hours, that made it six in the morning in L.A.

He grinned. He should call Maury. Wake him up. Serve him right. *Give me ethnic, baby.* He'd give him ethnic all right. Maybe he'd even get lucky and catch Maury in the middle of plunking some honey-blonde chorus line wannabe.

He wiped the sweat off the back of his neck. "I need a telephone and a beer," he said.

"There's a small Greek café half a mile or so from

here," Sam said. "When you're done there, find your way to the Sterkfontein Caves. Go on the tour. Amuse yourself by playing tourist. You'll like it. It's cool inside." He looked at Legs and smiled for the first time. "I mean temperature, not what you Americans call cool. There's an old mine dump behind the caves. You'll see a house. When the mine was working, the supervisor lived in it. Now I do. Meet me there in a couple of hours. If you get there first, just hang around."

Legs found the café with no trouble. The beer was warm, but at least it was wet. He took his bottle with him into the phone booth outside. The receiver was greasy and the booth smelled of old hamburger. Legs gagged, and held the door open with his foot. It didn't help much; the day had grown older, but no cooler.

"I'm bringing them in," he said, when Maury answered. "Ethnic, just like you wanted." He explained who and what they were, cutting to the chase so that he could get out of the telephone booth. "I'll have the contract signed over to me for eight of them. We'll leave sometime over the weekend. Private plane—part of the deal. We'll give them a day to get over jet lag, get them used to the stage. They'll be ready Tuesday night. Dingaan's Day."

"You did good, baby," Maury said, his voice raw. "Just one thing, what the fuck is a Dingaan?"

"You asked for ethnic. Go to a library, Maury. Look it up."

Chuckling at the thought of Maury in a library, Legs went back to the café. He used the bathroom, which was anything but clean, bought another beer, and asked for directions to the Caves. The last tour had already started, so he paid for a small, overpriced tourbook that lay atop a souvenir showcase near the entrance, and wandered inside.

Immediately, as if it called out to him, something drew him through an opening to his right and toward a cave painting at the far end of a small cavern.

The hair on his neck, on his arms, stood on end, and he shivered. He opened the guide book and identified the painting. "**Gemsbok**." *Cave painting of an oryx antelope, discovered by Sir John Barrow who . . .*

His vision blurred. Without realizing what he was doing, he sat down on the floor of the cave and crossed his legs Indian fashion, the way he had sat as a young boy in the Mojave, waiting for his spirit guide to show itself.

Which it had. A black buck, with a single horn— black and white and crimson.

His hand, scrabbling nervously in the dirt floor of the cave, touched something hard and cold. He picked it up and looked at it. Striated. Black at the bottom, white in the middle, the tip of the piece of horn red as blood.

Unhurriedly, Sam packed away his stilts, showered, changed, and left the compound. In his hand he held a map and a set of car keys. He left the area, turned the car around, and drove down the hill. At the first fork in the road he made a right and drove around the outskirts of one of Pretoria's prosperous white suburbs. It would take him less than half-an-hour to get back to the meeting place. Plenty of time. He slowed down and thought about the dragon-child of Negwenya, the Mother Lightning Bird.

He was half-brother to the dragon-child, or so it was said. As it was said that when the time was right the dragon child would come for him, Sam Mtshali. Might be, he thought, she would have to fly a sizable distance to find him.

Strange, how things worked out. He was finally part of the *in* crowd, a Zulu, a voter of consequence, and here he was about to go off with a red man to dance in the United States.

Besides, it was all just a story, told around the night fires. He had seen Negwenya once, during his sojourn in the Karroo; he had never seen her child, his half-brother. His childhood memories were of music and dancing, of fighting and loving. He hadn't even met their master, Nkolosi, until he'd joined the AFI, and then only briefly until the witchdoctor appeared today to take over The Zulu Warriors and inform him of his duty.

He started to turn up the music on his car radio, thought better of it, and headed down the stretch toward his destination, the abandoned mining compound. He had known it would be deserted, yet today he found its air of desolation disquieting. Letting his gaze travel over the low-slung barracks, their corrugated roofs buckled by the sun, he peopled the compound. He imagined it filled with black men who spent their days in the belly of the earth and their nights on cement bunks, longing for families departed for the homelands. Wondering if their babies had become children, their children young men and women with families of their own.

Driving past the end of a barbed wire fence, he turned off the road, and took a narrow dirt track to a house that lay hidden behind bulges of sand that grew like breasts out of the Transvaal dust. Usually, he thought, there are children around places like this, using the dumps as their personal playground. Here not even a stray dog or cat broke the silence.

The quiet disturbed him enough that he found himself actually looking forward to his meeting with Nkolosi, and the red man who was taking them to America.

The front door key slid in easily and he walked inside. Because this was the last night he'd be spending here, he took stock—seeing it with the red man's eyes, and saying his farewells. There was a table. A couple of chairs. A bed with a *coir* mattress and, downstairs in the cellar, rifles wrapped in blankets and lying like corpses on the dank floor.

He wandered aimlessly back upstairs, found a small transistor radio, and turned it to Springbok Radio. Since it was hotter than hell inside, he opened the front and back doors and plugged in the only fan he owned. Later, when an early evening thunderstorm darkened the sky, he sat at the window and watched the dust divert the rain into channels that ran down the grimy window panes. Then, wondering briefly what had become of Legs Cleveland, he lay down on the cot and dreamed of the smell of baking bread that sometimes masked the odor of poverty of his mother's kitchen. The sound of the rain on the tin roof had an hypnotic effect, and he was soon asleep. When he awoke, the sun was setting over the mine dumps and someone was knocking at the front door.

Sam opened it. "Come in, Mr. Cleveland."

"Call me Legs. Nick here yet?"

The red-skinned American put out his hand. Sam ignored it.

"Sorry I'm late," Legs said. He sounded nervous. "Fuckin' spooky around here."

Sam led him into the kitchen. There were only two chairs. Legs took one and indicated to Sam that he should take the other. When Sam did not do so, Legs said, "Okay, buddy. If you prefer to stand."

The Zulu lounged against the wall.

"Tell me about the Mining Company," the American said.

"They pay us well, by South African standards," Sam said. "In exchange, they demand a year's contract. Most of the time, the men don't have any idea what they're signing. They think they want to get out of the *kraal* and think they're going to get rich."

"I don't understand. They're equal now. They don't have to do it anymore."

"Do what?"

"Live in a compound, eat off tin plates, sleep on cement bunks . . . ?"

And laugh, and sing, Sam thought. And play the pennywhistle. Deprived and happy, until they begin to lust after the city and the cars— He said nothing.

"Hey, listen," Legs said. "We're gonna be working together. I need your cooperation, need you to keep the troops in line, if you know what I mean." Legs grinned. Put out his hand. "Can't we be friends?"

Still Sam said nothing.

Legs pressed on. "Don't hold it against me that I'm an American. My heart's the same color as yours." He gestured at Sam. "Besides, I'm Navajo. I understand what being different means, just like you men in barracks 536."

Sam moved gracefully away from the wall. "What is it you really want from us?" He looked at Legs and felt a fleeting compassion. He knew of Navajo, and of the

Reservations where the red man, like the Zulu, allowed himself to be turned into a performing bear for the tourists.

Legs flashed a gold-toothed smile, then grew serious. "Your war dances are something, Sam. All the beads and feathers and paint. Assegais waving. Terrifying the audience. Your ancestors and mine were probably related."

"Is that what you believe?"

Nkolosi had entered the room silently. His eyes held the hint of a smile at the look on Legs' face as the American whirled around in surprise.

"Here's your contract," Nkolosi said. "Signed and stamped. I even went to a shebeen and found you some pretty ladies who love to dance, and a good singer."

Legs took the contract from him, folded it carefully, and put it in his pocket. "Guess that's it then," he said, moving toward the door. "Have the men at the airport—"

"Today is Sunday," Nkolosi said. "Tuesday is Dingaan's Day, Mr. Cleveland," Nkolosi interrupted.

Legs shrugged.

"You have surely heard of Chaka Zulu?"

"Yeah, Nick. I saw the made-for-TV movie. Helluva fighter."

Nkolosi's smile did not reach his eyes. "Over a hundred years ago, Dingaan—Chaka's brother—defeated the Boer leader, Piet Retief. . . . Never mind. The details aren't important. To you. Just listen to me carefully. You'll see in the contract that I have stipulated that The Zulu Warriors must dance on Dingaan's Day." He paused for a moment, then went on. "No matter what happens or where they are, they have to dance—to remind themselves of their heritage."

"They'll be dancing. Don't worry about that."

"Yes. They will, Mr. Cleveland."

Fascinated by the encounter between snakes, Sam watched Legs walk out of the front door, stop, and pull out the contract to check it over. The light from the house stopped at the American's feet and he had to kneel to see the writing. As he did so, a lizard darted across the path of the light. He jumped. "Sooner we get of this country, the better—"

"For all of us, Mr. Cleveland," Nkolosi said softly. "For all of us."

The next morning, Sam led his fellow dancers through the service entrance of the Mining Company's working compound, a carbon copy of the deserted one, except that it was peopled by flesh-and-blood men rather than by his imagination.

Things went almost too smoothly. They wandered out of the same service gates he'd driven through the day before, astounded at the new lack of security under the coalition. No one stopped them, questioned them, asked to see IDs. Sam had the strange sensation that he didn't exist at all, that he was a figment of Legs' and Nkolosi's imaginations—not even his own. It was not so much a nightmare quality, but a disembodiment, as if he had nothing whatever to do with what was happening. Even on the flight, his first, he did not lose that sensation.

They were less than an hour away from Las Vegas when Legs appeared. He perched on the arm of the seat across the aisle from Sam. "Don't panic," he said.

"Panic?"

"The pilot just let me know that we're making an unexpected landing. I'm not sure what it's all about.

Something to do with heavy rains in Vegas. Flash floods at the airport—"

Legs looked pale, worried, but all Sam could feel was relief that he'd be able to walk around for a while, stretch his long limbs—anything that might force his mind and body to fuse.

Alex "Legs" Cleveland was the first to admit that he thrived on luxury. He was, therefore, not surprised that he was less than thrilled at the idea of sleeping on a rock in the middle of nowhere.

Well, not exactly nowhere. Don Laughlin's private airstrip was in the Mojave Desert, on the outskirts of Laughlin, the southernmost town in Nevada, right on the border of both California and Arizona. Hottest spot on earth where people actually live. Rarely got below one-twenty-five in midsummer. Still it was close enough to Las Vegas to be somewhere in Alex's lexicon.

Could be worse, Legs thought. It often had been.

He walked to the far end of the runway, leaned on a fence, and watched a helicopter marked "Riverside" take off in the direction of Vegas. Then he lit a cigarette, and glanced enviously at Sam Mtshali, sleeping comfortably on a large, flat rock just the other side of the fence.

Sam stirred and opened his eyes.

"That helicopter belongs to the man who built this town," Legs said.

Sam said nothing. He stared out into the desert.

He could see nothing around him except dust and sand and, in the distance, the blinking lights of a few high-rise hotels. He thought about the Karroo, where he had once spent a month listening for the voice of his ancestors. "Do you understand spirit-seeking, red man?" he asked.

"I have been part of it," Legs said. He pulled something out of his pocket, looked at it, and seemed about to show it to Sam.

"Then you know the desert. We are brothers after all."

Legs rubbed whatever it was he held in his hand, then replaced it in his pocket. In strangely companionable silence, he joined Mtshali on the rock. They lay together and contemplated the stars. Later, they talked quietly for a while of weeks spent alone in the desert, at the time of their initiations.

"I was taught that my ancestral guide would come to me in the form of an animal," Sam said.

"Did it?"

"Yes."

Sam was pleased when Legs did not ask for more explanation than that.

"My spirit guide came as a beast with one horn," Legs said. Again, he reached into his pocket. "I didn't know exactly what it was until the other day." He held up the small gemsbok horn—striated, black at the bottom, white in the middle, and tipped with red. "I found this in the cave in Sterkfontein, buried near that painted figure of a one-horned oryx antelope Sir John Barrow found on the cave wall, at least according to the guidebook."

He paused. "Can't imagine why someone hadn't found it before. An archaeologist. A paleontologist. A tourist. It was lying right there, saying pick me up."

"It was waiting for you," Sam said, matter-of-factly. "Africa is like that. Things do not call out *Mfune,* pick us up, until *they* are ready." He was silent for a while. "I, too, have only seen my ancestral guide once," he volunteered, surprising himself by his own loquacity. "She will come to me again when she is ready. Even here, the Lightning Bird will find me."

He stopped talking, and soon fell into an uneasy sleep, interrupted by voices and dreams—ancient voices and ancient dreams, of Africans and Indians, of white men and black, of blood and revenge.

Legs listened to the Zulu's sleep-mutterings. Sam mumbled a couple of times and rolled over. The Zulu was so different from him and yet, as it turned out, so much the same.

The same but different.

The night desert was cold, the sky brilliant with stars. He lay back down, closed his eyes, and allowed the stored daytime warmth of the rock to penetrate between his shoulder blades, but sleep eluded him.

Opening his eyes, he looked at the sleeping Zulu, examined the man's ear and earring, and imagined the close-up on *Geraldo*. A tall and stately man, dressed in a terra-cotta loincloth, earlobes embedded with circular discs which so stretched the lobes that they hung below the level of his jowls. He and Maury would license the sale of those earrings. Half of America would be wearing them. The new liberal button. He'd be rich. Very, very rich. And a hero for taking the troupe away from the Mining Company, where—he would say to *Entertainment Tonight*—they worked underground all week and made a mockery of their heritage for the tourists on Sunday afternoons. And all for pennies. He'd get them real money. Make them rich, what the hell. Maybe he'd run for political office, go back to his roots—

Mayor Alexander Cleveland. The key to Los Angeles. Better yet, Vegas. Maybe he'd marry, make a whole shitload of emancipated little Navajos. On the other hand, with all those broads, hanging around for a handshake, begging for a fuck . . .

. . . Yeah, Alex thought, as Sam stirred next to him. You'll love me, everybody will love me. I'll get stinking rich, send a big check to the Reservation—and stop making promises before I have the means to fulfill them. One of these days, I'll even stop looking for yesterday. Stop needing my Show Biz fix.

In a pig's eye.

He had tried every high—coke, morphine, booze. There was no high like this. Maury would love it. Vegas would love it.

Legs Cleveland was back in business.

He debated the walk into Laughlin, and quickly abandoned the thought. Hell, everyone else who'd been on the private jet, including the pilot, was sleeping. No point in doing anything until dawn, except try to rest. Just so there weren't any snakes around, he thought, lighting another cigarette. He reached into his pocket and once again removed the piece of gemsbok horn. What was it that Sam had said? *In Africa things do not say* Mfune, *pick us up, until* they *are ready*.

Mornings are no time for conversation, Sam thought. He shifted so that his back was squarely facing Legs, and opened his eyes. For a moment, as he'd awakened, Sam had thought he was at home. The thought was fleeting but comforting. He watched the mountains come alive into the dawn. This desert, the Mojave, Legs had called it, was like the Karroo. Yet it was different, too.

The same but different.

The real question was, why was he here?

Searching for an answer, he forced himself to relive what had happened in his life since he'd picked up Alex "Legs" Cleveland at the side of the road, mostly because he had never seen a red man in the flesh before. There was Nkolosi's appearance, the dances, the meeting—

—A streak of light brought the mountains into relief. The smell of Legs' cigarette penetrated Sam's retrospection. Keeping his back to the red man, he actively relived the rest of the time between the meeting with Nkolosi and the present. When he had caught up, he turned over, propped himself up on one elbow, and looked over at Legs. Then he stood up and stretched to his full height.

"It is Tuesday," he said. "Today we must dance."

Damn plane, damn storm. Damn everything, Legs thought, scrambling back over the fence. His relatively benign mood was disappearing fast with the renewed realization that he was stuck out here until noon. He headed for the plane to pick up his video-cam and to speak to the pilot.

Their conversation did not improve his mood any. No amount of effort had rustled up a bus that was available before noon. He was hot. Hungry. Thirsty. Vegas was only an hour or so away by car, yet he felt like he was stranded in the middle of Hell. Some place for an opening performance; bullshit, this Dingaan's Day stuff—like insisting on celebrating Custer's last stand.

How was he supposed to know how to deal with this bunch of fucking Zulus who insisted on dancing, right here, today.

A noise overhead broke the desert silence. He looked up, expecting to see Don Laughlin's helicopter returning.

"PRESS. CNN," he read out loud. "Come on down, guys. It's . . . da-da-da-da . . . Showtime!"

The helicopter banked to the right and circled.

Shifting his gaze a little, Legs blinked and refocused.

He got up and walked quickly toward the plane, where The Zulu Warriors were dressing. All he wanted was to get out of this place. His heart hadn't regained its natural rhythm since they got here.

He sat down and tried to concentrate on the voice booming over the plane's PA system. A familiar voice. Sinister. Sibilant. Nkolosi's, though it could not be.

"More than one hundred years ago," the voice said, "a band of Zulus attacked and destroyed Piet Retief and his white followers. The war dances which preceded that bloody battle are about to be recreated for you."

He hadn't authorized the announcements, Legs thought. Or had he? Suddenly he couldn't remember. He felt confused, lucky to remember his own name. If my friends could see me now, he thought wryly: Alexander "Legs" Cleveland, entertainment King of Laughlin, Nevada.

"Let's go," he yelled. He applauded too loudly. "It's showtime."

Sam listened to Legs' clapping and wondered if it reached into the barracks, to the friends he had left behind. He looked at the troupe, The Zulu Warriors, waiting to make their entrance. Their stage a desert airstrip. Only they weren't warriors. They were urbanites, whose ancestors once were warriors. Though he knew it shamed them to make a mockery of their tribal rituals, there were those among them who had long not given a damn.

Suddenly, he knew why Nkolosi had sent him here. Now. To get American television coverage for Nkolosi's statement against the Botha-Mandela coalition. Proof that the tribal heritage was being sublimated. This would be Nkolosi's platform statement, as the American called it, his first official bid for leadership of the new South Africa.

Sam mounted his seven-foot stilts, took out the knife he'd hidden in his belt, and conjured up feathered warriors, readying poison darts, and secreting them in plumed headdresses. Somewhere in the deepest level of his gut, he sensed their assegais quivering with the scent of blood.

He looked upward. Overhead, the sky had darkened and the circling helicopter had given way to his ancestral guide. At her side flew his half-brother, son of the Lightning Bird. Together, they had come to remind him and the other dancers that happiness in the afterlife depended upon having lived this life with pride.

"Kill the Wizards!"

Sam's cry broke out, loud and clear. An ancient cry, Dingaan's, it rose from his throat as it had risen from Dingaan's over a century before. He stared straight at Legs. "Kill the Wizards, and the world will bow before you and your ancestors!"

———⚔———

Legs sank to the ground. Cross-legged, sun beating down on his bare head, he stared through his video-cam lens at the bodies of the dancers—skin glistening with oils and unguents, assegais held loosely, tapping the beat with balls of unshod feet . . . the beat itself, moving from legato to staccato in preordained rhythms and played by one lone drummer. Behind the men stood the women, breasts exposed, heads raised, voices harmonizing in a language of loss.

Slowly, their movements ordered by centuries of tradition, eight men drove their bodies to the beat, drove them until they became Dingaan's marshals reborn.

They were all tall men to begin with. In their feathered headdresses, bobbing and gyrating as they circled the musician, they appeared gigantic. As for Sam, elevated above the highest head by his wooden stilts, Legs knew that the Zulu could see beyond the airport, across the desert that so closely resembled the land that had belonged to his father's father . . . the land of Legs' own tribe. In his own mind's eye, Legs saw cattle grazing and sensed that he was seeing what Sam saw. Feeling what Sam felt.

The rhythm picked up. Legs glanced across at the far end of the airstrip where a group of security guards stood stiffly erect. "Kill the Wizards!" Sam cried out.

"I am an American. I am one of *you*," Legs shouted, as the guards advanced and he realized he was sitting directly in their path. Move, schmuck, move, he told himself. He could sense the danger he was in, yet he sat on, his head filled with visions of axes and arrows—

And then it was too late.

The dancers were dancers no longer. Warriors now,

they charged. Swaying, Sam commanded his troops, and a guard's bullet found its mark.

Clutching his head, the Zulu began to totter. For a moment, impossibly, he maintained his balance. Raising his hands in the air, he released his assegai in what he thought to be the direction of the advancing guards. But the blood from his wound obscured his vision.

Legs, standing now, felt the assegai impale him. He watched the flow of blood from Sam's wound. Then together, like two telephone poles struck down by an electric storm, the black man and the red man fell to the ground.

Lying in the dust, Legs watched Sam trace his fingers in a pool of blood, theirs, and wet his lips. Our blood tastes the same, Legs thought, wondering why that had never occurred to him before.

He thought longingly of Las Vegas, the danger of the tables, the wonderfully blatant kitsch. Then he looked up at the Mother Lightning bird, its cousin the helicopter, and the child Lightning Bird, come with its Mother to guide the spirit of their son and half-brother, Sam Mtshali. Where the hell was *his* spirit guide when he needed it?

He reached into his pocket for the gemsbok horn. His hand came up empty. As the pain began, he narrowed his eyes and looked across the tarmac. A brightly colored object lay near the spot where he had climbed the fence. By sheer force of will, he dragged himself over to where it lay. He picked it up and lifted his head to the sky. For a moment his vision blurred and the three birds, the same but different, became one. Then his pain stopped. He looked down at his wound. To his amazement, the flow of blood had ceased.

Slowly, testing every movement, he stood.

"Black, white, Native American. All the same magic, isn't it, Mr. Cleveland?" Nkolosi's voice was soft inside Legs' head. Soothing. A grandfather, healing the cut on his grandson's knee by the gentle persuasion that a kiss could make it better.

Bloodsucking magician, Legs thought, knowing Nkolosi could hear him. He used me. *Used* me. Now what am I supposed to tell Maury?

He brushed himself off. For one thing, he thought, as he ambled toward the plane—stepping gingerly around several bodies, including Sam's—he would tell Maury to watch CNN News. He patted the video in his pocket, the one he had made of the one-and-only performance of The Zulu Warriors in the US of A. That would take care of *ethnic*, for the moment. They ought to be able to sell plenty copies of that, a few million at least, what with the killings and all. More than pay for the trip to Africa which, he decided, he personally would avoid in future.

So where next? He was fresh out of ideas . . . except, well, there was that kid he'd heard about, the one who claimed he could fly—no tricks, no gimmicks. A regular Mary Martin.

He took the piece of gemsbok horn out of his pocket, kissed it, and chuckled. "One thing you gotta say, Maury," he rehearsed out loud, patting his chest where the wound had been and holding the video-cam on high, "Alexander 'Legs' Cleveland puts on a helluva show."

CHARLES DE LINT

SEVEN FOR
A SECRET

Peter: As an occasional singer/songwriter/guitarist, it interests me to discover that several contributors to *Immortal Unicorn* have worked as far more professional musicians than I ever was. **Charles de Lint** is one: He currently plays in an acoustic band called Jump at the Sun, along with his wife, MaryAnn Harris. His consistently admirable fiction (*The Ivory and the Horn, Memory and Dream*) aside, I'm shamelessly envious of the fact that he plays Irish flute, fiddle, whistles, button accordion, bouzouki, guitar, and bodhran. He is also the proprietor/editor of Triskell Press, a small publishing house that prints fantasy chapbooks and magazines. Later for that—I want to find out how you get a sound out of that damn button accordion. . . .

Janet: I had read some of Charles de Lint's work before inviting him into this anthology, but obviously not enough. After reading this story, he's got me. I intend to read everything he has ever written. Since Charles is Canadian, I chose to leave the British spellings in his story. I think they add to the flavour.

Seven for a Secret

—◦◦◦◦◦◦—

> "It's a mistake to have only one life."
> —Dennis Miller Bunker, 1890

- 1 -

Later, he can't remember which came first, the music or the birds in the trees. He seems to become aware of them at the same time. They call up a piece of something he thinks he's forgotten; they dredge through his past, the tangle of memories growing as thick and riddling as a hedgerow, to remind him of an old story he heard once that began, "What follows is imagined, but it happened just so. . . ."

- 2 -

The trees are new growth, old before their time. Scrub, leaves more brown than green, half the limbs dead, the other half dying. They struggle for existence in what was once a parking lot, a straggling clot of vegetation fed for years by some runoff, now baking in the sun. Something diverted the water—another building fell down, supports torched by Devil's Night fires, or perhaps the city bulldozed a field of rubble, two or three blocks over, inadvertently creating a levee. It doesn't matter. The trees are dying now, the weeds and grass surrounding them already baked dry.

And they're full of birds. Crows, ravens . . . Jack can't tell the difference. Heavy-billed, black birds with wedge-shaped tails and shaggy ruffs at their throats. Their calls are hoarse, croaking *kraaacks,* interspersed with hollow, knocking sounds and a sweeter *klu-kluck.*

The fiddle plays a counterpoint to the uneven rhythm of their calls, an odd, not quite reasonable music that seems to lie somewhere between a slow dance tune and an air that manages to be at once mournful and jaunty. The fiddle, he sees later, is blue, not painted that colour; rather the varnish lends the wood that hue so its grain appeared to be viewed as though through water.

Black birds, blue fiddle.

He might consider them portents if he were given to looking for omens, but he lives in a world that is always exactly what it should be, no more and no less, and he has come here to forget, not foretell. He is a man who stands apart, always one step aside from the crowd, an island distanced from the archipelago, spirit individual as much as the flesh. But though we are all islands, separated from one another by indifferent seas that range as wide as we allow them to be, we still congregate. We are still social animals. And Jack is no different. He comes to where the fires burn in the oil drums, where the scent of cedar smudge sticks mingles with cigarette smoke and dust, the same as the rest of us.

The difference is, he watches. He watches, but rarely speaks. He rarely speaks, but he listens well.

"They say," the woman tells him, "that where ravens gather, a door to the Otherworld stands ajar."

He never heard her approach. He doesn't turn.

"You don't much like me, do you?" she says.

"I don't know you well enough to dislike you, but I don't like what you do."

"And what is it that you think I do?"

"Make-believe," he says. "Pretend."

"Is that what you call it?"

But he won't be drawn into an argument.

"Everybody sees things differently," she says. "That's the gift and curse of free will."

"So what do you hear?" he asks. His voice is a sarcastic drawl. "Fairy music?"

The city died here, in the Tombs. Not all at once, through some natural disaster, but piece by piece, block by block, falling into disrepair, buildings abandoned by citizens and then claimed by the squatters who've got no reason to take care of them. Some of them fall down, some burn.

It's the last place in the world to look for wonder.

"I hear a calling-on music," she says, "though whether it's calling us to cross over, or calling something to us, I can't tell."

He turns to look at her finally, with his hair the glossy black of the ravens, his eyes the blue of that fiddle neither of them has seen yet. He notes the horn that rises from the center of her brow, the equine features that make her face seem so long, the chestnut dreadlocks, the dark, wide-set eyes and the something in those eyes he can't read.

"Does it matter?" he asks.

"Everything matters on some level or other."

He smiles. "I think that depends on what story we happen to be in."

"Yours or mine," she says, her voice soft.

"I don't have a story," he tells her.

Now she smiles. "And mine has no end."

"Listen," he says.

Silence hangs in the air, a thick gauze dropped from the sky like a blanket, deep enough to cut. The black birds are silent. They sit motionless in the dying trees. The fiddler has taken the bow from the strings. The blue fiddle holds its breath.

"I don't hear anything," she says.

He nods. "This is what my story sounds like."

"Are you sure?"

He watches as she lifts her arm and makes a motion with it, a graceful wave of her hand, as though conducting an orchestra. The black birds lift from the trees like a dark cloud, the sound of their wings cutting through the gauze of silence. The fiddle begins to play again, the blue wood vibrating with a thin distant music, a sound that is almost transparent. He looks away from the departing birds to find her watching him with the same lack of curiosity he had for the birds.

"Maybe you're not listening hard enough," she says.

"I think I'd know if—"

"Remember what I said about the ravens," she tells him.

He returns his attention to the trees, the birds all gone. When he looks for her again, she's already halfway down the block, horn glinting, too far away for him to

read the expression in her features even if she was looking at him. If he even cared.

"I'd know," he says, repeating the words for himself.

He puts her out of his mind, forgets the birds and the
city lying just beyond these blocks of wasteland, and goes
to find the fiddler.

- 3 -

I probably know her better than anyone else around
here, but even I forget about the horn sometimes. You want
to ask her, why are you hiding out in the Tombs, there's
nothing for you here. It's not like she's an alkie or a squat-
ter, got the need for speed or any other kind of jones. But
then maybe the sunlight catches that short length of ivory
rising up out of her brow, or you see something equally
impossible stirring in her dark eyes, and you see that horn
like it's the first time all over again, and you understand
that it's her difference that puts her here, her strangeness.

Malicorne, is what Frenchy calls her, says it means
unicorn. I go to the Crowsea Public Library one day and
try to look the word up in a dictionary, but I can only find
it in pieces. Now Frenchy got the *corne* right because
she's sure enough got a horn. But the word can also mean
hoof, while *mal* or *mali* . . . you get your pick of what it
can mean. Cunning or sly, which aren't exactly compli-
ments, but mostly it's things worse than that: wickedness,
evil, hurt, harm. Maybe Frenchy knows more than he's
saying, and maybe she does, too, because she never
answers to that name. But she doesn't give us anything
better to use instead so the name kind of sticks—at least

when we're talking about her among ourselves.

I remember the first time I see her, I'm looking through the trash after the Spring Festival, see if maybe I can sift a little gold from the chaff, which is a nice way of saying I'm a bum and I'm trying to make do. I see her sitting on a bench, looking at me, and at first I don't notice the horn, I'm just wondering, who's this horsy-faced woman and why's she looking at me like she wants to know something about me. Not what I'm doing here, going through the trash, but what put me here.

We've all got stories, a history that sews one piece of who we were to another until you get the reason we're who we are now. But it's not something we offer each other, never mind a stranger. We're not proud of who we are, of what we've become. We don't talk much about it, we never ask each other about it. There's too much pain in where we've been to go back, even if it's just with words. We don't even want to think about it—why do you think we're looking for oblivion in the bottom of a bottle?

I want to turn my back on her, but even then, right from the start, Malicorne's got this pull in her eyes, draws you in, draws you to her, starts you talking. I've seen rheumy-eyed old alkies who can't even put together "Have you got some spare change?" with their heads leaning close to hers, talking, the slur gone from their voices, some kind of sense working its way back into what they're saying. And I'm not immune. I turn my back, but it's on that trash can, and I find myself shuffling over to the bench where she's sitting, hands stuck deep into my pockets.

"You're so innocent," she says.

I have to laugh. I'm forty-five and I look sixty and the last thing I am is innocent.

"I'm no virgin," I tell her.

"I didn't say you were. Innocence and virginity aren't necessarily synonymous."

Her voice wakes something in me that I don't want to think about.

"I suppose," I say.

I want to go and get on with my business. I want to stay.

She's got a way of stringing together words so that they all seem to mean more than what you think they're saying, like there's a riddle lying in between the lines, and the funny thing is, I can feel something in me responding. Curiosity. Not standing around and looking at something strange, but an intellectual curiosity—the kind that makes you think.

I study her, sitting there beside me on the bench, raggedy clothes and thick chestnut hair so matted it hangs like fat snakes from her head, like a Rasta's dreadlocks. Horsy features. Deep, dark eyes, like they're all pupil, wide-set. And then I see the horn. She smiles when she sees my eyes go wide.

"Jesus," I say. "You've got a—"

"Long road to travel and the company is scarce. Good company, I mean."

I don't much care for weird shit, but I don't tell her that. I tell her things I don't tell anybody, not even myself, how it all went wrong for me, how I miss my family, how I miss having something in my life that means anything. And she listens. She's good at the listening, everybody says so, except for Jack. Jack won't talk to her, says she's feeding on us, feeding on our stories.

"It's give-and-take," I try to tell him. "You feel better after you've talked to her."

"You feel better because there's nothing left inside to make you feel bad," he says. "Nothing good, nothing bad. She's taking all the stories that make you who you are and putting nothing back."

"Maybe we don't want to remember those things anyway," I say.

He shakes his head. "What you've done is who you are. Without it, you're really nothing." He taps his chest. "What's left inside that belongs to you now?"

"It's not like that," I try to explain. "I still remember what put me here. It doesn't hurt as much anymore, that's all."

"Think about that for a moment."

"She tells you stuff, if you're willing to listen."

"Everything she says is mumbo-jumbo," Jack says. "Nothing that makes sense. Nothing that's worth what she's taken from you. Don't you see?"

I don't see it and he won't be part of it. Doesn't want to know about spirits, things that never were, things that can't be, made-up stories that are supposed to take the place of history. Wants to hold onto his pain, I guess.

But then he meets Staley.

- 4 -

The fiddler's a woman, but she has no sense of age about her; she could be thirty, she could be seventeen. Where Malicorne's tall and angular, horse-lanky, Staley's like a pony, everything in miniature. There's nothing dark

about her, nothing gloomy except the music she sometimes wakes from that blue fiddle of hers. Hair the colour
of straw and cut like a boy's, a slip of a figure, eyes the
green of spring growth, face shaped like a heart. She's
barefoot, wears an old pair of overalls a couple of sizes
too big, some kind of white jersey, sleeves pushed up on
her forearms. There's a knapsack on the ground beside
her, an open fiddle case. She's sitting on a chunk of
stone—piece of a wall, maybe, piece of a roof—playing
that blue fiddle of hers, her whole body playing it, leaning into the music, swaying, head crooked to one side
holding the instrument to her shoulder, a smile like the
day's just begun stretching across her lips.

Jack stands there, watching her, listening. When the
tune comes to an end, he sits down beside her.

"You're good," he tells her.

She gives him a shy smile in return.

"So did you come over from the other side?" he asks.

"The other side of what?"

Jack's thinking of Malicorne, about black birds and
doors to other places. He shrugs.

"Guess that answers my question," he says.

She hears the disappointment in his voice, but
doesn't understand it.

"People call me Jack," he tells her.

"Staley Cross," she says as they shake hands.

"And are you?"

The look of a Michelle who's been called *ma belle*
too often moves across her features, but she doesn't lose
her humour.

"Not often," she says.

"Where'd you learn to play like that?"

"I don't know. Here and there. I just picked it up. I'm a good listener, I guess. Once I hear a tune, I don't forget it." The fiddle's lying on her lap. She plays with her bow, loosening and tightening the frog. "Do you play?" she asks.

He shakes his head. "Never saw a blue fiddle before—not blue like that."

"I know. It's not painted on—the colour's in the varnish. My grandma gave it to me a couple of years ago. She says it's a spirit fiddle, been in the family forever."

"Play something else," he asks. "Unless you're too tired."

"I'm never too tired to play."

She sets the bow to the strings, wakes a note, wakes another, and then they're in the middle of a tune, a slow reel. Jack leans back, puts his hands behind his head, looks up into the bare branches of the trees. Just before he closes his eyes, he sees those birds return, one after the other, leafing the branches with their black wings. He doesn't hear a door open, all he hears is Staley's fiddle. He finishes closing his eyes and lets the music take him to a place where he doesn't have to think about the story of his life.

- 5 -

I'm lounging on a bench with Malicorne near a subway station in that no-man's-land between the city and the Tombs, where the buildings are falling down but there's people still living in them, paying rent. Frenchy's sitting on the curb with a piece of cardboard cut into the shape of a guitar, dark hair tied back with a piece of string, holes in his jeans, hole in his heart where his dreams all escaped. He strums the six drawn strings on that cardboard guitar, mouthing "Plonkety, plonkety" and people are actually tossing him quarters and dimes. On the other side of him Casey's telling fortunes. He looks like the burned-out surfer he is, too many miles from any ocean, still tanned, dirty-blond hair falling into his face. He gives everybody the same piece of advice: "Do stuff."

Nobody's paying much attention to us when Jack comes walking down the street, long and lanky, hands deep in the pockets of his black jeans. He sits down beside me, says, "Hey, William," nods to Malicorne. Doesn't even look at her horn.

"Hey, Jack," I tell him.

He leans forward on the bench, talks across me. "You ever hear of a spirit fiddle?" he asks Malicorne.

She smiles. "Are you finally starting a story?"

"I'm not starting anything. I'm just wondering. Met that girl who was making the music and she's got herself a blue fiddle—says it's a spirit fiddle. Been in her family a long time."

"I heard her playing," I say. "She's good."

"Her name's Staley Cross."

"Don't know the name," Malicorne says. There's a hint of surprise in her voice, as though she thinks she should. I'm not the only one who hears it.

"Any reason you should?" Jack asks.

Malicorne smiles and looks away, not just across the street, it seems, but further than that, like she can see through the buildings, see something we can't. Jack's looking at that horn now but I can't tell what he's thinking.

"Where'd she go?" I ask him.

He gets a puzzled look, like he thinks I'm talking about Malicorne for a second, then he shrugs.

"Downtown," he says. "She wanted to busk for a couple of hours, see if she can't get herself a stake."

"Must be nice, having a talent," I say.

"Everybody's got a talent," Malicorne says. "Just like everybody's got a story."

"Unless they give it to you," Jack breaks in.

Malicorne acts like he hasn't interrupted. "Trouble is," she goes on, "some people don't pay much attention to either and they end up living with us here."

"You're living here," Jack says.

Malicorne shakes her head. "I'm just passing through."

I know what Jack's thinking. Everybody starts out thinking, this is only temporary. It doesn't take them long to learn different. But then none of them have a horn pushing out of the middle of their forehead. None of them have mystery sticking to them like they've wrapped themselves up in double-sided tape and whatever they touch sticks to them.

"Yeah, well, we'll all really miss you when you're gone," Jack tells her.

It's quiet then. Except for Frenchy's cardboard guitar, "Plonkety-plonk." None of us are talking. Casey takes a dime from some kid who wants to know the future. His pale blue eyes stand out against his surfer's tan as he gives the kid a serious look.

"Do stuff," he says.

The kid laughs, shakes his head and walks away. But

I think about what Malicorne was saying, how everybody's got a story, everybody's got a talent, and I wonder if maybe Casey's got it right.

- 6 -

"Blue's the rarest colour in nature," Staley says.

Jack smiles. "You ever look up at the sky?"

They're sharing sandwiches her music bought, coffee in cardboard cups, so hot you can't hold the container. If Jack's still worrying about magic and spirit fiddles, it doesn't show.

Staley returns his smile. "I don't mean it's hard to find. But it's funny you should mention the sky. Of all the hundreds of references to the sky and the heavens in a book like the Bible, the colour blue is never mentioned."

"You read the Bible a lot?"

"Up in the hills where I come from, that's pretty much the only thing there is to read. That, and the tabloids. But when I was saying blue's the rarest colour—"

"You meant it's the most beautiful."

She nods. "It fills the heart. Like the blue of twilight when anything's possible. Blue makes me feel safe, warm. People think of it as a cool colour, but you know, the hottest fire has a blue-white flame. Like stars. The comparatively cooler stars have the reddish glow." She takes a sip of her coffee, looks at him over the brim. "I make up for all the reading I missed by spending a lot of time in libraries."

"Good place to visit," Jack says. "Safe, when you're in a strange town."

"I thought you'd understand. You can put aside all the

unhappiness you've accumulated by opening a book. Listening to music."

"You think forgetting is a good thing?"

She shrugs. "For me, it's a necessary thing. It's what keeps me sane."

She looks at him and Jack sees himself through her eyes: a tall, gangly hobo of a man, seen better times, but seen worse ones, too. The worse ones are why he's where he is.

"You know what I mean," she says.

"I suppose. Don't know if I agree, though." She lifts her eyebrows, but he doesn't want to take that any further. "So tell me about the spirit in that fiddle of yours," he says instead.

"It hasn't got a spirit—not like you mean, anyway. It comes from a spirit place. That's why it's blue. It's the colour of twilight and my grandma says it's always twilight there."

"In the Otherworld."

"If that's what you want to call it."

"And the black of a raven's wing," Jack says, "that's really a kind of blue, too, isn't it?"

She gives him a confused look.

"Don't mind me," he tells her. "I'm just thinking about what someone once told me."

"Where I come from," she says, "the raven's an unlucky bird."

"Depends on how many you see," Jack says. He starts to repeat the old rhyme for her then. "One for sorrow, two for mirth . . ."

She nods, remembering. "Three for a wedding, four for a birth."

"That's it. Five for silver, six for gold . . ."

". . . seven for a secret never to be told . . ."

". . . eight for heaven, nine for hell . . ."

". . . and ten for the divil's own sel'." She smiles. "But I thought that was for crows."

He shrugs. "I've heard it used for magpies, too. Guess it's for any kind of blackbird." He looks up at the trees, empty now. "That music of yours," he goes on. "It called up an unkindness of ravens this afternoon."

"An unkindness of ravens," she repeats, smiling. "A parliament of crows. Where do they come up with that kind of thing?"

He shrugs. "Who knows? Same place they found once in a blue moon, I guess."

"There was a blue moon the night my great-great-grandma got my fiddle," Staley tells him. "Least that's how the story goes."

"That's what I meant about forgetting," he says. "Maybe you forget some bad things, but work at it hard enough and you forget a story like that, too."

They're finished eating now, the last inch of coffee cooling in their cups.

"You up to playing a little more music?" Jack asks. "See what it calls up?"

"Sure."

She takes the instrument from its case, tightens the bow, runs her finger across the strings to check the tuning, adjusts a couple of them. Jack likes to watch her fingers move, even doing this, without the music having started yet, tells her that.

"You're a funny guy," she says as she brings the fiddle up under her chin.

Jack smiles. "Everybody says that," he tells her.

But he's thinking of something else, he's thinking of how the little pieces of her history that she's given him add to his own without taking anything away from her. He's thinking about Malicorne and the stories she takes, how she pulls the hurt out of them by listening. He's thinking—

But then Staley starts to play and the music takes him away again.

"I was working on a tune this afternoon," she says as the music moves into three-four time. "Maybe I'll call it 'Jack's Waltz.'"

Jack closes his eyes, listening, not just to her music, but for the sound of wings.

- 7 -

It's past sundown. The fires are burning in the oil drums and bottles are being passed around. Cider and apple juice in some, stronger drink in others. Malicorne's not drinking, never does, least not that I can ever remember seeing. She's sitting off by herself, leaning against a red brick wall, face a smudge of pale in the shadows, horn invisible. The wall was once the side of a factory, now it's standing by itself. There's an owl on top of the wall, three stories up, perched on the bricks, silhouetted by the moon. I saw it land and wonder what owls mean around her. Jack told me about the ravens.

After awhile, I walk over to where she's sitting, offer her some apple juice. She shakes her head. I can see the horn now.

"What's it with you and Jack?" I ask.

"Old arguments never die," she says.

"You go back a long time?"

She shakes her head. "But the kind of man he is and I do. Live long enough, William, and you'll meet every kind of a person, hear every kind of a story, not once, but a hundred times."

"I don't get what you mean," I say.

"No. But Jack does."

We hear the music then, Staley's fiddle, one-two-three, one-two-three, waltz time, and I see them sitting together on the other side of the fires, shadow shapes, long tall Jack with his raven hair and the firefly glow of Staley's head bent over her instrument. I hear the sound of wings and think of the owl on the wall above us, but when I check, it's gone. These are black birds, ravens, a flock of them, an unkindness, and I feel something in the air, a prickling across my skin and at the nape of my neck, like a storm's coming, but the skies are clear. The stars seem so close we could be up in the mountains instead of here, in the middle of the city.

"What are you thinking about?" Malicorne asks.

I turn to her, see the horn catch the firelight. "Endings," I find myself saying. "Where things go when they don't fit where they are."

She smiles. "Are you reading my mind?"

"Never was much inclined for that sort of thing."

"Me, either."

That catches me by surprise. "But you . . ." You're magic, I was going to say, but my voice trails off.

"I've been here too long," she says. "Stopped to rest a day or so, and look at me now. Been here all spring and most of the summer."

"It's been a good summer."

She nods. "But Jack's right, you know. Your stories do nourish me. Not like he thinks, it's not me feeding on them and you losing something, it's that they connect me to a place." She taps a finger against the dirt we're sitting on. "They connect me to something real. But I also get you to talk because I know talking heals. I like to think I'm doing some good."

"Everybody likes you," I tell her. I don't add, except for Jack.

"But it's like Scheherazade," she says. "One day the stories are all told and it's time to move on."

I'm shaking my head. "You don't have to go. When you're standing at the bottom of the ladder like we are, nobody can tell you what to do anymore. It's not much, but at least we've got that."

"There's that innocence of yours again," she says.

"What the hell's that supposed to mean?"

She smiles. "Don't be angry."

"Then don't treat me like a kid."

"But isn't this like Neverneverland?" she asks. "You said it yourself. Nobody can tell you what to do anymore. Nothing has to ever change. You can be like this forever."

"You think any of us want to be here? You think we chose to live like this?"

"She's not talking about you, William," Jack says. "She's talking about me."

I never heard the music stop, never heard them approach, Jack and the fiddler, standing near us now. I don't know how long they've been there, how much they've heard. Staley lifts her hand to me, says hi. Jack, he's just looking at Malicorne. I can't tell what he's thinking.

"So I guess what you need is my story," he says, "and then you can go."

Malicorne shakes her head. "My coming or going has nothing to do with you."

Jack doesn't believe her. He sits down on the dirt in front of us, got that look in his eye I've seen before, not angry, just he won't be backing down. Staley sits down, too, takes out her fiddle, but doesn't play it. She holds the instrument on her lap, runs the pad of her thumb along the strings, toys with wooden curlicues on the head, starts to finger a tune, pressing the strings against the fingerboard, soundlessly. I wish I had something to do with my hands.

"See," Jack's saying, "it's circumstance that put most of these people here, living on the street. They're not bad people, they're just weak, maybe, or had some bad luck, some hard times, that's all. Some of them'll die here, some of them'll make a second chance for themselves and your guess is as good as mine, which of them'll pull through."

"But you chose to live like this," Malicorne says.

"You know, don't you? You already know all about me."

She shakes her head. "All I know is you're hiding from something and nobody had to tell me that. I just had to look at you."

"I killed a man," Jack says.

"Did he deserve it?"

"I don't even know anymore. He was stealing from me, sent my business belly-up and just laughed at me when I confronted him with it. Asked me what was I going to do, the money was all spent and what the hell could I prove anyway? He'd fixed the books so it looked like it was all my fault."

"That's hard," I say.

I'm where I am because I drank too much, drank all the time and damned if I can tell you why. Got nobody to blame but myself. Don't drink anymore, but it's too late to go back. My old life went on without me. Wife remarried. Kids think I'm dead.

"It was the laughing I couldn't take," Jack says. "He was just standing there, looking so smug and laughing at me. So I hit him. Grabbed the little turd by the throat and started whacking the back of his head against the wall and when I stopped, he was dead. First time I ever saw a dead person. First time I ever hit anybody, except for goofing around with the guys in high school." He looks at me. "You know, the old push and shove, but it's nothing serious."

I give him a nod.

"But this was serious. The thing is, when I think about it now, what he did to me, the money he stole, none of it seems so important anymore."

"Are you sorry?" Malicorne asks.

"I'm not sorry he's dead, but I'm sorry I was the one that killed him."

"So you've been on the run ever since."

Jack nods. "Twelve years now and counting." He gives her a long, steady look. "So that's my story."

"Do you feel any better having told us about it?"

"No."

"I didn't think you would," she says.

"What's that supposed to mean?"

"You've got to want to heal before you can get out of this prison you've made for yourself."

I'm expecting this to set him off, but he looks at the ground instead, shoulders sagging. I've seen a lot of broken men on the skids—hell, all I've had to do for years is look in a mirror—but I've never imagined Jack as one of them. Never knew why he was down here with the rest of us, but always thought he was stronger than the rest of us.

"I don't know how," he says.

"Was he your brother?" Staley asks. "This man you killed."

I've been wondering how she was taking this, sitting there so still, listening, not even her fingers moving anymore. It's hard to see much of anything, here in the shadows. Our faces and hands are pale blurs. The light from the fires in the oil drums catches Malicorne's horn, Staley's hair, awakes a shine on her lap where the blue fiddle's lying.

Jack shakes his head. "He was my best friend. I would've given him anything, all he had to do was ask."

"I'm sorry for you," Malicorne says, standing up. "I'm sorry for you both, the one dead and the other a long time dying."

She's going then, nothing to pack, nothing to carry, leaving us the way she came, with her hands empty and her heart full. Over by the oil drums, nobody notices. Frenchy is rolling himself a cigarette from the butts he collected during the day. Casey's sleeping, an empty bottle of wine lying in the dirt beside his hand. I can't see the black birds, but I can hear them, feathers rustling in the dark all around us. I guess if you want to believe in that kind of thing, there's a door standing open nearby.

"Let me come with you," Jack says.

Malicorne looks at him. "The road I'm traveling goes on forever," she says.

"I kind of guessed that, what with the horn and all."

"It's about remembering, not forgetting."

He nods. "I know that, too. Maybe I can learn to be good company."

"Nobody ever said you weren't," she tells him. "What you have to ask yourself is, are you trying to escape again or are you really ready to move on?"

"Talking about it—that's a start, isn't it?"

Malicorne smiles. "It's a very good start."

- 8 -

Staley and I, we're the only ones to see them go. I don't know if they just walked off into the night, swallowed by the shadows, or if they stepped through a door, but I never see either of them again. We sit there for awhile, looking up at the stars. They still seem so big, so near, like they want to be close to whatever enchantment happened here tonight. After awhile Staley starts to play her fiddle, that same tune she played earlier, the one in three-four time. I hear wings, in behind the music, but it's the black birds leaving, not gathering. Far off, I hear hoofbeats and I don't know what to make of that.

Frenchy gets himself a job a few weeks later, sweeping out a bar over on Grasso Street, near the Men's Mission. Casey goes back to the coast, says he's thinking of going back to school. Lots of the others, things start to look up a little for them, too. Not everybody, not all of us, but more than tried to take a chance before Malicorne came into our lives.

Me, I find myself a job as a custodian in a Kelly Street tenement. The job gives me a little room in the basement, but there's no money in it. I get by with tips from the tenants when I do some work for them, paint a room, fix a leaky faucet, that kind of thing. I'm looking for something better, but times are still hard.

Staley, she hangs around for a few days, then moves on.

I remember thinking there's a magic about her, too, but now I know it's in the music she calls up from that blue fiddle of hers, the same kind of magic any good musician can wake from an instrument. It takes you away. Calls something to you maybe, but it's not necessarily ravens or enchantment.

Before she goes, I ask her about that night, about what brought her down to the Tombs.

"I wanted to see the unicorn," she says. "I was play-ing in a pick-up band in a roadhouse up on Highway 14 and overheard somebody talking about her in the parking lot at the end of the night—a couple of 'boes, on their way out of the city. I just kind of got distracted with Jack. He seemed like a nice guy, you know, but he was so lonely."

"The unicorn . . . ?"

For a minute there I don't know what she's talking about, but then Malicorne's horsy features come to mind, the chestnut dreadlocks, the wide-set eyes. And finally I remember the horn and when I do, I can't figure out how I forgot.

"You know," Staley's saying. "White horse, big spi-raling horn coming out of her forehead."

"But she was a woman," I begin.

Staley smiles. "And Jack was a man. But when they left, I saw a white horse and a black one."

"I didn't. But I heard hoofbeats. . . ." I give her a puzzled look. "What happened that night?"

Staley shoulders her knapsack, picks up her fiddle case. She stands on tip toes and kisses me lightly on the cheek.

"Magic," she says. "And wasn't it something—just that little piece of it?"

I'm nodding when she gives me a little wave of her hand.

"See you, William," she says. "You take care now."

I wave back, stand there, watching her go. I hear a croaking cry from the top of the derelict building beside me, but it's a crow I see, beating its black wings, lifting high above the ragged roofline, not a raven.

Sometimes I find myself humming that waltz she wrote for Jack.

Sometimes I dream about two horses, one black and one white with a horn, the two of them running, running along the crest of these long hills that rise and fall like the waves of the sea, and I wake up smiling.

KAREN JOY FOWLER

THE BREW

Peter: **Karen Joy Fowler**'s "The Brew," which deals with both the miraculous and the absurdly horrible side of immortality, is one of my favorite stories in this collection. But Karen is probably best known, not for science fiction or fantasy, but for the excellent and unusual historical novel, *Sarah Canary*. She has also published a book of stories called *Artificial Things*. Karen lives in Davis, as I do; along with my wife and myself, that makes at least three people I know of who don't teach at the local branch of the University of California.

Janet: After the first time I read a Karen Joy Fowler story, I wrote her an honest-to-God fan letter, enclosing the story and asking her to sign it. We have since become friends. I still read everything she writes, still send her fan letters, only now I'm hard-pressed to know what I like most, Karen or her work.

The Brew

I SPENT LAST CHRISTMAS IN THE HAGUE. I HADN'T
wanted to be in a foreign country and away from the family at Christmastime, but it had happened. Once I was
there I found it lonely, but also pleasantly insulated. The
streets were strung with lights and it rained often, so the
lights reflected off the shiny cobblestones, came at you
out of the clouds like pale, golden bubbles. If you could
ignore the damp, you felt wrapped in cotton, wrapped
against breaking. I heightened the feeling by stopping in
an ice cream shop for a cup of tea with rum.

Of course it was an illusion. Ever since I was young,
whenever I have traveled, my mother has contrived to
have a letter sent, usually waiting for me, sometimes a
day or two behind my arrival. I am her only daughter and
she was not the sort to let an illness stop her, and so the
letter was at the hotel when I returned from my tea. It was
a very cheerful letter, very loving, and the message that it
was probably the last letter I would get from her and that
I needed to finish things up and hurry home was nowhere
on the page, but only in my heart. She sent some funny
family stories and some small-town gossip and the death
she talked about was not her own, but belonged instead to

an old man who was once a neighbor of ours.

After I read the letter I wanted to go out again, to see if I could recover the mood of the mists and the golden lights. I tried. I walked for hours, wandering in and out of the clouds, out to the canals and into the stores. Although my own children are too old for toys and too young for grandchildren, I did a lot of window-shopping at the toy stores. I was puzzling over the black elf they have in Holland, St. Nicholas' sidekick, wondering who he was and where he came into it all, when I saw a music box. It was a glass globe on a wooden base, and if you wound it, it played music and if you shook it, it snowed. Inside the globe there was a tiny forest of ceramic trees and, in the center, a unicorn with a silver horn, corkscrewed, like a narwhal's, and one gaily bent foreleg. A unicorn, tinted blue and frolicking in the snow.

What appealed to me most about the music box was not the snow or the unicorn, but the size. It was a little world, all enclosed, and I could imagine it as a real place, a place I could go. A little winter. There was an aquarium in the lobby of my hotel and I had a similar reaction to it. A little piece of ocean there, in the dry land of the lobby. Sometimes we can find a smaller world where we can live, inside the bigger world where we cannot.

Otherwise the store was filled with items tied-in to *The Lion King*. Less enchanting items to my mind—why is it that children always side with the aristocracy? Little royalists, each and every one of us, until we grow up and find ourselves in the cubicle or the scullery. And even then there's a sense of injustice about it all. Someone belongs there, but surely not us.

I'm going to tell you a secret, something I have never

told anyone before. I took an oath when I was seventeen years old and have never broken it, although I cannot, in general, be trusted with secrets, and usually try to warn people of this before they confide in me. But the oath was about the man who died, my old neighbor, and so I am no longer bound to it. The secret takes the form of a story.

I should warn you that parts of the story will be hard to believe. Parts of it are not much to my credit, but I don't suppose you'll have trouble believing those. It's a big story, and this is just a small piece of it, my piece, which ends with my mother's letter and the Hague and the unicorn music box.

It begins in Bloomington, Indiana, the year I turned ten. It snowed early and often that year. My best friend Bobby and I built caves of snow, choirs of snowmen, and bridges that collapsed if you ever tried to actually walk them.

We had a neighbor who lived next door to me and across the street from Bobby. His name was John McBean. Until that year McBean had been a figure of almost no interest to us. He didn't care for children much, and why should he? Behind his back we called him Rudolph, because he had a large, purplish nose, and cold weather whitened the rest of his face into paste so his nose stood out in startling contrast. He had no wife, no family that we were aware of. People used to pity that back then. He seemed to us quite an old man, grandfather age, but we were children, what did we know? Even now I have no idea what he did for a living. He was retired when I knew him, but I have no idea of what he was retired from. Work, such as our fathers did, was nothing very interesting, nothing to speculate on. We thought the name McBean rather funny, and then he was quite the skinflint, which struck us all, even our parents, as delightful, since he actually was Scottish. It gave rise to many jokes, limp, in retrospect, but pretty rich back then.

One afternoon that year Mr. McBean slipped in his icy yard. He went down with a roar. My father ran out to him, but as my father was helping him up, McBean tried to hit him in the chin. My father came home much amused. "He said I was a British spy," my father told my mother.

"You devil," she said. She kissed him.

He kissed her back. "It had something to do with Bonnie Prince Charlie. He wants to see a Stuart on the throne of England. He seemed to think I was preventing it."

As luck would have it this was also the year that Disney ran a television episode on the Great Pretender. I have a vague picture in my mind of a British actor—the same one who appeared with Haley Mills in *The Moon Spinners*. Whatever happened to him, whoever he was?

So Bobby and I gave up the ever-popular game of World War II and began instead, for a brief period, to play at being Jacobites. The struggle for the throne of England involved less direct confrontation, fewer sound effects, and less running about. It was a game of stealth, of hiding and escaping, altogether a more adult activity.

It was me who got the idea of breaking into the McBean cellar as a covert operation on behalf of the prince. I was interested in the cellar, having begun to note how often and at what odd hours McBean went down there. The cellar window could be seen from my bedroom. Once I rose late at night and in the short time I watched, the light went on and off three times. It seemed a signal. I told

Bobby that Mr. McBean might be holding the prince captive down there and that we should go and see. This plan added a real sense of danger to our imaginary game, without, we thought, actually putting us into peril.

The cellar door was set at an incline and such were the times that it shocked us to try it and find it locked. Bobby thought he could fit through the little window, whose latch could be lifted with a pencil. If he couldn't, I certainly could, though I was desperately hoping it wouldn't come to that—already at age ten I was more of an idea person. Bobby had the spirit. So I offered to go around the front and distract Mr. McBean long enough for Bobby to try the window. I believe that I said he shouldn't actually enter, that we would save that for a time when McBean was away. That's the way I remember it, my saying that.

And I remember that it had just snowed again, a fresh, white powder and a north wind, so the snow blew off the trees as if it was still coming down. It was bright, one of those paradoxical days of sun and ice, and so much light everything was drowned in it so you stumbled about as if there were no light at all. My scarf was iced with breath and my footprints were as large as a man's. I knocked at the front door, but my mittens muffled the sound. It took several tries and much pounding before Mr. McBean answered, too long to be accounted for simply by the mittens. When he did answer, he did it without opening the door.

"Go on with you," he said. "This is not a good time."

"Would you like your walk shoveled?" I asked him.

"A slip of a girl like you? You couldn't even lift the shovel." I imagine there is a tone, an expression, that would make this response affectionate, but Mr. McBean affected neither. He opened the door enough to tower over me with his blue nose, his gluey face, and the clenched set of his mouth.

"Bobby would help me. Thirty cents."

"Thirty cents! And that's the idlest boy God ever created. Thirty cents!!?"

"Since it's to be split. Fifteen cents each."

The door was closing again.

"Twenty cents."

"I've been shoveling my own walk long enough. No reason to stop."

The door clicked shut. The whole exchange had taken less than a minute. I stood undecidedly at the door for another minute, then stepped off the porch, into the yard. I walked around the back. I got there just in time to see the cellar light go on. The window was open. Bobby was gone.

I stood outside, but there was a wind, as I've said, and I couldn't hear and it was so bright outside and so dim within, I could hardly see. I knew that Bobby was inside, because there were no footprints leading away but my own. I had looked through the window on other occasions so I knew the light was a single bulb, hanging by its neck like a turnip, and that there were many objects between me and it, old and broken furniture, rusted tools, lawn mowers and rakes, boxes piled into stairs. I waited. I think I waited a very long time. The light went out. I waited some more. I moved to a tree, using it as a windbreak until finally it was clear there was no point in waiting any longer. Then I ran home, my face stinging with cold and tears, into our living room, where my mother pulled off my stiff scarf and rubbed my hands until the pins came into them. She made me cocoa with marshmallows. I would like you to believe that the next few hours were a very bad time for me, that I suffered a good deal more than Bobby did.

That case being so hard to make persuasively, I will tell you instead what was happening to him.

Bobby did, indeed, manage to wiggle in through the window, although it was hard enough to give him some pause as to how he would get out again. He landed on a stack of wooden crates, conveniently offset so that he could descend them like steps. Everywhere was cobwebs and dust; it was too dark to see this, but he could feel it and smell it. He was groping his way forward, hand over hand, when he heard the door at the top of the stairs. At the very moment the light went on, he found himself looking down the empty eyeslit of a suit of armor. It made him gasp; he couldn't help it. So he heard the footsteps on the stairs stop suddenly and then begin again, wary now. He hid himself behind a barrel. He thought maybe he'd escape notice—there was so much stuff in the cellar and the light so dim—and that was the worst time, those moments when he thought he might make it, much worse than what came next, when he found himself staring into the cracked and reddened eyes of Mr. McBean.

"What the devil are you doing?" McBean asked. He had a smoky, startled voice. "You've no business down here."

"I was just playing a game," Bobby told him, but he didn't seem to hear.

"Who sent you? What did they tell you?"

He seemed to be frightened—of Bobby!—and angry, but that was to be expected, but there was something else that began to dawn on Bobby only slowly. His accent had thickened with every word. Mr. McBean was deadly drunk. He reached into Bobby's hiding place and hauled him out of it and his breath, as Bobby came closer, was as ripe as spoiled apples.

"We were playing at putting a Stuart on the throne," Bobby told him, imagining he could sympathize with this, but it seemed to be the wrong thing to say.

He pulled Bobby by the arm to the stairs. "Up we go."

"I have to be home by dinner." By now Bobby was very frightened.

"We'll see. I have to think what's to be done with you," said McBean.

They reached the door, then moved on into the living room where they sat for a long time in silence while McBean's eyes turned redder and redder and his fingers pinched into Bobby's arm. With his free hand, he drank. Perhaps this is what kept him warm, for the house was very cold and Bobby was glad he still had his coat on. Bobby was both trembling and shivering.

"Who told you about Prince Charlie?" McBean asked finally. "What did they say to you?" So Bobby told him what he knew, the Disney version, long as he could make it, waiting, of course, for me to do something, to send someone. McBean made the story longer by interrupting with suspicious and skeptical questions. Eventually the questions ceased and his grip loosened. Bobby hoped he might be falling asleep. His eyes were lowered. But when Bobby stopped talking, McBean shook himself awake and his hand was a clamp on Bobby's forearm again. "What a load of treacle," he said, his voice filled with contemptuous spit. "It was nothing like that."

He stared at Bobby for a moment and then past him. "I've never told this story before," he said and the pupils of his eyes were as empty and dark as the slit in the armor. "No doubt I shall regret telling it now."

In the days of the bonnie prince, the head of the McBane clan was the charismatic Ian McBane. Ian was a man with many talents, all of which he had honed and refined over the fifty-odd years he had lived so far. He was a botanist, an orientalist, a poet, and a master brewer. He was also a very godly man, a paragon, perhaps. At least in this story. To be godly is a hard thing and may create a hard man. A godly man is not necessarily a kindly man, although he can be, of course.

Now in those days, the woods and caves of Scotland were filled with witches; the church waged a constant battle to keep the witches dark and deep. Some of them were old and haggish, but others were mortally beautiful. The two words go together, mind you, mortal and beautiful. Nothing is so beautiful as that which is about to fade.

These witches were well aware of Ian McBane. They envied him his skills in the brewery, coveted his knowledge of chemistry. They, themselves, were always boiling and stirring, but they could only do what they knew how to do. Besides, his godliness irked them. Many times they sent the most beautiful among them, tricked out further with charms and incantations, to visit Ian McBane in his bedchamber and offer what they could offer in return for expert advice. They were so touching in their eagerness for knowledge, so unaware of their own desirability. They had the perfection of dreams. But Ian, who was, after all, fifty and not twenty, withstood them.

All of Scotland was hoping to see Charles Edward Stuart on the throne, and from hopes they progressed to rumors and from rumors to sightings. Then came the great victory at Falkirk. Naturally Ian wished to do his part and naturally, being a man of influence and standing, his part must be a large one. It was the sin of ambition which gave the witches an opening.

This time the woman they sent was not young and beautiful, but old and sweet. She was everyone's mother. She wore a scarf on her hair and her stockings rolled at her ankles. Blue rivers ran just beneath the skin of her legs. Out of her sleeve she drew a leather pouch.

"From the end of the world," she said. "Brought me by a black warrior riding a white elephant, carried over mountains and across oceans." She made it a lullaby. Ian was drowsy when she finished. So she took his hand and emptied the pouch into his palm, closing it for him. When he opened his hand, he held the curled shards and splinters of a unicorn's horn.

Ian had never seen a unicorn's horn before, although he knew that the king of Denmark had an entire throne made of them. A unicorn's horn is a thing of power. It purifies water, nullifies poison. The witch reached out to Ian, slit his thumb with her one long nail, so his thumb ran blood. Then she touched the wound with a piece of horn. His thumb healed before his eyes, healed as if it had never been cut, the blood running back inside, the cut sealing over like water.

In return Ian gave the witch what she asked. He had

given her his godliness, too, but he didn't know this at the time. When the witch was gone, Ian took the horn and ground it into dust. He subjected it to one more test of authenticity. He mixed a few grains into a hemlock concoction and fed it to his cat, stroking it down her throat. The cat followed the hemlock with a saucer of milk, which she wiped, purring, from her whiskers.

Ian had already put down a very fine single malt whiskey, many bottles, enough for the entire McBane clan to toast the coronation of Charles Stuart. It was golden in color and ninety proof, enough to make a large man feel larger without incapacitating him. Ian added a few pinches of the horn to every bottle. The whiskey color shattered and then vanished, so the standing bottle was filled with liquid the color of rainwater, but if you shook it, it pearled like the sea. Ian bottled his brew with a unicorn label, the unicorn enraged, two hooves slicing the air.

Have you ever heard of the American ghost dancers? The Boxers of China? Same sort of thing here. Ian distributed his whiskey to the McBanes before they marched off to Culloden. Taken just before the battle, Ian assured them that the drink would make them invulnerable. Sword wounds would seal up overnight, bullets would pass through flesh as if it were air.

I don't suppose your Disney says very much about Culloden. A massacre is a hard thing to set to music. Certainly they tell no stories and sing no songs about the McBanes that day. Davie McBane was the first to go, reeling about drunkenly and falling beneath one of the McBanes' own horses. Little Angus went next, shouting and racing down the top of a small hill, but before he could strike a single blow for Scotland, a dozen arrows jutted from him at all points. His name was a joke and he made a big, fat target. His youngest brother Robbie, a boy of only fifteen years, followed Angus in like a running back, and so delirious with whiskey that he wore no helmet and carried no weapon. His stomach was split open like a purse. An hour later, only two of the McBanes still lived. The rest had died grotesquely, humorously, without accounting for a single enemy death.

When news reached home, the McBane wives and daughters armed themselves with kitchen knives and went in search of Ian. They thought he had lied about the unicorn horn; they thought he had knowingly substituted the inferior tooth of a fish instead. Ian was already gone, and with enough time and forethought to have removed every bottle of the unicorn brew and taken it with him. This confirmed the women's suspicions, but the real explanation was different. Ian had every expectation the whiskey would work. When the McBanes returned, he didn't wish to share any more of it.

The women set fire to his home and his brewery. Ian saw it from a distance, from a boat at sea, exploding into the sky like a star. The women dumped every bottle of whiskey they found until the rivers bubbled and the fish swam upside down. But none of the whiskey bore the unicorn label. Ian was never seen or heard from again.

"Whiskey is subtle stuff. It's good for heartache; it works a treat against shame. But, even laced with unicorn horn, it cannot mend a man who has been split in two by a sword stroke. It cannot mend a man who no longer has a head. It cannot mend a man with a dozen arrows growing from his body like extra arms. It cannot give a man back his soul."

The story seemed to be over, although Prince Charles had never appeared in it. Bobby had no feeling left in his hand. "I see," he said politely.

McBean shook him once, then released him. He fetched a pipe. When he lit a match, he held it to his mouth and his breath flamed like a dragon's. "What will I do to you if you tell anyone?" he asked Bobby. This was a rhetorical question. He continued without pausing. "Something bad. Something so bad you'd have to be an adult even to imagine it."

So Bobby told me none of this. I didn't see him again that day. He did not come by, and when I finally went over his mother told me he was home, but that he was not feeling well, had gone to bed. "Don't worry," she said, in response, I suppose, to the look on my face. "Just a chill. Nothing to worry about."

He missed school the next day and the next after that. When I finally saw him, he was casual. Offhand. As if it had all happened so long ago, he had forgotten. "He caught me," Bobby said. "He was very angry. That's all. We better not do it again."

It was the end of our efforts to put a Stuart on the throne. There are days, I admit, when I'm seeing the dentist and I pick up *People* in the waiting room and there they are, the current sad little lot of Windsors, and I have a twinge of guilt. I just didn't care enough to see it through. I enjoyed Charles and Diana's wedding as much as the next person. How was I to know?

Bobby and I were less and less friends after that. It didn't happen all at once, but bit by bit, over the summer mostly. Sex came between us. Bobby went off and joined Little League. He turned out to be really good at it, and he met a lot of boys who didn't live so near to us, but had houses he could bike to. He dumped me, which hurt in an impersonal, inevitable way. I believed I had brought it on myself, leaving him that day, going home to a warm house and never saying a word to anyone. At that age, at that time, I did not believe this was something a boy would have done.

So Bobby and I continued to attend the same school and see each other about in our yards, and play sometimes when the game was big and involved other people as well. I grew up enough to understand what our parents thought of McBean, that he was often drunk. This was what had made his nose purple and made him rave about the Stuarts and made him slip in his snowy yard, his arms flapping like wings as he fell. "It's a miracle," my mother said, "that he never breaks a bone." But nothing much more happened between Bobby and me until the year we turned sixteen, me in February, him in May.

He was tired a lot that year and developed such alarming bruises under his eyes that his parents took him to a doctor who sent them right away to a different doctor. At dinner a few weeks later, my mother said she had something to tell me. Her eyes were shiny and her voice was coarse. "Bobby has leukemia," she said.

"He'll get better," I said quickly. Partly I was asking, but mostly I was warning her not to tell me differently. I leaned into her and she must have thought it was for comfort, but it wasn't. I did it so I wouldn't be able to see her face. She put her arm around me and I felt her tears falling on the top of my hair.

Bobby had to go to Indianapolis for treatments. Spring came and summer and he missed the baseball season. Fall, and he had to drop out of school. I didn't see him much, but his mother was over for coffee sometimes, and she had grown sickly herself, sad and thin and gray. "We have to hope," I heard her telling my mother. "The doctor says he is doing as well as we could expect. We're very encouraged." Her voice wobbled defiantly.

Bobby's friends came often to visit; I saw them trooping up the porch, all vibrant and healthy, stamping the slush off their boots and trailing their scarves. They went in noisy, left quiet. Sometimes I went with them. Everyone loved Bobby, though he lost his hair and swelled like a beached seal and it was hard to remember that you were looking at a gifted athlete, or even a boy.

Spring came again, but after a few weeks of it, winter returned suddenly with a strange storm. In the morning when I left for school, I saw a new bud completely encased in ice, and three dead birds whose feet had frozen to the telephone wires. This was the day Arnold Becker gave me the message that Bobby wanted to see me. "Right away," Arnie said. "This afternoon. And just you. None of your girlfriends with you."

In the old days Bobby and I used to climb in and out each other's windows, but this was for good times and for intimacy; I didn't even consider it. I went to the front door and let his mother show me to his room as if I didn't even know the way. Bobby lay in his bed, with his puffy face and a new tube sticking into his nose and down his throat. There was a strong, strange odor in the room. I was afraid it was Bobby and wished not to get close enough to see.

He had sores in his mouth, his mother had explained

to me. It was difficult for him to eat or even to talk. "You do the talking," she suggested. But I couldn't think of anything to say.

And anyway, Bobby came right to the point. "Do you remember," he asked me, "that day in the McBean cellar?" Talking was an obvious effort. It made him breathe hard, as if he'd been running.

Truthfully, I didn't remember. Apparently I had worked to forget it. I remember it now, but at the time, I didn't know what he was talking about.

"Bonnie Prince Charlie," he said, with an impatient rasp so I thought he was delirious. "I need you to go back. I need you to bring me a bottle of whiskey from McBean's cellar. There's a unicorn on the label."

"Why do you want whiskey?"

"Don't ask McBean. He'll never give it to you. Just take it. You would still fit through the window."

"Why do you want whiskey?"

"The unicorn label. Very important. Maybe," said Bobby, "I just want to taste one really good whiskey before I die. You do this and I'll owe you forever. You'll save my life."

He was exhausted. I went home. I did not plan to break into McBean's cellar. It was a mad request from a delusional boy. It saddened me, but I felt no obligation. I did think I could get him some whiskey. I had some money, I would spare no expense. But I was underage. I ate my dinner and tried to think who I could get to buy me liquor, who would do it, and who would even know a fine whiskey if they saw one. And while I was working out the problem I began, bit by bit, piece by piece, bite by bite, to remember. First I remembered the snow, remembered standing by the tree watching the cellar window with snow swirling around me. Then I remembered offering to shovel the walk. I remembered the footprints leading into the cellar window. It took all of dinner, most of the time when I was falling asleep, some concentrated sessions when I woke during the night. By morning, when the sky was light again, I remembered it complete.

It had been my idea and then I had let Bobby execute it and then I had abandoned him. I left him there that day and in another story, someone else's story, he was tortured or raped or even killed and eaten, although you'd have to be an adult to believe in these possibilities. The whole time he was in the McBean house I was lying on my bed and worrying about him, thinking, boy, he's really going to get it, but mostly worrying what I could tell my parents that would be plausible and would keep me out of it. The only way I could think of to make it right, was to do as he'd asked, and to break into the cellar again.

I also got caught, got caught right off. There was a trap. I tripped a wire rigged to a stack of boards; they fell with an enormous clatter and McBean was there, just as he'd been for Bobby, with those awful cavernous eyes, before I could make it back out the window.

"Who sent you?" he shouted at me. "What are you looking for?"

So I told him.

"That sneaking, thieving, lying boy," said McBean. "It's a lie, what he's said. How could it be true? And anyway, I couldn't spare it." I could see, behind him, the bottles with the unicorn label. There were half a dozen of them. All I asked was for one.

"He's a wonderful boy." I found myself crying.

"Get out," said McBean. "The way you came. The window."

"He's dying," I said. "And he's my best friend." I crawled back out while McBean stood and watched me, and walked back home with a face filled with tears. I was not giving up. There was another dinner I didn't eat and another night I didn't sleep. In the morning it was snowing, as if spring had never come. I planned to cut class, and break into the cellar again. This time I would be looking for traps. But as I passed McBean's house, carrying my books and pretending to be on my way to school, I heard his front door.

"Come here," McBean called angrily from his porch. He gave me a bottle, wrapped in red tissue. "There," he said. "Take it." He went back inside, but as I left he called again from behind the door. "Bring back what he doesn't drink. What's left is mine. It's mine, remember." And at that exact moment, the snow turned to rain.

For this trip I used the old window route. Bobby was almost past swallowing. I had to tip it from a spoon into his throat and the top of his mouth was covered with sores, so it burned him badly. One spoonful was all he could bear. But I came back the next day and repeated it and the next and by the fourth he could take it easily and after a week, he was eating again, and after two weeks I could see that he was going to live, just by looking in his mother's face. "He almost died of the cure," she told me. "The chemo. But we've done it. We've turned the corner." I left her thanking God and went into Bobby's room, where he was sitting up and looking like a boy again. I returned half the bottle to McBean.

"Did you spill any?" he asked angrily, taking it back. "Don't tell me it took so much."

And one night, that next summer, in Bryan's Park with the firecrackers going off above us, Bobby and I sat on a blanket and he told me McBean's story.

We finished school and graduated. I went to IU, but Bobby went to college in Boston and settled there. Sex came between us again. He came home once to tell his mother and father that he was gay and then took off like the whole town burned to the touch.

Bobby was the first person that I loved and lost, although there have, of course, been others since. Twenty-five years later I tracked him down and we had a dinner together. We were awkward with each other; the evening wasn't a great success. He tried to explain to me why he had left, as an apology for dumping me again. "It was just so hard to put the two lives together. At the time I felt that the first life was just a lie. I felt that everyone who loved me had been lied to. But now—being gay seems to be all I am sometimes. Now sometimes I want someplace where I can get away from it. Someplace where I'm just Bobby again. That turned out to be real, too." He was not meeting my eyes and then suddenly he was. "In the last five years I've lost twenty-eight of my friends."

"Are you all right?" I asked him.

"No. But if you mean, do I have AIDS, no, I don't. I should, I think, but I don't. I can't explain it."

There was a candle between us on the table. It flickered ghosts into his eyes. "You mean the whiskey," I said.

"Yeah. That's what I mean."

The whiskey had seemed easy to believe in when I was seventeen and Bobby had just had a miraculous recovery and the snow had turned to rain. I hadn't believed in it much since. I hadn't supposed Bobby had either, because if he did, then I really had saved his life back then and you don't leave a person who saves your life without a word. Those unicorn horns you read about in Europe and Scandinavia. They all turned out to be from narwhals. They were brought in by the Vikings through China. I've read a bit about it. Sometimes, someone just gets a miracle. Why not you? "You haven't seen Mr. McBean lately," I said. "He's getting old. Really old. Deadly old."

"I know," said Bobby, but the conclusion he drew was not the same as mine. "Believe me, I know. That whiskey is gone. I'd have been there to get it if it wasn't. I'd have been there twenty-eight times."

Bobby leaned forward and blew the candle out. "Remember when we wanted to live forever?" he asked me. "What made us think that was such a great idea?"

I never went inside the toy store in the Hague. I don't know what the music box played—"Edelweiss," perhaps, or "Lara's Theme," nothing to do with me. I didn't want to expose the strong sense I had that it had been put there for me, had traveled whatever travels, just to be there in that store window for me to see at that particular moment, with any evidence to the contrary. I didn't want to expose my own fragile magic to the light of day.

Certainly I didn't buy it. I didn't need to. It was already mine, only not here, not now. Not as something I bought for myself, on an afternoon by myself, in a foreign country with my mother dying a world away. But as something I found one Christmas morning, wrapped in red paper. I stood looking through the glass and wished that Bobby and I were still friends. That he knew me well enough to have bought me the music box as a gift.

And then I didn't wish that at all. Already I have too many friends, care too much about too many people, have exposed myself to loss on too many sides. I could never have imagined as a child how much it could hurt you to love people. It takes an adult to imagine such a thing. And that's the end of my story.

If I envy anything about McBean now, it is his solitude. But no, that's not really what I wish for either. When I was seventeen I thought McBean was a drunk because he had to have the whiskey so often. Now, when I believe in the whiskey at all, I think, like Bobby, that drinking was just the only way to live through living forever.

GEORGE GUTHRIDGE

MIRROR OF
LOP NOR

Peter: **George Guthridge**'s story is not necessarily an easy read; it *is* a worthwhile one. His own statement regarding his remarkable diptych, "Mirror of Lop Nor," is well worth including here:

> "Lop Nor: Reflection" and "Lop Nor: Refraction" are meant to stand on their own, but also, mirroring one another, to form a third story. A mirror is a triad: subject, image, object. A unicorn looks in the mirror; a narwhal stares back. They eye each other without blinking. Which is the image, which the reality?

Janet: George and I met in the early eighties because of his Nebula-contending African-based short story, "The Quiet." We have essentially been writing together ever since. For multitudinous reasons, we're often called the hot-and-cold team. That we come at things differently is not surprising. I am, by nature, more European gypsy than anything else; he is an Eskimo at heart, internal and cautious. My training is as a journalist, his as a researcher.

What we do have in common is a serious love of words, a fascination for social and cultural anthropology, and an obsession with *The Great Gatsby*. George once counted the em-dashes in Fitzgerald's novel; I once fell in lust with a man—albeit briefly—simply because he, like Gatsby, looked wonderful in a pink suit.

Mirror of Lop Nor

For Noi

—reflection—

I
hear
your
hooves
above me,
cold as the
soul of the Khan.
Young, wild horses
brown as the land I
loved, manes the hair
of graves. Do not enter
here in search of Umber
or pasture, young horses.

THE AFTERLIFE IS A LIE. I KNOW: I AM DEAD, YET HAVE
no Khan to serve, no ghost horses to ride, not even the
memory of women lamenting me. No one knows where I
died except dust; and only wind wails for me, whistling in

mockery at my stupidity and despair. *Umber, who captured the Lin and witnessed the whinnying of the Lung-Ta! In whose arms do you lie forever?*

Such voices fill the desert.

In my silence I scream for them to stop, but they do not stop, the wind never stops shrieking. My only hope lies in salty waters: that Lake Lop Nor will crawl across the desert, engulf my bones, evaporate my soul, rain it down on the grasslands of my beloved Mongolia, so far, far away.

Do you love me? Bragda asked. *Taste my blood.*

I lie in terror of dark desert.

Taste my blood, Umber, she said.

So hard do I yearn for the lake that sometimes I hear it spill slowly southwest toward my release, the wind scalloping the edge, its waters filling the created cavity. Then I realize it is only the wind, always only the wind, and I rail as I remember how I scoffed at water while I lived, reminding me as it did of my father's pathetic prayers for summer rains for his sickly winter wheat.

"He who prefers water over kumiss should seek an oasis and sell pottery," I would say to Bragda after I became a Mongol. Was I not one of the Khan's Lightning Messengers, able to ride for days without stopping, riding even while asleep, the rhythm of the horse like Bragda in her abandon, breathy but never moaning? On long rides, when the water in the goatskin gave out, had I not tasted the hot sweet suck of horse blood?

My pride brash as brass in morning sunlight.

Like flies on a dead man's face.

Do you love me, Umber? she asked. *Taste my blood. The Mongols say it holds the soul.*

Now my pride is sand searing a throat whose flesh has shriveled to parchment. Wind exposes a skull, pelts my jawbone with sand, a million stinging insults. Such is the final field of the farmer's son who fancied himself Mongol, the wretch who lassoed the Lin, the husband who loved his wife but never told her so.

Instead, I left her among Mongols while I rode in joy across empire, my love seemingly only for danger and distance. Alone, she waited for my return or word of my death, surely always fearful, her face framed by a traditional headdress whose braids and bangles were strange to her, cooking mutton instead of meals of summer cabbage and winter wheat, everything foreign to her stomach and soul.

Not room enough in this great grave for so many regrets.

Come Lake Lop Nor.

Breach my bones.

Send me home to Bragda.

Taste my blood, she said.

How many days and dreams have passed since that late-winter night when last I slept beside her, warm against her flesh, warm beneath the sheepskin? Even now I see her silhouetted against the wall of the ger as the oil-lamp flickers and the squatty burkan gods watch from near the door. She disrobes: taut breasts, belly that sadly never stored a child, buttocks like mounds of black bread. I have returned from a thirty-day ride, so exhausted I want to sob like a weak woman, giddy from the pitching and yawing of the pony and the endless hours without real rest. Naked, she bows and places the small fruit offering I have brought home into the spirit house we keep in honor of our original heritage.

Then she kneels beside me, opens the boogda bag, the marmot kettled in its own skin, and with forefinger and thumb brings meat to my mouth. I am too exhausted to chew. I down the meal with marmot-grease broth, reach for her.

"A bad time," she whispers. "I am sorry. . . ."

I ignore her protest and take her roughly, stuporous with desire, thankful to be between someone else's legs rather than the horse between mine. After, she squeezes a drop of semen from me, touches it to her tongue.

"You are my lord . . . Umber."

She has never grown accustomed to my new name, for I have been Umber only since my twentieth year, son of a farmer whose name I have not spoken since that day I welcomed the enemy. He lost a son and I an ancestry the instant I took an assassin's arrow meant for Otogai, the Khan's third son—and lived to become Mongol.

I put my arm around her waist.

"It did not bother you that I am bloodied?" she asks.

I say nothing. It bothers me, but I say nothing.

Her eyes are lowered. A sign of respect. In her, a sign, I sometimes imagine, almost of reverence. It frightens me, her faith in me, and I remember again that day she stood with me when the Mongols came.

How happy I was when the army of the Khan breached the Great Wall and overran the lands of my former ancestry with its barren, barefoot fields of sickly winter wheat! It seemed that only Bragda and I did not flee before the invaders. My neighbors shook their heads at my foolishness as they herded toward the cities. "You would stay and fight for this land that yielded so little?" Father begged as he bundled our family possessions in his cart. "The Mongols have no love for farming. They will not remain. Soon we will return, my son. Do not sacrifice yourself."

Sacrifice? I stay to see the land trampled.

"You will die quickly, uselessly," he said. "A sword slash, and I will have lost my only child. And do you know what they will do to your beautiful bride?"

Why did you remain beside me amid that desolation, Bragda? You would never say.

I draw my fingers along her silken back. She shivers—quietly smiles—then touches herself between her legs and holds two fingers close to my lips. "Taste my blood, Umber," she says. "The Mongols say it holds the soul. Know me as no other man ever has—or ever will."

No woman should dare ask a man such a thing. Yet her fingers remain extended, and her eyes plead.

Her words shake me not only for what she asks but for the memory they instill. Not virginal when we wed, which was why my father, a poor farmer, was able to buy me such a beauty, her face round as the moon, soft as moonlight among lilies in bloom, feet so small you would have thought them bound, toes flexible enough that she sometimes uses them to massage my manhood, and she giggling. She has never hinted about who took her before I did.

Time ticks, her heart beating against my chest, and I sense fear emanate from her like warmth from a candle.

She lifts her eyes—moist with love, as the rest of her has so often been for me. Demean myself this way for her, I sense, and I will never lose her love no matter how many rides I might require—of her, away from her. I know not why it is important to her, yet I sense a gateway of our lives hinges on this moment. Just as it did that sun-scorched afternoon when we stood together—she behind me, trembling; I could sense her trembling—and watched the Khan's cavalry march a hundred abreast across the fallow, hallowed ground on which my ancestors toiled and dreamed and died.

I lift my head toward her fingers.

Am interrupted by the tent's wood-framed flap slapping open.

Bragda jerks her hand away, desperate to squirm beneath the sheepskin as Jailspur enters without knocking. There is no need for the formality of knocking. Commander of the Messengers, the warrior to whom Otogai himself gave the task of teaching me how to ride, Jailspur has treated me as the son he never had, and in return I have accorded him the respect my real father deserved. As usual he is impatient, suspicious, his scant mustache and beard seeming to give his aged, weathered face a perpetual sneer, but beneath that demeanor dwells the man who not only showed me how to handle a horse and how to survive, but also lovingly drilled into me tales of honor and of the yasak, the Khan's code of laws.

He glances around the ger as if expecting treachery, then haughtily peers down on us, the wrinkled folds of his eyelids like hoods. "You ride," he says.

"But I just returned."

"You would disobey me?"

"Of course not." Already I am rising, pulling myself into sheepskin cloak and felt socks, my joints sore and stiff. "Where would you have me go?"

"Khwarezm. You will tell Temujin that we have captured an Uighur monk who ciphers symbols."

To bring such a message to the Khan himself? My heart should skip as joyfully as a flat stone. Not only is it the highest honor to serve him personally, he rewards Messengers regardless of their message—one reason for his warfare success—rather than adopting the Chinese custom of executing bearers of bad fortune. The news will delight him. For has he not said that those who read and write hold the power of gods? *Find a scribe who can pen our history,* he has declared, *and our glory will live forever.*

Instead of skipping, the stone sinks.

At least another three months without Bragda, who now pokes her head from under the covers, staring in horror from me to Jailspur. He looks away, abruptly ill at ease, and in that instant she briefly shakes her head at me in terror. Fear emanates from her in even greater waves.

When he eyes her again, his gaze registers contempt, as though he sees her nakedness despite the sheepskin cover.

And suddenly I *know*.

He has had her, against her will, while I was away.

He who taught me that warriors guilty of murder or adultery or urinating on water so respect the yasak that they will announce their transgression and expect to be put to death without ever having been accused.

My Mongol father.

Turning, he stalks into the night, me stumbling behind, pulling on boots. Wanting to kill him but knowing I cannot accuse, much less condemn. He is a commander. And I, after all, a foreigner.

Above us the Eternal Blue Heaven, ear to so many Mongol prayers, is but a black bowl crusted with icy stars that twinkle in mockery.

He reaches his tent, pauses, walks on. Perhaps he

knows I am aware of what he has done but fears to involve his family. Perhaps he seeks a place where he can quietly murder me. If so, it would be a favor.

We wend through camp, he not acknowledging me behind him. The air, filled with the smell of smoke and butter and mutton, crackles with the cold. Snow snaps beneath our footfalls. I hear a woman humming, and I wonder what Bragda must be thinking. I wonder if she has snuffed the lamp and sits in darkness, humiliation emanating from her like heat.

When Jailspur reaches the edge of the huge camp, the clouds uncover the moon. It is as if he has ordered a curtain pulled back, nature acquiescing to his wishes. How many times in these five years since Bragda tugged the arrow shaft from my back and nursed me again to health have I witnessed Earth and Heaven side with the Mongols? I could kill him, but I cannot kill them all, and I have no power to fight the world.

On the grasslands, white-muzzled horses mill uneasily, many nervously pawing frozen ground, as if the renewed light has found out some conspiracy among them. There are five hundred of them—half the herd that was among the bounty from Kara Khitai, the enormous kingdom that once I called home. The rest are with the Khan. Rallying symbols as the Mongols march against Bukhara and Balkh.

Jailspur removes his caftan, tosses it onto the ground and, bare-chested despite the cold, spreads his arms, as if expecting the horses to come. They shy away, moving as with one mind.

"The finest steeds this side of eternity," he says, picking up his jacket and holding it in the crook of his arm as he gazes across the grasslands. "Were you or I born like the Khan, clutching a blood clot in our fist, then perhaps we, too, would own such an animal, eh Umber? Perhaps the Blue Heaven would smile on us as well."

I neither answer nor step up beside him as an equal. I remain behind, as a woman might. As an assassin might.

"I have delivered few messages these past years," he says. "I kept turning my responsibilities over to you. People have been laughing. I hear them say *old* behind their lips. What did you expect of me, Umber?"

"And yet you would have me go again."

This time it is his turn to be silent. He puts the caftan across his shoulder and, hunched as though burdened by the weight of the moonlight, saunters off toward a distant hill, the horses slowly scattering.

I watch him until he disappears into darkness, and when I turn to go back to my tent I am surprised to find Bragda behind me. She holds my leather armor and peaked metal helmet—my proudest possession other than the wife a poor, wise farmer chose for me—and I find myself trembling as I recall how she stood behind a husband branded a fool by his neighbors and insolent by his father, while the Khan's terrible cavalry came on. I tremble not from the fear I felt then but the love I feel now. Tremble so much that my teeth chatter. I clamp my lips shut.

She waits, eyes downcast, until I follow her cue and put on the armor and helmet. When she looks up at it there is a sad smile in her gaze. Perhaps she remembers how, when Jailspur gave me the helmet after a year's horsemanship instruction, she said I was a Ki, the horned horse of Chinese legend.

From beside her feet—bare toes curled upon the

snow—she lifts my saddlebags and leather drinking pouch. "I tucked a cabbage amid the dried meat and milk curds," she says. "I traded for it during"—the eyes again downcast—"during the time you were gone. It was to be your breakfast, after you were rested."

When she gives me the things our hands touch. The edges of her eyes tighten, a look of pain. "Go now, " she says.

"Bragda."

"Go. And do not look back, my love. The spirits will think you're not watching the trail, and will steal your eyes."

She backs away—hesitantly; now turning, hurrying off. I think I hear her crying, but it is only a mother humming a child asleep.

"I'll come back for you," I call out. "I will come back."

A dog barks. Smoke from a thousand tents rises into moonlight. I stand there until the day dawns violet against the hill toward which Jailspur walked, before I trudge to where the Lightning Mounts are hobbled and select the dapple-gray I often use for the first and last legs of journeys. I let the horse trot from camp, she seeming happy to be moving. Without nodding I pass women gathering dung for fires and boys tending horses and sheep. They eye me curiously. The ugly Chinese.

For three days I do not look back—not until I crest the summit of the eastern pass through the Heavenly Mountains and see Lung-Ta prayer-flags snapping in the wind, one color for each realm of the universe. All point back toward the northeast, the land of Khan. An odd, ill omen; winter winds usually blow south.

Rather than invoking the traditional prayer to the

passes, I murmur to the Wind Horse, guardian of the elements of self-control: body, speech, mind. "Be a steed for the spirits, Lung-Ta," I beg him. "Carry them to watch over my wife."

I switch ponies at Barkol, the dapple-gray about to drop. I have long since worked past exhaustion; hatred drives me on. I suck my anger like a pebble in a parched mouth.

Days wing by like the birds that sometimes come squalling out of the infinite blue, angry with the intruder. Their cries shake me awake; for the first time since I learned to ride long distances, I have given myself over to the horse's rhythm out of frustration rather than love. A golden-brown mare, she trots along as though unaware she carries anyone, much less a Chinese.

At Hami we cross the Silk Road, the ruts of a thousand years and myriad caravans etched into the desert, and continue southwest toward Lop Nor and the southern route—faster but more hazardous than going west through Kashgar, where camel drivers and shopkeepers might see the pain behind my scowl. I break into a gallop when I see the great salt lake shining like a coin beneath the sun, and pretend I am in an even greater hurry than I am when I change horses at the outpost on the northern shore. The two men stationed there raise eyebrows in hope of news or kind words, but I offer neither, dismounting and sending the next steed, a piebald, galloping as I run and leap on, the animal wild-eyed at my insistence, splashing through the salt marsh.

Dusk has oranged the horizon when we come to the southern end of the lake, where I pull up so abruptly that I yank both reins and mane.

Drinking from the salt waters is a Lin.

Reddish and shaggy, the mare has muscular shoulders, a swayed back, and huge haunches, as if built for fertility. She does not look up as I slide from my horse and approach, but watches me coolly, only a slight shake of her head indicating she is aware of me. Her horn—except for its fleshy tip, translucent as an icicle—catches the waning light. I squat, knees cracking, as if a lowered level will power blood to my brain and enable me to see that she is merely mirage. Or hallucination.

Now she lifts her head, a bundle of rushes between her teeth, her jaw working, water falling from her muzzle and splashing, disturbing the stillness. Bragda, I realize, was right. The Ki and Lin, male and female of the species, are real. As real as my dreams were false.

She canters away across the desert, the land flat and nondescript here, not the wind-tortured landforms deep within the Takla Makan, the desert from which no living thing returns. As if Eternal Heaven, angry over the uncaring and ugliness of the people below, slammed a fist between the Heavenly Mountains to the north and the Himalayas to the south, then twisted knuckles in despair. Such is the wretched land of the Takla Makan.

I jump onto the piebald and ride after her.

For days I follow her into the desert, my heart racing faster the more my mount continues to tire. It has become apparent that the Lin is leading me rather than being followed, for she never lets me closer than the length of my father's field, speeding up each time I kick the piebald into a panting gallop but slowing should I fall behind.

Why, I wonder, has she led me into the desert? To keep her pursuer from returning to alert others that she exists?

The brown expanse tufted with brush gives way to land knobbed with sandstone forms so grotesque they look like evil idols. It is as if I have entered a supernatural world. Calcite is crusted like opium, and shale set on edge curves up like talons or scimitars waiting to slice open the unwary. The piebald limps along, head and tail drooping, legs nicked in a dozen places.

When the Lin pauses at a tall stickery bush jutting like a flame between two ragged hills, I also halt. I spear my helmet into the soil, line it with hide torn from my saddlebag, pour precious water within, again pull myself onto the horse, ride away and wait. The Lin stops cropping the bush and slowly serpentines toward the offering. Knowing I cannot catch her unawares, I hope to win her trust, so that—against all logic: sun, exhaustion, and desperation having warped my reasoning—she will come to me of her own will.

She examines the helmet but does not drink. Then she snorts as if in disgust and wanders away, her gait less certain now.

When at last, disheartened, I go back to the helmet she is again a farmer's field away. I drop to the ground and consider the water instead of replacing it in the bag. Sunlight reflects off the liquid as though off a coin. I remember the gleam of Lop Nor, the lake that moves, its marsh-rushes like lashes around a glassy eye staring up from the desert as if scrutinizing God.

Salt. That is what drew her to Lop Nor! Salt—together with water: symbols of life and immortality. Elixir for a horned horse.

Salt fringed a dry watercourse along what is now the horizon, I remember. Heart thudding, I leap onto the piebald and race him so urgently, backtracking, that twice he nearly falls. When we arrive he is lathered and gasping. I wrench off a boot, scoop in salt and dirt, the Lin again, insanely, a field away, and gallop back to the helmet, holding the boot like a chalice. The Lin, once more cropping the spike bush, eyes me as I filter salt from sand, my fingers a sad sieve. I have witnessed her look before.

"Bragda," I utter through parched lips.

The sound so startles me that I cease working, pour half the boot-sand into the helmet. If the lake has a sandy bottom, why not my capful? I mount the piebald and, watching one another, the Lin and I ascribe a circle, she to the helmet, I to the bush. Up close I see that its main branches, white as poplar, are long and strong and straight. With my knife I whittle off the greatest length I can find as the Lin drinks, neighing her satisfaction, shaking her head, again drinking. From my saddlebag thongs I fashion a lasso, attach it to one end of the branch and at the other make a loop for my hand, reviewing with a kind of exultant anxiety the lessons Jailspur taught. How to ride upside down, dangling from a stirrup; or on my head, a shoulder snugged in the saddle; above all how to lasso a takhi—a wild pony. My sorriest skill. As though I had captured myself one sun-scorched afternoon as the Khan's cavalry rode toward me, and I had not the heart to capture anything else.

"Bragda," I repeat, under my breath. The Lin whinnies as if in answer.

I pat the piebald. He is spent. What horseman am I, using him up like this? I resolve to make his anguish up to him should we capture the Lin. Give him the remaining water and curds, walk before him rather than ride as we return to the Lop Nor station, and there order him rubbed down and fed, then set free. Even now the men would obey me, but report me to be punished. With the Lin in tow they will obey *instantly,* report me with pride. I will own the finest horse beneath Blue Heaven.

"Soon," I whisper in the piebald's ear, and mount him, he stumbling to hold me.

I kick him and ride down on the Lin like a thunder, the piebald struggling to respond. The mare seems reluctant to move from the salt water, as if it has drugged her senses. This time she eyes me in fear, not condescension.

Then, as though breaking from a spell, she jerks up her head and starts to bolt, tension rolling the length of her, power gathered in her hind legs.

"Bragda!" I shriek in a cracked, croaky voice as the piebald's hooves pound and dust boils up around me. The Lin hesitates—an instant too long before she lurches left. I am now so near I can see the sheen of sweat upon her flanks. I thrust the lasso forward. The noose dangles in the sun.

Then it is around her neck. She swivels on all fours, facing me, straining against the leash, legs spread, like a dog worrying a rag. Her snorts are desperate, high-pitched; she jousts at the branch with her horn, twisting her head from side to side.

"I've come for you!" I yell at her. "You see I came back!"

She kicks the helmet, sending it catapulting end over end, water wheeling into the air. I am jerked off-balance. The piebald lurches, trying to adjust himself to the rider, and in his exhaustion, stumbles. The mare lunges back— too late. The piebald pierces its neck on the mare's horn—and instantly rears, screaming. I tumble from the saddle, unsuccessfully fighting to keep my feet in the stirrups, hit the ground so hard my breath exits in a whoosh. As I lie trying to suck in air, the Lin watches as if in horror as the piebald collapses. Then the mare flees, pulling me with her.

Dirt covers my face, choking me, rocks rumble against my back and buttocks. I hang on whether I want to or not, my hand trapped in the loop. Far behind me the piebald is on the ground, kicking spastically, crying its pain and terror. Shadows slant like ribs across my face and then I am pulled through the bush, branches and brambles raking my skin and eyes. She drags me onward, and I know I would not let go even if I could. The mare, like Bragda, is all I have. Other than delusion.

I will die this way, I decide, here in a realm rendered evil by the elements. Not that death much matters, except for my not seeing Bragda again. What was I thinking when I shirked my duty as Messenger and followed the mare? That she would make me so respected my position would be elevated above Jailspur's? That he would be forced to dissemble before me and fear for his life?

Suddenly the Lin stops.

And lies down.

I clamber to my feet, spitting dirt, wiping grime from my eyes. Her back is toward me, chest heaving. Surely the sojourn in the desert could not have weakened her so!

She turns her head toward me, nostrils flared, her gaze more that of victim than victor. In her eyes I see darkness spreading. The wind has picked up, whining past my ears. As I peer at the sky, fear twists my insides like rope. Black clouds drive across the desert, sand furling before them. Takla Makan storms, infamous for their severity, arise so quickly that the only warning experienced caravaners have is when the older camels abruptly halt and thrust their mouths into the sand.

I claw at the loop, squinting around anxiously for shelter. As if taunting me for my travail, the sandstone idols waver and disappear behind the onslaught of sand. It assaults my face like needles. I cry out in pain—unable to hear my voice above the wind—and clutch my jacket's felt liner against my cheeks. I collapse to my knees, nuzzle my head against the mare. She does not resist.

The sand beats a furious percussion against my leather armor while I huddle, as concerned now for the plummeting cold as for the sand. I wriggle my right hand, still attached to the loop, beneath her head, and snuggle ever closer against her flanks, not unlike how I used to lie with Bragda, my groin cupping her buttocks, my left arm around her torso, hand on a breast, my right hand pillowing her head.

Though my eyes are clenched shut, the insides of the lids seem coated with dirt. As I struggle for breath, the mare's heat is a heaven I can almost taste but not touch with my lips, separated as it is from me by felt. I wonder if the sky is also felt, behind which lives the warmth and heart of God.

Bragda, my mind moils, and I wonder if Jailspur is upon her, absorbing her heat—never her heart. Why did I not plunge my knife into his back!

As abruptly as it began, the storm subsides. Here in the Takla Makan it is not like in the Gobi, where storms rage for days, sand browning the sky yet leaving the land unchanged. Here, storms slash like a Mongol sword, delivering death, carving up the world.

When I look up, coughing against the grit in my mouth and shoving away at the sand cloaked to my shoulders, I seem to have arisen in some other world. The idol-shaped sandstone formations are aproned with dirt, as though their essence has been pulled out of them.

I stand, shaking off the sand and fear. The mare also gains her feet, weak-kneed and unsure on the impermanent earth, neighing her dismay, softly tossing her head. I start to unloop the thong from around my wrist but decide against it; she seems resigned to the fate of the pole and noose. We trudge through sand together, awkwardly, my right arm across my chest; I am on the wrong side of her.

We crest the rise.

No sign of the piebald. A dune has avalanched, its alluvial fans spread across the depression in which the animal died—if indeed I am facing the right direction.

Needing a focal point, I search for the bush from which I cut the pole. The bush is also gone, as though the wind uprooted it and sent it flying like the arrow of an assassin. I dig among the alluvial for my goatskin bag, but to no avail. We will have to reach the Lop Nor station without water.

I do not, dare not, let go of the loop. We head off in what I hope is the right direction. Above, as if in contradiction to the cold, the sun blazes. I have the ugly sense that the desert is how the sun wants the world: scoured clean of life, reduced to sandscape. Beneath the glare, everything looks white, the color of mourning. Not even the most hardened Mongol would enjoy such austerity. There is a greater feeling of death here than I have ever known. Temujin's bloodbaths pale beside it.

The mare and I stumble on, she perhaps as physically

and spiritually lost as I, keeping close to me as we move across the barrenness. The cold continues to deepen. Plumes of breath hang momentarily from her nostrils like fine feathers, and in her horn, sunlight coalesces like warmth congealed. I am tempted to take hold of it, but I would no more touch it than I would a fellow Buddhist's head, highest point of the body and thus residence of the soul. For me, the highest point was not head but helmet, which I had thrust into dirt. Perhaps wisely, perhaps an insult to ancestors.

We crest another hill; beyond lies the sharpened shale, which seems to stretch forever. Was it such an expanse when we came? How obsessed was I with the Lin!

We start forward, though I know I will never survive the crossing. The shale will slice my boots, pierce my feet. The mare balks: from fear, I think at first, but when she tilts her head and then lowers it, throatily snorting, I grasp her intent.

Wants me to ride.

She shivers and turns in an uneasy circle as I mount, her eyes full of fear, her whinnying seemingly one of subtle lament, not insult. The storm seems to have scoured me of whatever pride or joy I should feel at mounting such sublimity, and yet a thought occurs: if I gifted the Lin to the Khan, could he not mate her with stallions of the Kara Khitai herd? Might he not elevate me to the top of the empire? Perhaps even make me his fifth son?

But the thought fades, another lone bird squalling above desert only to wing away, and for the first time in my life I feel at peace. The mare starts forward through the ragged rocks without my urging, hooves clinking against stone like the chime of a Buddhist bell. Who shod her, and why? The Eternal Blue Heaven, seeking to keep all creatures bound to the earth?

Around us, shale wavers like fingers of demons or the dead reaching up to protest our passing, and suddenly I know why the region seemed smaller before. Death is not to be denied. Was the area more compact during our first crossing, hoping to draw us into a trap—or wider now, attempting to hold us within?

The Lin provides a path.

Then I can see Lop Nor, shining in the sky and reflecting the ground—a trick not uncommon in the desert—though the lake is still many days away. There, salt water awaits the mare; and, too, a stall. For should we reach the station, I will never release her. I am not strong enough for that. I came for her; I will never let go.

We thread among shale for a day and into darkness. When dawn blooms along the horizon, sand and crusted earth greet us; we have completed the crossing.

The mare does not try to shake off her human weight, as I expected she might. Desire for the elixir of Lop Nor, I suspect, drives her despite the looming loss of freedom. Above us, the lake blinks in and out of existence, as though now and again closing its eye to the world.

"Bragda," I whisper, and pat the mare's neck.

Her head, already hanging, lowers even further as if in acquiescence.

That evening, as the first clouds I have seen since the storm lie like coiled cloth along the horizon, the winking of the lake escalates my thirst. I had thought myself no longer capable of saliva. Even now, though saliva spumes in my cheeks, I cannot swallow, so parched and swollen is my throat. As I lie beside the mare, seeking warmth, I fight the desire that pulses in that throat, that finally pulses up and down my body, like taut nerves struck with a tuning fork. I fight, but my body is too aflame with thirst. *Why not?* tolls like a bell in my brain. *Why not drink of her, Umber? What harm could come of it!*

I pray to the Eternal Blue Heaven, to Bragda, to my father son of a farmer son of a farmer for release from greed; but the day is dark, Bragda is not listening, the prayers to my father and my fathers before him are plaintive laments from beyond a far, far field.

I press tightly against her, trying to commune with her. What is she thinking? *How* does she think? The desire for water makes my heart race. Even my skin tingles with the craving. *Forgive me,* my inner voice whispers, but I do not mouth the words, for fear she will hear and, understanding, flee.

I slide my knife from its sheath, quickly cut a tiny slit along the right gaskin, and lower my lips to the wound. She neighs her dismay and starts to rise, but I am up with her, and then the effort seems to expel from her and she lies down again. The drug that is her lifeblood courses through me. My mind feels the emollient; though my limbs heat up, listlessness suffuses me—a reaction the opposite of what I would have believed.

As she gains her feet I easily stand, but the desert appears to slant to and fro, as if my mind is water a child is attempting to hold in a shallow pan. Careless yet careful, I again mount, aware with heightened senses of the world around me. Each grain of sand looms large. Each, a miracle.

How wonderful the elixir that is the blood of the mare!

We will make the station, I know; and I can give the Khan the essence of the Lin without my having to give her up. Sequester the mare, dole out her blood to Temujin a vial at a time. Who then would be the more powerful—he, or Umber?

I could buy my father and neighbors out of their bondage at Jinquan. Again they will have farms and freedom. I will send searchers into the opium dens, whose windows, below street level, look out on the world but see nothing. We will find Bragda's father, and surely with the goodness and grace of the blood of the Lin he will escape his addiction.

And Bragda will love me.

And forgive me for leaving her.

A distant whinny assails us, dissipating my daydreams.

The Lin halts. Together we look around, she seemingly as confused as I over the new sound.

Then we see a stallion, nimbused by the sun, upon a bluff whose stark sides have been riven by the wind. He lifts, kicking at the air. Fastened to his back, what at first looks like the spiked bush sparkles darkly. Not a bush, I realize, but a triad of wish-fulfilling jewels, elongated and egg-shaped, set as though in a lotus-flower saddle.

The Lin whinnies and keeps turning toward the stallion, regardless of how hard I kick her onward toward Lop Nor. Curiously, I feel no fear; perhaps the blood-drug lodged in my gut has calmed my heart. I blink at the realization of good fortune—who but the dead and dreamers have witnessed the Lung-Ta?—and close my eyes.

Drowsiness descends, and abruptly I am on the ground, gasping and looking up at Lop Nor shimmering in the sky directly above me. My reflection peers down from the lake. I could cry, had I moisture enough for tears.

The Lin lowers her head and nuzzles me as if to assure I am alive. I groan; the sound seems to spill from outside my body, echoing beneath the bowl of Heaven. "Go away," I manage to say.

She nudges my ribs more insistently, attentive even to an enemy.

"Bragda?" I ask, and let the loop fall from my grip.

I know now why Bragda stood behind me that day the Mongols came. Not in support but in hope that together we would run away.

Perhaps she will be better off with Jailspur: among Mongols, stealing another's wife is not so much infamy as tradition. He might not love her as I did but at least he if leaves her he will say good-bye.

When I stagger to my feet, I see the mare bound up the bluff toward the white stallion. How else but by freeing her could I keep her from the Khan?

I walk toward Lop Nor, and when darkness descends I lie down against the cold, my blood chilling, never to warm again. I have the spirit but not the physical skills to go on. In my dreams I see the Lin and Lung-Ta canter across clouds.

I awaken not into daybreak but into death. Sand whistles through my rib cage and fills the cavity of my pelvis. Desert-spiders and, once, a hare scuttle across the expanse and find sustenance in my shriveled flesh. The giving makes my jawbones sag open in a smile. I know the karma in that, know it literally in my bones, and when I look up through eyeless sockets at Lop Nor, I am not afraid. Not even of Mongols whose ghosts might ride the wind.

Another storm comes, so ferocious that it sends rocks running. I laugh at its weakness. Sand covers my bones, as though the world is incensed at my insult. I lie awaiting Lop Nor.

Instead of water, I hear hooves. They pass again and again across my grave, gradually revealing my face. The herd is golden brown, offspring of a silver-white stallion and a russet mare. So fine-limbed and sleek-bodied is the herd that their hooves barely touch the earth as they roam the Takla Makan—now home to mustangs not even a Mongol could ride. I am happy as I await the lake, for in dying I have learned to live; and by drinking the Lin's blood have learned that, except for escape, there is no evil.

—refraction—

I
am
amid
narwhals'
whistles and
terrified wheezes,
like elders coughing;
flukes slapping, kayak
creaking, ice converging
as froth and fear pull me
into waves in whose tangled
hair sea mammals breed and
bear: the world's watery roots.

I DO NOT FIGHT THE DROWNING. IT TROUBLES ME NO more than the failure of the research project. Without sorrow or solace I remember how, before the narwhals collapsed the kayak, this sea and my soul were calm as a mirror, the narwhals mirrors of the world's fragility, their flanks a map of time.

My eyes and lungs bulge, salt water and bile burst into my mouth, bubbles escape as if seeking a higher life-form to inhabit. I am oddly at peace despite the pain, as though, like water bending light, the fjord refracts my past. As sea and ice give way to darkness, I imagine the kayak's skirt hugging my waist, thinking *there is no life without winter.* Moon the color of snow, glaciers lying like predators along the fjord. Whalesong—and spray from the narwhals' spouting. Do only we Eskimos see the value of the white world? Jerac was right: women should hold the animal's legs while their husbands skin. He was wrong about everything else. As I was, about everything.

I imagine myself again paddling in the polynia, the narwhals in a rosette around me, flukes toward the kayak, tusks outward. I barely dip the paddles, awed by what might drive whales to such a geometric. Display of com-munal well-being, or does an enemy lurk? Will an orca surface or polar bear pad out from among icefall? I lift my paddle in an absurd attempt at defending myself.

I sigh at my naïveté, put down the paddle; the whale-song is not one of fear. I let the kayak drift as I admire the tusks. Slender and spiraled, brittle and exquisite. Small wonder why Medieval Europeans used them as scepters and believed them imbued with Grace: capable of curing impotency or ague, able to detect and neutralize poison. Symbols of imperial power, they brought a king's ransom.

Today, for as little as three thousand krøner, you can hang one in your den; for only fools believe in unicorns. The educated pontificate about rhinos being the basis of the myth, while the real unicorns go on dying—harvested for horns, or their tusks caught in cod and salmon nets.

The wind comes up as if to chill my anger, reminding me that the world of ice pack and ice cap, though filled with retribution, is without remorse. The living cannot retrieve the dead.

I am chilled despite my polypropylene, sweater, down coat, anorak. My perspiration has begun to freeze. As usual I am overdressed—as I was at Copenhagen's Polytekniske except for my freshman year. After Jerac left school, I discarded my jeans for skirts and pressed slacks. I became the Eskimo who had discarded her culture. Jerac and the Arctic taught me nothing, nothing; but I learned less at the university. Heat, not cold, kills earliest on the ice; I know that much. It is opposite in academe.

Maybe as a grad student I should have attempted to radio-tag Jerac instead of narwhals. Perhaps I could have kept track of him. And he, me.

We met at Polytekniste as freshmen, both never out of Greenland before. Right off the ice, as they say. He was gorgeous: skin like moist terra-cotta, physique that brought him the gold in the knuckle-hop at the Eskimo Olympics, eyes so dark our heritage could not account for their depth. "A magician in bed," my dormmates told me. "Makes your inhibitions disappear."

We became lovers back home the following summer, while working at the cannery in Godthåb. Rather, he worked—on the slime line sixteen hours a day—and I was paid for delivering coffee and bad jokes. "Happy slimers are safe slimers," I had convinced the corporation, proving to myself, and any worker I could browbeat into listening, that the fishing industry's executives had the brains of beat-up humpies seeking to spawn.

Perhaps if he were not always giving up precious sleep to sleep with me, our weekend on the tundra would have gone differently. Jerac packed the basics, I brought my usual: Walkman with mini-speakers, freeze-dried kung pao chicken, leather flask filled with chablis. And mushrooms, this time.

An experimenter back then, I was anxious to try some, but only if Jerac joined me. At first he shook his head. I delayed asking again until after we made love to exhaustion—my exhaustion, anyway—in that endless light while the summer wind sighed against our tent. At last he lay with his head on my belly as we talked and snacked on pickled mangtuk. "About the mushrooms," I asked again, and he became silent; lay looking at the ceiling.

"They say that's what caused her problem," he said bitterly.

"I thought you said she'd eaten too much stink flipper. Or was drunk."

"She *couldn't* have been drunk."

His face hardened, but it was I who was annoyed—he invoking *her* again. For someone who never existed, the woman from Qingmiuneqarfik often came between us. For Jerac she existed.

He took the last piece of whale skin from his mouth, replaced it in the Tupperware. He had temporarily lost his taste for its flavor of hazelnut and cloves. "Only if we do it the old way," he said.

"God, Jerac."

I was not so town-Eskimo that I did not know the tradition. The woman ingested the mushrooms, her liver filtering out toxins but not the hallucinogens. The man drank her urine.

It was crazy. It was also *culture*.

I hesitated. I realized there were boundaries to what I'd try. That, more than the danger and attendant humiliation, gave me pause. I felt old. But not like Eskimos are supposed to feel old.

"Never mind," he said. After a moment he added, in an awkward attempt at levity, "If the sexism bothers you, we could switch roles."

I laughed, but it was forced, reluctant. I sighed, lay down alongside him, head to toe. I gathered my courage and foolishness. "Would you fill a cup, or would I have to drink from the faucet?"

"You're certain."

I wavered: finally shut my eyes.

"It's too gross."

I waited to be caressed and cajoled. But Jerac misunderstood; silence filled the tent. He slowly sat up, put the film canister containing the mushrooms back into the side pouch of my pack, and crawled from the tent. Head, shoulders, bare butt, bare feet, gone.

"God, Jerac," I said, to the ceiling.

There were tears in my eyes.

I wouldn't cry, I never cried. Not for a man, anyway.

When my father died I was stone. Stone when my brothers and uncle died. As the boys in my high school at Godthåb dropped like dominoes—suicide and accident, accident and suicide; and how do you classify Russian roulette?—I had stonehood polished to perfection. The gleam in my eyes at graveside reflected my heart. It was not caused by tears.

I refused to follow Jerac outside. I crossed my arms as though to keep my will in place, and tightly shut my eyes.

Sleep slowly enveloped me. Not exactly sleep, but not daydreaming. I lay in the stupor of considerable sex and too little empathy. For the first time I could recall, I dreamed of deserts.

He lies on the ground while sand skirls in the wind, his tattered jacket and puffy pants billowing, the goatskin boots full of holes, his toes and hands and face shriveled to parchment. The lips are gnarled, eye sockets empty. Sand builds along the windward side of his legs, spreads over the knees and thighs, angles across the jacket. Only the feet and face remain uncovered. When the wind abates, a bird lands on his chest, and after walking around as though nervously testing the stability beneath its feet, tears off the upper lip as if pulling up a worm. The bird flies toward a lake lying on the horizon like a shiny coin. The ravage has unhinged the jaw; it sags open. The man appears to be desperately grinning. Dusk brings the wind. Shadows and sand fill the mouth.

When I awakened I felt a sense of loss, whether only from Jerac's absence I wasn't sure. I pulled on my things and crawled outside.

As if unmindful of the chill, he lay naked and seemingly asleep on the lichen-covered slope beyond the tundra marsh. I slogged over, padded up the hill, nudged his foot with my boot.

"Good way to get hypothermia."

He turned his face toward the ice cap along the horizon. The moon was silver-blue, the sun pale and distant. My watch buzzed. *Midnight.*

"You going to play *shrug?*" I demanded.

He would sometimes go silent and rigid, in the way Eskimo men often do, infuriating everyone with their silent fury, communication reduced to slight shoulder movements.

He shrugged.

I returned to the tent, lay remembering the discussions my girlfriends and I sometimes had. Many Eskimo men were dysfunctional. Was it wise to marry or have children by one? But there were voices that blew down from the ice cap, whispering *for the good of the culture.*

He returned an hour later. We shared the tent, but we might as well have slept on opposite sides of Greenland, the ice cap between us.

The wind lulled my anger away.

The man staggers against sand blowing across the desert, his cheeks so puffy with sunburn that his eyes are slits. A lake seems to shine in the sky, winking as he stumbles. He passes a swollen tongue across his lips. "Bragda," he utters, and collapses to his knees.

He crawls on, hands turned in, shoulders bowed like those of a lizard. Then his elbows give way; abruptly, his face is on the ground. When he lifts his face, sand covers his left eye, clinging to the mucous. He brushes desperately, again collapses. "Bragda." He clutches at sand.

I awoke to an ATV stuttering across the tundra. Outside, I found Jerac watching as the machine pitched and yawed across the niggerheads. His eyes were hard and narrow.

Jailspur was at the throttle, face burnished by the midnight sun. He shut off the machine and slapped his gloves down among the gas cans strapped to the rear luggage rack.

"Brought you something," he told Jerac.

He grinned, held up a baggie filled with fish strips. He was unshaven, his teeth green with grime, a front one missing.

"You came ten miles to bring smoked sheefish," I said suspiciously.

"Breakfast ready?" he asked Jerac.

Icily: "Tea and pilot bread."

"Sounds fine to me."

We ate sitting on rocks, not speaking. The slabs of snow and ice that dotted the summer camp seemed appropriate. Jerac stared at the bag of fish strips, holding it by the ends as if it were evidence. He ate nothing.

"You have the papers," he said finally, not looking at the older man.

Jailspur took a folded sheaf from his jacket and held it toward Jerac, arm's length, between forefinger and thumb. Jerac looked at the papers as if appraising their weight, the way he looked at the bar during gymnastic meets. He lowered his eyes and reached for the papers.

Jailspur pulled them back, Jerac's fingers closing on air.

The Dane laughed. Jerac seized the papers, held them before Jailspur's face as though to slap him with them, then walked to the edge of camp, where he clutched the papers against his stomach and stood looking across the tundra. A fulmar circled, screeching, angry at having humans near her nest. Jerac did not look up.

The papers, I was sure, were his long-awaited boat title and commercial permit. He could now sell fish on the open market. But Jailspur's unsubtle choreography with the fingers was not lost on me. Prohibitively expensive in our world of limited-entry cod and salmon openings, the papers had come at a price beyond the percentage of profits Jerac would owe his benefactor.

When Jerac was a boy, Jailspur briefly was his foster parent—until the courts decided Jailspur was not fit to be anyone's parent.

The Dane was back in Jerac's life.

Jailspur zippered his jacket, put on his gloves, slipped a leg over the machine with the exaggerated extension of someone mounting a Harley, yanked the starter cord. The ancient Honda roared into life.

I pulled the key from the ignition, the tundra again still except for the fulmar's cawing. "This could have waited," I told him. "He hasn't finished school. Tend to your fucking boat yourself. Leave him alone."

He held out his hand for the key, his body language insolent. I cocked my arm, ready to throw the key out into the tundra muck.

"Go back to Copenhagen—Bunnuq," he said, using my Eskimo name.

"Jerac goes with me," I answered.

"He knows where he's from. That's where he belongs."

Jerac had grown up in Qingmiuneqarfik—the village in which, it was said, a woman mated with dogs and produced the white race, nearly human outside but monstrous within. Only non-Eskimos would fail to understand such shame. Jerac's accomplishments paled by comparison.

"They should have locked you up," I said. "Jerac told me what you did."

Jailspur looked up at me from the tops of his sockets, brows pulled down.

"Never did nothing. The court said so. So did Jerac."

"Not anything anyone could prove. Or would testify to."

He smiled. It was haunting, and I sensed it would go with me when I returned to the university, even if Jerac did not.

I pitched the key as far as I could.

His face reddened even more. I thought he would hit me. I had been in a few fights, growing up in Godthåb, but they were mostly scratch-and-hair affairs, few fists. I never had been punched by a man. I wasn't ready, but in a way I wished it would happen.

Instead he sneered, reached into his rubber coveralls, withdrew a wallet, took out another key. He started the machine. "Jerac's a big boy."

He roared away, spewing mud and exhaust. The machine listed like a dog raising a leg as he traversed the nearest niggerhead. He raised a middle finger.

I looked for a rock or stick, but ended up throwing insults.

"He's not a boy! And he never was *your* boy!"

The finger remained up like a flag. I strode toward Jerac, thinking that perhaps I *had* eaten mushrooms, that the world was unreal. I wanted him to do *something*—tear up the papers, tear off Jailspur's finger.

His back to me, he was looking at the sun, red and diamond-shaped. "Only a share of the profits," he said. "That's all he'll want."

I looked around his shoulder—withdrew to keep from embarrassing him and having him walk away from me again. His eyes were so moist I half expected a tear to form upon his lashes. I put my cheek against his shoulder blade. "That's all he'll want," he said. He was quivering.

"You needn't accept what he's offering."

His body shook convulsively. "Even if I get a degree—how long before I raise enough cash for another chance like this?"

"You can always subsistence-fish."

"And my children?"

"You don't have children."

"But I will! And they will!"

He was talking crazy.

"You're sounding like a white man—always worried about the future."

"What am I, but a white man!—*masquerading*. What am I, anymore."

He walked away, and I couldn't have gone to him even had he wanted me to.

What were we—any of us—all of us.

When he returned to the tent, his reticence was more profound than before—he did not even shrug when I spoke to him. I ran my tongue along the length of his palm; he did not respond. Finally I eased his sweatpants down.

He was the only man I'd slept with who hated having

orgasms. In bed he had an obsessive desire to please. I think Jailspur had taught him too well.

When he came, he gripped my hair.

"Leah," he said. "Leah."

It was my Christian name, and he hated it.

When I slept, the warmth and salt of him still in my mouth, I was again transported from the tundra to a hotter and far more foreign desert.

The man faces the wind, cheek crusted with sand, eyes and lips tight, arms out. His hands are fisted. Between him and the lake, amid the furling sand, rears a muscular reddish unicorn, forelegs kicking, its tusk translucent as an icicle. The man rocks as though inebriated and sits down in the sand, shoulders slumped, arms sagged, hands listless in his lap. "Everything I had," he mutters. "You ruined it all."

His eyes close as of their own accord. Sand peppers his face, but he seems not to notice. "If I get back to Mongolia . . . I'll kill you with my bare hands."

Back at the cannery, Jerac took to wearing mirror-like sunglasses, a baseball cap on backwards, jeans with holes in the knees: things he had seen on TV. He no longer laughed at my jokes or invented horrible similes to describe my coffee, and everyone on the line was faster with a fillet knife. We slept separately. When we were together we ate salmon instead of anything special, and did not talk much.

We flew back to Copenhagen, but he stayed less than a quarter. He skipped practices, and his grades slipped. None of my girlfriends asked about him anymore.

The night he left for Greenland, the Berlin Wall was officially coming down. Everyone who was anyone flocked to Germany, as though some Teutonic migration had begun. The flight to Reykjavik, where he would change planes, was nearly empty. "I'll stay if you beg me," he said. "I'll do anything you want if you beg me."

I reached to remove his sunglasses before he kissed me, but he backed away, hands up defensively, then compounded the slight by bowing and attempting to kiss my hand like some stupid European.

That night, Woman Without Face came to me for the first time.

The man staggers into the wind, snow, not sand, billowing around him. "Kill you," he mutters. At the edge of the lake in the distance stands a figure in a thick hooded coat, spear raised. The figure motions him forward. As he stumbles closer, he sees that the beckoning hand is the color of mourning. White as a fish's belly. He squints against the sun, trying to discern the figure's face, but except for a curve of slitted wood where the eyes should have been, the face is lost in the hood's darkness.

The figure points toward the lake—rimmed and chocked with huge ice chunks that float in a surface that mirrors the sun. Great fish-like creatures break the surface, noisily spouting, their geysers forming rainbows.

Jerac's promised letter-a-month became postcard-a-season, then ADDRESSEE UNKNOWN. The next summer I remained in Denmark, on a work-study stint that, appropriately, considering the omnipresence of Hans Christian Andersen, had me counting swans. That the other researchers called me Ugly Duckling did not stop several married ones from asking me out. I slept alone, and badly, and studied so much that I found myself with a galloping GPA I ultimately rode into grad school.

My proposed dissertation, *Echolocation: Acoustical Analogues in the Narwhal (Monodon monoceros)*, was my undoing. The day my committee approved the topic I stood amid tanks that reeked of formaldehyde, and in concert before a hundred watchful specimens remembered with trembling clarity my last afternoon with Jerac, beneath the down comforter in my dorm room. The moment just prior to climax, *I had* told myself *he's only another partner only a partner until* I accidentally willed my orgasm away.

"You all right?" my committee head asked as she scrawled her signature.

Momentarily speechless, I pointed to the title, which I realized I had unintentionally typed in boldface. The subtext implied I would be returning to Greenland, for research. Straining against the weakness the memory instilled, I said, "I'll need money."

She stifled a smile at my non sequitur and glanced at her colleagues.

"Of course you do. All grad students do. Goes with the territory."

"What you're really here to learn," the second smiled at his own incisive humor, "is how to live with being poor. Then we watch you jump through research hoops."

The third, balding except for gray around his ego, had spent much of his research the past year trying to determine how to get into my pants. "You're *Eskimo*," he said. "Apply for Northern Studies Institute funding. Americans love to throw money at anything *Native*. They think it assuages some collective guilt."

My non sequiturs. My youthful enthusiasm. My culture. Ultima Thule, the world they called Grønland. Such were the amusements in the mausoleum of higher education.

Under their tutelage and titles, I was to beg funding from some government, oil or Arctic shipping company, or environmental group. There was little difference, for money fueled them all; all knew the value of priming the pump with research. I would do most of the fieldwork, with one or more committee members occasionally visiting the research site. It would be a late-spring operation, when the ice pack had broken up enough to allow Zodiac launches but before the summer thaw made it difficult to locate the animals. I'd submerge hydrophones to record their songs, then put a year in the lab: decipher signals, check frequencies, search out correlations between songs, write the dissertation. Finally a journal article, my name bylined last.

Unless I proved exceptionally worthy, and a committee member fucked me not only intellectually but actually. Rather than my merely being the research assistant, the article then would be coauthored. Which meant my name would still be bylined last.

Woman Without Face had armed me for this moment.

"I have figured out how to radio-tag a narwhal," I said.

No one had succeeded at subjecting narwhals to telemetry.

The three monkeys looked up in unison from behind the lab table, so startled that Mr. Ego rocked on his stool.

Metaphorically I kicked the chairs out from under all of them.

"During winter," I said and, exiting, added, "A lot of money."

That night, Woman Without Face, as I had come to think of her, visited me again. As she had so many nights during the past four years, as mindful of my bedroom needs as Jerac had ultimately proved negligent.

Except for the slitted wooden sunglasses, her face, framed by the hood of wolverine and polar bear fur, is dark as death, her hands white as mourning. The man from the desert is gone. I am beside her. She shows me an agloo hole, where seals come to breathe, then faces me toward the narwhals, which arc in syncopated water ballet in an ice-free hole in the frozen sea rather than in a lake. Their tusks catch the sunlight.

She points to the dots arrayed along the flanks. "My children have a chance if I'm not their mother," she whispers. As the tails glide beneath the sea, she pushes me forward. "Approach their pain, not their pleasure."

When I awoke I lay looking at the Atlantic Whales poster above my bed. Over the years the picture had sagged on its pins, as if from the sea's weight. I, too, felt pulled down—by pride. I pushed my hair back and breathed deeply. *Stay centered.*

My center: into the ice-free polynia, like Alice through the looking glass, into the world where narwhals fed and moaned whalesongs as if in mourning for whatever narwhals mourn. Sometimes, staring at the poster, I imagined myself one of them, ugly duckling turned cetacean swan, jousting lance jutting, the dots along my marbled flanks like points on a map of eternity.

Those dots were what Woman Without Face wanted me to see. She was the woman from Qingmiuneqarfik; I had guessed the identity long ago. I was to look beyond lineage. Perhaps we are not products of our parents, she was telling me. Perhaps parents are merely *agloo* holes through which our centering spirit flowed—each child not a reincarnation but rather drawing into itself spirits of the dead depending on its capabilities and charisma, like a sculptor freeing a statue from the stone.

"My children have a chance if I'm not their mother."

As Jerac Johnnie would, if I raised enough research capital to buy out Jailspur's interest in the boat. I would give Jerac that chance as much for myself as for him.

I picked up the phone.

That Jerac proved easy to find did not surprise me. Most Eskimos do not drift far from their center unless alcohol absorbed them.

For Jerac, as with many, his center was his boat.

Even though it wasn't his.

Four months later he was showing me around *Qing-miuneqarfik;* Jailspur had insisted upon the name. An uneasy ebullience had displaced Jerac's depth. He prattled about draft and decking, ship tonnage and salmon poundage, weather along Inglefield Gulf. Jailspur watched us from the wheelhouse. Fishing regs dictated that the permit holder be aboard during the season, but the season was over. Jerac was a glorified deckhand.

"Why is *he* piloting?" I asked when we were behind the net winch. "That wasn't part of the deal."

"You told me you needed transport to . . . to Kanger-lussuaq." He avoided saying "Qingmiuneqarfik," at the fjord's mouth. "You didn't insist on our going alone." He glowered, the ebullience gone like so much bilge, and lit a cigar, smoking Greenland-style: three puffs, put it out with spit, bite off the end of the ashed tobacco, chew. All the men in my family had smoked that way. First came the failure to wipe the tobacco juice at the corner of the mouth, then bathing declined, pants hardened with fish blood and snot went unwashed as each year the drinking extended further into the fishing season. "Why must you go *there*," he said morosely. "There're polynias . . . other places."

"Not in a fjord with so many narwhal, there's not."

"Fuck it." He glanced toward the wheelhouse as though needing an excuse to get away from me. Jailspur signaled with two fingers. Jerac gave me a hard look, climbed onto the main deck, and went inside.

Exhausted and discouraged, I slept that night in the bow's cramped cubby while the men loaded my equipment. Back in Copenhagen, everything seemed so straightforward. I would arrive in Thule, we would chug off into a bouyant sunrise, and after we reaped the research's rewards and I bought out Jailspur, I would only ask two things of Jerac.

That he rename the boat.

That, if possible, he love me.

My plan regarding the narwhals was simple, but required someone with knowledge of the fjord. Unlike other whales, narwhals do not migrate south during winter, except to journey from their summer range near Canada's Baffin Island to their winter quarters among Greenland's polynias—the never-freezing upwellings along the west coast.

Each year, narwhals entered Kangerlussuaq in search of halibut, their favorite food, but risked being trapped by advancing ice. That some trapped narwhals survived the winter was an enigma no one had studied. The expense, the isolation, and the possibility of not finding trapped narwhals were too great. Perhaps, some theorized, they escaped by ramming through the ice or by piercing it with their tusks. But a meter of ice imprisons a narwhal, and the tusk is too fragile to break anything except itself.

Woman Without Face, doomed by her sin never to enter the watery afterworld, had shown me the answer.

A polynia—usually an oceanic occurrence—existed in Kangerlussuaq Fjord. The animals would be trapped but not desperate, which meant they could be approached. Like other whales, narwhals love being scratched; crustaceans dig hooked legs into cavities not directly exposed to water flowing over the narwhal's body. Vigorous rubbing with a brush or even a hand seems to provide relief from an itching of literally leviathan proportions.

"*. . . their pain, not their pleasure . . .*"

Attempts at telemetry had consisted of placing collar-like radios around the tusk. The narwhals slipped them off in minutes. I would glue a radio tag where the crustaceans thrived. The tag would be better protected, and perhaps the narwhal wouldn't notice it among the general discomfort.

The next day dawned cold and clammy, the stench of diesel so pervasive it seemed to cling to the skin, the engine's droning making my head drum. I peed in the coffee can Jerac had provided, pulled on my anorak, and climbed through the wheelhouse. I nodded to Jerac's grunted hello, stepped out into the stinging air, emptied the can overboard. Jailspur, at the wheel, stared at his reflection in the hole he had sleeved in the fogged-up front window, never looking at me.

We threaded among ice floes and icebergs, puttering through fog. The temperature continued to drop. Soon my teeth were chattering. Jerac exited the wheelhouse, crossed to my kayak, checked the straps binding it across the stern, stood contemplating the craft for several minutes. The kayak was traditional—walrus stomachs rather than fiberglass. I'd have thought he would examine it with a connoisseur's excited eye, but he just stared. Then he walked back to the wheelhouse. Before entering he gave me an ugly look.

Minutes later, Jailspur was laughing, his hand on Jerac's shoulder. Jerac stared into the windshield. When I went inside, wet and cold to the skin if not the soul, Jailspur stopped laughing and took his hand away. Jerac kept looking at the windshield. I went below. Condensation had formed along the bulkhead nearest my bunk; my bag was damp. I climbed in.

The only way to the rest of the boat was through the wheelhouse, so except for making sandwiches and emptying the can, I stayed in bed three days, ice occasionally sliding past the porthole. Woman Without Face brought dreams, and I thought about the man in the desert. Some relation to me, I was sure, but whether a literal or metaphysical one I couldn't tell. I thought about the dots on narwhal flanks.

Perhaps, like lineage, time is not a continuum but rather random acts the mind, seeking the satisfaction we call sanity, coalesces to sustain itself. Like beads threaded on a nonexistent string. Accept that the beads are scattered, and the past could lie ahead of us as easily as behind. We might impact not only the future, but the past.

Ibn Khaldun and Mahmoud Al-Hassan said as much a millennium before, in their appreciation of Allah—an idea only now catching on in the Western world, with its wormholes to parallel worlds whose time frame might not coordinate with our own. Though I felt little for Islam except scorn, given its excesses and view of women, I had found comfort in parts of its philosophy during the years of having Woman Without Face and not Jerac in my bed. Allah creates and destroys everything at each instant, but perhaps to demonstrate His omnipotence He leaves scattered beads.

The boat stopped. I went topside.

Qingmiuneqarfik's dozen tar-papered huts lay like crumbs before the fjord's maw, the village usually deserted during winter but now deserted permanently. The only sounds were from guy wires humming in the wind. No dogs came to investigate the boat out in the calm water.

"We'll anchor here," Jailspur told Jerac. "Then you take the skiff and find us a decent shack."

Check out your old place, is what he meant.

"The ice is firming up," I said hopefully, pointing toward the fjord's mouth. "Maybe we can get the radio tags in place sooner than I thought."

Savssats can occur quickly. Shore-fast ice is capable of growing across the mouths of fjords at a furious rate and expanding toward its head. It is not surprising that animals become trapped.

Moments later we were moored, and Jerac stood holding the line of the skiff we'd been pulling. His back was to the village; he was gazing across the fjord, his head hanging. Except for the tiny wake the skiff left, the sea was still, mirroring an orange sun bulbed atop the granite walls.

Jailspur slid open the wheelhouse door with a thud.

"What's keeping you! She's paying you to do a job. Paying *us*."

Jerac let the skiff line go slack. The smaller craft drifted several meters before pulling around and creating another wake. Despite his bulk, Jailspur left the wheelhouse and bounded along the boat edge with a dancer's dexterity. He put a hand on Jerac's shoulder, and for a time the pair looked like father and son, the elder quietly giving advice. Jerac nodded as if in resignation and pulled the skiff alongside. Jailspur's hand trailed down Jerac's jacket to the back of his jeans. Jerac's head jerked up. He glared at the older man, and made a fist. Jailspur backed away. Jerac stepped down onto the bow of the skiff, crossed to the stern, lowered the motor, connected the gas hose, and pulled the starter cord.

He sat hunched, gray as the sea, as he puttered toward the village.

During the next hours I sometimes glanced at the launch sitting on that lonely snow-dusted beach before the empty houses, but mostly I watched the savssat. The ice spreading across the fjord's mouth looked like something created by time-lapse photography. One minute the sea was quiet and gray; seemingly the next it ran thin and shallow, as if a shelf had floated from the depths. Except for a couple of channels, the ice blocked the mouth and was broadening up into the fjord.

Now and again Jailspur emerged from the wheelhouse and watched the village, at first with coffee, then a cigarette, then with thumbs thrust into the sides of his coveralls. He rocked on his heels. "The little fuck. I have to beg him to get anything done right."

The sun had eased around the bowl of sky, never rising more than a few degrees off the horizon. It hung to the west, as clear as the day was cold. "I'll go see what's taking him so long," I said.

"The hell."

I didn't know if that implied agreement, but I unstrapped my kayak. I managed to lower it into the water without his help, climbed down, and climbed in with difficulty. As I pushed away with the paddle, he returned to the wheelhouse and yanked the door shut.

Wandering among the shacks was like being in a world of the dead. I half expected to see people peer from the windows or doors creak open, hands inviting me inside, but the windows just stared blankly and the only activity in the doorways was when a breeze rippled a plastic sack.

Jerac's footprints went from house to house, rarely in a straight line. Meandering. A quarter mile past the village, someone had built a traditional sod house, perhaps a desperate attempt to attract tourists. Such projects are common in remote villages, where even a few visitors a year can boost the economy.

The place was unfinished or, more likely, had fallen in. The whalebone stays looked bleached in the dying light. Seal and caribou hides lay haphazardly on the sides; others had slipped to the ground. The arctic entrance had no door.

Jerac's footprints led to the hut.

White people who hang themselves leave a question behind. Did they change their minds after stepping off the stool—panicking before their neck snapped? Among my people, there is no such issue. We tie twine or thin rope to a chair or door handle—any object—and, on hands and knees, lean forward, the noose around our necks. Change our minds, we stand up.

You have to *want* to die to die that way.

Jerac used his shoestrings, knotted together and neatly half-hitched around a whalebone. He still had on his tennis shoes, his legs tucked tightly beneath him, hands fisted as though in determination. Only after I untied him and laid the body on its side did I think to uncurl the fingers.

I opened the hands with difficulty. He had a treble fishhook in each fist, the barbs jammed into the flesh.

Until then my nerves had kept me moving, my emotions sealed in stone, but when the barbs tore from the skin I sank to the floor amid hides slick with rot and quietly cried, his head in my lap.

Had I not lowered my head, crying over him, Fric Jailspur would have killed me.

Somehow I never saw him crawl through the arctic entrance. He suddenly was standing over me, swinging a bone sled runner he had found somewhere. He missed my head, the bone slamming my shoulder. Pain screamed through me but I managed to lurch sideways as he swung again. Again he missed—hit Jerac across the top of the nose. There was a *thuuk* as bone shattered and blood splattered me.

"Now look what you've done," Jailspur said in a hollow voice, dropping the sled runner and falling to his knees. He lifted Jerac's hand and held it, fishhook and all, against his cheek. "You and your goddamn narwhals. Killed my precious boy."

He picked up the sled runner. I scrambled on hands and knees through the arctic entrance, then raced through the village, the empty houses watching unconcerned.

The *Qingmiuneqarfik* was moored close to the shore, the skiff beached beside my kayak. I chose the boat that best guaranteed survival, not speed, and pushed off, paddling furiously toward the savssat. Looking back to see Jailspur lumber from between the shacks, I cursed myself for not disabling the skiff. *Forget it. Stay centered.* I bent into the work.

The kayak hit the shore-fast ice with a bump I thought would crack the ribbing. The boat bellied, then slid into the slush and freestanding water atop the ice shelf. The ice was only a dozen meters wide; I jumped out, kept my weight across the kayak as best I could as I splashed along. I reached open water again just as Jailspur brought the skiff's motor screaming to life and sent the launch flying across the sea, spewing a rooster tail, the bow lifted.

I had thought the fjord would save me, but I was wrong.

Jailspur roared along the ice, found a lead, brought the skiff around in a spraying arc and headed up the channel. In an instant he would clear the savssat. My only hope was that he would run me down, killing me quickly.

Halfway across the ice shelf, the skiff bottomed out in a screech of metal, and Jailspur was abruptly without water. Cursing, he pulled up the motor, climbed from the boat, and shoved the craft forward. It moved easily across the ice, his strength apparent.

Suddenly he was not beside the boat. It sliced into freestanding water and slid forward. Only Jailspur's head and arms were visible. He was thrashing wildly. "Bunnuq! You bitch! Help me!"

I braced myself against my initial reaction and paddled forward. I climbed onto the ice, sloshed to his boat and somehow untied the launch line, then crawled toward him, the coiled rope slapping as I moved.

"That's a girl." He clawed at the ice shelf. "Keep coming."

When I was close enough to assure a good throw, I heaved the lifeline.

For a moment his thrashing stopped. He looked at the shoestring I had thrown, then at the rope still at my side. I smiled and backed away.

Few people can pull themselves from ice without help. There is nothing to grip. The hands bloody, the thrashing becomes more desperate. Cold inexorably seeps upward—Satan's frigid hand reaching through the torso for the soul thudding in the throat.

Jailspur almost succeeded in climbing out unassisted.

He had dug his nails into a tiny crack in stable ice, and his upper half was out of water when he discovered a new way to die.

There are three ways to kill a man who has fallen through the ice. You can leave him there, haul him out but let him freeze, or, if the weather is extremely cold, you can kick him in the spine and it will snap like a stick.

Fric Jailspur found another way.

I saw a man—or what had been a man—emerge behind him in the sea. The skin was parchment, the eye sockets empty, the upper lip torn off, revealing crooked teeth. Sand was crusted across the cheek, despite the water. He wore a tattered goatskin jacket from which water streamed as he rose—reaching around Jailspur's head, sinking gnarled fingers into Jailspur's eyes, pulling him backward. Jailspur gurgled, clawing at the ice. Then both men were gone, only a small swirl to mark their passing.

Regardless of the thin ice, I retrieved Jerac's shoe-string and slipped it into my pocket. Then I returned to my kayak and paddled into the fjord instead of recrossing the shelf.

It was almost dark. I could hear the honking of seals and the narwhals' pulsed whistling and clicks that bespoke social communication rather than the shrieked wheezes associated with fear or feeding. My paddle caressed the fjord's easy current. I was alone among the animals and the stars.

Somehow I knew the ice would continue advancing. The polynia would not hold. I could return to the gillnet-ter, but I kept heading east. The *Qingmiuneqarfik* was home beside the village whose name she bore. There was nothing for me there except legend, nothing anywhere beyond. I was home in Kangerlussuaq. I would drown when the ice closed in and frenzied fear seized the narwhals. But for the first time in my life, I would live.

ELLEN KUSHNER

THE HUNT OF THE UNICORN

Peter: **Ellen Kushner** is another person I'm always sure I know better than I do, because of having met her so often at science fiction and fantasy gatherings. She's the author of a fine fantasy novel, *Thomas the Rhymer,* which reflects her lifelong interest and experience with music, song, and singing. As I recall, that's mainly what we talk about in all those hospitality rooms. . . .

Janet: I echo what Peter said—I always feel that I know Ellen better than I do, and for the same reason. Also because we seem to have so many common friends and acquaintances. In the cover letter Ellen sent with her story, she wrote:

> This story is actually a sequel to the first story I ever published, "The Unicorn Masque." The month it appeared, another dream of mine came true: I got to meet one of my writing idols, Peter S. Beagle, at a convention in California. I nearly fainted when he told me that he'd actually read my story in the anthology (*Elsewhere,* Vol. 1,

edited by Terri Windling, 1980), and the generous praise he gave it still makes my heart beat fast. I think the Renaissance writers whose work inspired these stories would approve of the perfect circularity of my writing the next one in the sequence for him, and I thank him for the encouragement, and the opportunity to do so.

The Hunt of the Unicorn

BEROWNE ALSO IS HERE IN NANTES, EXAMINING RUGS newly off the vessels from Turkey. His family could well hire an agent to do this foreign collecting for them, to furnish the walls and tables of their houses at Hastings, Ardmere, Little River . . . not to mention his own apartments at court. Perhaps they assign him such tasks as consolation for the real work already being accomplished by his elder brother, whose movements I know you concern yourself with. What, after all, can the young Berowne do but occupy himself with ornament, being himself nothing but an ornament currying grace and favor at the court of the Baseborn Queen? My lord, you shall be kept well aware of his movements here, and those of all the rest of your countrymen as they touch these shores, to the greater future of our noble enterprise, which cannot fail to thrive.

As for our Quarry, I have several reports to hand, but none of good repute. Your servant while I live—

Lord Thomas Berowne was indeed in Nantes, though not at the moment examining anything particularly beautiful. He was in a dockside tavern where even the beer was stale to match the air. He wore a heavy cloak to hide the splendor of his clothes and was much too hot. With one gloved hand he cracked a vent in its folds for air, and received a warning glare from his manservant, Jenkin. Lord Thomas sighed, and looked around again for the stranger who earlier that day had offered him a chance at a rare carving. Berowne was on time for the rendezvous, and the stranger was not—unless he'd managed to disguise himself as a redheaded barmaid with a squint, or a one-legged sailor with a greasy beard. Over by the poor excuse for a fire, two men sat playing cards. One, with his back to the light, was nothing but a shape, and that not the shape of the antiquities dealer; the other was a heavy-built fellow who seemed to be mostly voice: he was on a losing streak, and as his cries of annoyance grew louder, other taverners emerged from the shadows to watch the fun.

"Yer an imp!" the loser roared. "Foreign devil, magicking away a sailor's good money, yer not a man at all!" This provoked predictable comments from the watchers that drowned out his opponent's answer. The loser was drinking heavily, and Jenkin muttered that there might be a fight toward, and perhaps they'd better go now?

Berowne cast another annoyed look toward the door. Still no sign of the stranger and his Hermaphrodite Venus.

"Yes, all right, Jenkin." But as the disguised nobleman rose, so did the drunken cardplayer, stumbling back from his bench and holding up a glittering knife. The spectators drew back, the winning cardplayer drew his sword—or tried to.

Thomas could see the other now. He was a study in black and white with his dark clothes and pale skin, pale hair. Only the low glow of the fire created a faint flush along his right side, running along his emerging blade, while above it his ivory fingers were sketched in charcoal, and his eyes a smear of shadow over high, wide-set cheekbones. Even the swordsman's movements were like the most graceful poses imaginable—and that was the problem: he moved as if he were in a court ballet, slow, deliberate, beautiful, and at about half the speed required for him to survive the encounter.

"Draw!" Lord Thomas ordered his servant; "I know this man!"

At the sight of two outsiders taking an interest in his quarrel, the drunken sailor turned tail and fled, stumbling and cursing his way out of the tavern.

The swordsman turned his head slowly to look at his rescuers. His eyes widened.

"Oh, no," he said.

But they managed to get him out of the smoky tavern and into the sharp night air. Jenkin lit their way down several streets, always away from the wharves. At length they stopped under a cooper's sign, leaning against the shuttered windows of his shop.

"I am not drunk," the beautiful swordsman explained meticulously. "Drink does not affect me. My hands are perfectly steady, and I know exactly where I am."

"Yes, yes." Berowne was delighted to free himself of the heavy cloak and wrap him in it. "I've heard this before, remember? When you were in my rooms at court, drinking my claret and beating us all at cards. You weren't well then, either, though I agree your hands were perfectly steady."

"I am perfectly all right."

"No you're not. You're white as a sheet, and you keep looking at your own hands as though you're not sure whether they're flesh or marble. Which they might well be; Carrara, I think, with the blue veining . . ."

"Ahem," said Jenkin.

"Yes." With an effort, the fair man moved his hand slowly down out of his sight. "Thank you, I must go now."

"I don't think you'll get very far," Berowne said patiently. "Besides, that sailor might have friends. You'd best come home with me."

And so Lazarus Merridon awoke the next morning in an enormous curtained bed, the kind he had slept in in his days at court, and in his master's house. The bed hangings were brocade, patterned with doves and ivy intertwined; he pulled them back and found a vase of white roses by the bed, and a pitcher of water flavored with rosemary, and a blue silk bedgown hung over a chair.

His own clothes were nowhere in sight, which was a pity; he couldn't leave the house clad only in silk, nor yet without his sword. Jenkin was no doubt washing and brushing the clothes; perhaps he was polishing the sword as well? Lazarus rose easily from the bed. He felt fresh and whole again. The tavern had been a regrettable mistake; most regrettable, now. He had thought no one from his past would find him there. A whim of fate had brought the young nobleman. For which he supposed he should be grateful, considering what a fool he had been, drinking more even than he could handle. He wished he were like other men, to whom strong drink brought the mercies of folly and forgetting.

He was thirsty, and drank nearly all the water that was in the pitcher. From the courtyard below his window, women's voices drifted up, laughing and bantering. He went to the casement, and looked out through the cloudy diamond panes. He saw the women as bright spots of color, fetching water at the well. He knew that their lives were not carefree, but in this moment they were happy in the day, in their task, in one another's company. He wished that he might join them then; but that choice had been lost to him.

"Ah, good! You're up."

Lord Thomas Berowne stood in the doorway, neat in brown satin modishly piped with velvet and trimmed with pearls.

Lazarus was wearing nothing. The nobleman was staring. In the moment when he realized it, Thomas turned to the roses and busied himself with rearranging them. The fair man crossed the room, and slipped the blue silk robe over his naked body. If he looked now like a Knight of Love resting between bouts, at least he resembled less a pagan god new-minted in flesh.

"Good morning," he said smoothly to his host. "I slept very well. I'm sorry I disturbed your household. If I might disturb them once more to the tune of my sorry possessions, I'll quit all disturbance hereafter."

"No, no." Thomas broke off a rose, occupied himself pinning it to his doublet. Lazarus couldn't help smiling, to see the young lord again with his hallmark. Last winter at court the nobleman had seldom been without his precious flowers out of season, just as Lazarus had seldom been without his lute. Thomas smiled back. "Your linen is drying, and you must be starving. Stay at least for a meal. This cook does a very nice omelette, and the rolls are fresh, I just tried one."

Lazarus nearly laughed at the man's disingenuousness. Instead, he set his teeth. "I will not strain your courtesy."

"Strain my—? No, it's no trouble, I'll be eating myself."

It was the fair man's turn to stare. "You are very bold, Lord Thomas. Stay me with omelettes, comfort me with apples if you will; I do trust that while you so stay me your hospitality does not extend to finding me better lodgings on a prison ship bound back for home, but only that you take some weird joy in dining with a traitor."

Lord Thomas looked evenly at his guest, all mirth gone from his round and pleasant face. "Are you a traitor, Master Merridon?"

"I loved the queen, it is well-known."

"As do we all."

"No." With one hard word Lazarus froze the practiced courtesy. "As no one else did."

"That is not treason. You served her majesty's pleasure," Thomas said quietly. "As do we all."

"And when she took sick, and like to die, I fled the court."

"That was unhappy."

"Poison was spoken of."

Berowne shrugged. "Strange if it had not been. But

she will not hear it in the same breath as your name."

At that, the fair man's composure faltered; but only for an instant, while he drew a breath and closed his hands tightly on nothing.

The nobleman said carefully, "It was a wonderful winter for many, when you were there."

"If my love had been her death, you would not say so."

"I watched you all last year, and heard you play your music. The queen has many enemies. I never thought that you were one of them."

Lazarus turned away from his steady gaze. "Thank you."

"You're welcome."

"And yet," Lazarus Merridon turned his eyes full upon Thomas, "you do not know me at all." His eyes were wide, fringed with heavy lashes, the blue almost silver. Thomas met them, although it was not easy to look into them and speak at the same time.

"I would like to know you. I would like to be your friend."

"Would you?" Agitated, he paced the room, trying to keep his anger away from this generous man. "Because I play the lute, and sing, and can dance, and handle a sword, read Latin and some Greek; in short, play the gentleman in each and every part?"

Lord Thomas smiled fondly. "No, you fool. Because I like you."

"You—*like* me?" Even poised on the edge of confusion, head cocked, brow furled, hands taut, Merridon looked only as if he were performing some complicated dance turn. "What kind of reason is that?"

"The only reason. The very best."

Lazarus let the robe fall open. "Come, know me, then."

Berowne's face paled to match his own, then flushed. "Is this what you want?" he asked hoarsely. "I hadn't thought . . ."

"Come," said Lazarus Merridon, and sighed once as he felt the white rose being crushed between their two breasts.

My lord, I dispatch this in haste only to tell you that the Quarry is Sighted.

They awoke in the late afternoon sun, amid a tangle of sweaty sheets.

Thomas sighed. "I did not think that I could be so happy."

"You've had other lovers, surely."

"But none like you."

Lazarus smiled wryly. "Certainly none like me."

Thomas looked at his own well-tended hand; it seemed brown, even coarse against the man's pale, soft skin. "You are so beautiful. It's almost hard to believe that you are real."

"Let me help you to believe it." Lazarus kissed him, and they spoke no more until the sun was set.

A discreet tap at the door woke them only from their contemplation of one another.

"Yes?" answered Thomas, because it was his house.

Jenkin's rusty head appeared around the doorframe. "My lord, I wondered if you wanted supper. And if the gentleman wanted his clothes."

"Yes," said one voice, and "No," said the other.

Jenkin understood them perfectly.

There was bread, and cheese, and sausage, and white wine to wash them down with, stony and cold. Because they had slept enough, they lit the candles and they talked.

"I wish that I had known you all my life," said Thomas. "Come, tell me: what were you like as a little boy?"

"I don't remember," Lazarus answered.

"I was rather pious." Thomas rested on his lover's chest. "I like for people to like me, and most of the people I knew were adults. Even my brother, Stephen—he's always been very grown-up. He's virtuous and brave, like an old-fashioned knight: he's studied fighting, and tactics, and history and all. He is the heir, and a good thing, too. I am only a second son—a fifth, actually, but I'm the one that lived. Have you brothers and sisters?"

"No. I was hatched. From an egg—or maybe an alembic. I was an experiment."

Thomas laughed. "Of course. Your patron, Lord Andreas, always liked to dabble in the weird sciences." Lazarus shuddered. "Quite," said his friend. "Something about all those rings, crammed on his puffy fingers . . ."

"Oh, Thomas! You dislike him only because he is not beautiful."

"Well, I am sure that there are many other reasons to

dislike him." Thomas rolled over, and wrapped his arms around his companion. "You let me talk and talk, and you don't say a word. You are so brilliant, so accomplished; is there not one good memory for you to share? Some piece of music heard for the first time; a kindly tutor; a lover; a warm spring night?"

Lazarus pressed his knuckles to his eyes, as though he would squeeze tears out of them. "Oh, do not ask me. Be my friend and do not ask me that."

Of ships in the harbor here, full xiv are provisioning to the benefit of our enterprise under pretext of an Eastern Expedition, and idle men are easy come by to man them; expecting one profit, they will rejoice to find another! . . . Meanwhile, I will make it my business to create the occasion for some idle conversation with the Quarry, to know which way his mind tends concerning our affairs. That he is skillful and clever I well believe, since he contrived to elude me for so long. I will do all I can not to start him into further flight, knowing his value to yr ldshp.

They woke to midmorning sunlight. The curtains were drawn, the roses were fresh, and Lazarus' clothes lay neatly folded on a chest. Even his sword had been polished.

Thomas Berowne said, "It's funny, how much more interested I was in Turkey carpets two days ago. But I suppose I had better finish my dealings, since I've begun. Dress and come with me; you can tell me which ones to buy."

But Lazarus shook his head. "I think that would be unwise."

"Why? You have excellent taste."

The fair man smiled. "Thank you. But I will stay here."

"Ashamed to be seen with me, are you?" Berowne teased. "Afraid we'll fall to it in the street, is that it?"

"That is exactly it."

"Oh, come, you're a model of self-control. I've seen you at court, where the thing is truly tested."

Lazarus sighed, laughing. "Oh, Thomas . . . ! Just because you think me blameless doesn't mean others do. Shall I spell it out? People are looking for me."

"But the queen has called off the search, I was there."

"Enemies of the queen, then."

"And you the great swordsman that you are, to fear them!"

"Much service I would do her, being taken up for quarreling and murder in a foreign country."

"I can protect you, Lazarus. I promised."

"But who will protect you?"

Thomas raised his eyebrows. "You?"

"And there you have it"—Lazarus nodded—"a perfectly closed system. Pretty in two places only: philosophy and bed. Go on; be off with you and buy your carpets. I will be here when you get back."

Lord Thomas looked at him gravely. "Will you?"

"Yes, I will. I like it here."

Welcome, my lord, to these shores, blessed by our most sovereign lady. I rejoice in your deliverance from the realm of the Baseborn Queen, and hope you will return there soon in triumph at the side of our gracious lady her sister, whose true right to the throne of her father is incontestable.

It was late that night under a full moon when Lord Thomas returned to their room. What he saw made him catch his breath: a man seated on the windowseat, fair head bent over a lute, all silvered by moonlight, the strings shimmering like liquid as they were plucked.

He stood still, listening to the music, wishing it could go on and on; but Lazarus looked up, and set the lute aside. "There you are. I went back to my old lodgings to rescue a few things."

Around his neck a gold chain gleamed. Thomas approached, and lifted from his chest a jewel, a heavy pendant of a unicorn crusted with gemstones and pearls.

"The queen's jewel. You have it still."

"I was thinking of pawning it."

"But you did not."

"No." Lazarus laced his fingers with Thomas's, closed together around the gaudy unicorn. For a long time, he looked at them. He opened his mouth, closed it, then wet his lips and said, "Tell me—how is she?"

"Truly? She is sad. She reads philosophy, and speaks no more of masques, nor yet of love."

"Poor lady."

"Her younger sister, the Gallish queen, has an eye to her kingdom as well; rumors of invasion are common as starlings in June. Because the Gallish woman has sons, and in her pride seeks kingdoms for them all, while our sweet lady sits alone—"

"And will not wed. I know."

Thomas's fingers tightened around them both. "She still wants you. My family serves her, and always has," he said earnestly. "Lazarus, I can—I can arrange certain things. A passage. A pardon. You might return to her."

"No. It would kill her."

Thomas knelt at his feet, to look up into his moon-silver eyes. "Sweet, why do you say so? I know you are a good man. You may not love her, but you value her happiness, as I do. You would never seek to harm her."

Lazarus looked back at his friend. His pupils were huge and dark. "It has to do with Andreas. With my guardian, my patron."

"He is no longer your patron. He cast you off when you fled."

"No. He did not," Lazarus said bitterly. "Never mind what he told the court. He did not cast me off and never will."

"Sweet, what is it? Are you his son?"

The fair man barked a laugh. "God, no! I made a bargain."

"It can be broken. Whether you are bound by money, honor, duty—Lord Andreas is a rotten man, and a greedy one; it is not right for such as you to owe him anything! Tell me, only tell me, and I will see to it; I am not so very unworldly that I cannot do that for you."

"No. This bargain cannot be broken. And if it were to be, you would not like it." Lazarus smiled thinly. "I promise you that."

"Riddles, my love." Thomas unknit his fingers from the overwrought jewel, and smoothed his hand like a kitten, or a rumpled sheet. "I wish that you could tell me. I wish that I could help. . . ."

"You do." Lazarus' voice was muffled by Thomas's shirt. "Oh, you do. But there are things I cannot say—I cannot *tell* you, Thomas!"

Thomas kissed the back of his neck, where the fine hair grew like down. "What is it? What is so terrible? Are you a murderer? An adulterer? Father of a hundred bastards?" Lazarus laughed against his chest. "I know you do not kick small children in the street. What is this terrible thing you cannot tell?"

But the glib-tongued man was silent.

"Let me ask you questions, then. These painful secrets, kept too long, will fester; and, like old worms, begin to feed on that which is their home. I will ask, and you will answer as you may." He felt the fair man stiffen in his arms. "Right. Then cut straight to the heart. Lazarus, why did you flee the court?"

"For the harm I did the queen."

"What harm is that?"

"I did not mean to—I did not know—And when I knew, I fled."

"What did you do?

He turned his head away. "I poisoned her."

"You did. And by what means?" Thomas asked patiently.

Lazarus swallowed, and in a muffled voice said, "It is my love. My love that poisons."

Thomas nearly shook him, but wrapped his arms around him tighter instead. "Nonsense! People have only told you that . . . angry people, people you've hurt who want to hurt you. But you mustn't listen to them," he soothed; "they are wrong, it isn't true—"

Lazarus wrenched himself from his lover's grasp.

His face was nothing but eyes and hollow angles, unnatural and lovely, like cut glass. "But it is true, Thomas. Not some quaint conceit—or maybe that is exactly what I am: the poetic *love that kills* made flesh, walking the earth. A lover's song incarnate."

"How is that possible?

"To be a dream made flesh? I do not know. Ask Andreas and his alchemical friends. But I am perfect, am I not? You have said so yourself. Created for a queen to be her death. And maybe I will be yours as well."

"How?" Lord Thomas only stared. "I do not understand."

"Because you do not want to understand! Look at me, Thomas, only look at me and think. I have no past, no childhood, no store of memories but dreams. I cannot get drunk, I cannot be killed, by poison or by the sword— instead of getting drunk, I go to sleep; my wounds close up as soon as they are made. I am not a man, Thomas, so do not waste your sympathy and your kind understanding on me. I'm not a man like you, or Jenkin, or the beggar in the street!"

Thomas sat, impassive. "And the queen?"

"I carry poison in my flesh. For others, not for me."

"I see." Thomas nodded. "Yes.

Moonlight flashed across his lover's body as he paced back and forth between the shadows and the window.

"But you were mortal once?"

"Of course. Only God can make a human soul from nothing," Lazarus said scornfully. "Do not ask me what I was before; it comes to me in dreams, but that is all."

Thomas said slowly, "I've taken no harm of you thus far."

"Nor did the queen, at first."

"Yes."

Lazarus stopped his pacing. He stood in the shadows, watching Thomas in the moonlight. Thomas rose, and turned from him, pressing his forehead to the moon-washed glass, hands raised above his head against the panes.

"There," Lazarus said. "You asked, and now you know." Lord Thomas's eyes were closed, his face washed blue, like someone in a tomb. "You will not want to see me, now. It is disgusting, I know."

"No," Thomas spoke, his cheek against the cold glass. "Oddly enough, that isn't true. I've heard all that you have said, and I think that I believe it. But I find I do not care. It makes no difference. And that surprises me."

"Ah," said Lazarus with a bravado he did not feel. "I have frightened you at last."

Lord Thomas smiled. "Oh, no, my dear; you do not frighten me." His face was warm enough to melt the cold-ness of the glass; but still he stood where he was, cheek pressed to the night.

Lazarus came to him, slowly and gently, and turned him in his arms, and sat him down, and laid his bright head in his lap.

It is a wonderful thing, how Berowne scarcely ven-tures from his house, and yet he is not Ill, save with that disease common to bridegrooms and green girls! Neither do any come in to him, and so yr ldshp's thought that he might be passing and receiving information under cover of his collecting may be disproved. Let him do our work for us the whiles, for as a Keeper he does excel any that Art or Nature could provide!

They had flowers and wine, music and conversation, darkness and light, and the warmth of one another's breath in the silences in between action and talk; they had all that they needed to make them happy.

In the dark, they talked of everything that came to them, or ever had. Thomas learned to know the rhythms of his lover's body, his breathing and his silences; when he needed comfort, when passion; when he might be taken, and when it was necessary to give.

Lazarus, too, learned to see without eyes, and to make music for one person only. *Pretty fool*, Thomas called him; and, knowing he could outmatch Thomas at anything but love, Lazarus found he liked that.

Thomas tended his love like a garden. He pulled the weeds out from among the fragile shoots, careful not to tangle with their roots. Thomas asked, "Is it true you cannot die?"

Lazarus shrugged. "Only time will tell. It adds a certain spice to life. I think that I cannot be killed—except, perhaps"—he frowned—"by those who made me. My making was expensive; they told me so many times. They are unlikely to waste their labor by undoing me."

Thomas stroked the length of his body, infinitely precious now in light and dark. "I would like to think no one can touch you now."

Lazarus laughed gently. "No one but you."

My lord has in the past had the kindness to credit me with some good sense, and so will not think me derelict or negligent, particularly when the good resolution of our enterprise is so very near, that I have not contrived, by accident or by design, to meet with and hold some conversation with the Quarry. And yr ldshp's warnings about his prodigious skills at arms and clever speech have not made me timid, nor lax to do yr bidding, but only cautious not to betray my interest lest some word of this come to Berowne. After all, the thing now is under way, and cannot be stopped, least of all by two such inward-turning fellows. Yr ldshp's concern that the Quarry not return to his Baseborn love, lest he in his great gifts should prove of service against us, I think unfounded. Your further uses for him you may achieve when you sit at the hand of the True Queen, whose enterprise will surely thrive. Meanwhile, so long as he remains the chief toy and jewel of the young lord, and they do content themselves with one another, then why not trust the words of the old adage, and "Let sleeping dogs lie"?

But the end came, as it so often does, with news of the outside world. They were at breakfast, a meal of honey and golden sunlight, both making golden patches on their skin, and oranges, and country butter on rolls hot from the oven.

Thomas wiped a trickle of honey from the other's chin, and regarded him critically. "Hmm," he said; "you are, if possible, even paler than before. Fresh air is what you need, and if you must go out disguised, it won't be in that ridiculous black hooded cloak."

"I must not be recognized with you—"

". . . too dangerous, I know, I know. We must find some way of altering your looks that does no lasting harm—a wig? A wig . . ." The nobleman's smile stretched into a gloat of pure mischief. "Certainly a wig; a nice long one, and a veil, and paint to your eyes, and a lovely gown, green, I think!"

"Oh, excellent!" His friend's hilarity held a note of near-hysteria. "Disguise me as that I am!"

"Well you're hardly a courtesan, my dear, though some might call you my mistress—"

"My lord."

Jenkin stood holding a folded parchment bound about with tape and wax. "This is new come off the boat for you, my lord. A man waits below for your reply."

Thomas broke open the heavy seals. Lazarus knew the device stamped into them; the family crest was on Berowne's dagger, his goblets, his plate. He waited quietly across the room, until Thomas lifted a drawn face to him.

"My father—My brother—It seems I must come home."

"Are they ill?"

"No, no. But this is not a time for me to be abroad." Lord Thomas glanced down at the letter, and forced a smile. "They like the rugs I chose."

Lazarus felt it then, the hard-edged border between what he was to Berowne, and what a man's family was: the loyalties held, the confidences understood. "Well," he said. "You will close up this house?"

"I must." Thomas walked around the room, rapping at things with the parchment: the wall, a chair, a chest, the bed. "From what they say, I will not be back soon."

Lazarus felt his stomach lurch with understanding. "Good. I'll send you some music."

"Music?" Thomas looked at him with amazement. "What music?"

"For the procession. The banquet." With pride, Lazarus noted that his own voice held light and steady. "It will be a gift between us."

"My dear, what on earth are you talking about?"

"Now that your family has found you a bride."

"A— Oh!" Thomas laughed with his fingers spread over his face. "Oh, no. I wish it were that simple, that would be easy."

Lazarus saw that he was not laughing after all. He knelt at his side. "My dear, tell me—what is it?"

Thomas handed him the letter. Skimming over the salutations, the family news, Lazarus Merridon read:

". . . that Her Majesty's sister plans invasion is now certain, and the time will be soon. Although we could wish you safely away, your place is here."

Berowne is closing his house up very suddenly. Doubtless he returns home to join ranks with the Baseborn Queen. Should the Quarry seek to accompany him thither, I will take those measures yr ldshp instructed me in.

"Come with me," said Thomas. "Please come."

"I will be more use to you here. Hidden in the taverns, I can collect reports—"

"I do not care for use! I want you by me."

In the dark, Lazarus put his fingers to his lover's mouth, stilling the words on his lips. "I dare not come. I dare not. If the queen sees me— Or anyone thinks I've hurt her— If those who made me find me . . ."

"Come under my protection— Come disguised— Do you mean to live an exile all your life?

"An exile? You speak as though I had a home."

"In love, you do. In love and honor."

"Oh, Thomas . . . ! I am not a man of honor. I am not noble, as you are, in any sense of the word."

"You are loyal, to those you love. You would not suffer the queen to be harmed through you."

"Pride," Lazarus dismissed it. "I would not be used. If I go back, they will try to use me to harm—to harm those around me.

"You will not let them. You know now that you did not know before. You're strong, my love, and true."

The slender fingers clenched in upon themselves, biting half-moons in his perfect flesh. "*I do not know what I will do.* You must understand, Thomas, try—I do not know fully what I am. My limits or my strength. Andreas knows. I am afraid, Tom: afraid of him, afraid to let him find me."

"My dear, how long must you live thus?"

"I need time, I must have time to find out what I am in truth."

"I will kill Andreas when I see him! He is a traitor, and a pig besides. He never told you, he and his friends, what you were made of?"

"They gave me what they promised me."

"Lazarus—what did they promise you? What did you trade yourself away for?

"It was to be that which I am. The form, the grace, the

gifts, the skills—all of it. I desired it above all things," the beautiful man said with bleak defiance. "I thought I would be happy."

"Poor Lazarus!" He heard the smile in Thomas's voice, but the man's warm hands were all comfort and affection. "You may not be mortal, but I fear that you are human after all."

Lazarus rolled in his lover's arms. And where one held the other and where one was held, was a thing indistinguishable as hair from hair in a braided coronet, or the interlaced twining of vines in the bower.

Lazarus spoke at last. "Go home and do what you must do. If it is done well, I will be free to return. If ill—then you will come to me, and we will go adventuring together the wide world over."

The Quarry is fled. The trail is cold. I rejoice in your victory, and that of our most Sovereign Lady.

In a tavern in another harbor town, Lazarus Merridon heard of the fall of the crown, and the death and attainder of many of its noble supporters. Among the dead, the Berowne heir; the parents fled to friends across the sea. And their surviving son, attainted traitor, awaiting now the new prince's judgment in a little room behind the thick walls of a tower, encircled with woven rushes in a field of flowers.

MICHAEL MARANO

WINTER REQUIEM

Peter: **Michael Marano** writes that he ". . . was born in 1964, the youngest of nine children. His interest in horror is, therefore, self-evident." Hard to argue the point. As a home-made, half-assed medievalist myself, it intrigues me to learn that he began studying alchemy and Kabbalah while pursuing a degree in medieval history at Boston University.

Janet: Nothing about Michael is simple. He is one of the most intense and loving people I have ever met. What's more, he supplies me with coffee beans and fascinating manuscripts, in about equal quantity. This may be the first time you read one of his stories. My guess is, it won't be the last.

Winter Requiem

—To the memory of Lee Marshall

DAVID WATCHED A STREAK OF RED NOVEMBER sun-set become a bloody serpent hung in the darkening sky.

He knew, sitting in the wine-colored dusk beneath the eaves of a great oak, that the serpent was an illusion conjured by the toxins in his blood. He did not dispel the vision by blinking or glancing away. It did not threaten him as did most others; it was neither disturbingly vivid nor clear, but had, rather, the quality of art. He found comfort in the serpent's rich color and its smoke-like undulations.

To him, it seemed a guardian of this time of change, ushering the day into night, summoning stars from the darkening east, and winter from the dying fall. He wished, in the way that he had once prayed, that such a guardian would see him through the coming end of his life.

When dusk gave way to moonlight, and the scent of autumn's dead leaves meshed with smoke from distant fireplaces, and the sound of the brook that ran through the grove of oaks to the south became sharper with the cold night air, David stood and leaned on the branch he used as a walking staff. In his youth, not so very long ago, he'd called this hill "Weathertop," and carried a tall branch of birch as a prop when he imagined himself a peer of Gandalf. Now he needed a staff to negotiate the terrain; the illness that had turned his blood to slow poison had also given him gout.

He hobbled down the hill toward the house where he'd grown up. By the time he reached the yard he was sweating with exertion, despite the night air. Drowsy grayness filled the corners of his sight, as if another phantom would step from the shadows to accost his senses. At the door, he stood a moment, and breathed deeply until the grayness passed.

When he entered, he saw his work, the sheets of music he'd been composing, crumpled and torn and strewn about the living room. The piano bench had been toppled and flung to a far corner. The piano itself was dented and banged, its rich wood splintered and scuffed from the blows of the poker that lay upon it. A bottle of ink had been thrown against the far wall, leaving a smear like a blue handprint upon the white paint and shards of glass upon the wood floor.

David stood aghast. The clatter of his staff as it fell from his hand brought him out of his shock.

He limped to the center of the room, turned in circles, filled with panic, filled with fear, filled with rage. He was about to phone the police when an ugly thought struck him.

He could have done this himself, while made drunk by the disease that was killing him—enraged that the degradation of his mind would not allow him to compose a musical legacy before his body destroyed itself. He had been frustrated, angry for most of the day, unable to focus on his work or play musical phrases on the piano.

He had no memory of what he'd done before he'd left the house—no memory of actually leaving. He recalled only a need to be outside, to feel wind and see the sky before he resumed composing.

He searched the house for signs of a break-in. Who would break into a house in the middle of the woods? There were no forced or broken windows, no splintered wood on the doors.

Fear washed over him. A fear of losing himself, his music, his identity to mumbling, premature senility, and madness.

Not wanting to cry, feeling lancing pain in his gouty joints as he kneeled, David gathered the sheets off the living room floor, unrumpled them, and placed them on the mantel. He righted the piano bench and took the poker away from the scarred piano. He cleaned and tidied the room, but left the stain on the wall, for fear that trying to wash it off would make it worse.

Afterward, he put on his favorite recording of Mozart's *Requiem* and pressed a razor against the blue veins of his forearm.

The hunt was on.

Across wailing regions of Hell, his pursuers mocked him by signaling the chase with horns.

The deposed commander of twenty-nine scattered legions ran through living muck that screamed and writhed under his monstrous footfall. He crossed a swampy river as a horse would ford churning waters, his head and neck craning and bobbing with the strokes of his arms. The horn set upon the brow of his equine face rose and fell like a mast without a sail.

A new crash of horns came like a storm wind across the marsh. He stopped swimming and listened, looking back the way he'd come. Through the thick, perpetual fog of that starless, sunless place, he saw a signal fire flash atop a watchtower on the shore he had just left.

Ahead he saw answering fires upon the ramparts of the city of burning red iron on the shore before him.

He wanted to bellow his rage, scream his fury. But he dared not give away his location. Then he thought to make his position known in a manner that could save him.

He sounded the brackish water, warm as fresh blood yet laced with Death's cold touch, and pulled from the slime at the bottom something corrupted and tortured.

He broke the surface, and held aloft by one hand the screaming ghost he had pulled from below, hiding most of his bulk under the water, yet keeping his gaze above the surface.

The debased soul, able at last to shriek the agony it had felt since it had dropped to this spiritual vomitorium, summoned the river's guardian. Fast as an arrow from a bowstring, the guardian's skiff skimmed the water. The twisted gray creature on board smiled, eyes alight with the color of ice as he poised his oar like a weapon at the screaming soul's breast.

"You are *mine*!" said the guardian.

The prince lashed out. Hurling the ruined soul aside, he crashed his head and his spiraling horn against the skiff's prow, and gripped the prow in his claws. The guardian shouted, raised his oar overhead, and was about to bring it down on the prince's claws when the prince hissed, "I'll sink you!"

The boatman froze, teeth clenched.

"I'll sink you!" said the prince. "Think how all your little charges will be upon you, biting, gnashing, and clawing."

From the shore, the crash of horns came again, so close it made the air shudder. The twisted boatman smiled and leaned upon his oar.

"There's no room in *this* ark for you, either."

The prince growled, splintered the prow's lip, and rocked the skiff to and fro. He spoke in an intonation he had used in cold defiance of the Archangels. "Enough theater. Take me to the safe shore."

Without a word, the boatman piloted the skiff along the shores of the city of burning red iron. In the shallows, far from the city's ramparts and gate, the prince let go the skiff and waded ashore through water choked with rotted souls, putrescent as stalks of decayed kelp. Standing upon the bank, he pried several of them from his limbs, his chest, back, and genitals.

Soon he was running again, the hoofbeats of creatures both two- and four-legged thundering behind him.

The razor broke David's skin as the voices of the chorus gave earthly expression to the sound of Heaven. Blood ran down his wrist, baptizing his hand in red warmth.

He stopped the razor's path through his flesh.

If I survive this, I won't be able to play, he thought.

His riot of emotions fell quiet as he watched red drops make sudden blossoms upon the deep kitchen basin. *The tendons will be cut. I'll have nothing left. Nothing. Not able to play or compose. Or I'll be put in a ward somewhere, not allowed anything sharp as a pen to compose with on scrap paper. . . .*

If he died now, there would be no meaning or point to his life. Nothing left behind. A few minor compositions, already performed, that his teachers and a few critics had said showed a hint of greatness. But nothing that would endure as a testament to the sacrifices his family had made for him and his music.

He set down the razor and inspected the wound.

It was minor. No vein had been opened. He flexed his fingers. No tendon had been cut. He washed the wound under warm water, and watched currents of red flow within the stream. A thought struck him as the bloody water swirled into the drain and the *Requiem* played itself out. He took a wineglass from the cabinet beside the sink. He let his blood flow into it, clenching his fist around a dish towel as he did so. He made a tight bandage around his forearm with gauze, and carried the glass to the living room. There, he took from the shelves the books of magic bound in dusty leather that had belonged to his mother, and the large clay bowl she had had made for her by an artisan who lived near Jerusalem. Dust covered the vermilion lines of concentric letterings inside the bowl—letterings in Hebrew, Aramaic, and other languages David did not know.

He wiped away the dust and set the bowl in the center of the room. With dull pain in his joints, he knelt over the books and began to read.

The prince ran through a forest of those who had, in life, made a gibbet of their existences, and had ripped their souls from out of their bodies so that they dropped here and germinated to twisted, black trees. Knotted branches inlaid with tendons and veins quivered with unreleased suffering. Blood spurted from the branches that he broke as he ran, and the blood wept, vibrating softly as if each drop were a tiny throat pressed upon his skin.

The prince stopped and listened for his enemies. He did not hear them above the steady cries that hung thick in the forest's air, or filled the bloody trail he had beaten behind him. Harpies, perched in the upper branches, pecked at the trees, taking communion in small bites from the ruined souls transubstantiated to twisted wood.

The sounds of the forest were restful, calming to the prince. They reminded him of the dark places where the newly-dead congregated, wandering like sleepwalkers, mourning the sudden loss of their bodies. In happier days, he would often run through this antechamber, scooping up souls like bundles of wood to give as playthings to his followers.

The prince crouched low and rested, thinking of how he would orchestrate sufferings that would make his enemies envy the damned they'd once had charge over.

His punishments would be hailed as atrocities, legendary in their cruelty, even in Hell. He would make of his enemies living standards, erect cathedrals to his own honor from their bones.

Those who hunted him served The Enfolded One, the great unthinking idiot that held sway in this world, of late.

He could elude and defeat The Enfolded One's lackeys, and in time he would partake of the route of The Enfolded One with other princes and their armies.

But first he had to escape the hunters who craved his blood and coveted his horn, the emblem of his power that he wore upon his brow.

The cries from the trees closest to him quieted. The cries of his trail fell into the regular rhythms of the forest. Absently, the prince etched his mark upon the trunk of a tree. The soul inside cried softly in a tune he found sooth-ing as he pressed his claws into the bark. Perhaps he should enlist aid from the Master of Fraud, he thought. Sound a clarion call while riding on his back as they flew in a gyre to the deepest pit of the abyss. If he doubled back, Hell's Gatekeeper would allow him to weave music from the suspirations of the newly-dead that would—

A sound rose from the way the prince had come, like a great wave breaking, the fabric of thunder meshed with the roar of the sea. And beneath that sound, the screams of his enemies as they crashed through the wood and the cries of the trees they wounded. The prince stood and, with the speed of a hunting cat, climbed the tree he had been scarring.

In the distance, he saw hundreds of points of light spread in a line. Some were, he knew, the flames of torches held by those who hunted him, darting, curving in a wide ribbon among the bleeding trunks. Others were the burning faces of yith hounds, black hunting bitches mad-dened with the need to rend and tear and wound.

The prince dropped to the ground, but did not run. He was a strategist, a tactician. Nothing he did now could be without thought. He stifled the sound of his pursuers in his ears, reached out with his senses for *anything* in the ether that could help him. And found it. Something informed so slightly by the aura of this place of suicide that, at any other time, he would not dare pursue it.

He had no choice.

At the trunk of the tree he had climbed, he kneeled like one about to take communion and forced his hands into his mark, pulling open within it a portal made possible by the dim invocation of his name.

"There are no such things as demons, Mother. Or angels. There is only us."

His mother had taught him to believe in magic, that the world was full of hidden wonders. As he grew older, he believed only in the wonders of the mind, that what she called "magic" was the product of focused will. Ritual and formula were crutches to focus that will.

He needed such a crutch to free his mind and thought from his sickness. Kneeling on the living room floor, David read aloud the Latin incantations of his mother's books, and also the Hebrew she had phonetically scribbled upon sheets of yellow legal pad and inserted within the pages. Toward the end of his ritual, he took the wineglass that held his blood and poured a few drops in the center of the bowl, so they were surrounded by the concentric lines of script.

He turned the bowl over and read a final Hebrew incantation.

There was a change within David's mind. A flowering of images and feelings that unfurled like a white rose. A vista of alabaster filled his vision, and a sound, distant at first as the tread of a ghost, became louder and more tangible.

He knew it to be the sound of snow.

A memory rose like mist from his childhood, of lying with closed eyes upon the white blanket of a winter field. Even the wind itself had been hushed. In that unreal, timeless quiet, he heard the breath of the sky itself, the whisper of the dome of gray clouds above, and the voice of each crystalline feather of snow as it fell, alighting upon the earth, his face and lashes. The snow had a delicate poetry, but he could not fathom its language. It was a language he both heard and felt, that touched him as the morning of the year's first frost touched him, telling him of its presence the instant before he woke.

David remembered the sound of snow, and remembered the person he had been when he had heard it: the boy who believed, as his mother had taught him to believe, that magic lay hidden everywhere around him. This, as revealed by the snow, was the essence of what he was trying to compose, yet he had not been able to name it before.

He could grasp it and give it musical form. He would make it a requiem, a remembrance of his mother's teaching created in the twilight of his own life.

David wept, with relief and joy. And with pain, for the memory had been pulled from his deepest sense of self.

The white vista faded from his sight, but in his mind the sound of snow maintained. Grew louder.

David wiped away his tears and listened. A shiver ran up his back as strands of mist, like wisps of white hair, streamed from beneath the bowl, flowing into a smoky pool by the hearth.

The wineglass vibrated as the sound grew, as if a tuning fork had been touched to it. The vibration had a rhythm separate from the sound that David knew. He felt it inside himself.

It was the rhythm of his own breath, as if the blood in the glass were still within his veins, pulsing with his body.

Winter filled him, coursed in a February wind through his torso, his limbs, filling each capillary, collecting in an icy fist in his heart.

He screamed. The sound endured past David's scream. He tried to stand and run, blindly, into the cold November night. But he couldn't rise from his knees; the rotting joints of his legs gave way under him.

A hump formed in the pool of white smoke by the hearth, as if the pool were a sheet and a man stood up from a crouch beneath it.

The form became solid. The sound fell silent.

A hunched abomination stood before David.

"Yes?" it said.

With that one word, the sanity of David's world was torn away.

I'm hallucinating, he thought. *Be rational. This is nothing. This is a dream. This is a ghost. It comes from the sickness.*

The thing rose to its full height, towering above him. Fine mist came off its heavily muscled body, off its chiseled legs, its arms, off the torso that looked as if it had been sculpted in marble. Up to its neck, its skin was white as bone. Coarse hair with the sheen of sea-foam grew over the throat and the bestial head was at once like that of a horse, and that of a deer and of a goat. A mane of human-like hair fell in foppish bangs around the great spiraling horn that grew from its brow and that glowed like mother of pearl in candlelight.

It's not real. It can't be. It's a demon from one of Mother's books. A demon. You saw its picture and you . . .

The monstrosity fixed David with eyes violet as the cusp of a January dawn. Again, it spoke.

"Yes?"

The square animal mouth moved, making human speech that didn't vibrate as sound in the air but *occurred* in David's mind, like a premonition given grammar and cogent thought.

David tried to speak. His jaw trembled, as if from cold, and the beast cocked its long, equine head, never taking its gaze from David's.

David clenched his jaw, turned his gaze to the floor and forced words from his lips.

"You're not real. I don't believe in you."

He looked up, hoping, knowing, his words had banished the thing with the other phantoms his sickness had created.

David was again held by the violet gaze.

"But I believe in you."

David fought the urge to drown in those eyes and made himself speak.

"You don't exist."

"Oh, but I do."

"I didn't call you. I didn't summon you. You're nothing. I'm dreaming you."

The demon glanced away, freeing David from its opiate stare. It leaned forward; its horn lowered like a pike before David's face. Its great lion-clawed hand lifted the bowl from the floor as David would lift a teacup from a shelf. It turned the bowl over in its palm and pointed with a claw of its free hand to the red inscriptions inside.

"You did call me. And politely, I came. If you look closely here, you will see my name. You invoked it. Of course, if you do look closely, you will also find the name of a very splendid Nazarene carpenter. I'm afraid he's too busy knocking together cabinets and tables for his dear tyrant of a father to answer your call. I, however, am free this evening, and so accept your invitation."

"I . . . revoke my invitation."

"After I have come all this way? Why? Have I been rude? Of course I have! I have come empty-handed. Allow me to give you a gift."

It brought its horn down on David's shoulder, as if the horn were a sword and the creature were knighting him. David's every muscle clenched, his every tendon pulled tight. From his knees, he fell backward, unmoving on the floor.

The thing stood above him, its horn almost touching the ceiling. "There. Now I am a decent guest. But I am sure there are other exchanges to be made between us. Does this go here?"

The thing held out the bowl to David, and turned partly to place it on the mantel. "Ah! You compose!" it said as it set down the bowl. It picked up the rumpled sheets and read. And David, gripped by nightmare paralysis, could not scream when he saw upon the thing's back another atrocity.

The thing turned to face David. It stepped forward, looked down at him and said, "I am a patron of composers. I have stood invisible at the side of great maestros, guiding their batons. I have revealed my secrets to composers

whom you venerate. I have woven melodies from the footfalls and the clatter of wheels upon the cobblestones of
great cities—melodies that have touched the entire world.
I would be happy to help you with this." It held David's
rumpled compositions out to him and made a bow, like a
courtier. "I am Amduscias."

The thing that had clung to the demon's back fell
wetly to the floor. David tried to shut his eyes, to look
away as the spectral body of a young woman, torn in half,
reached out to him. She tried to speak, but no sound came
from her mouth.

The thing that called itself Amduscias snatched the
torn woman by her hair. "I've tracked mud into your
home," it said coolly. "Forgive me." The woman continued her wordless pleading. She raised her arms over her
head, trying to free herself from the demon's claws.

The buzzing grayness of disease filled the edges of
David's vision. He embraced it, willing it to blot out what
he saw. The light in the room changed, became dappled,
like afternoon light in a deep forest.

The demon held the mauled ghost aloft, almost level
with its head. In the dappled light of David's hallucination, Amduscias looked like a poacher holding his catch
in a wooded glen. The demon's animal face looked with
sickeningly human contempt upon the woman. It looked
back to David.

"Since, as you say, I do not exist, I am a product of
your mind," it said. "Therefore, if you were to *allow* me to
possess you, no harm could come of it. I would be one
part of your mind returning home. A part of your mind
you've lost touch with, that otherwise would help you
create sweet music such as this." The claw that did not

hold the woman held forward David's compositions. "Allow me to demonstrate my musical ability."

It drew the sheets over its heart and the room filled with snatches of music. David's music. The bars, the sketches, the phrases he'd been working on performed faultlessly by invisible musicians. The air shimmered as if from the heat of a fire. The dappled forest light glinted as it shook with the music's resonance.

The music stopped with a gesture of the demon's hand.

"Think what I could do inside your mind," it said. "Think what I could liberate."

It shook the woman as a sadistic child would shake a cat held by the scruff of the neck. Bits of cloudy, dust-colored flesh dropped to the floor.

The demon came down to one knee. "There must be blood here somewhere for you to have called me. If it's fresh, I can make a gift of her. A little aid to help with your composing. Ah! Just so."

It set David's sheets down and lifted the wineglass. The dappled light grew dimmer as the demon held the glass to its eye. "I'll do what I am able with this. Watch what is possible when two agents meet to create something new and wonderful. Imagine what could happen if you and I were to join."

It set the woman like a broken doll on its knee, and with one claw forced open her mouth and poured the blood down her throat.

Her flesh shrank, took on the texture of a wet scab. The demon began sculpting her, molding her as if she were clay. "She will be of great use to you. For how long I can't say. We'll make the best of what we have."

Welcome hallucination suffocated David's senses, eclipsing the violation of sanity before him. He floated in a world of twilight. Among burgundy clouds, he saw the red serpent again, and longed for the comfort it had given him as he had sat upon the hill. Dimly aware of himself, he followed the snake to a place he knew was safe.

Amduscias watched dreams move like föhn winds through the ether.

After stepping over the inert form of the conjurer who had summoned him, he settled upon a wooded hill that overlooked the conjurer's home. The place was special to the conjurer; he could smell the conjurer's spirit invested among the oaks. He hunched down beneath the tallest oak to watch for signs of his pursuers.

It was then he saw the dreams rippling through the nonphysical landscape the way sunlight moves through water. The dreams were sent by his enemies. They would drift through the night to settle upon the minds of sleepers, and so make the sleepers the vessels of his enemies.

His enemies would clothe themselves in the sleepers' bodies and souls, and so continue the hunt through the living world.

Amduscias tasted the dreams as they passed. They were dreams of redemption, of hunting and coursing a snow-white beast with a divine horn, and being made clean and whole and pure by the beast's blood. The dreams would make the sleepers hungry for such healing, and this hunger would be used to make the sleepers long for the prince's blood and horn.

The prince was not alarmed. This was expected. His

pursuers could not follow him here without being summoned into materiality. He would be ready for them when they resumed the chase as avatars moving through the bodies of others. Several nights would pass before the dreams took root.

By then, he would have safe harbor in a willing soul. The conjurer had a ripe and fragrant soul, full of vibrancy and poetic insight. The prince would use his soul both as a shield and a weapon. He would create within it a fortified tower from which he could attack. He would cleave to and cleave through the man's soul, make it a source of *élan* to face those who hunted him and crush them for their arrogance in taking arms against him. He would descend upon them as the Great Archangel who routed him and his followers had descended, just before The Expulsion.

It was a simple matter of time before the little conjurer capitulated, before he invited the prince to transmigrate into the chamber of his soul where his music was born, into the realm of his spirit where the prince would have complete dominion. Forced or insinuated possession would shatter his soul, make it useless.

Soon the sickness of the conjurer, or the desperation it inspired, would vaporize the rich metal of his will. All just a matter of time.

David's fountain pen glided over the staff paper.

The requiem's first movement would be carried by the piano, creating a foundation for the sound of snow translated as music. Wagner's *Das Rheingold* was his model; he would invoke sky and snow as acoustic collage the way Wagner had invoked the slow, deep power of a river. The piano would build a layer of sound echoing the heartbeat and breath of the person hearing the snow. Slow heartbeat, quiet breath . . .

After waking in the entryway dazed and stinking of fear, David had found the pen on the living room floor, beside a stack of freshly transcribed notations, copies of the sheets he had destroyed.

. . . breath that is soon joined with the breath of the sky, articulated with a French horn . . .

Several steps away, he'd found a moist, thick blood-stain.

. . . and the breath of the sky would fall into harmony with the steady notes of a flute . . .

The bloodstain had the vague outline of a small human body.

("She'll be of great use to you.")

. . . and the flute would change, creating a counter-point to the piano and the French horn . . .

("A little aid to help with your composing.")

. . . a counterpoint that would parallel the opening of the senses of the person hearing the snow . . .

David undid his stiff, brown bandage, to see if his cut could have produced enough blood to make a stain that size.

("Watch what is possible when two agents meet to create something new and wonderful.")

. . . and the soft notes of a guitar would paint the movement of snowflakes falling through still air . . .

The wound was closed.

("Let me give you a gift.")

. . . soon joined by another guitar to suggest layers of snow . . .

The joints of David's legs no longer ached.

("You will feel like a new man in the morning.")

David's hand jerked; the nib of the pen cut through the staff paper.

"It didn't happen," he said out loud. He paced as dusk filled the room, and made arguments to himself that what he had experienced was delirium. When he had convinced himself, he sat down to work again.

He could not focus.

The feeling of guilt and unfulfilled obligation was too great for him to bear. He went to the trash and fished out the soaked, bloody rags with which he'd cleaned away the stain. He buried them in the yard, straining with the shovel to break the hard soil.

The pleading eyes of the torn woman stayed with him though, well into the night.

Amduscias walked among the trees.

He heard, among the sounds of the night, the voices of his enemies in a whispering cacophony. They were nearer, tonight. He could smell them wandering without substance, uttering murmuring orisons that would bloom into the dreams that would give them a foothold within living souls.

The foothold would not be enough. He would destroy them, their purloined bodies, and the stifled souls within those bodies. It would be a great victory, and great blow against The Enfolded One.

Perhaps he should shove the little conjurer's soul into one of these oaks when he was done with it. Give it a home like the one it would have had if the conjurer had taken a few steps closer toward the bloody wood where the prince had heard his call. He'd use the spent soul as a conduit, a portal to this wood if ever he had need to escape the abyss.

He walked to the edge of the wood and looked down at the conjurer's home. He felt in the ether the process of sickness, the touch of madness. The prince's host from the night before was having another of his episodes.

Splendid.

He could never resist a dramatic entrance.

The prince crouched down and waited for an opportune moment to leave his body and invade David's weakened mind, and so invade his soul.

David fought the coming delirium with his music. He stood up from the piano bench as his senses reeled, focusing on the sheets of his composition, reading his notes and willing the tranquillity of the sound of snow to fill his mind. He would not face another horrific episode like he had last night.

The music surrounded him, held him with joy and a sense of being healed. The layers of the requiem built upon each other, and the room changed, became from the peripheries of his vision a great concert hall. The hall was empty, but his music filled the air. He faced the orchestra pit, and read until he reached the end of what he had composed.

"Bravo!"

David spun around.

The towering thing he knew as Amduscias walked the aisle toward him. It walked erect, with a grace that belied the monstrosity of its form. Its grace offended David. Revolted him.

"Bravo! You are touched with magnificence."

The demon stood a few steps from David. It turned its animal head, looking about with human intelligence. "What a lovely hall you've made. A special place, is it? A place of hidden dreams and lofty ambitions? A lovely hall. With lovely acoustics."

The monster threw back its head and sang with many voices part of an *"Ave"* with impossible pitch and clarity, as if an angelic choir found outlet in its throat.

When it was done, it pulled its animal mouth into a sickeningly human grin.

David looked away, spoke in a steady, even tone.

"I banish you. I cast you out."

"Do you?"

He looked back at the demon.

"Our Father, who art in Heaven, hallowed be Thy name. . . ."

The demon cocked its head.

"Thy kingdom come, Thy will be done . . ."

"On Earth as it is in Heaven!" said the demon. "But this is neither Earth nor Heaven. This is the place of your dreams."

David gripped the sheets of music tightly in his hand. They were a tether to the world that was real.

"What do you want of me?"

"I want what you want. I want to be returned to you. I want to help you with your great work."

"You can't have my soul."

"Why not? You share your soul through your music. Let me return to your mind. Let me free what's inside your soul so it can touch the souls of others. So your music can be shared with the world."

"What do you gain from this?"

"Joined with you, I would be a heavenly creature again. I would be pure and splendid. Able to sleep again upon the laps of maidens and heal the sick. Able to resurrect kings and foretell the birth of prophets." It raised its powerful arms skyward and turned joyfully. "You would not wish to deny me salvation, would you? I have healed you, have I not? At least partly? Imagine what I could do within you, what healing powers I could liberate. I might be able to save your life."

"You don't exist."

The demon looked at David as it had looked at the torn ghost-woman who had writhed at its feet.

It made a slow fist with its clawed hand before his face. "What have you to lose?" it hissed.

David stepped backward, toward the pit. He heard his sheets of music fall to the floor.

"What you have to gain."

With incredible speed for a beast its size, the demon lunged at David and reached for his throat. Its claws were almost on him when it looked up, startled as the sound of hunting horns reverberated through the room. It turned and was gone as the hall faded to dim shadows.

Amduscias pulled himself from the conjurer's mind, stood, and looked down from the hill he had claimed for himself.

Scrambling up the hill from the west were the human vessels of his pursuers. He could see pressed around their fleshy bodies the shadowy forms of those who had hunted him across vistas of damnation.

Mass possession like this was not possible. Not so soon. The dreams could not have taken root.

The prince looked up and saw a churning cloud like a swarm of insects blotting out the sky.

The Enfolded One had come.

Horns crashed through the ether.

Amduscias ran, the thunder of many footfalls behind him.

David picked up his sheets of music from the floor. He would play part of the piece. Get his mind working on the fine points. Focus, and gain control.

The entryway door burst open, and Amduscias forced his towering bulk through.

"ENOUGH!" David shouted. He picked up the piano bench and hurled it at the monster. "GODDAMN YOU! *ENOUGH!* I BANISH YOU! I EXILE YOU! YOU'RE NOTHING! YOU'RE—"

David was seized in the beast's claws. Lifted. Pressed against the cold plaster of the wall. The spiraling lance on the demon's brow hovered inches from his breast.

"Enough theater!" it said. "Do you hear them? Listen! They'll be at the door. The barrier I evoked will not hold them. They are my enemies. They will destroy us both unless you admit me to your soul. I cannot ward them off without you."

"No. This isn't real! You don't—"

The demon pulled him from the wall and smashed him back against it. "You don't know what's at stake!"

There was a crash in the entryway and David saw, over the demon's shoulder, his neighbors, people from town, old teachers and classmates standing at the door.

They pressed into the room, and for an instant, David thought he was saved.

The monster that held him in its claws looked toward the people piling into the room, then back at David.

Rage burned like diamond fire in those violet eyes.

It bellowed and pulled David onto its horn.

David screamed, back arched, arms out to his sides. He felt the horn pass through his flesh, his lung, his heart, his back. A fire coursed through him. He began to die as the horn that was killing him cleansed his blood.

His mind was freed from the sickness as his lungs filled with blood. He tried to cry out to the people below.

The demon's claws gripped David, its voice echoed in his mind.

"Give me your soul! You will live! We will live!"

The people in the room snarled like dogs and leapt upon the demon, rending and biting and tearing.

David fought the demon, joined to it by its horn, its mind groping, lunging, trying to cleave to his soul as its horn had cleaved through his flesh. The horn kept him in his body. His soul did not rise. He felt his being change as he and his enemy fell to the floor under the crush of bodies.

"Yes! Give me your soul! I can spare you from this!"

Hands were upon David, pulling, ripping.

The demon pressed into David's spirit through his sundered heart, through the strength of its will and David's longing for the agony to end.

David felt the atrocity of the thing's mind within his

own mind. With his last act of will as his body tore, David reached out with his soul, pleading for salvation. Before his dimming eyes, he saw the red serpent—the guardian of change and benevolent passage. David embraced it with his spirit as his arms were pulled from him.

Between life and death, David joined with the demon. The serpent moved through him, and he knew it to be a thing of his own creation, part of his own mind given form, his own strength given tangible shape.

He put the demon down as his existence ended. The serpent's red glow transmogrified him, burning away what he had been, cleansing the demon's contamination of his spirit.

In an unnamable limbo, he knew the quiet of snowfall . . . and the dead ethereal form of his enemy.

He made them both his own as he heard the cries of tortured living souls around him.

A November sunrise, burning with secret fire and the rich amber of autumnal light, touched the faces those who had been a mob as they drifted across the countryside, covered with blood, covered with flesh, covered with scraps of skin and torn clothing.

As the songs of larks echo across a valley at dawn, so did their screams, cries, and sobs echo among the fields. Some of the wanderers fell to their knees, some tore their hair, some curled into fetal balls upon the cold, hard ground.

Their souls had been mauled by the things that had possessed them and filled them with blind lust for the blood they had thought could redeem them.

Gray clouds drifted from the west, towering in the sky like cliffs of granite, dimming the sun's light. The cold rains the clouds brought drove the people home like slow-moving animals. The rain did not wash away the filth that clung to their spirits.

What happened among them was kept secret, in the way witch hunts and midnight lynchings are. The house where the torn flesh of their prey lay piled thick upon the floor was burned several nights later, as was part of the fields around it.

The fire's glow brought a false dawn to the moonless sky; the clouds of smoke carried with them the scent of sulfur and rot, of burned hair and sickness.

A spiritual plague hung like choking fog over the countryside. A plague that would have warped and killed the souls of all whom it touched, had it not been for the visitation in dreams of a magnificent snow-white beast that came to each of them. That touched their hearts and souls with the healing light of its horn at the moment when the burning clouds of sunset seemed to have coiled among them a great serpent the rich color of cinnabar.

The beast came to them atop a hill crowned with a grove of oaks that was held by the eternal rebirth of spring. The coming of the creature was heralded by music. Sweet music, reminiscent of the sound of snow falling upon quiet winter fields, of the breath of the sky, and the voice of each crystalline feather as it alights upon the earth.

ELIZABETH ANN SCARBOROUGH

A RARE BREED

Peter: **Elizabeth Ann Scarborough** really was a near-neighbor of mine when I lived on Bainbridge Island, six miles of Puget Sound from Seattle. What I particularly like about her story, "A Rare Breed," is the manner in which she sketches her special part of coastal Washington: a uniquely funny and touching mix of tourists, Old Inhabitants, aging hippie burnouts, and the walking wounded of one war or another, declared or otherwise.... In the bio she sent us, she calls herself, "... a child of the sixties ... gray, fat, and nearly fifty." *Nearly* fifty? *Gray?* In the words of today's youth, "Been there. Done that."

Janet: "Been there, done that," myself. I don't know Elizabeth personally, though after reading her story I feel as if I do—and wish I did. She made me laugh when I was under extreme pressure, and for that, alone, I thank her.

A Rare Breed

I MET MY FIRST UNICORN, APPROPRIATELY ENOUGH, when I stepped into an enchanting forest glade. It was enchanting for a couple of reasons.

The first reason was that it was out of shouting and phone distance from my place, where an unexpected visitor snoring in my bed reminded me never to wish for anything too much lest it come not only to pass but to remain for an indefinite stay.

The other reason was that I normally don't venture out in the morning too far from the house because I take blood pressure medicine. This medicine displaces the pressure on your heart by creating pressure on another bodily system. That morning, however, I had to go out or go nuts, so even though I did think of it before I left home, I had a certain personal function to perform. The strategically placed trees surrounding the glade provided cover from the road as well as from the hiking trail.

It requires a little extra agility for a female wearing sweatpants to assume the position in semibondage without falling over, of course, but I'd had considerable practice while living in the woods in Alaska. With sufficient privacy, such a moment can be ideal for achieving a calm, earthy oneness with nature. However, the occasion is not, as I discovered, the ideal moment for a close encounter with a unicorn.

Up until recently, unicorns were never a problem. No one I knew had seen one except in the movies or in books. Then all at once, people started seeing unicorns. This was my first one. I wasn't crazy about its timing.

It lowered its head, its little goatee quivering and its long spiral horn aimed right at me. Before I could—er—point out to the beast that it was supposed to be mythical, extinct, or at the very least an endangered species and therefore should have better things to do than menace me, it charged. Fortunately it was a good few yards away—the enchanting forest glade was a largish one.

I stood, hastily rearranging my attire for maximum mobility, and did a bullfighter twist to one side at the last minute as the damned thing galloped past me.

Undeterred, it turned, gave me an annoyed look, and lowered its head to charge again.

Clasping my garments to my loins, not from modesty but practicality, since they weren't properly fastened and would hinder movement otherwise, I recalled my meager store of woods lore and pondered my strategy.

With a mountain lion, you're supposed to make yourself big like an angry cat and back, not run, slowly away. This will make the lion think you're too big to swallow in one handy bite-sized chunk. With a bear, you make a lot of noise and hope it really is as scared of you as you are of it (though it couldn't possibly be). If it's a mother bear, you don't interfere with cubs. If you're camping, you hide your food in a sack in a tree well away from where you sleep, praying the bear eats your food and ignores you, mummied in your sleeping bag. But what in the hell you were supposed to do in the event of a unicorn attack had never been covered in any literature I'd ever read.

The unicorn galloped forward again, an ornery look in its green eye. "Hey, you," I said to it, sidestepping awkwardly. "You just cut that out. I didn't do a damned thing to you that you should go harassing me. Go find a virgin to impress!"

Shaking its head and emitting a snort that sent a cloud of steam rising from its nostrils, it turned to charge again. I ducked behind a tree long enough to fasten my pants, and prepared to duck again, but by this time the unicorn was pawing—or rather hoofing—at the place where I'd formerly positioned myself. It was covering my—er—scent, the way a cat would cover its scat.

"Prissy damn critter!" I muttered, and used its preoccupation to scoot away back to the road. I was not followed.

I definitely needed human company then and a latté. My guest would no doubt follow his lifelong custom and sleep till noon, so I headed down to Bagels and Begonias Bakery. It was Wednesday and on winter Wednesdays particularly, when the tourists were all back at work in their own towns, groups of friends met to gossip and pour over the Port Chetzemoka *Listener,* our town's weekly newspaper.

I grabbed my latté and a plain bagel and joined a table. Conversation was already in full swing but I broke in, which was okay etiquette for Wednesdays at the bakery. "You'll never guess what happened to me!" I said to the two people nearest me while Ramona Silver continued to regale everyone with the problems her friend

Cindy had been having since her fifty-something boy-friend had gone back to drinking. The AA group in Port Chet has a much larger and more prestigious membership than any of the lodges with animal names.

Ramona stopped in mid-sentence and turned to me, "What?" she asked.

"I got attacked by a unicorn."

"Where at?"

"Walking up the Peace Mile at Fort Gordon. It just came out of the woods and tried to gore me." I didn't mention the circumstances. It didn't seem important then.

"Oh, well. The paper's full of that this morning," Inez Sunderson said, and directed me to the front page.

Local authorities, the *Listener* said, attributed the recent proliferation of unicorns in urban areas to the effects of deforestation and development.

"It's said that a unicorn won't even step on a living thing," Atlanta, the real estate saleslady turned psychic reader told us.

I snorted. "If that were true, they'd only walk on concrete. The one I saw walked on grass and was getting ready to walk all over me—after it shish kebobbed me, that is. I think the only thing that kept me from panicking was that I couldn't believe it was real. I've been writing about unicorns for a long time now and I always thought they were make-believe."

"Oh no," Randy Williams said. "The Raven people have several legends in which the unicorn is an important transformative figure. Of course, they refer to unicorns as the One-Horned Dog."

"Surely they're not *indigenous*?"

He shrugged. "The legends are pretty old. Of course, they might have been prophetic instead of historic, I guess. I don't speak the Raven tongue very well."

"You mean the Indian legends maybe foretold that the unicorns would be here?" asked Ramona, a jeweler and artist who, like every other artist in town, works four minimum wage jobs to sustain herself. She twiddled the silk flower she always wore in her hair, an orange one today. She always twiddled when she was thinking particularly hard. Her "Wow" was so reverent I understood it to actually mean "Far out."

Lance LaGuerre, our former Rainbow Warrior and present head of the Port Chetzemoka Environmental Council, said, "That doesn't necessarily mean the unicorns are indigenous or even a naturally occurring species. Some Indian legends also foretell such events as space travel and nuclear disasters, isn't that true, Randy?"

Randy just gave him a look. He doesn't like Lance very much. Lance is the kind of guy who would probably have grown up to be a religious–right-wing industrialist if his father, whom he detested, hadn't been one first. So he brought all of his genetic judgmental Calvinistic uptightness over to the other side. Thus he was a liberal, except that he wasn't awfully liberal when it came to being empathetic or compassionate or even reasonable with anyone who didn't agree with all of his opinions. And he had an awful lot of opinions.

"I mean, now the forest service is acting as if they knew about the unicorns all along but up until now, who ever heard of them? I'll bet they're the result of a secret genetic engineering program the government's been conducting . . ."

"Yeah," Ramona said, "Or maybe mutants from toxic waste like the Ninja Turtles."

Lance nodded encouragingly, if a bit patronizingly. I doubt the patronizing had anything to do with the Ninja Turtles. I don't think he knew who they were.

"Well, whatever they are," said Inez Sunderson, "they've been stripping the bark from our trees, digging up my spring bulbs, and terrorizing the dogs, and I mean to plug the next one I catch in our yard."

The men gently, supportively encouraged her to do so. Inez, you have to understand, gets that kind of response to everything she says. I think the reason is that she is one of those incredibly ethereally beautiful Scandinavian blondes who look really good in navy blue to match their eyes. She used to be a model, I know, and was almost as old as me, but she looked about twenty-five. She is also intelligent and well-read in the classics and has a good knowledge of music and only watches PBS when she deigns to watch TV and never sets foot in a mall. All that is fine but sometimes her practical, stoic Norski side makes her sound like Eeyore.

I didn't say much more. I was still bemused—and amused, because by now the incident seemed funny to me—by my first meeting with a unicorn. I wasn't quite ready to go home and face my other problem, though, so I hung out till everyone left, though Randy was over at another table talking with some of his other friends. He's lived in Port Chet for years and has all these close personal ties with the other folks who worked for the Sister Cities group, were with him in South America with Amnesty International, or used to live in school buses at the same time he did.

My alma mater is a little different from that of most of my friends. I wasn't living in school buses and going to peace marches. I was nursing in Vietnam. So was Doc Holiday, whose real name is Jim, but since he was a medic in Nam, and has sort of a Sam Elliot–gunfighter presence, everyone calls him Doc. It's appropriate. He's the local Vietnam vet counselor, Amvet coordinator, *and* how-to-avoid-the-draft-should-it-come-back-into-fashion resource person. He's a Virgo, which Atlanta has explained means he's very service oriented.

He walked right past me and sat down at a table by himself.

I figured he didn't see me and I wanted to tell him about the unicorn, so I got up and walked over to his table and said. "Hey, Doc. How ya doin'?"

"Hey, Sue," he said, shaking his head slowly. I could tell right then that he'd sat down where he was because he figured he was best off alone. He gets these depressions sometimes, but then, so does Randy. They belong to the half of the town that isn't already on Prozac. "Not so good, lady. I lost another one."

"I'm sorry, Doc." He was referring to clients. He told me once that more than twice as many Vietnam vets had died from suicide since the war as died in battle during. He still lost several more the same way every year.

"Can't win 'em all, I guess," he said with a deep sigh.

Randy wandered back our way just then. "Doc, hi. Sorry. I heard about Tremain."

Doc shrugged. "Yeah, I'm sorry about your buddy, too."

I hadn't heard about that one. "Flynn?" I asked. They both nodded. "God. AIDS is so awful," I said completely unnecessarily. But then, most things you say about how someone dies are unnecessary.

Randy's mouth quirked. "Well, hey, we never thought we'd live to thirty anyhow and look at us—old farts now. I guess it's just the time when your friends start dropping. But we never thought it would be us."

"Too cool to die," I said. "Old Boomers Never Die They Just—finish that sentence and win a free all expense paid trip to Disney World."

They nodded. We all understood. The three of us were graying lone wolves. Armchair analysts would say we had each failed to bond due to post-traumatic stress disorder—Doc's and mine from the war, Randy's from a number of things including the wars he observed with Amnesty. Actually, I think I'm in the club under false pretenses—I bond only too well and stay bonded, whether it's a good idea or not. Doc and Randy didn't care, as long as I didn't try bonding with them in any significant way, but it was good having a woman in the group since they both felt they had a lot of shit to work out about women. So, okay, it's tokenism, but nobody ever asked me to make the coffee, so I didn't care.

"Doc, you know what happened to me this morning? I got charged by a unicorn."

He gave me a slow grin. Twenty, thirty years ago it would have made my heart flip-flop. Fifteen years ago it would have sounded fire alarms that my feminist integrity was about to be breached. But now I just waited politely as he asked, "Oh, yeah? What was the offense? Did you get his badge number?"

"Very funny. I see my first unicorn after all these years of writing about them and all I get is cop jokes."

Doc's known me for, what? seven or eight years now, but he still takes my joking kvetching seriously.

"Sorry, Sue. I'd be more impressed except that our facility down by Port Padlock is about overrun with the critters. They're all over the place, and they fight constantly. It's sort of hard to teach people to be at peace with themselves when there's all these unicorns going at it cloven hoof and horn out in the back forty. Makes me want to get out my huntin' rifle again, but I swore off."

"I think I'll go for a walk. See if I can spot any," Randy said, and left. I followed reluctantly. I didn't want to go home.

Jess Shaw, my houseguest, was on his first cup of instant coffee when I returned. He had the remote control to my TV in his hand and was clicking restlessly between channels. The MUTE sign was on the screen. None of the cats were in sight. I think the smell drove them off. They're not used to people who reek of cigarette smoke and whiskey fumes, half masked by men's cologne. There was a time I couldn't get enough of that scent. Now I wanted to open a window, even though it had started to rain and the wind was whipping up the valley from the Strait. It wasn't that I didn't care about him anymore, it was just that ever since my first youthful infatuation more than twenty-five years ago, the emotion I felt toward this man was something like unconditional ambivalence. It was requited.

After not bothering to pick up the telephone for the last couple of years, the man had just driven two thousand miles to see me. In the years I'd known him, he'd gone through several live-ins and marriages. Since my own divorce, I'd done a lot of thinking about who and what I was and who and what the man I'd married and the men I chose tended to be, with the result that I'd pretty much retreated into my own private nunnery. So I just said, "Is your own remote at home broken? Is that why you came to see me?"

"Mornin', darlin'," he said, his voice as soft and growly as ever. The darlin' was nothing personal, however. To him everything that can be remotely construed as being of the female gender is darlin'. He sighed deeply and kept flipping channels.

"You'll never guess what I saw on my walk this morning," I said.

He obviously didn't give a rat's ass.

"A unicorn," I said.

"That's nice," he said.

"It almost killed me," I said.

"Huh," he said.

But two cups of coffee later he was up pacing a dented place in my splintery softwood floors and talking a mile a minute. He wanted to get his gun out of his van and go looking for the critter.

"Not a good idea," I said. "In this wind, a tree could fall on you."

"Well, bring the sonuvabitch on then," he said in that bitter tone he gets when he's both grieved and pissed about something. "It's not like I'm gonna live that long anyway."

"You've made it farther than I thought you would," I told him, a little tartly. He's like a quadruple Pisces and prone to throwing pity parties, so I wanted to head him off at the pass.

He stopped pacing and sipping coffee long enough to

look over at me and grin. "Yeah, me too," he said. Then he shrugged. "But I pushed the edge of the envelope, babe, and now the doc says I've ruptured the sonuvabitch."

"What do you mean?"

"The big C, darlin'."

"You've got cancer?" I asked. "Where?"

"Liver," he said. "Just like you always told me."

I used to warn him about cirrhosis but after all the ups and downs he'd been through, I figured he was probably made from good old pioneer protoplasm and would end up grossing out the staff of a nursing home some day. I also figured I might hear about it from one of the mutual friends I was still in contact with. Funny that I hadn't. Now I didn't know what to say. Finally, I resorted to being clinical. "Did you get a second opinion?"

He lifted and dropped a shoulder. "Yeah. No good. They wanted me to go through chemo and all that crap but I figured, hey, I'd rather keep what hair I got and go finish up a few things while I feel like it."

I swallowed. "You know, doctors are wrong about a lot of stuff. And I have several friends who were supposed to have cancer and just got over it. How about alternative therapies? Have you tried that?"

He just shook, kind of like a dog, kind of like someone was walking over his grave. Now I noticed that his color under his tan was terrible. He'd always been thin but now he looked like he was made of matchsticks. He took a long shuddering breath and said, "It hurts, Sue."

"I'm real sorry," I said. Another friend I would have offered a hug but though he always talked like he could barely wait to jump any woman in his vicinity, he was weird about hugs when he was upset. So I put my hand in the middle of the kitchen table and waited to see if he'd take it. It seems to me that we had always taken turns being White Fang. He being wild and needing to trust and me being, at least in some ways, blindly loyal.

He took my hand and gripped it hard for a moment, then got up to pace again. By that time the wind had died down a little and the rain was just a drizzle. "Look," I said, "do you want to walk someplace instead of just around the room? That way you can smoke and I'll show you where I saw the unicorn."

"It's still raining," he said.

"We'll be in the trees. Are you up to it?"

"I ain't dead yet," he said.

His breath was even shorter than mine but he enjoyed the walk and picked up the unicorn's tracks right away. We followed them back into the woods, but then it started pouring rain again and I felt bad because I'd encouraged him to come out and he was shivering, despite his Marlboro man hat and sheepskin jacket, by the time we got back to the house.

I felt worse (and so did he) when the his chill didn't go away, in spite of a shower and being tucked back in bed. The cats showed up again and curled up next to him. He seemed to appreciate the warmth. I asked him for the name of his doctor but he wouldn't give it to me, said he was going to "ride it out." Well, I respected that, but by the second day, when he still hadn't improved, I called my own doctor as well as the mutual friends to find out if any of them had any ideas. He had no kin left, I knew, except for a couple of ex-wives. Finally Brodie Kilgallen told me that Jess had walked out of the hospital, telling the doctors what they could do with their tests and treatments, and that was the last anyone had seen of him down there. Brodie knew the name of the hospital, so if everything went well, I could have my doctor call and get his records from there if need be.

He slept all through the day while the wind drove the rain against the windows, made the trees do the hula and the wind chimes ring. I tried to write but finally, after the storm outside caused two brownouts and one brief power failure, I gave it up for fear my computer would be ruined. The TV's old, though, so after dinner I settled into my nest of pillows on the end of the couch and with cats, remote, hard-wired phone and a bag of pretzels, flipped on the evening news. The wind was booming now, window-rattling, and house-shaking, a thug growing bolder in the dark.

According to the news, the storm was raging throughout the Puget Sound area. Trees were across the roads, across power lines everywhere. One motorist had been killed already. Highway 101 was closed along the Hood Canal, and both the Hood Canal Bridge and the Narrows Bridge, which joined the Olympic and Kitsap Peninsulas with the mainland, were closed. They often were, especially the Hood Canal Bridge, during high winds. Right after the bridge was built, the first big storm blew it away and people had to drive around or take a ferry for a couple of years until it was repaired. With 101 closed, you couldn't even drive around now.

Pretty soon Jess padded into the room, wearing only his jeans. He walked into the kitchen and put the kettle on for his first transfusion of the day, then, for a wonder, came and sat down on the couch next to me.

"I didn't know y'all got hurricanes up this far north,"

he said, and we sat in one of the only companionable silences I can remember in our association, just touching, watching the tube. He didn't drink or pace or smoke or anything but watch the tube, making a brief remark occasionally or responding to one of mine without rancor at me for interrupting the sacred broadcast.

Then the kettle went off and he got up to fix his coffee, even inquiring if I wanted any.

Just as he returned with the cup, the TV winked off, along with the lights and the fan on the propane stove and we were left staring at a ghostly blue screen.

I found a flashlight, lit a couple of candles, and called the power company. The line was busy, of course.

Jess started telling me about hurricanes he had lived through along the Gulf of Mexico and continued into a rambling story about his boyhood. I'd heard it before, many times. He always revises it in the retelling. I opened the blinds to try to see how far the power loss extended. The whole neighborhood was dark, as was the hill above us and the streets all the way into town, as far as I could see.

"Jess?"

"Yeah, babe?"

"Play me something, will you? I haven't heard you play since you've been here. You up to it?"

"Hell, yes," he said, and got out his guitar and began playing a song about the death of the Nez Perce Appaloosas. He kept on singing one after the other, songs he had learned since I'd last seen him, songs he used to play constantly, new songs he admired but had only learned bits of. I heard a sort of tapping sound and looked toward the window.

Four whiskery mouths were pressed against the glass, above them the tips of four horns. I touched Jess on the shoulder and turned him, still singing, to look. He caught his breath and gave me the same "Oh, my god," look he'd worn when we saw the Marfa Lights together. But he kept singing, segueing from "Blowin' in the Wind" to the Shel Silverstein unicorn song. At this the critters gave a collective snort and turned tail for the woods between my house and my northernmost neighbor's.

"I never cared for that one myself, actually," he said, shaking his head. "Damn, Susie-Q, what the hell do you folks do around here when this happens?"

"I was thinking we might go see my friend Doc and seeing if he's up to a visit," I told him. "He's a vet counselor who lives out in Port Padlock at old Fort Chetzemoka, which is a pretty interesting historical site. I think you'd like him and find the area interesting."

"Okay with me. You think he's got a beer?"

"Could be," I lied. Doc's been dry for fifteen years, six months and he'd have to tell you the rest. "We should take some candles though."

Soft light glowed from Doc's windows when we drove into the park grounds. Several pale four-legged shapes lurked at the edge of the woods, down by the water, and behind the house and the caretaker's buildings at the park. Randy's truck was in the driveway beside Doc's.

I felt immensely relieved. Randy and Doc would know how best to help Jess. I could get him medical help, of course, but Jess has been in the habit most of his life of turning over the unattractive practical details of daily existence to some woman until she had control over all of his associations, jobs, and where he'd be and who he'd be with at any given time. Then he'd rebel and sabotage her, chewing his own foot off to escape from the trap he'd laid for himself. I was too old for that game and he was too sick. I wasn't going to turn my back on him, and I didn't want to do a whole codependent number either. What was left of his life was his to do with as he wished and if he was going to drink it away, I was going to need backup to deal with it.

"Hi, Doc," I said, sticking my head in the door. Doc likes to adapt Indian ways when he's off duty and it's rude to knock. Usually you try to make a lot of noise outside the door but there was no way we'd be heard over the storm and I wasn't going to expose Jess to another chill.

Doc and Randy sat in the recycled easy chairs Doc keeps by the fireplace. A candle burned in the window and on the table between them.

"Don't you have sense enough to come in out of the rain, young lady? Getcher buns in here," Doc said.

I walked in, half pulling Jess behind me and as we shook the water from our ponchos I introduced him.

Randy said, "I was just warning Doc to start filling up water containers, Sue. I heard on the scanner that the floodwater's reached the point where it's within an inch or two of compromising the reservoir."

"Holy shit," I said. "That'll shut down the town *and* the mill."

"You betcha," Doc said. "I got some extra jerry cans though. I could let you have a couple."

"I wouldn't want to run you short," I said, "but I'd appreciate it."

Jess was standing at the window, staring out at the

rain and the pale shapes dancing in it. Randy looked over his shoulder. "Wonder where they all come from."

"I don't know, but they're getting bolder," I told him. "Jess was singing me some songs and they came right up out of the woods and crossed the yard to listen."

"No kiddin'? They're music lovers?"

"Good to know they like something besides destroying trees and flower bulbs," Doc said. "You folks want some coffee?"

"Sure," Jess said, his hand going to the jacket pocket with his flask.

"I'll hold a flashlight for you while you find stuff, Doc," I told him, catching his eye with a meaningful look that he met with a puzzled one. But he nodded me toward the kitchen and we left Randy and Jess to stare at each other.

"So, you're going to tell me who this guy is, right? Long-lost love?"

"Close enough," I said. "He's lost anyway." I filled Doc in while he made loud noises crashing around the shelves of the white tin cupboard he packs both dishes and nonperishables in. The coffee was instant, not that big a deal.

Randy was regaling Jess with some of his better stories about Central America. Like Jess, Randy can be so quiet you can't get a word out of him or so garrulous you can't get a word in edgewise.

Jess seemed content to just sit and listen. Doc handed him his coffee and after giving his a splash from his flask, he offered it to the others. He didn't have any takers.

By the time the coffee was gone, Jess, Doc, and Randy were swapping stories. Jess felt compelled to keep his hand proprietarily on my knee, though I knew from long experience he had no interest in that knee at all—it was a territorial thing, about as romantic as your cat pissing on your shoe. But aside from that, everyone was getting along famously. Both Doc and Randy liked music and at one point someone said something that reminded Jess of a song with a yodel in it and he started singing again, but this time he winked and half turned to the window. Sure enough, there was a whole herd of unicorns out there, their faces blurred impressionistically by the rain.

"That's the damnedest thing I've ever seen," Doc said. He peered more closely at the creatures in the window. "You know, I haven't looked at these guys this close up before. There's something a little funny about them."

"Funny how?" Randy asked.

"Funny familiar," he said. "I'm getting one of those psychic things I used to get in Nam—"

"Maybe we ought to call Atlanta," I said facetiously. "We could have a storm party."

Doc turned away, chewing his lip. Without another word, he pulled on a slicker and went out in the yard. I watched through the window while Randy and Jess pretended not to notice he'd done anything out of the ordinary.

The unicorns scattered at first, then Doc hunkered down beside a mud puddle and waited. I thought, oboy, he's going to look like a sieve by the time they finish with him. A couple of them did feint towards him and I saw his mouth moving, his hands making gentling gestures.

After a bit Randy asked, "What's he doing?"

"Talking to the unicorns."

"What about?"

"Your guess is as good as mine." So then he had to go

out, too, and Jess put on his coat again to join them. I wanted to say, don't go out there and stand around in the rain like the other damn fools, you'll catch a chill and die this time and then I guessed he probably knew that. I used Doc's phone book, found Atlanta's number, and called.

"Sue! How nice of you to call. Do you have power at your place yet?" she asked.

"Not that I know of. Actually, I'm out at Doc Holiday's in Port Padlock."

"He caretakes the grounds at old Fort Chet doesn't he? Is he okay? No trees down on the house or anything?"

"No. Nothing like that. But he said something about thinking he was having a psychic experience with the unicorns."

"Really? I haven't gotten close enough myself to pick up anything specific but there's definitely *something* about them. I'm not the only one who's noticed it, either."

"No," I said, looking out the window at the three men sitting on their haunches in the rain, a loose circle of unicorns surrounding them. "Do you think you could come out here?"

"In this?"

"Yeah, I know. And it might be for nothing. But it could be interesting, too."

"Okay."

I put on my own coat and went out in the yard to join the boys. Two unicorns danced skittishly sideways to let me inside the circle. They were learning manners since my first encounter, maybe? I was as skittish as they were. I didn't hunker down either. My knees aren't that good. The rain was letting up at least and the wind quieting a little.

None of the men said a word. They stared at the critters. The critters stared at them. Then the lights came back on and the unicorns, startled, scattered to the edges of the woods surrounding the house. About that time, Atlanta arrived.

Doc seemed to have a hard time snapping out of his trance but he did give her a little wave and say, "I was just thinking about you."

"So Sue said," she said, not smiling but looking sympathetic and receptive. "Where are the unicorns?"

He nodded toward the woods. Some of them were creeping back out, watching. A couple were brawling up in the north corner of the property.

"Will they let me touch them?"

"I think so, maybe. I'll come with you."

The two of them headed for the nearest of the beasts while the rest of us stayed behind for fear of spooking the one Doc and Atlanta were stalking.

"Well, so much for the virgin thing," I said, surprised to hear myself sound so disgusted. "They're not real unicorns."

"Of course they are," Randy said. "Just because they don't do what you were led to expect they would doesn't mean they're not real."

I felt let down and excited at the same time. On the one hand, they weren't turning out to be what I thought they should. On the other hand, it promised to be a kick seeing what they did turn out to be, other than a nuisance.

Doc approached the unicorn first, and it let him lay his hand on its neck in a friendly way. With his other hand, he took Atlanta's forearm and guided her hand toward the beast's nose.

The unicorn tolerated that closeness for a second or

two before it bolted. Doc and Atlanta rejoined us.

When we went back inside the house, the phone was ringing and Doc's TV, set on our local news bulletin board, was saying that the recent rains had caused the flooding to overflow the reservoir and we should all used bottled water for drinking until further notice.

Doc apologized for not getting out his jerry cans sooner. I introduced Atlanta to Jess and he gave her the best of what charm he still had to call on, to which she responded with girlish confusion. I fought off a pang of jealousy and asked, "What did you think of the unicorn?"

"I think Doc's right," she said.

"Right about what?" Randy asked.

Jess just sank back onto the dilapidated couch and closed his eyes. His mouth and nose had that strained look about them I've seen so often on people who were suffering but afraid to ask for pain meds. After a moment, he drew out his flask but, from the way he shook it, I could tell it was empty.

Doc cleared his throat. "I know this sounds a little crazy, but the unicorns remind me of some of my clients. I'm pretty sure the one I was trying to talk to at first out there in the yard was Tremain."

"It would explain why you have so many of them around here, anyway," Doc said.

And these were the guys I turned to for practical help for Jess! "You think that's what they are too, Atlanta?" I asked her.

She did a Yoga inhale-exhale number then said, "They're frightened. Disoriented. And—I don't know how to say this. They aren't quite real."

"What do you mean, not real?" Doc asked.

"They're all adult males for one thing, and none of them seem to have been unicorns very long. They're not sure what to do, where to go, how to act. They're like souls in limbo."

"So you think they're reincarnations of the vets?" I asked. "Then why did one try to attack me while I was taking a leak in the park the other day?"

"Maybe that one was the reincarnation of LaGuerre's old buddy Jenkins? Remember? The guy who took pot-shots at the sewage plant when they started building over by the lagoon?"

"Yeah," Randy said. "He didn't want you polluting the pristine parkland, I bet."

"I still don't get it," I said. "Why should they come back as something that was just mythical before? I mean, even taking reincarnation as a given, why not come back as another person, or a worm if you've behaved in a pretty unevolved fashion, or one of my cats if you deserve to be spoiled?"

Atlanta shrugged. "I don't know. But it seems to me like maybe, well, because there's too many of them dying at once? Maybe there isn't really an established place for them?"

"Yeah," Doc said. "And a lot of these guys weren't bad or good, just confused. Maybe Great Spirit didn't know what to do with them either. Take Tremain. He was well educated, for a while after Nam he was a mercenary, then he switched and became an agent for the Feed the Children foundation, meanwhile going through three families before he tried settling down and working as an electrician. Then he kills himself. Who'd know what to do with a guy like that?"

Atlanta nodded soberly. "There's a lot of people that way now. Too many maybe. Well educated, semi-enlightened, lots of potential but just never could quite find a place among so many others—even after, I guess . . ." her voice trailed off as she looked out the window toward the woods again.

"So all our contemporaries who are dying are coming back as horny old goats?" Randy asked, chuckling. "I like that. That's real interesting, folks. I think I'll wander over by Flynn's place and see if he's around. Maybe he'd like a game of ringtoss."

These were the people I was counting on for practical help with Jess? They were nuttier than I was. I just wrote about this stuff. They believed it.

"So what do you think of all that?" Jess asked in the car on the way back to my place.

"I hate to say it but I think the sixties were way too good to some of my friends," I said.

"Maybe that's why they're comin' back as unicorns," Jess laughed. "They're all hallucinations."

"Or something," I said.

"If I come back as one, I promise not to gore you when you try to pee, darlin'."

"Gee, thanks."

Just as we were pulling into the drive he said, "Susie?"

"Yeah?"

"Say your buddies are right about the unicorns. Why are they only around here?"

He was serious now. And it occurred to me that questions about the afterlife, however ludicrous they might sound to me, were probably of urgent interest to him right now. So I said, "I dunno. Maybe because there's such a high concentration of guys kicking off around here, but it's a small place. Maybe it's like some sort of cosmic test area or something."

He nodded, very soberly for him.

While he slept in the next morning I spoke with my doctor, with a friend in hospice work, trying to figure out what to do if Jess chose, as he seemed to be doing, to die at my house. I half wished they'd tell me it was against the law. It had taken me a lot of years and miles to find a place to work and be peaceful while I got over him. I didn't much want it polluted with his death. On the other hand, I wouldn't be able to live with myself if I sent him away. Ordinarily, I'd figure whatever ulterior motive brought him to me would take him on his way soon enough, but now he was dying and I knew about that. The bullshit stopped here.

Ramona called me about two that afternoon. "Sue, it's awful. They're going to start shooting the unicorns."

"Who?" I asked.

"The public works guys from the city. They're trying to get in to fix the reservoir and the unicorns won't let them."

"I don't think they can do that legally, Ramona," I said as soothingly as possible.

"They don't f-ing care! They're going to just do it and take the consequences afterward. I'm calling everybody to get their butts up there and stop it."

"Okay, okay. When?"

"Now!"

"What's to stop them from doing something after we leave?"

"I'm not leaving," she said, but she was a little over-wrought. In her hippie days she could have chained herself to a tree. Now she's got a son to think of and an elderly mother to care for.

I was just debating whether to wake Jess or to go by myself and leave him a note when Doc and Randy drove up.

"Jess still here?" Doc asked, without even greeting me.

"Yeah," I said. "But he ought to be up soon. You can stay and wait for him if you want. Ramona just called and said the city workers are planning to kill the unicorns blocking work on the reservoir and they're organizing a protest."

"I know," Randy said. "I called Ramona."

About that time there was the sound of bare feet hitting the floor in the bedroom and Jess padded out and peered benignly but blearily around the corner before disappearing into the bathroom. A few noisy minutes later he was back out. In the light of day he looked worse than he had before, his skin stretched tight and dry over his cheekbones, his eyes feverishly bright. The smile he greeted us with was more like a grimace and he walked stooped a little, his hand pressed to his side.

I didn't want him to go, but for once he didn't insist on six cups of coffee. He took one with him. He threw it up on the ground outside when we got to the reservoir.

Armed men in uniforms squared off with Ramona, yellow silk flower quivering with indignation, and a small crowd of people, only some of whom I recognized from the bakery. Lance LaGuerre for one, Eamon the Irish illegal, Mamie who used to run the gallery downtown, lots of others. A rerun of the sixties, except for the unicorns stomping, splashing, bleating, fighting, kicking, biting, and diving in and around the reservoir and the flooded river overrunning it.

Doc strode over to talk to the city workers. Some of them were clients of his, others Amvet buddies. Gun-hands relaxed a little. Randy hauled Jess's guitar out of the back of the truck.

He nodded at Jess, Jess nodded at him and spent a minute or two tuning.

"Shit, oh dear, they're gonna sing 'Kumbaya' at us," one of the city guys said.

Instead, Jess swung himself and his guitar into the back end of the truck while Randy started the engine. I joined the protesters, as Jess began to sing in a voice that never did really need a sound system.

The unicorns that were in the reservoir climbed out and dried off and followed the others, who were already trotting down the road after the truck while the pied piper of Port Chet sang the national anthem. Doc saluted and the city workers put their hands over their hearts while the unicorns, brown, black, white, spotted, dappled, gray, and reddish, their horns uniformly shining white, passed by. Jess kept singing the national anthem until they were well down the hill and into the trees (and out of rifle range). Then I heard him launch into Hamish Henderson's "Freedom Come All Ye" in lowland Scots with a fake Irish accent.

"Wow," Ramona said. "Some guy. How'd he do that?"

I shrugged. "He's been doing it all his life."

"For unicorns? He got some special thing with them?"

"I don't know. I expect a ghetto blaster with loud

rock 'n' roll will work as well for some of them, or maybe the Super Bowl on a portable TV, but we already knew they were attracted to Jess's music so this'll get them out of harm's way while everybody cools off. Maybe someone would like to call a lawyer for the unicorns and get a restraining order against the city? Before Jess runs out of breath and the critters return?"

But that wasn't necessary. Five o'clock came first and the city workers climbed back into their vehicles and went home, and pretty soon the protesters did, too. Doc hitched back into town to help Ramona see about hiring the unicorns a lawyer. He asked me to stay and see if any of the beasts came back or new ones came. He said Randy and Jess were supposed to come back for us when they'd taken the unicorns safely off into the national forest on some of the back roads Randy knew.

It wasn't a bad wait. The water was so pretty and clear that even the turbulence of the river mingling with the still water couldn't mar its beauty. You could still see clear to the bottom, like in a mountain stream. And the reservoir was plenty deep.

It was getting dark by the time the truck returned for me, and it had started to rain. I picked up the lights all the way down the road and Randy parked and honked for my attention. When I stood up, Randy yelled, "We got to get back to your place. Jess wore himself out—he's running a fever and he's looking pretty bad."

But about that time there was a thump and a crunch of gravel and a splash.

"Where is he?" I asked, peering into the cab.

"Still in the back."

But he wasn't. His guitar was there. I ran to the reservoir. He was lying facedown in it, the ripples still circling away from him in the pallid moonlight beyond the truck's headlights.

When I pulled on his arm, it was hot as a poker. Randy leaped out and helped me and did mouth to mouth and got him in the truck. I couldn't help thinking on the way to the hospital that it was a blessing this had happened. He'd apparently gotten delirious from fever, half drowned himself trying to cool off, and now we *had* to turn him over to someone else.

My relief turned to anger and dismay when they took him away from us into ICU and not even Randy's friends on the nursing staff could help. Nobody but next of kin allowed. Randy took me home and I sat there crying and hugging my cats, waiting for a phone call to tell me my friend—my oldest, dearest love who was now my friend—had gone out with his boots on and was now, if Atlanta and Doc were right, on his way to unicorndom to be chased through a country where he had no real niche, even in the afterlife.

The call came at about six in the morning.

I scared all three cats grabbing for the receiver. "Hello?"

"Sue Ferman?"

"Yes?"

"Mr. Shaw in bed six wishes to check himself out now. He said to call you."

The damned fool, I thought, briskly brushing the tears away and cleaning my glasses so I could see to drive, he was determined to die here. I drove into the hospital lot and walked through the door, afraid of what I might see. What I saw was Jess arguing with an orderly that he didn't need a goddamn wheelchair, he could walk out on his own two feet.

"Susie-Q, get me outta here, will you?" he said. "I thought I told you no hospitals."

"Yeah, well, you didn't tell me you were gonna drown yourself," I said, hugging him whether he wanted me to or not. He did. And to my surprise his hug was strong, and cool, if not as fragrant as usual. I took a good look at him. His eyes were tired and lined and he was still thin, but the pain was gone from his face and when he stood up to get into the car, he stood erect as he ever had, moving with an ease I'd almost forgotten he possessed.

He hung around another day or two to see if the unicorns returned but you know, they never did. We're still not sure why. Then he said, "Well, darlin', I love the audiences you got around here but I guess if I ain't gonna die, I'd better haul ass home."

I surprised myself by laughing, not even bitterly. "Yeah, we already know we can't live with each other."

He grabbed me and hugged me and kissed my ear rather sloppily. "I know it. But I sure do love you. I don't know what the hell you see in me though, I truly don't."

I returned his hug and kissed him on the bridge of the nose where I kiss my cat and where his horn would one day sprout if the present trend continued. "I don't either except that you're almost always interesting as hell."

"I'll stay if you want me to," he said, like he was going to make the ultimate sacrifice. "You damn near saved my life."

"Nah," I said. "I love you more than I've ever loved anyone but you get on my nerves. Go back and find some younger woman who's not got to cope with you and menopause at the same time."

And he did.

He's called every so often since then, however, even though he hates the phone, just to stay in touch.

"How's our horny little friends?" he asked the first time he called back from the road in Boulder. "Do they miss me?"

"They must," I told him. "Since you led that bunch off that day, nobody's seen much of them. Do you suppose Atlanta was right and they were just on their way to some other place?"

"Either that or it was just the cosmic testing ground like somebody said and somebody else saw the test was failin'."

"Well, it's the city that feels it's flunked now," I told him. "Do you know, when they tested that water, even after the flood supposedly polluted it, they found it was free of all impurities? We had the taps turned on again right after you left. Three cases of hepatitis C, two cases of AIDS and several more cancers supposedly made miraculous recoveries in that time, but then, of course, the good water got all flushed out of the system. The city would *pay* the unicorns to come back now. But I guess you can't just have magic when you want it."

"Nope, which brings up somethin' I been meanin' to discuss with you. Do you know that ever since I got out of the hospital, I haven't been able to enjoy a good drink? It's like it turns to water the minute it touches me."

I expressed my sympathy with cheerful insincerity and hung up to take a couple of bags of daffodil bulbs out to the woods, just in case.

ROBERT SHECKLEY

A PLAGUE OF UNICORNS

Peter: I first read **Robert Sheckley** in the early 1950s, when I was twelve or thirteen—*Untouched by Human Hands*, it was—and I've been a devoted admirer of his ever since. In that so-called Golden Age of science fiction (all Golden Ages are so-called, by definition), he and William Tenn and Avram Davidson stood out as, to my knowledge, the only writers who consistently dared to introduce humor, off-the-wall satire, and plain absurdity into their work. I used to read his short stories to my children, who were warped enough then to appreciate them, and are totally bent now, thanks in part to Mr. Sheckley, who remains, straight through his three recent collaborations with Roger Zelazny (*Bring Me The Head of Prince Charming, If at Faust You Don't Succeed,* and *A Farce to be Reckoned With*) the treasured weirdo he always was.

Janet: I know that Bob doesn't remember this, but I first met him when Ed Bryant took me to a party Bob threw in a Greenwich Village loft. It was a mighty strange party, which I'm sure was his intent. This story is almost as strange, but then anything else from Sheckley would be a profound disappointment.

A Plague of Unicorns

CHILDREN, IT IS ONLY FITTING THAT YOU SHOULD know the stories of your ancestors. Here is the legend of Ctesiphon, who sought the unicorn's horn of immortality for his beloved, Calixitea.

Ctesiphon lived in the ancient days of our civilization, in the great city of Aldebra. One day while listening to speeches in the forum he met the fair Calixitea, daughter of Agathocles and Hexica. The attraction between them was immediate and imperative. Love struck them as unexpectedly and powerfully as lightning. From that first day they were inseparable. Within a month Ctesiphon had approached Calixitea's parents to ask her hand in marriage, asking for himself since his own parents had died in the great plague of '08. Since the young man was well-born and had a reasonable income, the parents consented. A date was set. And then Calixitea fell ill.

The finest doctors were consulted, as well as specialists from Asmara and Ptolomnaeus, where men are skilled in such things. Their diagnosis was immediate and conclusive: Calixitea had contracted the rare disease known as galloping anisthemia. There was no cure. The victim would be dead within a week.

Ctesiphon was beside himself with grief and rage. When no reputable doctor would offer any hope, he went to the wizards, whose controversial practices were a frequent topic of discussion in the forum. And here he did not begin at the bottom, or even mid-list, but went straight to Heldonicles, reputed to be the greatest mage of his generation.

Heldonicles answered the door himself, since his latest apprentice had just recently left him after winning a million talents in the Aldebran Lottery. Not even wizardry is entirely proof against good fortune, though if Heldonicles had anticipated it, he might have done something about it: Agatus had been a good lad, and might have made a decent wizard himself. But it was always difficult to keep a good apprentice.

"What can I do for you?" Heldonicles asked, ushering Ctesiphon into his sitting room and gesturing at one of the low blocks of marble that served for seating.

"It is my sweetheart, Calixitea," Ctesiphon said. "She is suffering from galloping anisthemia and the doctors say there is no cure."

"They are correct," Heldonicles said.

"Then how am I to save her?"

"It will be difficult," Heldonicles said, "but by no means impossible."

"Then there is a cure!"

"There is not," Heldonicles said. "Not in the generally accepted meaning of the word, anyhow. To cure her, you must go to the root of the matter. Mortality is the real problem here."

"And how am I to do anything about that?"

Heldonicles settled back and stroked his long white

beard. "To preserve one from mortality, a state of immortality must exist."

"That's impossible," Ctesiphon said.

"Not at all," Heldonicles replied. "You've heard of the unicorn, no doubt?"

"Of course. But I always thought it was a myth."

"In the realm of magic," Heldonicles said, "myth is the merest statement of fact. Ctesiphon, there exists a country where the unicorn dwells. The unicorn's horn is an infallible conferrer of immortality. If you go to that country and bring back a horn, or even so much as a sliver of horn the size of your fingernail, that will suffice to save her."

"If this is possible, why is it not done more generally?"

"There are several answers to that," Heldonicles said. "Some men are simply too lazy, and would not stretch out their hands if heaven itself were within their grasp. Others might make the effort, but would not know that the opportunity exists. Because opportunity, young man, is a darting and an uncertain thing in the domain of magic. What was never possible may be done today, and not be possible again tomorrow."

"Is that the only explanation?"

"There are others," Heldonicles said. "Perhaps you'd care to study them someday. I have quite an interesting book on the subject. For now, there is a clear and immediate choice. Either you bring your beloved some unicorn horn or she is doomed."

"And how do I go about that?" Ctesiphon asked.

"Ah, now we're getting to it," Heldonicles said. "Follow me to my laboratory."

In the familiar surroundings of his laboratory, with its creaky wooden tables loaded with alembics, retorts, furnaces, and the bodies of small animals, Heldonicles explained that unicorns had once existed in this world, but had become extinct due to uncontrolled hunting of them. This had been a long time ago, and people had known a brief golden age when unicorn horn was plentiful, so the stories ran. Mankind had been extremely long-lived back then. What had happened to the Immortals? Heldonicles did not know. He had heard that ordinary people had resented them, for there was never enough unicorn horn for everybody. They had tortured many of them, and if they could not kill them, had contrived to make their lives so unpleasant that death itself seemed a tolerable alternative. Until at last the remaining Immortals had contrived a way to leave their home planet, to get themselves elsewhere, together with their herds of unicorns, to another world in another realm of reality, where unicorns could thrive in abundance and everyone shared in the benefits they brought.

"What is this place?" Ctesiphon asked.

"It is sometimes referred to as the country behind the East Wind."

"And how does one get there?"

"Not easily," Heldonicles said.

"I understand that. I suppose there's no regular service between this place and that one."

"Oh, there's regular service, but only spirits can avail themselves of it. This place exists in another region of space and time entirely, and has no regular connections with our own. Not even traveling on the back of a dragon could get you there. However, there is a way for a person of much determination who is willing to risk everything for his beloved."

"I am that person!" Ctesiphon cried. "Tell me what I must do."

"The first requirement for this, as for most other enterprises, is money. I will need all you have, all you can beg, borrow, or steal."

"Why is so much wealth needed?" Ctesiphon wanted to know.

"To buy the materials that will be used when I cast the spell that will send you where you want to go. I ask nothing for myself. Not at this point."

"Are you sure this magic will work?" Ctesiphon asked. "I have heard bad reports on magic."

"Most of it is plain humbug and tomfoolery," Heldonicles admitted. "But there is some, the very oldest, that works. To go that route is expensive, however, since the dearest ingredients are needed in conditions of utmost purity, and such does not come cheaply in this day and age."

Heldonicles had to find money to buy oil of hyperautochthon, and two tail feathers from the Bird of Ill Omen, and seven crystalline drops of anciento, wrought at great expense from the inner bark of the hinglio tree, itself rare, and stored in little flagons of amber, themselves worth a king's ransom. And there were more ingredients, the least of them too dear by half.

Ctesiphon procured these articles over a frantic two days, taking out a crippling loan at usurious rates to secure the final money he needed. At last, by the morning of the third day, he brought them all to the wizard, who declared himself satisfied and led Ctesiphon into his laboratory.

There he asked Ctesiphon if he was ready for this journey. Ctesiphon said he was but asked what price Heldonicles wanted for himself.

"I'll let you know when I'm ready to name it," the wizard said.

"But you won't tell me what it'll be?"

Heldonicles shook his head. "Magic is spur-of-the-moment, and so are the practitioners of it." And with that Ctesiphon had to be content. He had often heard that when you dealt in magical matters, you had to beware the double whammy. But he saw no way of avoiding that, whatever it might be.

"If you help me save Calixitea's life, you can have what you want of me. Even my life. Even my soul."

"Perhaps it won't go quite that far," Heldonicles said. "But you're thinking along the right lines."

The actual ceremony was elaborate and tedious and more than a little painful at times. But the wizard assured Ctesiphon that it was a one-shot; to return, Ctesiphon would need only click his heels together four times (reports of three heel clicks being all that was required are false; such reports have corrupted the ancient formula for the sake of a false simplicity) and say aloud, "Home again!"

Ctesiphon thought he could remember that. And then he was no longer able to think of anything, because the multicolored smoke of the wizard's fires, burning in tall braziers, curled around him and he had to squeeze his eyes tight shut and sneeze violently. When he opened them again, he was in a different place.

Ctesiphon found himself standing on a high mountain pass in a place unknown to him. Behind him were deep mists. Ahead, there were sloping meadows dotted with clumps of ancient oaks and cut through here and there with bright streams of water. Scattered across that plain in their thousands he saw herds of unicorn.

Like a man in a daze, Ctesiphon picked his way through the mild-eyed creatures, and the wonder of them was still on him when, further down the plain, he came across and entered the low stone city of the immortals.

The people had noted his progress and were waiting for him. "A visitor!" they cried, for even in the Land of the Immortals a tourist was a welcome sight. And this place was somewhat off the beaten track that leads to the twelve most famous sights of the Universe of Invention, and whose names cannot be spoken here.

In this land everyone looked about thirty years old and in the prime of life. There were no old people, and no children, either, for this race had lived so long that they had given up procreation as boring and old-fashioned, and even perversion had at last turned banal. But they were always ready for novelty, and the idea of giving some unicorn's horn to Ctesiphon was clearly the most novel idea that had come along in a long time.

Everyone knows that unicorns shed their horns from time to time, or lose them in battle with the griffins; and everyone remembered that the immortals picked up these horns whenever they came across them, and put then in a special place. But what place was that? Hadn't they buried them in a bronze casket under the northernmost point of the city wall? Or was that what they had done a century ago? No one could remember.

"But haven't you written it down somewhere?" Ctesiphon asked.

"I'm afraid not," said Ammon, a citizen who had appointed himself as spokesman.

Ammon hastened to reassure Ctesiphon, lest he think the less of them, that they all had excellent natural memories, nor had age robbed them of a scintilla of their intelligence. But the sheer accumulation of fact and detail, year after year, for uncounted centuries, left a mass of material in their brains too dense to navigate with the simple tool of natural recall. So they had all learned the art of forgetting old nonessential things so they could recall newer things, perhaps equally nonessential but at least current. One of the losses had been the location of all the shed unicorn horn.

Then someone remembered that they had devised a system to help them remember facts that weren't of immediate importance but might be wanted someday. But what was the system? No one could remember, and their voices rose in the air, arguing, disagreeing.

Then a man stuck his head out an upper story window and said, "Excuse me, I was asleep. Did someone ask something about remembering something?"

"We need to know where the unicorn horns are kept!" they called back to him. "We devised a system to help us find facts like that."

The man in the window nodded. "Yes, you devised a system, and you asked me to remember the system for you. That was my job and I am happy to say I did it well."

"Then tell us where the unicorn horns are!"

"I do not know anything about that," the man said. "I was only supposed to remember the system that would tell you who remembered that information."

"Out with his name, then."

"Do you want me to tell you the system?"

"No, you obtuse idiot, we only want the name of the man who remembers it for us and to hell with the system!"

"Don't get so excited," the man said. "What you need is safely stored in the head of Miltiades."

"Which Miltiades? Miltiades what?"

"The Miltiades you want is where you put him, in the Temple of Memory."

"Never heard of it. Temple of what?"

"Memory. You see, I remembered that for you as well, and it wasn't even required. It's straight down the street, first left, second right, can't miss it."

To many in the crowd it didn't seem the right way to go, but they followed the man's directions, and, bringing Ctesiphon with them, went to the indicated place.

It was an abandoned building. They entered it and went through to an inner courtyard. Here there was nothing except a largish box.

Ammon opened the box. Within was the head of a man, in his thirties like the rest of them, and apparently in the prime of life despite the loss of most of his customary parts.

"You've come for me at last!" the head cried. "But what took you so long?"

"Sorry, Miltiades," Ammon said, "I'm afraid we forgot you were here until that other fellow, I didn't catch his name, the one who remembered you, told us to come here."

"You mean Leonidas," Miltiades said. "Bless his

incredible memory! But why did you come now?"

"This fellow here," Ammon said, indicating Cte-siphon, "needs a unicorn's horn, and we've got plenty of them somewhere, and by a natural chain of association we came to you to find out where they are kept."

"Unicorn horns?" Miltiades said.

"Yes, we always used to save the unicorn horns, don't you remember?"

"Of course I remember," Miltiades said.

"Didn't forget about the unicorn horns, did you, lying there in the dark?"

"Not a chance. What else was there to do but think about unicorns' horns?"

"Specialization has its merits," Ammon said, in an aside to Ctesiphon. "He would never have remembered otherwise."

He turned to Miltiades. "Now be a good fellow, Miltiades, and tell us where they are."

"Ah," Miltiades said.

"What do you mean, 'Ah'?"

"I mean, let me out and I'll tell you."

"Out of the box?" Ammon said.

"That's right, out of the box."

Ammon thought for a moment. "I don't know. I haven't thought about it."

"Well, think about it now."

"I can't. I'm thinking about this fellow and the unicorn horn he wants. And anyhow, what would you do outside your box? You haven't got a body, you know."

"I know. You fellows cut it off, back when you were fooling around. But it'll grow back once I'm free of the box."

"I still don't see how you lost your body in the first place."

"I'm telling you, you fellows cut it off when you wanted to get me to remember where the unicorn horns were kept. I didn't want to, you see. It was also an experiment to see how far you could push immortality."

"This far, anyhow, without trouble," Ammon said.

"That's right. But now I've done my turn. Now experiment on somebody else. Let somebody else remember for a while."

They decided that was only fair and so they set Miltiades free, and Miltiades told them what they needed to know and then closed his eyes, waiting for his body to grow back. So the rest of them left and followed his directions to a cellar door at the end of a tiny cul-de-sac deep within the city.

The place was empty. Half-concealed in the trash on the cellar floor there was a large bronze box.

They pushed back the heavy lid, and revealed by flickering torch light a veritable treasure trove of unicorn horns.

Ammon selected one horn and handed it to Ctesiphon. "Do you know how to use this?"

Ctesiphon said, "I think so, but please tell me anyhow."

"You shave off an amount equivalent to your thumbnail, powder it, and dissolve it in a glass of wine."

"Thank you," Ctesiphon said. "I'll be on my way now."

"It's been nice meeting you," Ammon said. "After you and your bride take the stuff, why don't you come back? It's always nice to live among your own kind."

Ctesiphon said he'd think about it. But the city of the immortals seemed to him like an old people's home. Although they looked young, there was a mixture of vagueness and querulousness about them that was more than a little off-putting.

Ctesiphon tucked the unicorn horn securely into his belt, clicked his heels four times, said the magic words, and so appeared again in his native city of Aldebra.

There was genial rejoicing when Ctesiphon returned with the unicorn's horn. The local savants declared that a new age had begun, one which would bestow the blessings of infinitely extended life on all citizens. Enthusiasm abated suddenly when it was realized that one unicorn's horn would only serve a limited number of people. Ctesiphon was criticized for not bringing back a sufficient quantity for everyone—though no one explained how he might have accomplished this.

Ctesiphon ignored this groundswell of popular opinion and went to his beloved's bedside. There he shaved scraps of unicorn horn into a glass of the famous black wine of the Eastern Provinces, itself said to have salubrious qualities. His beloved drank, and Ctesiphon waited anxiously for signs of its efficacy.

He did not have to stay long in doubt. Within minutes, Calixitea was ready to get out of bed and take up her normal life again.

Her parents, noticing the change, asked for unicorn horn for themselves. Ctesiphon couldn't refuse them, nor did he want to. He supplied them with the necessary shavings, and made more available for Calixitea's aunts and uncles and cousins and nephews and nieces, finally drawing the line at a third cousin twice removed.

Ctesiphon had planned to reserve some of the horn for the immortalizing of great geniuses and public benefactors of the sort that turn up only once or twice in a generation. But before he could carry out that scheme, a city official arrived at his door, demanding and receiving the municipality's due share, which was promptly ingested by the mayor, his wife and family and nearest relatives, and the foremost members of the town council, all of whom felt they deserved immortality due to their important positions and good intentions toward the public at large. Ctesiphon gave without stint, and was more than a little surprised to see how quickly the horn was dwindling.

And then the king of the region wanted his share, and some for his wife, her sister, his wisest councilor and his wiliest general.

Finally there was just enough unicorn horn left for Ctesiphon to take his own dose. But before he could do so there was a knock at the door. It was Heldonicles the wizard.

Ctesiphon was a little embarrassed because he hadn't called on the wizard since his return. He had been too busy handing out shaved unicorn horn to the many claimants.

"Went well, then, did it?" Heldonicles enquired.

"Well indeed," Ctesiphon said. "And I have you to thank for it. How can I ever repay you?"

"Easily enough. Just give me that bit of horn you have left over."

"But that's the last of it!" Ctesiphon exclaimed.

"I know. It makes it all the more valuable, and therefore desirable."

This was a difficult moment for Ctesiphon, and yet not so difficult after all, because he had already considered who would be his partners in immortality if he took the horn. They would be in-laws and politicians for the most part, and he had no great desire to spend immortality with them.

He gave the bit of horn to Heldonicles and asked him, "Will you take it now or later?"

"Neither," Heldonicles said and left.

Ctesiphon was confused by this but he had fulfilled his primary purpose—to save Calixitea's life.

However, when he visited her, he found that things had changed. Calixitea had decided, in consultation with her parents and relatives, that although Ctesiphon was a fine young man, and would no doubt make an acceptable husband for a single lifetime, he left something to be desired as a husband for all eternity.

Calixitea wasn't at all sure she would even want to marry another immortal—that could be sticky in a country with no divorce, and no death to substitute for it.

She needed, at the least, someone who could provide for her, not only in the years to come, but in the centuries that lay after those years, and the centuries after that. What the family had decided upon was a rich man who would already possess the basis of a fortune sufficient to keep Calixitea and her family secure throughout eternity.

There was nothing personal in this decision, and no criticism of Ctesiphon was intended. But circumstances had changed, and Ctesiphon had no one to blame but himself.

Feeling decidedly strange, Ctesiphon returned to his house to try to figure out what to do next. He wasn't home very long when there was a rap on the door and the wizard Heldonicles was there.

Ctesiphon asked him in, poured him a glass of wine, and asked him how it felt to be immortal.

"I wouldn't know," Heldonicles said. "I didn't take the powdered unicorn horn for myself, but to sell. The richest man in the country paid me a very good price for it."

"I'm surprised you didn't want to use it," Ctesiphon said.

"You shouldn't be. It should be apparent to you by now that immorality is delusive. In fact, it's a game for weak-minded people who haven't thought the situation through."

"What are you going to do?" Ctesiphon asked.

"With the money I got for the horn, I've bought the materials that will let me travel to the Land of Infinite Possibilities."

"I never heard of it," Ctesiphon said.

"Of course not. You're not a shaman. But it lies at the heart of all men's dreams and hopes."

Ctesiphon mused for a moment, then asked, "In this Land of Infinite Possibilities, is anything at all possible?"

"Just about."

"Eternal life?"

"No, that's the one thing the Land of Infinite Possibilities can't deliver. Without death, you see, nothing is really possible."

"But aside from that—"

"Yes, aside from that, anything is possible."

Ctesiphon said, "Wizard, will you take me along?"

"Of course," the wizard said. "That's what I've come here for. It's what I was planning all along."

"Why didn't you mention it before?"

"You had to suggest it yourself."

"But why me?" Ctesiphon asked. "Am I so special?"

"It's got nothing to do with that. It's difficult to find a decent apprentice these days. One with the necessary mixture of naïveté and cunning, but not too much of either quality. One who could be interested in the work of wizardry for its own sake."

And so the wizard and his new apprentice rode off into the blue in search of the ineffable, and for all we know are there still, exploring the kingdoms of the possible for new and ever newer knowledge and delight. They left behind Calixitea and her insufferable parents and a few rich people with their immortality, and from that choice all of us are descended, and all of us live out our endless years in boredom and apathy, because nothing new can ever happen.

Still, the outlook is not entirely grim, children. We believe that Death will return some day and relieve us of the vast tedium of our lives. This is a matter of faith with us. We can't prove the existence of Death, but we believe in it nonetheless. Someday, children, with a little luck and God's mercy, all of us will die.

DAVE SMEDS

SURVIVOR

Peter: I'm going to take the liberty of including in full **Dave Smeds'** statement explaining why he wrote "Survivor."

> War is something that stays with soldiers even after they come home. That's especially true of the Americans who fought in Vietnam. Soldiers of the nation's other wars typically served for the duration. In Vietnam individuals were yanked from the field of fire whenever their DEROS date (Date of Expected Return from OverSeas) rolled around, often being thrust within twenty-four hours into a peacetime milieu they no longer felt a part of. That we ultimately lost the war is only part of the point. Those men never had the satisfaction of knowing they had stayed until the job was done.
>
> May each of the half million guys who went find their closure.

Janet: Dave Smeds is a big guy with a black belt, a love of fantasy and science fiction, and the ability to be fully devoted to whatever he is writing, be it a novel or a short story. He is yet another member of The Melville Nine, one who became—and stayed—my friend after I said good-bye to the group and took off for the West Indies. As you will see from this story, he is an excellent and painstaking writer, with a hearty respect for the old traditions of storytelling. His stories inevitably have clarity, directness, a sense of knowing where they are headed. I like that. I also like the fact that, as a writer, he is never satisfied by giving anything but his best.

Survivor

———⚬≈≈≈⚬———

1967

G.I. BOB'S QUALITY TATTOOS, THE NEON SIGN declared, luring customers through the Bay Area summer fog with a tropistic intensity. Tucked between a laundromat and an appliance repair shop in lower Oakland, the studio was the only place of business on the block open at that hour. Troy Chesley scanned right and left as if he were on patrol, dropping into a firefight stance behind a parked car as a thin, dark-skinned man strode up to the nearest intersection.

"Easy, man." Roger, Troy's companion, grabbed him by the collar and yanked him toward the door. "We ain't back in 'Nam yet."

Troy's cheeks flushed. He had been doing things like that all night. No more booze. It wasn't every grunt that got a furlough back to the mainland in mid-tour, even if it happened for the worst of reasons. The least he could do was stay sober enough to acknowledge he was out of the war zone.

Troy was no longer sure why he had let Roger talk him into this. Nabbing some skin art was one thing; doing it in such a seedy locale was another. He jumped as the little bell above the lintel rang, announcing their entrance.

A man appeared through the curtains at the back. "May I help you?" he asked.

The hair on the nape of Troy's neck stood on end. Or would have, except that his father had insisted on a haircut so that he would look like a proper military man for his mother's funeral. (*"Your lieutenant lets you look like that on the battlefield?"*) "Shit," he blurted, "It's a gook."

No sooner had the words left his mouth than he knew it was the wrong thing to say. Yet the tattooist merely blinked his almond eyes, shrugged, and said calmly, "No, sir. Nobody but us chinks here." He spoke with no more than a slight accent, and with an air that said he was used to the ill grace of soldiers.

"Sorry. Been drinking," Troy mumbled. But drunk or not, it wasn't like him to be *that* much of an asshole. For some reason he felt menaced. The man was such a weird-looking fucker. He appeared to be middle-aged, but in an odd, preserved sort of way. His shirt was highly starched and black, his skin dry as parchment, his fingertips so loaded with nicotine they had stained the exterior of his cigarette. He sure as hell wasn't G.I. Bob.

He had no tattoos on his own arms. What kind of stitcher never applied the ink to himself?

"Come on," Troy said, tugging Roger's sleeve. "Let's get out of here."

Roger slid free. "We came all this way, Chesley my boy. What's the matter? Are the guys in your unit pussies?"

Those were the magic words. Troy barely knew Roger—their connection was that they had shared a flight from Da Nang to Travis and, in seven hours, would share the return leg—but he was his buddy of the moment, and he couldn't let the man say he lacked balls. He was a god-damned U.S. of A. soldier heading back to finish up eight months more In Country.

"All right, all right," Troy muttered.

"Do you know what design you want?" the stitcher asked. When both young men shook their heads, he opened up his books of patterns. "How about a nice eagle? Stars and Stripes? A lightning bolt?" He opened the pages to other suggestions he thought appropriate. To Troy, he seemed to give off a predatory glee at the prospect of jabbing them with a sharp instrument.

In less than two minutes Roger pointed to his choice: a traditional "Don't Tread on Me" snake. The artist nod-ded, propped the book open on the counter for reference, and swabbed the infantryman's upper arm with alcohol. To Troy's amazement, he did not use a transfer or tracing of any sort. He simply drew the design, freehand, crafting a startlingly faithful copy. The needle gun began to whir.

The noise, along with Roger's occasional cussword, faded into the background. Troy turned page after page, but the designs did not call to him. It had finally struck him that he would be living with whatever choice he made. A sign above the photos of satisfied customers warned, A TATTOO IS FOREVER.

Whatever image he chose had to be right. It had to be him. He finished all the books: no good. They contained nothing but other people's ideas. He needed something he hadn't seen on anyone else's body.

It came to him clearly and insistently. "Can you do a unicorn?" Troy asked.

The artist paused, dabbing at Roger's wounded skin with a cloth. "A unicorn?" he asked, with the seriousness of a man who used powdered rhinoceros horn to enhance sexual potency.

"A mean son-of-a-bitch unicorn, with fire in its eyes and blood dripping from its spike." Troy chuckled. "That'd be hot, wouldn't it, Rodge?"

"That's affirmed," Roger said.

The stitcher lit a new cigarette, sucking on two at once, and blew a long, blue cloud. He closed his eyes and appeared to tune out the parlor and his customers. When he roused, he reached into a drawer and pulled out a fresh needle gun, its metal gleaming as if never before used. "Yes. I can do that. But only over your heart."

Troy blinked, rubbing his chest. He hadn't considered anywhere but his arm, but the suggestion had a strange appropriateness to it. "Yeah," he said. "Okay."

The artist pulled out a sketch pad and blocked in a muscular, rearing horse shape, added the horn, and then gave it the intimidating, man-of-war embellishments Troy had asked for.

"That's fabulous," Troy said. He bared his upper body and dropped into the chair that Roger had vacated.

The man penciled the design onto Troy's left breast, with the unicorn's lashing tail at the sternum and the point of his horn jabbing above and past the nipple. He performed his work with a frenzied fluidity, stopping only when he reached for the needle gun.

"Point of no return," he said, which Troy thought odd, since he hadn't given Roger that sort of warning. It was at that moment he realized why the symbol of a unicorn had sprung to his mind. During the funeral, while the minister droned on, Troy had been thinking of an old book in which the hero was saved from death by a puff of a unicorn's breath.

His mind was made up. He nodded.

The needle bit. Troy clenched his teeth until his mouth tasted of metal. As the initial shock passed, he forced himself to relax, reasoning that tension would only worsen the discomfort. The technique worked. The procedure took on a flavor of timelessness not unlike watching illumination rounds flower in the night sky over rice paddies fifty klicks away. Detached, Troy watched himself bleed. He could handle anything, as long as he knew he was going to survive the experience. Wasn't that why he was there—proving like so many G.I.'s before him how durable he was? To feel anything, even pain, was a comfort, with his poor mother now cold in her grave, with himself going back into the jungle hardly more than a target dummy for the Viet Cong.

To be able to spit at Death was worth any price.

"What the hell is *that*?" asked Siddens, pointing at Troy's chest.

The squad was hanging out in a jungle clearing a dozen klicks west of their firebase, enduring the wait until the choppers arrived to take them beyond Hill 625—to a landing zone that promised to be just as dull as this one. They had spotted no sign of the enemy for a week, a blessing that created its own sort of edginess.

Troy, bare from the waist up, held up the shirt he had

just used to wipe the sweat from his forehead. The tattoo blazed in plain sight of Siddens—the medic—and PFC Holcomb, as they crouched in the shade of a clump of elephant grass.

"It's a unicorn," Troy said, wishing he had not removed the shirt. "You know, like, 'Only virgins touch me'?" He winced, too aware of being only nineteen. The joke had seemed so good when he thought of it, but in the past three weeks, the only laughing had been *at* him, not with him.

But Siddens did not laugh. "You got that back in the World?" he asked.

"Yeah."

The medic turned back to Holcomb, obviously continuing a conversation begun before Troy had wandered over to them. "See? Told you it had to be something."

Siddens and Holcomb were a study in contrast. Siddens was wiry, white, freckled, and gifted with a logic all his own. Holcomb was beefy, black, handsome, and spoke with down-home, commonsense directness. But Troy thought of them in the same way. Siddens was the kind of bandage-jockey a grunt relied on. Dedicated. He was determined to get to medical school, even if his family's poverty meant taking a side trip through a war. Holcomb was steady as a rock. He wrote home to his widowed mother and eight younger siblings back in Mississippi five times a week—he had a letter-in-progress in a clipboard in his lap at that moment.

Troy, who had dropped out of his first semester of college, and who had managed to write to his mother only three times between boot camp and her death, wanted to be like both these men.

"What the hell are you talking about?" Troy asked.

Holcomb smiled and pointed at the tattoo. "Doug here thinks that's your rabbit's foot. Your four-leaf clover. Ain't nothing gonna touch you now."

Troy laughed. "What makes you think that?"

"We been watching you since you got back. Remember that punji pit you stepped into? How do suppose you landed on your feet without getting jabbed by even one of them slivers of bamboo?"

"Just lucky, I guess."

"And where you figure all that luck comes from?" Holcomb asked. "You were never that lucky before. Remember your first patrol? You be such a Fucking New Guy you poked yourself with your own bayonet. You slashed your ankle on that concertina wire."

Troy nodded slowly. The story of his life. Broken leg in junior high. Burst appendix at fifteen. Nobody had ever called him lucky. Little mishaps plagued him all the time.

But not for the past three weeks. Not since he had acquired the tattoo.

"Causality," Siddens intoned. "Everything happens for a reason. Remember Winston?"

Troy remembered Winston very well. When Troy was first assigned to the platoon, the corporal had been a short-timer just counting the days until his DEROS. He used to meditate on which boot to put on first. Some mornings he started with the left, some days with the right. When he doubted his choice, he was jittery as a rabbit. On one patrol, his shoelace broke. His cheeks turned the color of ashes. A sniper wasted him that afternoon.

"He knew he was fucked," Siddens said. "Nothing could have saved him. You're just the opposite. You've got the magic right there on your chest. It's locked in. You're invulnerable, Bozo. You're immortal." His voice dropped. "And there isn't a damn thing you can do about it."

Troy rubbed his chest, frowning, wondering if the two men were just trying to mind-fuck him. But Holcomb just nodded sagely, adding, "Some folks get to know whether their time acomin'. The rest of us, we just keep guessing."

Siddens was right. It was as if there were a force field around Troy. Even the mosquitoes and leeches stayed off him. When he and some other grunts from the platoon spent an R&R polishing their peckers in a Saigon whorehouse, Troy was the only one who didn't need a shot of penicillin afterward.

Troy began leaving his shirt off, or at least unbuttoned, as often as possible, until he realized his tan was obscuring the tattoo, then he covered up again. He began to smile and make jokes. He even volunteered to be point man on patrols. At first the lieutenant let him, but later shitcanned the idea: Troy wasn't cautious enough.

Then, as the summer of '67 dribbled into late autumn, the North Vietnamese began to get serious about the war. Suddenly the enemy's presence meant more than an occasional sniper, a punji pit, or a land mine in the road. It meant assaulting fortified bunkers in the face of bullets and heavy artillery.

As the whole Second Battalion was swept into the midst of the firefight in the hills surrounding Dak To, Troy huddled in a foxhole, trying to banish the noise of the bombs from his consciousness. A five-hundred-pounder from a U.S. plane had accidentally wasted thirty paratroopers over on Hill 875—"friendly fire"—trying to dislodge the NVA from their hilltop fortifications. A brown, sticky mass stained the crotch of his fatigue pants—it had been there for hours. Hunger gnawed at his stomach—no resupply had been able to reach them for two days. Over and over he repeated the words Siddens had told him: *"Don't worry. You got the magic."*

He so needed to believe.

Dusk was falling. Staff Sgt. Morris passed a hand signal back. The platoon was going to advance.

A cacophony of machine guns and grenades filtered through the vegetation ahead. Somewhere, other elements of the battalion needed help. Troy gripped his rifle tightly as he rose from his foxhole. Crouching, he joined Holcomb and Siddens. They sprinted forward a bit at a time, heading for the base of the next large tree.

Troy was consumed by the urge to shut his eyes and clap his hands to his ears. No sooner had he done so than the ground erupted in front of him. Blinking, ears ringing, he realized only after the fact what he had sensed.

"Incoming!" he shouted.

His yell came too late. The smoking crater was already there. He was covered with specks of heavy, red laterite clay. He whirled to his right. There, still upright, stood the pelvis and legs of Doug Siddens. The medic's upper body lay somewhere in the brush.

Troy spun to his left. Leroy Holcomb was trying to scoop his intestines back into his abdomen with his remaining arm. Troy caught him just as he fell. His buddy let out a sigh and went limp, his blood and life soaking into the ruptured soil. He didn't even have time to utter a last sentence.

Troy cradled Holcomb's head in his lap. Sgt. Morris was yelling—probably something about retreating to the holes—but the words sailed right past. Troy examined his arms, his legs, his torso. Not a single cut. He had been the closest man to the explosion, and all it had done to him was get him dirty.

"Who'd have thought those gooks could whup our asses like this?" muttered Warren Nance, the radio telephone operator.

Troy raised his finger to his lips. The RTO should not have been talking. The jungle was fearsomely still, but that did not guarantee that the enemy had all fled.

The Battle of Dak To had ended suddenly. One moment the NVA were there, blasting with everything they had; the next moment they had melted into the earth, leaving the cleanup to the Americans. At present, Troy and the other survivors were scouring the jungle for the wounded and dead, a gory process that a Special Forces sharpshooter at the base camp had called "Shaking the trees for dog tags" due to the unidentifiability of some of the remains.

After the adrenaline overdose of the past week, the quiet did not seem real to Troy. Coherent thought was impossible. He still touched himself here and there, confirming that no pieces were missing. He felt no victory, no elation, no horror, no fear. All he knew was that he was here. The only emotion he was sure of was relief: What was left of Siddens and Holcomb had been zipped into body bags and shipped off. The KIA Travel Bureau was the wrong way to leave Vietnam, but at least he knew they were no longer rotting on the ground a million miles from home.

Why them? were the words rolling over and over through his mind. *Why them and not me?*

Whenever he considered the question, his hand rose up and scratched the left side of his chest. Sometimes it almost felt as if the unicorn were rearing and stamping its feet. Today the impression was stronger than ever.

They came to a gully containing the body of a dead U.S. soldier lying on his side. Flies crawled from his mouth and danced above the gaping wound in his back. As Nance bent to roll the corpse flat to check the tags, Sgt. Morris grabbed him by the radio and hauled him back two steps. "Hold it!" he hissed.

Morris knelt down, shifted a few leaves next to the front of the dead man, and uncovered a trip wire. "It's booby-trapped."

"Damn," Nance said. "Sure saved my ass, Sarge."

A burst from an AK-47 blistered the foliage around them. Nance jerked and fell.

"Down!" Morris yelled.

The squad hit the ground. Instantly half a dozen men trained their weapons in the direction from which the attack had come and began emptying their clips as fast as they could without melting their gun barrels.

Troy knew the bullets would continue to fly for minutes yet, even longer if the sniper were stupid enough to shoot back rather than play phantom. Meanwhile Nance was lying next to him, choking. A slug had torn through the back of the RTO's mouth.

What do I do? Troy thought. Nance was dying, and they had no medic; Siddens had not yet been replaced.

Troy's tattoo quivered violently. Abruptly the knowledge he needed came to him. He checked in Nance's mouth and confirmed that his upper breathing passage was too damaged to be cleared. Surgeons would have to do that after the medevacs airlifted the wounded man to a field hospital.

Nance's skin was turning blue. Troy pulled out his knife, located the correct notch near his buddy's Adam's apple, and sliced. Holding the gash open with his finger, Troy nodded in satisfaction as air poured directly into Nance's trachea. The RTO's lungs filled.

The panic in Nance's pupils faded to mere terror. Sgt. Morris managed to get to the radio on Nance's back and used it to request a chopper. Troy sighed. His buddy would live.

And then, with brutal suddenness, he understood why he had felt so certain of a medical procedure he had never before attempted. A presence was hovering inside him. He had been aware of the sensation for days, whenever the tattoo stirred, but he had not realized what it was. All he had known was that, from time to time, he felt as though he were looking at the world with different eyes.

The presence was not always the same. There were two entities. The visits had begun the night Siddens and Holcomb had died.

His buddies had not left him, after all.

1972

Specks of red Georgia clay marred the knees of Troy's baseball uniform. He bent down and brushed with his hands, but the dirt clung. With an abruptness just short of frantic, he tried again.

"Chesley!" The booming voice came from the rotund, middle-aged man near the dugout. "Where do you think you are? Vietnam? Pitch the damn ball already!"

"Sorry, Angus," Troy called, straightening up.

Troy had made the mistake a few days back of telling Angus that a lapse of attention had been caused by thinking of the war. Now the old fart accused him of more of the same any chance he could.

Troy shrugged off both the insult and the distraction that had provoked it. The ball was cool and dry in his hand, a tool he knew how to use. He wound up and let fly. The batter, suckered by Troy's body language, swung high and missed. Strike two.

Angus nodded. That was the kind of quality he expected of a prospective pitcher. Troy tipped his cap at the talent scout. Everything under control.

Troy had been thinking of Vietnam, though. Specifically of a buddy named Arturo Rivas with whom he had served during his second tour.

"When I get out of this puto *country, I'm going to do nothing but play baseball," Rivas said, huddling under a tarp. Thanks to the monsoons, the platoon hadn't breathed dry air in four days.*

Troy noted his companion's ropy muscles and gracile hands and, with a friendliness borrowed from Leroy Holcomb, said, "You mean as a pro, don't you?"

Rivas shrugged and smiled. "Why not? My uncle, he played in the minors for five years, and I'm better than him." He winked, full of young man's bluster. Troy could tell he believed what he said.

"I want to see you get there," Troy responded with sincerity.

That was five weeks before Rivas lost three vertebrae and too many internal organs in a nameless village in the Central Highlands. He had been the last one. First Siddens and Holcomb, then Artie Farina, Stewart Hutchison, Dennis Short, and Jimmy Wyckoff. Seven men dead from bullets, mortar rounds, and claymores that could have, should have killed Troy.

Dirt on his pants. He could wash a million times, and never lose the traces of those men.

Troy wound up, reading the batter's desire for another sinker like the last one. Troy laid it in straight and fast. Strike three.

"I want to see you get there." When Troy had made that comment, it had been intended merely as polite encouragement, but it had since gone beyond that. Arturo was with him. He guided Troy's arm through its moves, told him what the batters might be thinking, gave him speed when he ran around the bases. He was the one Angus was impressed with, the one the scout might reward with a contract.

The tattoo itched. *No,* Troy thought. *Not now.* But his wishes were ignored. The mind-set of a pitcher vanished. Arturo had phased out. He was Troy Chesley again—an indifferent athlete with no real knack for baseball.

The new batter was waiting. Troy hesitated, drawing another of Angus's infamous glares. No choice but to pitch and hope for the best. He flung the ball toward the plate.

The gleam in the batter's eye said it all even before he swung. The crack of wood against leather echoed from one side of the stadium to the other. The ball easily cleared the left field fence.

The next few pitches were not much better. The batter

let two go by wide and outside, then with a whack claimed a standing double. Luckily the player after that popped out to center field, sparing Troy any more humiliation.

That ended the three-inning minigame. Angus and his assistants reconfigured the players into a brand new Team A and Team B. Troy waited by the dugout for his assignment, but it didn't come. As the other aspiring pros hit the turf or loosened their batting arms, Angus pulled Troy aside.

The scout spat a brown river of tobacco juice onto the ground. "I know you don't want to hear this," he said gruffly. "You've got talent, Chesley, but no consistency. One moment you're hot, the next you're a meathead. Until you can keep yourself in the groove, you might as well forget about this camp. Put in some time on your own, get the kinks out, and maybe I'll see you here next year."

Angus turned back to the diamond. His posture said that as far as he was concerned, Troy no longer existed.

Troy slapped the dust from his mitt and trudged into the locker room. Next year? Next year would be no different. No matter how hard he tried to keep Arturo Rivas at the forefront, sooner or later he, Troy, would reemerge—he or one of the other six.

He was living a total of eight lives. Out there on the diamond, he had been Arturo, as intended. This morning while shaving Artie Farina had surfaced, and he had whistled a tune learned during a boyhood in Brooklyn, three thousand miles from where Troy Chesley had grown up. At least he thought it was Artie. Sometimes there was no way to really know. He simply *was* one guy or another, without any sort of command over the phenomenon, his only clue to the transition consisting of an itch or warmth or tingle in the area of his tattoo.

He opened his locker, took out his kit bag, and began shoving items inside, changing out of his togs as he went. No shower. He wanted out of this place. Already he knew what he would feel the next time Arturo emerged—the shame, the disappointment, the anger. The ambient stink of sweat and antifungal powder attacked Troy's nostrils, making him crave clean air.

"I'm sorry," Troy whispered. "I tried."

How he had tried. This time with baseball, for Arturo. Last year in pre-med courses, aiming for the M.D. that Doug Siddens had wanted. In his biochemistry class he had sailed through the midterm, propelled by the mental faculties of a man determined to learn whatever was required to become a doctor. On the final, the unicorn remained as flat and dull as plain ink, and as mere Troy Chesley he scored a dismal thirty-two percent, killing his chance of a passing grade.

As he peeled away his shirt, the tattoo was framed in the small mirror he had mounted on the inside of his locker door. He touched it, as ever feeling as though, no matter how much it was under his skin, it wasn't truly part of him.

A good luck charm? Oh, he'd survived all right. Through the war without a scratch. He had all the life and youth he could ever have imagined. Seven extra doses. But as usual, the rearing shape gave him no clue what he was supposed to do with so much abundance.

1975

Troy's dented Pontiac Bonneville carried him out of New Orleans, across the Pontchartrain Causeway, through the counties of St. Tammany and Washington, and over the boundary into southern Mississippi. As he drove along country roads beside trees draped with Spanish moss and parasitic masses of kudzu, the sense of familiarity grew ever more intense, though he had never been to this part of the South.

He unerringly selected the correct turns, having no need to consult his map. His destination appeared through the windshield. Hardly a town at all, it was one of those impoverished, former whistlestop communities destined to vanish into the woods as more and more of its young men and women migrated to the cities with each generation. By all rights he should never have recalled the place name; it had been mentioned in his presence no more than twice, all those years ago.

There were two cemeteries, the first dotted with old family mausoleums and elaborate tombstones—a forest of marble. He went straight to the second, a modest but carefully maintained site overlooking a river. The caretaker stared at him as if he had never seen a white man on the grounds before, but he was polite as he directed Troy to the graves belonging to the Holcomb family.

Leroy's resting place was easy to find. Eight years of weather had not been enough to mute the engraving of the granite marker. A few wilted flowers lay in the cup. He lifted them to his nose, catching vestiges of aroma. Not yet a week old. After eight years, someone still remembered this particular dead man. That brought a tightness to his throat.

He had a fresh bouquet with him, but he placed it at the head of a nearby grave marked Lionel Holcomb, 1919–1962.

"Rest in peace, Daddy," he whispered.

A woodpecker hammered in the oak tree on the river side of the graveyard. The air thrummed with an invisible chorus of insects that could never survive in the San Francisco Bay Area, where Troy had been raised. Seldom had he felt anything so real as the smell of the grass at his feet or the humidity sucking at his pores.

He turned and walked determinedly back to his car and drove into town. A block past the Baptist church, he pulled up at a house. The clapboard was peeling, but the lawn was mowed and the roof had been recently patched, showing that while no rich folk lived here, the occupants cared about the property.

Troy stepped up onto the porch. The urge to rush inside was next to overwhelming, but he stifled it. The body he inhabited was the wrong color, the wrong size. No matter what, part of him was always Troy Chesley, even when he didn't want it to be so. He knocked politely.

A stout black woman in a flower-print dress opened the inner door and stared at him through the screen mesh, her eyes widening at his stranger's face.

Mama! I love you, Mama! Troy forced down the words in his mind and uttered the pale substitutions circumstances allowed. "Mrs. Holcomb?"

"That's me," she said.

I missed you, Mama. "My name is Troy Chesley. I served with your son Leroy in the war."

The woman lifted her bifocals out of the way and wiped her eyes. "Leroy," she said huskily. "He was my firstborn, you know. Hard on an old widow to lose a son like that. What can I do for you, child?"

"I have a few questions, Ma'am. I was wondering . . .

what kind of plans Leroy had? What he wanted to do with his life? What do you think he'd be doing right now, if he'd come back from over there?"

She shook her graying head firmly. "Now what you want to go asking me those kinds of things for? All that will just remind me he ain't here. The war is over, Mr. Chesley. Go on about your business and don't bother me no mo'." She shut the door.

"But—" Troy raised his hand to protest, but blank wood confronted him. *You don't understand, Mama. Troy's got all my chances.*

"I've got everybody's chances," he murmured as he turned, shoulders drooping, and stumbled back to his Pontiac.

1978

The bathroom mirror showed Troy a twenty-one-year-old self. No traces of the beer belly or the receding hairline his younger brother was developing. No need for the corrective lenses his sister had required when she reached twenty-five. His greet-the-day erection stood stiff as a recruit being screamed at by a drill sergeant: a kid's boner, there even when all he wanted to do was take a piss.

He was aging eight times slower than normal. He was thirty now, a point when other two-tour vets often looked forty-five. At least he *was* aging. That proved he wasn't literally immortal. Just as he wasn't totally invulnerable, or the razor wouldn't have nicked him the day before. He didn't think he could bear it if the tattoo didn't have *some* limits.

He showered, dried, and drifted into the living room/kitchenette wearing only a pair of briefs—the summer sun was already high, and the apartment had no air-conditioning. Slicing an apple and eating it a sliver at a time filled the next three minutes. The clock above the stove ticked: the heartbeat of the room.

So many years to live.

Troy pulled open the file cabinet in the corner of the room that served as his home office and ran his fingers across a series of manila folders marked with names. He pulled out one at random.

It turned out to be that of Warren Nance, the RTO whose life he had saved with the emergency tracheotomy. That is to say, the one Doug Siddens had saved using Troy's hands. Clippings dropped out onto the floor, covering the threadbare spots his landlord described as "a little wear and tear." He sat down cross-legged and glanced at them as he put them back in the folder.

Warren was a realtor these days. The first clipping was a Yellow Pages ad for his business, describing it as the largest in the Texas panhandle. A pamphlet of houses for sale listed Warren's name as agent more than two dozen times. The third item, a newspaper clipping, praised him for a large donation to help people with speech impediments.

A dozen files in Troy's cabinet told similar tales. Sgt. Morris was now an assistant county superintendent of schools. Crazy Vic Naughton, now clean-cut and much heftier than he had been in Vietnam, was a sports commentator for a television station.

The one thing the files did not contain was direct correspondence, save for a Christmas card or two. Troy had seldom attempted to contact old buddies; he had abandoned the effort altogether after the incident with Leroy Holcomb's mother. As happened throughout the veteran community, the connections he had established in Vietnam disintegrated within the milieu of the World, no matter how intense those ties had been in the jungle.

It worked both ways. Troy had received scores of letters during late '69 and early '70. All from guys still In Country. He barely heard from those men once they arrived stateside. As the saying in 'Nam went: "There it is." And there it was. Soldiers sitting in the elephant grass watching the gunships rumble by overhead needed to hold in their hands replies from someone who made it back, just to have written proof that it was *possible* to make it back. Once they came home themselves, they didn't want to be reminded of the war. Now, with North Vietnam the victor, the silence was even more entrenched. Troy saw no reason to disrupt the quiet, and many reasons not to.

But still he kept the files. The other drawer contained only seven, but they were inches thick, filled with all the information he could collect on Leroy, on Doug, on Arturo and the others who had died beside him. This morning that drawer remained locked. He was thinking about the men who had lived. The other survivors.

They were making something of themselves.

Here he sat. He didn't even have a savings account. He was employed as a short order cook at Denny's, a job he had had for two months and one he would probably quit before another two months had gone by. Where his buddies had found focus, he had found dissipation, his efforts spread too thin in too many directions.

Too many chances. Those other men knew the Grim Reaper would catch them sooner rather than later, so they got down to business before their youth and energy raced away. Troy was missing that urgency.

On the other side of the wall he heard the reverberation of feet landing on the floor beside the bed and padding into the bathroom. The toilet flushed. The shower nozzle spat fitfully into life, and a soprano voice rose in song above the din of the spray and the groan of the plumbing: "Carry On Wayward Son" by Kansas.

A hint of a smile played at the edges of Troy's lips. Troy let the folder in his hands close. He cleared the floor, stowed the materials in the file cabinet, and locked the drawer. Before sitting back down, he lowered his briefs and tossed them on the couch.

Maybe he could make some sort of progress after all.

Hardly had the thought coalesced in his mind than his chest began to itch. He scratched reflexively, fingernails tracing the outline of the unicorn. No. He would not let anyone surface. This was his moment. With a firm act of will, he drew his hand away, brought his attention back to the sound of faucets being shut off in the bathroom. The doorway to the bedroom seemed to grow larger and larger until his girlfriend emerged wrapping a towel around her glossy brunette mane, her bare skin rosy from the effect of the hot water.

Scanning his naked body with an appreciative eye, she migrated forward with the boldness that had originally lured him into their relationship. He clasped her wrists, easing her down beside him and patiently thwarting her attempts to fondle him.

"Lydia, do you love me?"

She tilted her head, humming. "I will if you let go of my hands."

"I'm serious."

She blanched as the gravity of his tone sank in. "I . . . oh . . ." She hiccupped.

"I take it that's a yes?" he said as he released her wrists.

Head turning aside, arms hugging herself, and cheeks ablaze with uncharacteristic shyness, she nodded. "You weren't supposed to know, you fucker." He realized the drops on her face were not drips from her wet hair. "Not until you said it first."

"Will you marry me?" he asked.

Her nose crinkled, as if she were going to laugh or sneeze. She lay back on the ratty carpet and spread her legs. "You sure I can't distract you enough to make you forget you said that?"

"Not a chance," he said firmly. "Does that mean you're turning me down?"

"I'm . . . stalling." Her features hardened. "I don't want you to say one thing today, and another tomorrow, Troy. If you mean to follow through, then of course I'll marry you."

The puff of his pent-up breath almost made the walls shake. Shifting forward, he accepted her body's invitation.

1983

"You can't be doing this," Lydia said, yanking at the tag on his garment bag.

"Don't. You'll rip it." As he snapped his briefcase

closed, she let go of the tag, spun, and marched to the window of their apartment. The Minneapolis/St. Paul skyline stretched flat beyond her—the nearest mountain a billion miles over the horizon. They had moved here when she landed the hospital job, but after almost two years he still couldn't get used to the landscape. He wanted geographical features that could daunt the wind, and most especially slow the approach of the summer thunderstorms whose booms reminded him too much of artillery.

"Darling, we discussed this," he said. "I'll be back by suppertime tomorrow. It's a little late to change plans."

"You didn't even ask what I thought of the idea. You didn't even think about the budget when you bought the plane ticket." Lydia tugged the curtain to the side and frowned. "The taxi's here." She turned back, meeting him eye to eye, freezing him in place instead of tendering silent permission to pick up his luggage. "What is so important that you have to spend money we don't have?"

"We have the money."

"Barely. There are other things we could have done with that cash."

He sighed and, denying her spell, carried his things to the front door. "This is something I need to do. You act like I'm way out of line."

"You're going all this way for a guy you knew for a few months? Doesn't that strike you as a little obsessive?" She patted her abdomen, highlighting the prominent evidence of pregnancy. "Don't you think you have bigger priorities at home right now? Christ, Troy, I feel like I'm living with a stranger sometimes. I don't know you right now. You're someone else."

Troy turned away before she could see his reaction.

Her glare drilled a hole through the back of his head as he walked out the doorway, and the wound remained open throughout the ride to the airport, the takeoff, and the climb to cruising altitude. How he wanted to tell her: about the unicorn, about the seven lives he lived besides his own. Everything.

Even Stu wanted to tell her. That's who had emerged earlier in the week. Stewart Hutchison, his squad leader after Sgt. Morris had rotated to the safety of rear echelon duty. Stu understood Troy's needs the way Troy understood his.

He lowered the lunch tray and tried to write his explanation out in a note. He began by admitting that he had lied: This trip was not for a funeral. But when it came to speaking of all he had been holding in throughout their relationship, he kept crossing out the sentences, finally giving up when he noticed the woman seated next to him glancing at the paper.

He wasn't the person he needed to be in order to write it. Much as Stu tried to cooperate, the words had to be Troy's and Troy's alone.

After a troubled night in a motel room, he reached his exact destination: the stadium bleachers at Colorado State University, Fort Collins. He was among the throng gathered for the graduation of the class of '83. Patiently he waited as the university president announced the names, until he called that of Marti Hutchison, highest honors, Dean's List.

Stu had *had* to emerge this week. This was an event the man would certainly have attended had he not been killed in the Tet Offensive. Marti Hutchison had been a toddler when Stu enlisted, an action he had taken partly in

order to support his young family. That day at the recruit-
ment office the war had been only a spark no one believed
would flare into an inferno. He had never expected to be
removed so far from his child; that was not his concept of
the right way to do things. A man needed to Be There, as
he had said when he learned he had knocked up his high
school girlfriend and heard her suggest giving the baby up
for adoption.

He was Being Here today. Troy kept his binoculars
pointed at the freckled face until she reached the base of
the podium and vanished into the sea of caps and gowns.
The eyepieces were wet with tears as he lowered the
glasses, and it felt like somebody was pushing at his rib
cage from the inside. The sensation recalled an occasion
when he had sat in a bunker all night, so scared of the
incoming ordnance that his heart tried to leap out and hide
under the floor slats with the snakes. Or was that something Stu had experienced?

It wasn't fear he was feeling now, though. It was pride.
He let the emotion cascade through him, yielding fully,
allowing his buddy to savor every particle of the joy.

A memory came to Troy hard and potent, one of those
that he and Stu shared directly: *Stu was sitting next to him
in the shade of a troop carrier, speaking fondly of his wife,
who was due to rendezvous with him in the Philippines
during a long R&R the sergeant had coming up.*

*"Gonna try for a boy." He grinned. "On purpose,
this time."*

Troy shut his eyes tight, reliving the moment when
the claymore wasted his buddy, ten days before that R&R
came due. No boy. Perhaps Troy and Lydia's child could
make up for that, though that was not something he could

control. At least he had this much. He caught a glimpse of Marti over the heads of several female classmates—she was almost as tall as her father had been. Again came the heat to his eyes and the tightness to his throat.

"Do you feel it, Stu?" His murmurs were drowned by the din of the names continuing to boom from the loudspeakers, though to his right a grandmother in a hat and veil glanced at his moving lips with puzzlement. "It's for you, buddy. You gotta be in here, feeling this."

Stu felt it, indulged in it, and as a sharp throb hit Troy on the left half of his chest, the dead man slipped back into limbo.

A peace came over Troy, a faith that he had done what he was supposed to. Because of him, seven men had their own taste of immortality.

Lydia would tan his hide if he went on more trips soon. But there was so much more to do. He still had never been to the California/Oregon border, where Doug Siddens was from, nor to Artie Farina's old digs in Brooklyn, nor to . . .

Surely there was some way to balance it all.

1989

"Do you ever really feel anything for us?" Lydia asked.

The abrupt comment made Troy jump. He had been gazing at the clouds out of the windows of their rental suburban tract home, lost to the moment. He always seemed to be lost to the moment.

Outside, his daughter Kirsten, resplendent in ruffled

skirts and pigtails for her final day of kindergarten, swung vigorously to and fro, fingers laced tightly around the chains, calling to him to watch her Go-So-High as he had promised to do when she headed for the backyard. Had that been thirty seconds ago, or several minutes?

"What do you mean?" He cleared his throat. "Of course I do."

"Do you?" Lydia hid her expression by stepping to the stove to remove the boiling teakettle from the burner. "That's good." She said it deadpan, which was worse than overt sarcasm, because it implied a measure of faith still at risk upon the chopping block.

"What makes you ask such a question?" He wanted to let the subject drop, but somewhere he found the courage to listen to the answer.

"You let yourself trickle out in a million directions," Lydia said, reaching into a cabinet for the box of Mountain Thunder. She put two bags in her mug and poured the water. "But it's not because you don't know what discipline is. You make trips, you subscribe to all sorts of small newspapers, you make scrapbooks. You even hired a private detective that time—all to find out more about some guys in your past. If that isn't ambition, I don't know what is. But you don't apply yourself to what you've got right here."

Lydia's jaw trembled. "It's like you're not even you, half the time. You're a bunch of different people, and none of them are grown-up. When you're in one of those moods, it's like Kirsten and I don't count. Are we just background to you?"

"I love you both," he said. "I'm just . . . not good at remembering to say so."

Lydia turned away, sipped her tea, and spat the liquid into the sink because it was far too hot. Testily, she waved toward the backyard. "Go push your child. You only have half an hour before you're supposed to go to that job interview."

"Oh. The appointment," he said. "Almost forgot."

"I know."

1991

As Operation Desert Storm progressed and U.S. ground troops poised on the border of Kuwait, Troy grew painfully aware of the frowns of the senior citizens at the park where he walked on afternoons when the temp agency failed to find work for him. Those conservative old men were undoubtedly wondering why someone as young as he wasn't over there kicking Saddam Hussein's ass, showing the world that America hadn't forgotten how to win a war. There was no way to explain the truth to them.

Just as there was no way to tell Lydia, not after all this time.

The day the Scud missile went cruising into a Jerusalem apartment building, Lydia emerged from the bathroom holding an empty tube of hair darkener, the brand Reagan had used during his administration. "Do you want me to get the larger size when I go to the store?"

"What do you mean? You're the only one who uses that stuff," he replied.

She blinked. "Me? I'm not the one going gray."

Troy swallowed his answer. No use confronting her.

Four years younger than he, she was having a hard enough time dealing with her entry into middle age. She smeared on wrinkle cream every morning. She examined her body in the mirror each night after she undressed, bought new bras with greater support features, wore a one-piece bathing suit instead of a bikini so that the stretch marks below her navel would not show.

"Hey," he said consolingly, "it's all right, you know. It doesn't matter to me how you look."

Slowly she held up the tube to his face, her expression a fluctuating mix of anger and pity. "Troy, Troy, Troy—*this isn't even my hair color.* When are you going to stop playing these games?"

She had said it once too often. "It's not a game, Lydia." He choked back, not daring to say more. He regretted saying that much, but he couldn't let something so important be denigrated that way.

She tossed the empty tube across the room toward the general vicinity of the wastebasket. "Troy, you're forty-four years old. No matter how well you maintain your looks, let's face it—you're getting old. I don't like it any better than you do, but there it is. I've put up with a lot of weird shit from you in thirteen years, but this little fantasy of yours has gone far enough. I think it's time you saw a therapist."

Troy just looked at her in stony silence. The unicorn reared and snorted, though if it heralded the arrival of one of the guys, the latter held back, letting Troy keep command.

"No?" Lydia asked. "All right then, try this: You move out. I've done what I can. You get help, you make some changes, then maybe you can come back." She whirled and stalked out of the room the way she had come.

Troy hung his head. He did not go to the bathroom door, did not try to get her to change her mind, though he knew that was what she was hoping for. She would give him a dozen more chances, if only he would promise to change. But how could he do that? The facts were the facts.

He dragged himself into the bedroom and began to pack a suitcase—just a few things, so that he could get out of the house. He would arrange to come back for other possessions when Lydia would not be home.

He did not want to leave. This was yet another casualty in his life, and he was tired of making up for a choice he had made when he was nineteen. When would he be through paying the price?

1995

July the fifteenth arrived in a blaze of heat and humidity that recalled the jungle. It was Saturday, one of the special days. He pulled up to the curb outside what had once been his home and honked the horn. Kirsten, a lean and spry eleven-year-old, bounded out to his car with a grin on her face.

She still idolized him. He gazed at her wistfully as she buckled her seat belt: flat-chested, a bit under five feet tall, not yet one of those adolescents who had no time for parents. She would remain his girl-child for another year or so.

Troy thought of all those times he had failed to be a

good father. He used to fall asleep trying to read her books at bedtime. He would forget to pick her up after school. She always forgave him.

"Mom says I need to be back by ten," she reported.

"Good," Troy replied, drawing heavy, damp air into his lungs, letting the dose of oxygen lift his spirits. The deadline was later than ever; it was, in fact, Kirsten's weekend bedtime. "Is your mother feeling generous, or what?"

"I made a bet with her." Kirsten giggled. "She said you'd be late. I said you'd show up on time. She promised that if you did, I could stay out until ten."

He chuckled. Kirsten had, as usual, asked him to be on time when they had spoken over the phone on Friday, but he had to admit, most times he managed to be late no matter what.

They went to the lake for swimming and boating, then returned to town to pig out on pizza and Diet Coke.

"Mom always gets vegetables on pizza," Kirsten said with a scowl. She beamed as he ordered pepperoni, sausage, and Canadian bacon. One of the few good things about being a divorced father was that he didn't have to bother with the hard stuff like enforcing rules, helping with homework, taking her to the dentist. He got to be the pal.

They finished their evening at the bowling lanes, where Kirsten managed not to gutter a single ball, beating him two times out of three. She danced a little jig as she landed a strike in the final frame.

He hugged her, noting with regret that it was 9:30 P.M. "Come on, Shortstuff. Let's get you home."

"I had a great time with you, Daddy."

Yes, Troy thought. It had been a good day. He felt like a real father. A competent, mature person, seeing to his offspring's needs. He had hope there would be more days like it. Leroy and Doug and the others emerged less and less as the years went on. What was the point of living in his body when they couldn't truly follow their paths? Troy actually found himself looking forward to the next decade or two, to seeing what sort of adult Kirsten would evolve into.

Chatting with his girl, he drove along the familiar streets toward Lydia's house, through intersections and around curves that were second nature to him. Three blocks from their destination, he stopped at a signal, waited for the green light, and when it came, pressed on the gas pedal to make a left-hand turn.

Headlights blazed in through the right-hand windows of the car, appearing as if out of nowhere. An engine whined, the noise changing pitch as the driver of the vehicle attempted to make it through a light that had already changed to red. Kirsten screamed. As fast as humanly possible, Troy shifted his foot from accelerator to brake. He had barely pressed down when metal slammed into metal.

Troy's car, hit broadside on the passenger side, careened across the asphalt, tires squealing, the other car clinging to it as if welded. Finally the motion stopped. Troy, hands frozen on the steering wheel, body still pressed against his door, looked sharply to his right and wished he hadn't.

Onlookers had to pull him away from his seat to keep him from uselessly trying to stanch Kirsten's bleeding. Numb, he finally let them drag him to the sidewalk.

Nearby lay the dazed, yet intact, driver of the other car. The reek of alcohol rose from him like fumes from a refinery.

Troy had a bruise on his left shoulder and had sprained a wrist. That was all.

The way Troy saw it a day later, Kirsten had been a natural target. What better life essence to steal than that of the very young? The unicorn had probably had it in for her from the moment she was born.

He should never have called the tattooist a gook. The man had cursed him. For so many years, he had seen the unicorn at least partly as a blessing, when in fact the tattoo must have instigated all those deaths around him.

Causality. Everything happens for a reason.

The warnings had been there yesterday, but he had been blind to them. First there had been his uncharacteristic promptness. Then, Kirsten's smile in the bowling alley had reminded him all too much of Artie Farina grinning over a joke right at the moment the bullet struck him. Troy should never have kept his baby out late, should have taken her home in the daylight, before the drunk was on the road.

It was his fault. If not for the curse, reality would have taken a different path. The drunk would have come from the opposite direction, would have smashed into the driver's side of the car. Troy would have died, and his daughter would have lived.

It had been his fault in Vietnam as well. If he had taken the death assigned to him then, maybe all of his buddies would have lived.

He would not accept the devil's reward this time. He would not continue on, wandering through the decades, living glimpses of Kirsten's life, the one she would never live directly.

Blood seeped from the edges of the bandage on his chest. He pressed the gauze down, added another strip of tape from his shoulder to his rib cage. Pain radiated in pulses all the way down to his toes, but he paid it no more heed than he had when the stitcher's needle gun had impregnated him with ink back at G.I. Bob's.

He had been afraid, when he picked up the knife, that his skin could not be cut, that the invulnerability would apply. But it was done now, and the tears of relief dribbled down the sides of his face. Soon he would pick up the phone—to call Lydia, or contact the hospital directly. The docs could patch him up whatever way they wanted, recommend plastic surgery or let the scars form. All that mattered was that the tattoo was gone.

He had done the right thing, he told himself, wincing. He knew he could have scheduled laser surgery, could have gone to one of those parlors advertising tattoo removal. But it needed to happen before anything came along to change his mind. Now that he had found the courage, even one minute's delay would have been too much.

And it was working. He leaned toward his bathroom mirror, his reflection sharpening as he came within range of his nearsighted vision. There—little crow's feet radiated from the corners of his eyes. Gray roots showed like tiny maggots at the base of his hair. His joints ached, and his midriff complained of all the years held unnaturally taut and firm. He was back in the time line, looking as if he had never left it. Tomorrow's dawn would mark the first time in twenty-eight years that he would wake up as Troy Chesley and no one else.

His breath caught. Over the bandage, he faintly detected a glow. It coalesced into a horselike shape with a spike protruding from its head. It hung there, letting him get a good look, then it sank into his body. As it did so, his spine straightened, his hair thickened, and an unholy vibrancy coursed through his bloodstream.

His newfound sense of victory drained away. The ordeal had not ended. Some part of him was still willing to do anything to have a suit of impenetrable armor. The marks upon him had long since gone beyond skin deep.

A tattoo was forever.

"No," he whispered. His hand flailed across the countertop until his fingers closed on the knife. "I won't let this go on." If cutting off the unicorn was not enough to destroy its power, there was another way, and he would take it. He raised the knife to his throat. . . .

The weapon clattered to the floor. Troy stared at his image in the mirror. It had changed again. Though it was his same—youthful—face, his aspect now radiated an impression of intimidating, heroic size, as if he were looking at himself from the perspective of someone smaller and dependent.

"My God," he moaned.

The glow over his wound had done more than restore his immortality; it had brought an entity to the forefront. Troy reached toward the floor, willing his knees to bend, but they would not. The person possessing him would not allow a knife to point at the flesh of the man she had adored her whole brief life.

Leroy and Doug and Arturo and the others might have permitted him to consign them to oblivion. But this new one did not understand. She was frightened of death. Whatever shred of existence remained to her, she wanted to keep.

How could he deny her?

Troy stumbled into the second bedroom, lay down, and tucked up his knees. Overhead hung posters of cartoon characters. The coverlet was pink and trimmed with ruffles. He pulled Brown Bear off the pillow and hugged him close, beginning to cry as only an eleven-year-old, afraid of darkness and abandonment, could do.

S. P. SOMTOW

A THIEF IN
THE NIGHT

Peter: **S(omtow). P(apinian). Sucharitkul** is plainly a one-man show and a three-ring circus at the same time. His career as a composer and musician includes symphonic and operatic works, and conducting positions with the Holland and Cambridge Symphony Orchestras, the Bangkok Chamber Orchestra, and the Temple of Dawn Consort. He has published twenty-five novels. In his third life, he is a screenwriter and film director. I freely confess that I envy him his energy, his diversity, and the talent—not to speak of the moxie—that went into the extraordinary story he sent us.

Janet: I first stumbled across Somtow—a relative of the Royal House of Thailand—in the lobby of a hotel in Phoenix. It was around 120 degrees outside, and he was taking shelter at the keys of a grand piano, playing oldies but goodies, interspersed, if I recall it correctly, by jazzed-up bits of Liszt, Chopin, and Bach. I sat down next to him on the piano stool and started making requests. He spoke to me in a variety of languages as he played. Apologizing for what he called his lack of skill as a pianist, he addressed me in German, French, Dutch, Afrikaans, and was delighted when I answered him in kind. That was a lot of years ago. We still challenge each other by the language switches, we still talk of my joining him during one of his commuter trips to Thailand and showing him South Africa on the way back to the U.S. Beyond all of that, I consider Somtow to be one of the best contemporary writers around. Perhaps because of his classical education (Eton College and Cambridge), even the most thematically bizarre of his literary departures has a traditional beginning, middle, and end, and is highly readable. You'll see. You'll see. . . .

A Thief in the Night

I T'S TOUGH TO BE THE ANTICHRIST. NOBODY EVER feels for the villain.

Without the eternal dark, they can never shine, those messiahs with their gentle smiles and their compassionate eyes and their profound and stirring messages.

Without me, they have no purpose.

And I'm older than they are; I'm the thing that was before the billion-stranded web of falsehoods that they call the cosmos was even a flicker in some god's imagining . . . some *dark* god's.

In a house by the sea in Venice Beach, California, I wait for the second coming. Not really the second, of course; there have been many more than one. But the millennium is drawing near, and one tends to make use of the tropes of the culture one has immersed oneself in; ergo: in a house, a white house, by the sea, a placid but polluted sea, I wait, by a sliding glass door that opens to a redwood deck with shiny steps that lead down to the beach, for the second coming.

A unicorn led me here.

I can tell that the unicorn is very near. I can't see him directly, of course; I don't have the kind of stultifying purity that allows that. But we've achieved a kind of symbiosis over the eons. He works for me. What he does for me is very obvious, and very concrete. He leads me to purity so that I can destroy it.

What *he* gets out of this I do not know.

Today, a summer day, a cloudless sky, an endless parade of Rollerbladers down the concrete strip that runs beneath my window, I feel him more than ever. When they breathe, there's a kind of tingling in the air. Sometimes you see the air waver, as in a heat-haze. Today the shimmering hangs beside the refrigerator as I pour myself a shot of cheap chardonnay.

"Where is he?" I ask the air.

I hear him pawing the carpet. I turn in his direction. But already, he's just beyond my peripheral vision. I don't know how he manages it. One day I'll be too quick for him. But it hasn't happened in three billion years.

I hear him again. To my right. I slide the doors open. I squat against the redwood railings. I look to my right.

Against the slender trunk of a palm tree, the sharp shadow of a horn. Only a moment, but it is disquieting. A shadow is all I can normally see, or sometimes a hoofprint in the sand, or sometimes a piercing aroma that is neither horse nor man. The one who is purity personified is very close. Like an arrow on the freeway, the horn's shadow points me home.

He is a youth with long blond hair. He is Rollerblading up and down the pathway. He wears only cutoffs and shades. I've seen many messiahs. This one does not seem that promising.

Sex is usually their downfall. I think that's how it's going to be this time. I go to my closet and pick out what

I'm going to wear. I'm going to be as much like him as I can. His type. I select a skimpy halter top, and as I slip into it my breasts start morphing to strain against the cotton; I squeeze myself into Spandex leggings, strategically ripped; in the back of the closet, which after all does stretch all the way to the beginning of time, I find a pair of Rollerblades.

In the mirror, I am beautiful. Too beautiful to be true. I am California herself. The sandy beaches are in my hair. The redwoods are my supple arms and torso. My breasts are the mountain lakes and in my eyes is a hint of the snow on the summits of the Sierras. My scent is the sea, the forest, and the sage. I am ready to go to the new messiah and fuck him into oblivion.

Outside: I follow the hoofprints which linger but a moment before dissolving in the fabric of reality. I glide along concrete. The wind gathers my hair into a golden sail. I pass him. I don't think he recognizes me. His eyes are childlike, curious, wide. I whip around a palm tree, cross paths with him again; he looks longer, wondering if he's ever met before, perhaps; then, a three-sixty around the public toilets, a quick whiff of old piss and semen, passing him for the third time, calling out to him with my mind, stop, stop, stop, at the palm tree, tottering, slipping, slamming down hard against the pavement, have to make it look good now, me, the mother of all illusion.

I look up. Shade my eyes. The shadow of the unicorn crosses his face. You can tell; the sun is blazing, there's no shade, but his countenance darkens and then, moving up and down his face, the telltale stripe that shows the unicorn is standing between us somewhere, bobbing his head up and down, pawing at the sand perhaps, for there's a flurry of yellow dust about his heels.

Oh, he is beautiful.

Now, sensing something wrong, he shimmies across the concrete, smooth as the wind.

Bends over me. I groan.

"Are you hurt?"

"Only a scratch."

I look up with what I know to be a dazzling smile, one that has toppled empires. It is not a glad smile; it's a smile that knows all the sadness of the world. But he counters my smile with a smile of his own, a smile like sunlight, a smile like the sea. Takes off his shades, lets them dangle around his neck on a gold chain.

"Let me heal you," he says softly.

"Nothing can heal me," I say.

"It's a gift," he says.

He touches me where it hurts. I have made sure to be hurt only in the most strategic places; where he touches, I murmur arousal. He only smiles again. His hand wavers over my breast, just scabbing over, and the wound closes in on itself.

"How did you do that?" I ask him.

"It can only be temporary," he says. I know now that he must be the one I'm seeking. He has the long view. He really knows that the cosmos will crumble to nothing one day, and it grieves him. He has compassion.

I moan again. "What's your name?" I say.

"I don't know," he says, "I just live here."

"On the beach?"

"Mostly. Don't remember how I got here."

"You just popped into existence?"

"No, I do remember some things. Parents kind of a blur I guess. Social worker talked to me once, took me to McDonald's. I ordered a bag of fries. Everyone had some. It was cool how long those fries lasted, you coulda sworn there was five thousand people in that restaurant. Okay so the social worker, she's totally trying to dig some kind of trauma out of me, you know, drugs, molested by daddy, whatever, but she made me remember a couple of things."

"Like?"

"Dunno like, pieces of a jigsaw. Can't see the whole picture. There's a dove over my head. Keep thinking it's going to shit. That's good luck, isn't it? My mother . . . I only remember her a little. Kissing me good-bye at the bus station. I don't know who my dad is."

"Do you sometimes think he came down from above?"

"Oh, like an alien? Sure. But that don't make sense either, bad genetics. I ain't so dumb."

"I feel a lot better." The air is chill; it's the unicorn breathing down our necks. He's impatient, maybe. He doesn't like to work for me that much. He is a slave, in a way. His shadow crosses the boy's face.

How old? I still can't tell. So blond, you don't know if there's hair in his pits. "Old enough," he says, "if that's what you're thinking."

I'm thinking: what are you telling me, you stupid beast? After all these eons, you're coming down with Alzheimer's? This is the purest heart in the world, and he's staring at me with knowing eyes, and his smile turns into an earthy grin and I don't think he's any stranger to sexuality? I remember the one that got away, two thousand years ago. Now there was purity. Is this the best you can do? I cry to the unicorn in my mind; but though he hears me, he seldom answers.

But I might as well see this through. The Antichrist can leave no stone unturned.

"You've made me feel, I don't know, so *healed*," I tell him. "All warm and tingly." I'm not even lying. "Is there something I can do for you?"

"Is that your condo over there?"

"Yeah."

"Maybe Coke?"

"I'm all out. I might have enough for a couple lines."

"You're so funny. I mean Coke as in pop."

A smidgen of purity at least. I laugh. "Come on over," I say. There are possibilities in this after all.

So we're standing in the room by the glass door that leads to the deck with the stairway down to the sand and he has his soda in his hand and then, always smiling, he sort of drifts over to where I'm standing, almost as if he still has his Rollerblades on, that's how he moves. He kisses me; his lips are very sweet as if they've been brushed with cherry lip gloss; his kiss draws pain from me, each nugget of pain almost more painful to pluck out than it was when it lay festering inside me. I feel myself respond. It's a strange thing. I don't feel passion over what I do, but now, oddly, I'm vibrating like a tuning fork, and he hasn't even taken off his clothes, although I have, of course, temptress that I am, and yeah, there's a dick down there somewhere straining against those frayed cutoffs. But what's happening to me? Aren't I supposed to be sucking his purity out of him? Aren't I the vampire darkness that ensorcels, poisons, and consumes? I bite into sweat and sand. He laughs. It's like hugging a tree. I yank down on the denim, no underwear, pull him into the jungle chaos that seethes inside, and his eyes are closed and I think yes, yes, yes, you see now, I am killing the god-child in you, killing the future, closing the circle of the world, shoving the serpent's tail into his jaws. Oh, I cry out in an ecstasy of conquest. I exult. One more that didn't get away. It's child's play, I tell myself, as I let him empty himself into me. I feel a fire down there. I've never felt that before. It's never been so good to destroy.

But then he opens his eyes and I know something has gone wrong. Because he doesn't seem to have lost his purity at all. What I see is not the dullness of a flame extinguished. I see compassion. We're still standing there, flesh to flesh. Perhaps the flame that raged through me was not victory. Perhaps I was not detached enough. Perhaps he has actually caused me to have an orgasm. I am not sure. My thighs are throbbing.

Gently he leads me to the futon. It's black, naturally, L.A.'s most fashionable color. The pine frame is glazed black, too. He sits me down. And he says, very softly, "Sex is a beautiful thing, you know. Sometimes, when I'm with a stranger, I feel I'm giving away all of myself, and yet there always seems to be more to give."

I stare at him dumbly. Have men evolved that much, then? Have I given them too much freedom of thought? It has only been the blink of an eye since St. Augustine equated original sin with filthy sexuality. In his purity, this boy is completely innocent of such an idea. To me, what has transpired has been a wanton reveling in flesh and fluids; to him, I realize in astonishment, it has been an act of love, even though it was consummated with a stranger.

"You needed me," he says. "I heal people."

And turns away from me, and whistles, and I see the pointed shadow on the wall, and he walks away in his cutoffs with his blades slung over his shoulder, and the shadow follows him, and I wonder who the unicorn works for, and what he is getting out of all this, after all.

At the sliding door he says, "Oh, later. And I'm Jess. I don't know *his* name." He can see that creature as clearly as I see him, and he assumes everyone else can. A sure sign of a prophet, the ability to see such things. In the nineties they also call it schizophrenia.

I don't look up. I hear him slipping the blades black on and thudding down the wooden stairs.

I work myself into a frenzy. He has to be destroyed. I sit by the sliding door and gaze down onto the sand, and I see him whooshing past, a can of soda in his hand, and his hair streaming.

Sex is still the answer, I tell myself. That's still what the Garden of Eden thing means, isn't it? Though he seems to have found a way out of the Augustinian dilemma. He's found a way of imbuing sex with the attributes of divinity. There's deep theology here somewhere, but what do I know of theology? I am not God. The rules of the game keep changing. How was I to know you could have sex and still retain your purity?

Sex. But somehow it's got to be made more potent. And keep love out of it. And make it so I can't be healed.

I think I have an idea.

Evening.

It's easier to follow the unicorn in the night, in a crowded wharf, on a narrow walkway crammed with vendors of beachwear and hot dogs and incense and sunglasses and car shades. In a sea of faces, an equine shadow stands out. Practice it sometime. Watch the dark patches that ripple across walls, past people's gray complexions.

I follow. But I'm not a beautiful woman anymore. I'm a man old before my time. Too thin for the wrinkled Armani that sags on my skin and bones.

He's squatting between two trash cans; above his head, two dope dealers are squabbling. He looks up at me; I'm not sure if he recognizes me or not. He's mumbling something to the unicorn. The crack dealers hunch together over him and I realize that, shoulder to shoulder, they make the outline of a unicorn.

But the moment the image gels in my mind, the two men break apart. The one with the mohawk that seemed to be the horn of the beast, that one goes north while the other goes south, toward a hot dog stand. All that remains of the unicorn is the shadow of a torso in a pile of trash, flickering between the moonlight and the strident neon of a coffeehouse.

Does he recognize me? I think not.

"Hi," I say.

"You forgot 'sailor'," he says.

"Am I that obvious?"

"Do you need to be healed?"

"No."

"I think maybe you do."

"A drink somewhere?"

"A drink? But you're dying."

"Is it that obvious?"

"Yes," he says.

We go to a bar. It's a leather bar, sleazy as shit. I have

a glass of Scotch, and he asks for a glass of Evian. "Nothing stronger?" I say.

"It's as strong as it feels," he says, and waves a hand over the long-stemmed goblet. I wonder if he's turned it into wine. "Do I know you? You remind me of someone I met once."

"I remind a lot of people of people."

The waiter leers at us. And why not? A dirty old man and a beautiful youth. Actually I thought he was going to get carded. But no. We sit on leatherette stools, swimming in smoke. It's grim. I'll be waiting forever if I don't charge ahead. "Do you know what I want?" I ask him.

I make my eyes still and cold. The way people imagine a serial killer's eyes to be, though in reality they are sad people, lost on the fringes of fantasy. "You want to fuck me?" he says. Ingenuous. He smiles again as if to say, sure, anything, because I'm here to make you whole, I'm the caulk that will bind your soul.

"I want to kill you," I say. "I've got it. You know."

"I know." Still the smile. He always knew and yet he followed me. Was that a swizzle stick in the bartender's tray, or was it the horn of the unicorn? The smoke swirls like the tail of the beast.

"I'm riddled with Kaposi's. I have lesions on my lesions. If I fuck you, you will die. But I don't want to play safe. I'm bitter. I'm angry. I want to kill the world. I want to kill God."

If sex is not enough, I think, then sex and death together should do it. They are the twin pillars of the human condition. The error in making the Word flesh is that flesh is necessarily flesh.

"Will it be enough," he says, "to kill me?"

"I don't know. I'm raging. I don't know if you'll be enough. I could pretend you're the world. I could pretend you're God. Maybe that's what it will take."

"I don't like to say that I'm God."

"Are you?"

"People have said it."

"What people?"

"The little girl that the one-eyed man was pimping said it. I healed her up inside, totally. She closed her eyes and said, *God, God.* The social worker found her on the beach. She was staring up at the sun. I think she's blind now. But when I visit her in the group home, she says she can see. I don't know what kind of seeing it is because she's always walking into walls and tripping over coffee tables. I know she sees me okay, she never bumps into me. Except when she needs to be held."

"Is that a parable?"

"You mean, did it really happen? When I say a thing, somehow it gets to be true. But I've never said who my father is."

He is a profound enigma, this youth with the flowing hair and the deep, unfathomable eyes. "But you mean it," I say. "You *will* consent to die." I know that he cannot lie to me. "You will yourself to die."

"If that's what it takes to heal your rage."

I take his cup from him. I drink it in one gulp. It *is* wine, one of the faceless California whites.

I take Jess back to the where I found him earlier, the trash cans, the sea; now there is no one there at all. Behind us, the unicorn canters; I can hear the hoofclacks on the concrete, not a clippety-clop of an iron-shod horse, but a softer sound. It is almost the sound of raindrops on the leaves of a banana tree. And then, with alarming suddenness, it *is* the sound of rain.

He bends over, spreads his arms across the garbage can lids, and I pull down his cutoffs. There is no love here. There is no compassion.

There is no desire save the need to kill. There is no passion except fury. The rain is our only lubricant. I am the battering ram with the horned head. I am all anger. I squeeze the disease into him, a billion viruses in every spurt of semen. If I can't suck the purity out of you, I think, I'll fill you to bursting with my own impurity. I'll soil you with sin. Sex may no longer be the ultimate crime, but surely I have tricked him in seeking out death, and that is a mortal sin. Surely, surely. The rules of the universe do not change that much.

The rain pours down. I feel the exultation of victory. I pull away, kick the trash cans, send them rolling down the pavement and Jess slumping to the concrete, facing the sea. I didn't just give him AIDS, it's a kind of mega-AIDS and it works right away. The lesions sprout up in a hundred places on that bronzed flesh, and they spread with every raindrop; he blackens; he shits blood; he vomits; he writhes; he is in utmost torment.

He crumbles. The rain washes him down to the sand and sea.

I go back to the condo and make myself a double espresso.

In three days he is back.

It's not by the sea I see him, but down in Beverly Center, uppermost level, food court, me coming out of one of those artsy Zhang Yimao movies, ice cappuccino in hand. He's standing in the window of Waldenbooks, at the foot of the escalator I'm about to go down. Rollerblades slung across the shoulder, black tee shirt blazoned with the logo of some Gothic band.

Why hasn't he gone away?

He's coming up and I'm going down, we're crossing paths, I look at him, he looks at me, perhaps he knows me; I reach over, a glancing, electric touch of hand on hand for a split second, and I say, "Aren't you supposed to be dead?"

And he says, "I heard a rumor about that."

And passes out of earshot.

I go back up the escalator. I catch him coming down again, this time in more of a hurry. "I know you," he says, grabbing on to me; I am not sure who he sees, because I have not had time to change my shape. I run down the escalator the wrong way. We reach Waldenbooks, and the unicorn's shadow crosses the entrance. "But I don't seem to know anything else anymore."

I stop. I'm getting an idea. "You lost your memory?"

"It's more than that. Sure, like, I wandered into a homeless shelter this morning and I didn't know my own name. They thought it was maybe I was off my medication? But they didn't have anyone with authority to dole out Xanax or whatever it is, flavor of the week. So like, I'm here."

"I can tell you who you are."

"Do I want to know?"

"You know the answer to that."

He looks at me. He is disoriented. I have no shape, and he has just awoken from the sleep from which there is no awaking. But behind his confusion I can see that that demon compassion is about to come to life. I don't have much time. I have to do it soon, or it will be like that fiasco in Jerusalem. But I need to prepare myself.

I tell him I'll pick him up where Venice meets the sea, tonight, Friday the thirteenth.

Moonrise. I go to him as myself. I can hear the unicorn's breath above the whisper of the Pacific. His Rollerblades are stashed against the wall of the public men's room, and he is squatting on an old recycle bin, speaking to a withered hooker. For a while, I stand beyond the periphery of his vision, listening to what he has to say.

"Tell you a story," he's saying to her. "Because you think you've thrown away your youth, lost your beauty, and now you're this mangy old bitch yapping at tourists for a ten-dollar handjob. I knew this rich dude back East, and one day his daughter runs away from home, and she ends up somewhere around Sunset and Cahuenga, turning tricks, not cheap tricks at first, but later when she's totally lost her looks and been around the block too many times to count, they do get cheap and like, she's doing crack and everything. And she starts to miss her dad, so one day when she's completely bottomed out, she checks out of the women's shelter and hitches all the way back. And thirty-nine blowjobs later she walks in the front gate of the estate, and her dad's all sitting at the dining room table with her brothers and sisters, and her mom's dishing out this pudding which is all flaming in brandy, because it's Christmas. And everyone's crying and saying, you walked out on us, see how much you made us suffer, what did we ever do to make you do this to us." I can't help smiling. The homespun stories never change. He goes on, "But the dad says, it's okay, honey. I'm not going to ask what you've been through. I'm just going to say I love you, and welcome you home." He plants a chaste kiss on the prostitute's brow, and says, "That's what you have to do, babe. Go home to your dad."

"My dad's dead."

"There's a dad in your heart. That's the dad you have to go home to."

She weeps, and I interrupt them. "Another true story?" I ask him. She takes one look at me, stifles a scream, scurries away across the sand. He looks at me too. I don't know if he is afraid; if he is, he hides it well.

"True story?" he says.

"Oh, I remember now. When you say a thing, somehow it gets to be true."

"That sounds familiar."

"This morning, before the sun came up, Jess, you were still dead."

"I knew it had to be something like that! I woke up and it was like I'd been in a dark place, fighting monsters. The whole place was on fire but the fire gave no light. Was that hell?"

"Yes, Jess. You harrowed hell."

"No kidding."

"I tell stories too, you know. You'll have to tell me if you think they're true. I've been called the father of lies, but that's kind of a sexist thing to say; I'd rather be the mother of invention."

The tide is coming in.

"You keep changing the rules on me," I tell him. "First I thought sex would do the trick; it's worked every time for a couple of thousand years. And then there was death. I was sure death would work, because to seek death is the ultimate sin. Death and sex together. But you screwed me over by letting your death purge me of the cancerous anger that I'd worked up inside myself."

"I don't remember," Jess says. "I can't even see you too clearly. I look at you and all I see is a void. I know you're there because I can hear you inside my head. Does that mean I'm a schizophrenic?"

"Most people like you are."

"Don't I know it."

"All right. Are you hungry? I'll take you out somewhere."

We go to a Mongolian barbecue on Wilshire because he seems a bit hungry. It's a no shirt no shoes no service kind of a place but I happen to have an old lumberjack shirt in the backseat of the Porsche that seems to have my name written on it in the Venice Beach parking lot, don't ask me how, probably just another of this world's whimsical illusions.

Jess eats a lot: a lot of meat, a lot of vegetables, about five ladles of each sauce, and a triple side order of rice. I watch him. Sipping my water, I detect a hint of the vintner; it's still him all right, and he's still full of the power that comes from his ultimate innocence.

"I'm starting to remember a bit more," he says. "I guess seeing you was, what do they call it, a catalyst."

"What do you remember?"

"I'm a healer."

"How do you heal?"

"Sometimes with love. Sometimes by letting the world fuck me. Sometimes by telling stories. The stories just come to me, but I know they are true. I've got a direct line to the source of the world's dreams. Don't I? That's who I am."

He's starting to know. He's coming out of living dead mode. I toy with a piece of celery, flicking it up and down the side of the bowl with my chopsticks. "Did the unicorn tell you this?" I say, not looking into his eyes.

"No," he said, "we don't talk much. He doesn't, you know. He's not people. I do all the talking."

The shadow of the chopstick; the horn of the beast. In the distance, waitresses gibber in Chinese. But maybe it's Spanish. I say, "There is something you really need to know. You're dying to know. But you can't know it because you're not fully human. The thing that you want to know is a wall that separates you from the human race."

After sex and after death, there is only knowledge.

Knowledge is the greatest of all tempters.

"You know," he says, "you're right. Maybe."

He smiles. Is he humoring me, or does he already see it? The breath of the unicorn hangs in the air; it's not cigarette smoke, because it's illegal to smoke in restaurants in L.A. For a moment, his eyes lose that I-will-heal-you look. "But if I tell you what it is," I say, "then everything's going to change."

"How?" he says. "You might be lying. Tomorrow you'll still find me Rollerblading up and down the beach, pulling lost souls out of the fire. One day I'll rescue every soul in the whole world, and everyone'll shine like the sun, and the sea will part for us and we'll go into it and we'll see a crystal stairway and it'll lead all the people into the arms of our father."

"Whose father?"

Your father is not my father, I think. I pop a wafer-thin slice of lamb into my mouth.

"So tell me your story," he says.

But first he gets up, fills up a third bowl with goodies, and hands it to them to cook. The restaurant has emptied out. When he comes back, I can see the doorman switching the sign to CLOSED, but they don't seem to be kicking us out. Jess waits.

"Once upon a time," I say, "there was a perfect place."

"Like Paradise?"

"Kind of. You can imagine it as a garden if you want, but I'd like to think of it as a big mansion with hundreds of rooms. Super Nintendo. Videos. Edutainment. Roller coasters. Discovery and laughter everywhere you turned. And there were two children who lived in the house, a boy and a girl. They were like brother and sister. Their father was a weird old man with a long white beard, and he lived on the top floor, and he had a lab where he experimented with creating life. Every time he made a new creature, the kids got to name it. Every day was an adventure, but the estate was surrounded by a stone wall, and there was no gate. The father loved them so much that he wanted them to stay with him forever. He knew that there was only one thing that would cause them to leave. He shut that thing up in a room in the basement of the house. They weren't allowed to go into that room. Not that it was locked or anything. That would have been too easy.

"The kids played in the house for a million years. It wasn't boring. It wasn't that they lacked things to do. But somehow they started to get fidgety. It was time for me to come to them. And I did. 'Adam,' I said, 'why haven't you gone into that room yet?' And he said, 'It's against the rules.' And I said, 'If your father had really wanted you not to go into that room, he would have locked it and thrown away the key.' So the boy talked it over with his sister for a long time, and eventually I took them all the way down there, slithering down the clammy stone steps, and I watched them go in, and I watched the door close behind them, and I waited.

"Sex and death were in that room, Jess."

"I remember now!" He's exhilarated. "They were kicked out of the house, and I've come to fetch them home."

"Oh, Jess," I said, "that's the illusion I've come to strip away; that's the one piece of knowledge in *your* dark basement room—we all have them, those basement rooms—and I've come to give it to you."

"Oh," says the boy, and the light begins to drain from his eyes.

"You see, the boy and the girl went upstairs to tell their father they'd broken the rule. The old man was very sad. He said, 'You can stay if you want. We can work this out. I don't want to lose you.' Adam and Eve looked at each other. Strange and grand new feelings were surging through their bodies. At last, Eve said, 'We have to go, Dad. You know we do. That's why you didn't lock the door.' And the old man said, 'Yes. You're human beings. You can't be children forever. You have to break the rules. It's human to defy your parents. It's human to strive, to seek new worlds, to leave the nest, earn a living, make love and babies, filter back into the earth so that it can nourish more human beings. You're dust and you must turn into dust again one day. It's a sad thing. But it's not without joy. But look how dust dances in the light. You are beautiful because you are not immortal. I'm the one who can't change. I'm the one who has to go on forever. Pity me, children. Pity your poor old father.'

"The knowledge the children gained was the gateway through the stone walls and into the world outside. They lived in the real world after that. Not always happily, and not ever after.

"And Paradise became an empty nest, and the old man realized that the perfect place he had built was a private hell from which he would never escape."

Jess doesn't speak for a long time. They are turning out the lights, but a different light suffuses us, the light from the unicorn's eyes. At last he screams out, "Oh, God! Why did you send me here? Fuck you—you told me I was here to love them and redeem them and really you want me to chain them up and throw the key into the ocean and—"

"You're talking to the unicorn?"

"Sometimes I think the unicorn is my father."

That's never occurred to me in all those years.

"Good-bye," Jess says softly, and he's not speaking to me. I've robbed him of his innocence at last. And now, for a few brief seconds, it is I who am pure: I am all the goodness that was once in the boy, I am his hopes and dreams, I am his sacrifice, I am his redeeming love. Only in that moment, as his vision leaves him, do I see the unicorn.

The restaurant has dissolved into thin air and the great beast is running toward the waves. The sea splashes against his moon-sheened withers. His horn glistens. The wind from the Pacific whips Jess's hair across his bare shoulders. He looks down at the sand. "I'm naked," he says at last. "Can't you hold me?"

The unicorn has dissipated into mist.

I cradle Jess in my arms, and he weeps. In that

embrace, without sex and without death, I drain the last dregs of divinity from him. We love each other.

Maybe God *is* their father. But they are my children, too, and I'm a lot older than God. Because darkness is the mother of light.

I love them just as much as he does. More. My nest is empty, too. But *he* just won't learn to let go. He just won't let them be. He always wants to meddle in their affairs. But he always lets me have my three temptations.

They think they want to live forever. They think they want eternal bliss. But what they really want is to love and to die. That is their real nature. That is the truth that God can never face, and that's why this little war has to go on, why there'll always be an Antichrist.

Yesterday he was the savior of the world, but today Jess is just another lost boy. Tomorrow I'll give him the keys to the Porsche and the title deed to the house by the sea, so at least he can go Rollerblading to his heart's content, and have somewhere to come home to when he falls in love and raises a family and forgets that he ever had the power to mend broken souls.

I'm not the villain in this war.

Tomorrow I'll go someplace far away and I'll sit and wait for a hundred years until one day I'll hear the leaves rustling and see the darting shadow and the hoofprints in the sand, or the snow, or the forest floor. It's always been this way and it always will be. World without end. Amen.

MELANIE TEM

HALF-GRANDMA

Peter: **Melanie Tem** is the author of five novels as well as much short fiction. She is also a grandmother and was a social worker for over twenty years. That figures. I find more and more that the fiction that reaches me most immediately tends to be written by people living real lives—not the alligator-wrestling, freight-hopping dust jacket sort, but lives connected to a daily world with other people in it, other lives to be concerned with. The wisdom, tenderness, and quiet authority that inform "Half-Grandma" didn't come from books or TV or the Internet. . . .

Janet: Once upon a time, in one of my many incarnations, I had a small literary agency. That was how I met Melanie. I was, I am proud to say, her first agent. She's a tough lady with amazing courage, an indomitable spirit, and an overdose of talent. I'll never forget how she reamed me out—firmly, but ever-so-gently—when I called her "Mel." She ain't scared of no one, this woman. I cried (happy tears) a couple of years ago when I happened to be present when she won a Bram Stoker Award.

I cried again when I read the story you're about to read—because it touched my heart. I knew it would when I asked her to write one. I was right in the first place: She's a heck of a broad and a helluva writer.

Half-Grandma

THERE WAS A STRANGE HORSE IN THE PASTURE. White. White and swift. White as concentrated light and swift as sound.

Amelia had been gazing distractedly out her kitchen window at the backyard scene at which she'd gazed distractedly for so many years. It wouldn't have been accurate to say simply that she no longer really saw it; she saw it now in her mind's eye quite as clearly and in as much generous detail as with her physical eyes, and lived it in her bones.

Almost always there had been horses in the pasture—her sons', until they lost interest in horses, too; her younger grandson's, but that had been more her idea than his, and he probably hadn't ridden more than half a dozen times; her own until perhaps ten years ago when she'd decided, with surprisingly little disappointment, that she was too old to risk riding anymore; then a series of boarders. So it took a while this time for the fact to register that there was a horse in the pasture that didn't belong there.

She went on fixing supper for herself and Brandon—mostly, if truth be told, for Brandon; she was hardly ever hungry these days—and contented herself, for the moment, with a discouraged sigh. She'd rented the pasture for two horses, and now, without saying a word to her, they'd put in a third one. Pretty little thing, from what she could see through the trees, but nobody was paying for it to be there. Now she'd have to decide whether to charge extra for it or not, whether to have an unpleasant confrontation.

She resented being put in the position of having to make a moral choice which by rights was not hers. She just wished people would be honest. Maybe she was wrong, but it seemed to her that people as a whole had been more honest in her day. Odd, sobering way to think of it, as though *this* day were not hers.

The back door slammed and Brandon came clattering up the stairs, talking before he even got into the room. His energy delighted and tired Amelia. They were no kin to each other, had known each other only since his family had moved into the neighborhood—which was, though, more than half his life. He'd taken to referring to her as his "half-grandma." It gratified Amelia no end that people could consciously form relationships like that; sometimes, it also saddened her that they had to. "Look what I found!"

He had a bird, pin-feathered and apparently uninjured. His small grimy hands imprisoned it—carefully, tenderly, but imprisoned nonetheless. "Oh, he's beautiful, Brandon," Amelia told him, paying full attention. The waffles would wait. Trying to sound interested and not accusatory, she asked carefully, "Where'd you find him?"

The bird was emitting tiny frantic chirps that urged Amelia to set it free. But Brandon, clearly, was enchanted. He lifted the hollow ball of his fists to his ear and listened intently, face alight. "Hear him? He likes me!"

"He's scared," Amelia countered gently. She sat down at the table and pulled him onto her lap. He didn't resist, but he was far more interested in the bird than in her. "He might be hurt. Did he fall out of the nest?"

Brandon shook his head. Plush gray light through the south window played across the downy back of his neck and on his tousled sandy hair. "I climbed up and got him out."

Amelia caught her breath in alarm. Brandon squirmed when he felt her stiffen, but knew not to look up at her. "Where?" she asked, afraid to know.

Brandon said happily, "He's my *pet*," and slid down. Amelia started to object, but he was already out of the kitchen, down the noisy wooden stairs, out of the house. Temporarily bested, she went to plug in the waffle iron, mulling ways she might explain to a ten-year-old the concept of respecting another creature's place in the universe.

Brandon loved waffles. Whenever he came to her house, he wanted waffles—for breakfast, lunch, and dinner if he was staying a while, for snacks if he was just visiting. Amelia always added one or more healthful things to the basic batter, so he got bananas, bran, yogurt, walnuts, raisins, without her calling attention to them. Among his mother's numerous complaints about him was her assertion that he was a fussy eater, and Amelia guessed that was so, but she noted rather smugly that he'd never turned up his nose at her waffles, no matter what she'd sneaked into them. He'd been known to consume as many as eight at a sitting. Amelia hadn't mentioned waffles to his mother.

Now when she called out the window for him to come in for supper, he answered, "'Kay!" but he didn't come. She made another waffle, which pleased her by coming out in perfect quarters, and then called him again; he answered again, but he still didn't come. Less annoyed than amused by the vagaries of boyhood, predictable through at least four generations of boys she had more or less known—brothers and cousins; sons less well, as it had turned out; grandsons almost not at all—she stacked the waffles on a plate, covered them with a napkin, put them in the oven on "Lo," and went out to get him.

He was down the hill at the edge of the pasture, staring up at the roof of the shed with his arms crossed and a glower on his face. He was such a perfect picture of outrage that Amelia wanted to laugh, but of course she didn't. As she made her way to him she glanced into the pasture. The renter's two horses were there, the black filly and the bay, but she didn't see the white horse. Uneasily she wondered if it had gotten out, then told herself sternly it wasn't her problem, it wasn't even supposed to be there, and went to stand beside Brandon. "Waffles are ready."

"He ran away," the little boy announced unhappily.

Relieved, Amelia nodded. "He went back where he belongs."

Brandon shook his head vehemently. "He belongs to *me*. He was my *pet*."

"What if he didn't want to be your pet?"

This idea was quite beyond him. "Why not?"

"He's a wild thing. It's not in his nature to be anybody's pet."

"But I didn't want him to go away." Brandon was close to tears. He cried easily, a trait which Amelia found

endearing although she guessed that many other adults—
and, for different though related reasons, children—did
not.

She took his hand, and together they walked back up
the hill toward the house and the peach-yogurt waffles.
Amelia felt and acknowledged the brief shooting pain in
her chest that had lately become familiar. Acknowledged:
did not welcome, but did not deny, either. It might be
nothing. It might mean her heart, or something less dis-
crete and definable than an organ at the heart of her old
body, was preparing to stop.

Brandon wasn't done. "But I wanted to *keep* him!" he
wailed.

"I know you did, honey." Amelia smoothed his hair,
reflecting tenderly that there would be—probably already
had been—countless other things in his life he would
yearn to hold on to.

He stayed quiet and teary through his first waffle.
After a few unsuccessful attempts to distract or cheer him
up, Amelia did her best to respect his feelings and
restricted herself to a pat on the hand and an extra dollop
of sugarless strawberry preserves. By the time he'd
started on the second waffle, hot from the griddle, he was
chattering again, telling about his numerous friends at
school, all of whom were, as far as Amelia could tell, his
best friends. She tried to explain that "friend" was too
important a word to be used carelessly, that people didn't
become your best friends just by being in the same room
at the same time, but he would have none of it.

When he pushed his chair back and pronounced himself full, he'd eaten only four and a half waffles, which
worried her a little. Wasted food made her feel sad and

guilty; maybe the horses or the little wild cats who lived in the shed would eat them.

Brandon wanted to watch TV. More than she ought to, Amelia found herself lying on the couch with the television on; the pseudo-presence of voices and activity assuaged loneliness if she didn't think too much about how phony they were, and often she just didn't feel alert enough to do anything else, even read. Sometimes she was mildly resentful when visitors dropped by, generally one of her three sons who currently lived in town or her older grandson; she did not always want to extricate herself from the murky state of semiconsciousness into which she more and more easily sank, and television provided a host of handy excuses: "I must have dozed off." "It really does turn your brain to mush."

There was practically nothing on that she thought a boy Brandon's age ought to be watching, and she was somewhat appalled by the number and types of shows with which he seemed to be on intimate terms. Finally they agreed on a nature show, and she settled down in the rocker to watch it with him.

For a minute she was dizzy and sick at her stomach. Gripping the arms of the chair and staring fixedly at the regular repeated pattern of granny squares in the last afghan her mother had crocheted, nearly twenty years ago, she dreaded another days-long siege of feeling not at all well. But it passed. There would come a time, she supposed, when such things would not pass. When that happened, she would manage, but she was just as glad it was not now.

As the television program and Brandon and her living room came back into focus, out of the corner of her eye she glimpsed a white horse's head. It wasn't there when she looked directly out the window.

The simple cast of light could give rise to odd shadows and reflections. Years ago she'd had a dog named Jake, one in a long line of dogs and cats all of whose names and idiosyncrasies Amelia remembered fondly, who'd chased mirror reflections and the double circle of a flashlight shined on the ceiling; at certain times of the day at certain times of the year, plain light through the picture window had kept him leaping and mock-snarling for half an hour at a stretch.

Sitting on the floor at her feet, Brandon allowed her to stroke his hair a few times before he pulled away. Obediently she put her hands in her lap, not wanting him to break contact altogether. Really, though, she didn't think that was likely. Brandon wasn't the least bit skittish or reserved; it wasn't as if she had to win him. Still, her satisfaction was deep and sweet when he tipped companionably back against her knee.

It wasn't necessary or even wise to pay close attention to the program, although Amelia was rather interested in astronomy. Brandon would tell her all about it anyway. His memory and enthusiasm impressed her, so that she could put up with, even enjoy, his determination to recount every detail, not necessarily in sequence, not caring if she'd heard it the first time from the primary source. He did that with movies he'd seen, too, and cop shows, which she found considerably less fun to listen to.

Last summer Brandon had gone with his parents on vacation to the Southwest, where he'd learned about Kokopelli, the hump-backed flute player of Navajo legend, whose likeness he'd seen everywhere, from ancient pictographs on the walls of Canyon de Chelly to postcards for the Santa Fe tourists. Brandon had brought her a pair of Kokopelli earrings. "He makes girls have babies!" he'd chortled, and Amelia had laughed, hoping he knew what really made girls have babies. "I told the man they were for my half-grandma, and he said Kokopelli makes people live a long time, too. Live forever." She'd heard a lot about Kokopelli for a while there, and she wore the earrings every time Brandon came over, though he didn't often notice anymore.

It still made her smile to imagine the clerk, doubtless bemused by Brandon's term of relationship to her. Frequently she was saddened—mildly most of the time, but once in a while profoundly, heartbreakingly—that she wasn't his *whole* grandma, his *real* grandma. But his exuberant claiming of her, quite as though there were no need for blood or legal bonds between them, also raised her spirits and renewed her often flagging hope, for him, for herself, and for the world in general. All this from one small boy. Amelia smiled and reached around to pat his cheek. She felt him grin.

She dozed. The older she got the more irregular her sleep patterns became, so that she was asleep when most people were awake and awake when they were asleep a good deal of the time. This accentuated her feeling of being not entirely of this world, and for a while she'd struggled against it, forcing herself to stay awake when she craved sleep, lying sleepless in her bed because it was the appointed nighttime hour. But lately it had come to seem not a problem.

"I want a constellation on my bedroom ceiling," Brandon declared.

"Maybe we can find a poster or stickers," Amelia agreed.

"No, I mean a *real* constellation. Orion the Hunter." He made a sort of all-purpose gesture of aggression.

"A constellation is huge," she pointed out. Surely he knew that. "It wouldn't fit on all the ceilings of all the rooms of all the boys in the whole city."

"Okay, then a star." She could tell he was playing, but there was a real dreaminess in his expression that made her want, foolishly, to give him a star. A real star. "I want a star for my very own."

"Stars belong to everybody. They have their own places to be. When they fall to the earth they aren't stars anymore," Amelia told him, and immediately softened her tone. "You can't own a star."

He was openly unpersuaded, and he was also abruptly bored with TV, for which Amelia was glad. "Can I feed the horses?"

Amelia readily gave permission, and got herself up on her feet to accompany him to the pasture. His parents insisted he have supervision, a parental caution that Amelia recognized as more symbolic than functional, since she wouldn't be able to do much to protect him anyway. But she liked watching him, and she loved the horses, and it was good for her to have an excuse to walk that far. When she stood up her ears suddenly rang, her vision blackened, and her head swam, but she steadied herself on the unsteady arm of the rocker until the danger of fainting had receded, for now.

Brandon ran ahead down the hill and then circled back, solicitous of her without seeming to be. He stopped now and then to stuff his pockets with stuff—bugs, flowers, caterpillars, shards of shiny rock and metal—that wouldn't be the same when he put them on his shelf. A bit unsteady still, Amelia kept her gaze mostly on the ground and on her own feet, so Brandon was first to see the white horse in the pasture. "Oh, cool!" he cried. "You got a new one! And look! He likes me!" Indeed, the white horse had come right up to Brandon and was nuzzling his proffered hand. "Hi," he crooned. "Hi, there."

Setting aside her feeling of unwellness and her refreshed annoyance at being taken advantage of by the underhanded renter, Amelia stood back and gladly watched the boy and the horse. Such a lovely tableau they made that there was a sensation of etherealness about them, an out-of-this-world quality at the same time that they seemed utterly, thoroughly, *here* and *now* and of her life as well as their own.

The soft gray coverlet of clouds had come untucked in the west, and the setting sun made an edge there like yellow satin. Brandon's hair and skin shone, and he stood very still to receive the horse's greeting; Amelia almost couldn't bear his stillness, for she understood what it cost him and what he was longing for in return.

The horse's coat shimmered like mother-of-pearl. The animal's movements were so graceful that Amelia found herself thinking of them as poetic, musical. It was light-footed, sure-footed, and its neck arched finely, its mane and tail flowed. Amelia took a step and put her hand out to touch it, not wanting to displace Brandon but suddenly yearning to lay her palm on that smooth irides-cent neck right where the flesh curved inward under the jaw.

"It's a unicorn," Brandon whispered, just as Amelia,

too, saw the protrusion from the delicate forehead, above and between the huge limpid brown eyes.

Her heart sank, as much for Brandon as for the horse. Something was wrong with this creature. It had been injured. It had a parasite under its skin. It had cancer or some other terrible condition that would cause growths like that.

Now there was an ethical principle at stake far more important than honesty. Keeping animals was a responsibility not to be taken lightly. This poor thing needed medical attention, and, indignation at the renter flaming into outrage, Amelia thought she would just call her own vet to come tend to it and send the renter the bill.

"It's a unicorn, right?" His tone was obviously intended to have shed all awe, was almost taunting now. But he wasn't looking at her. He was fascinated by the horse, which was now making as if to eat out of his hand, never mind that he had nothing to feed it. Amelia all but felt the vellum-soft nose in the creases of her own palm, the warm breath so deceptively like her own and Brandon's from a creature utterly unlike them.

"No, something's wrong. Come here. baby. Let me see." She had enough time to note that the lump was hard and pointed before the horse tossed its head out of her reach, making its mane undulate with light fractured into rainbows more brilliant than she would have expected this close to dusk. It whinnied, peculiarly melodious and high-pitched, then pawed the ground in preparation for flight.

"No, no," Brandon admonished, as if he were training a dog, and put a restraining hand on the glimmering withers. "You stay right here."

The beast shivered his hand off and backed away, nostrils flaring, ears straight up and deeply cupped. It tossed its head again, and the knob below its forelock caught the fading light, sharpening and elongating.

"That's a good horse," Brandon breathed, gently, desperately. "You're not going anywhere."

The animal ducked its head in a gesture whose message was indecipherable—if, indeed, it had a communicative meaning and wasn't simply a muscle stretch or a quick survey of the ground for edibles. Amelia couldn't help but notice that the thing protruding from its forehead was long enough to score the earth, and that when it did so it bent.

"Look!" Brandon was thrilled. "It's bowing to me!"

But then the animal faded into the dusk. Amelia was a little shocked that it vanished so completely; she'd have thought its white coat would collect and reflect what little light remained.

"It was mine!" Brandon cried after it, outraged.

Amelia felt dizzy, found herself sitting and then lying on the ground. It didn't seem an unnatural position to her, and Brandon scarcely took notice. She shook her head against the moist twilit grass and dirt, but couldn't bring herself to enunciate anything.

Dimly she realized that she didn't know what to expect from him now, whether because she really didn't know him very well or because of the essential unpredictability of significant events. He might have sprung at her. He might have stalked away. Instead he sank beside her, the warmth of him seeping under her skin but not all the way into the reservoir where she was neither warm nor cold.

There was a silence that seemed long. Brandon ran his hand, then both hands very lightly over the tufted grass, barely disturbing it, not picking a blade. Amelia drifted with the motion of his hands, the motion of the grass. Brandon said finally, "I just want to keep things I love forever."

Amelia reached for his hand, not knowing whether she took it or not. They stayed there together until it was all the way dark.

Eventually she was able to get to her feet, with considerable help from Brandon. Vaguely it surprised her that she didn't mind relying on him for support and orientation, wasn't embarrassed by her own need or frightened by her own dependence. It seemed to her equally acceptable if they did or did not make it back to the house, equally likely that being with her in this way would prove of value to Brandon as that it would traumatize him.

"What's wrong? What's wrong?" he kept asking. Her arm around his sharp shoulders and her side pressed against his much thinner side, she could feel his whole body shaking.

It took several tries before Amelia could tell him clearly enough to be understood. "I think I've had a stroke," she meant to say, but only a single syllable actually emerged; she hoped it was a useful syllable.

Apparently it was, for he said, "What's that?"

"Something with my brain," was the best she could do, because, in fact, something untoward had happened in her brain, and this was her brain commenting on itself.

In the flat glare of the halogen light over the back door, she saw his wide eyes flicker up to the top of her head, as though he might see what was wrong with her brain. When his gaze slid back down, it didn't quite fix on her face. "Don't die," he said. She understood that she was supposed to assure him, but she had no desire to do so even if it had been possible.

They could not get up the steps. Interminably they tried it on foot, but Amelia, though it was clear to her that these were steps to be climbed, could not comprehend what was wanted of her or by whom. More than once Brandon exhorted, "Pick your foot up. Just pick your foot up." He even bent and grasped her ankle and lifted her leg and deposited her foot on the first step, but then they were stuck in that position, even more precarious.

Amelia, however, did not feel especially precarious; in fact, she felt quite safe. Knowing that the boy was increasingly anxious, she wished she could do something about that but knew she couldn't and was aware of the wish flowing out of her head.

They tried crawling. Brandon tried pushing and pulling her. By now he was panting, crying. Amelia was aware of being chilly, and of bumps and bruises and scratches where probably there had been none before, but the discomfort was minimal. "I can't," Brandon admitted. He sat down beside her, slightly above her on the step.

A warm breeze came over her like breath. Her pulse was like very distant hoofbeats, hesitant then quick. Something soft lay across the back of her neck, not moving away but becoming so immediately and thoroughly familiar that she wasn't aware of it anymore. "Call." This time she said as much as she thought, just the verb with no conception of an object for it or even, once she'd murmured it, of a subject.

Brandon was gone then. Maybe he'd gone into the

house to call. Amelia lay in her yard. Her house rose above her, solid and out of her reach and therefore not her house anymore. There came the sensation of warmth above her, then beside her, as the white horse settled down. Amelia wasn't surprised, though she hadn't been expecting it, either.

Sleek hollows. Pliable horn tracing the outline of her face and body as the creature bent its head to her, and the rainbow fringe of its mane. The aroma of horseflesh and flowers without a name. A nickering at the border of words.

The creature snorted and leaped to its feet. A noose lowered around its neck and Brandon crowed wildly from the top step where he stood with braced feet and held the other end of the rope in both hands, "Gotcha!"

The animal reared, hooves like stars and high clear voice. The rope snapped. Brandon gave a heartbroken little shout and flung himself off the steps. He managed a handful of mane, pulling the horse's head sharply around and the lithe body offstride, so that he was knocked down and a flashing hoof just missed his back. He wrapped his arms around a stamping, glancing leg and held on like a much younger child, whimpering.

Amelia knew horses. This one, though she conceded it was not precisely a horse, was spooked. Either she maneuvered around to the side of the frantic beast opposite the frantic boy, or the two of them together whirled; she was now pressed against—into—the glistening, quivering flank.

The animal shrieked and spun on her, wrenching itself free of Brandon, who shrieked, too. Amelia thought to flatten herself among the flying hooves and fists, but couldn't be sure that she had. In some way, though, she was between beast and boy, protecting one from the other, and then the unicorn broke into a seamless canter that carried it between the dark earth and the dark sky where it disappeared.

"You let it go!"

Amelia intended to tell him, "Yes." She had the impression that he held her accountable not only for this abdication but also for the escape of the bird and the inaccessibility of stars. And there was something to that. She wasn't to blame for the impermanence of things, of course, but she had assumed the role of messenger, and she concurred with Brandon's instinct that a certain moral responsibility accrued.

So she made an enormous effort and gathered him to her. He came easily. She couldn't stay with him much longer. "Don't go," Brandon whispered.

She was floating and flashing like stars. She meant to tell him, "Good-bye" and "I love you," but there was no way for either of them to know if that was what she said.

TAD WILLIAMS

THREE DUETS FOR VIRGIN AND NOSEHORN

Peter: **Tad Williams**, one of the best and best-known fantasists currently at work, writes that he "grew up in Palo Alto, a small but fiercely self-congratulatory (with some reason) town in Northern California . . ." (*Privileged editorial digression*: No, it *hasn't* any bloody reason—I've lived there myself.) He now lives in London, ". . . where they seem to have grown bored by the insane panoply of weather types with which we Americans indulge ourselves and have sensibly limited themselves to two: 'gray and wet,' or 'gray and very, very wet.'" After giving up on an early dream of being an archaeologist, having discovered that it involved work, he sensibly decided to settle for being hugely famous, "skip(ping) over all the irritating intermediary bits . . ." He is also half-owner of a multimedia company called Telemorphix, Inc. "We produce an interactive television show called *Twenty-first Century Vaudeville.* It's too weird to explain. . . ."

Janet: Here is another writer I have known forever, one of whom I can truly say, "I knew him when. . . ." Mostly we'd meet at BayCon, a medium-sized SF convention which I used to attend for pretty much the express purpose of playing catch-up with old friends. Tad was always there, hanging around, talking about writing, and being hopelessly intelligent and—dare I say it—*nice*. Then one year he announced that he was writing a novel. He did. And the rest, as they say, is (*New York Times* bestselling) history.

As for this story, it's an absolute delight—a little scary, a little history, and a lot Tad.

Three Duets for Virgin
and Nosehorn

FATHER JOAO CONTEMPLATES THE BOX, A WOODEN
crate taller than the priest himself and as long as two men
lying down, lashed with ropes as if to keep its occupant
prisoner. Something is hidden inside, something dead yet
extraordinary. It is a Wonder, or so he has been told, but it
is meant for another and much greater man. Joao must
care for it, but he is not allowed to see it. Like Something
Else he could name.

Father Joao is weary and sick and full of heretical
thoughts.

He listens to the rain drumming on the deck above his
head. The ship pitches forward, descending into a trough
between waves, and the ropes that hold the great box in
place creak. After a week he is quite accustomed to the
ship's drunken wallowing, and his stomach no longer
crawls into his throat at every shudder, but for all of his
traveling, he will never feel happy on the sea.

The ship lurches again and he steadies himself
against the crate. Something pricks him. He sucks air
between his teeth and lifts his hand so he can examine it

in the faint candlelight. A thin wooden splinter has lodged in his wrist, a faint dark line running shallowly beneath the skin. A bead of blood trembles like mercury where it has entered. Joao tugs out the splinter and wipes the blood with his sleeve. Pressing to staunch the flow, he stares at the squat, shadowed box and wonders why his God has deserted him.

∞   ∞   ∞

"You are a pretty one, Marje. Why aren't you married?"

The girl blushes, but at the same time she is secretly irritated. Her masters, the Planckfelts, work her so hard that when does she find even a chance to wash her face, let alone look for a husband? Still, it is nice to be noticed, especially by such a distinguished man as the Artist.

He is famous, this man, and though from Marje's perspective he is very old—close to fifty, surely—he is handsome, long of face and merry-eyed, and still with all his curly hair. He also has extraordinarily large and capable-looking hands. Marje cannot help but stare at his hands, knowing that they have made pictures that hang on the walls of the greatest buildings in Christendom, that they have clasped the hands of other great men—the Artist is an intimate of archbishops and kings, and even the Holy Roman Emperor himself. And yet he is not proud or snobbish: when she serves him his beer, he smiles sweetly as he thanks her and squeezes her own small hand when he takes the tankard.

"Have you no special friend, then? Surely the young men have noticed a blossom as sweet as you?"

How can she explain? Marje is a healthy, strong girl,

quick with a smile and as graceful as a busy servant can afford to be. She has straw-golden hair. (She hides it under her cap, but during the heat and bustle of a long day it begins to work its way free and to dangle in moist curls down the back of her neck.) If her small nose turns up at the end a little more than would be appropriate in a Florentine or Venetian beauty, well, this is not Italy after all, and she is a serving-wench, not a prospect for marriage into a noble family. Marje is quite as beautiful as she needs to be, and yes, as she hurries through the market on her mistress's errands, she has many admirers.

But she has little time for them. She is a careful girl, and her standards are unfortunately high. The men who would happily marry her have less poetry in their souls than mud on their clogs, and the wealthy and learned ones to whom her master Jobst Planckfelt plays host are not looking for a bride among the linens and crockery, have no honorable interest in a girl with no money and a drunkard father.

"I am too busy, Sir," she says. "My lady keeps me very occupied caring for our household and guests. It is a difficult task, running a large house. I am sure your wife would agree with me."

The Artist's face darkens a little. Marje is sad to see the smile fade, but not unhappy to have made the point. These flirtatious men! Between the dullards and the rakes, it is hard for an honest girl to make her way. In any case, it never hurts to remind a married man that he is married, especially when his wife is staying in the same house. At the least, it may keep the flirting and pinching to a minimum, and thus save a girl like Marje from unfairly gaining the hatred of a jealous woman.

The Artist's wife, from what Marje has seen, might prove just such a woman. She is somewhat stern-mouthed, and does not dine with her husband, but instead demands to have her meals brought up to the room where she eats with only her maid for company. Each time Marje has served her, the Artist's wife has watched her with a disapproving eye, as if the mere existence of pretty girls affronted Godly womanhood. She has also been unstinting in her criticism of what she sees as Marje's carelessness. The Artist's wife makes remarks about the Planckfelts, suggesting that she is not entirely satisfied with their hospitality, and even complains about Antwerp itself, making unfavorable comparisons between its weather and available diversions and those of Nuremberg, where she and the Artist keep their home.

Marje can guess why a cheerful man like this should prefer not to think of his wife when it is not absolutely necessary.

"Well," the Artist says at last, "I am certain you work very hard, but you must give some thought to the other wonders of our Lord's creation. Virtue is of course its own reward—but only to a point, after which it becomes Pride, and is as likely to be punished as rewarded. Shall I tell you a story?"

His smile has returned, and it is really a rather marvelous thing, Marje thinks. He looks twenty years younger and rather unfairly handsome.

"I have much to do, Lord. My lady wishes me to clear away the supper things and help Cook with the washing."

"Ah. Well, I would not interfere with your duties. When do you finish?"

"Finish?" She looks at his eyes and sees merriment

there, and something else, something subtly, indefinably sad, which causes her to swallow her sharp reply. "About an hour after sunset."

"Good. Come to me then, and I will tell you a story about a girl something like you. And I will show you a marvel—something you have never seen before." He leans back in his chair. "Your master has been kind enough to lend me the spare room down here for my work—during the day, it gets the northern light, such as it has been of late. That is where I will be."

Marje hesitates. It is not respectable to meet him, surely. On the other hand, he is a famous and much-admired man. When her day's work is done, why should she (who, wife-like, has served him food and washed his charcoal-smudged shirts) not have a glimpse of the works which have gained him the patronage of great men all over Europe?

"I will . . . I may be too busy, Sir. But I thank you."

He grins, this time with all the innocent friendliness of a young boy. "You need not fear me, Marje. But do as you wish. If you can spare a moment, you know where to find me."

She stands in front of the door for some time, screwing up her courage. When she knocks, there is no answer for long moments. At last the door opens, revealing the darkened silhouette of the Artist. "Marje. You honor me. Come in."

She passes through the door then stops, dumbfounded. The ground-floor room that she has dusted and cleaned so many times has changed out of all recognition, and she finds her fingers straying toward the cross at her throat, as though she were again a child in a dark house listening to her father's drunken rants about the Devil. The many candles and the single brazier of coals cast long shadows, and from every shadow faces peer. Some are exalted as though with inner joy, others frown or snarl, frozen in fear and despair and even hatred. She sees angels and devils and bearded men in antique costume. Marje feels that she has stepped into some kind of church, but the congregation has been drawn from every corner of the world's history.

The Artist gestures at the pictures. "I am afraid I have been rather caught up. Do not worry—I will not make more work for you. By the time I leave here, these will all be neatly packed away again."

Marje is not thinking of cleaning. She is amazed by the gallery of faces. If these are his drawings, the Artist is truly a man gifted by God. She cannot imagine even thinking of such things, let alone rendering them with such masterful skill, making each one perfect in every small detail. She pauses, still full of an almost religious awe, but caught by something familiar amid the gallery of monsters and saints.

"That is Grip! That is Master Planckfelt's dog!" She laughs in delight. It is Grip, without a doubt, captured in every bristle; she does not need to see the familiar collar with its heavy iron ring, but that is there, too.

The Artist nods. "I cannot go long without drawing, I fear, and each one of God's creatures offers something in the way of challenge. From the most familiar to the strangest." He is staring at her. Marje looks up from the picture of the dog to catch him at it, but there is something unusual in his inspection, something deeper than the admiring glances she usually encounters from men of the Artist's age, and it is she who blushes.

"Have I something on my face?" she asks, trying to make a joke of it.

"No, no." He reaches out for a candle. As he examines her he moves the light around her head in slow circles, so that for a moment she feels quite dizzy. "Will you sit for me?"

She looks around, but every stool and chair is covered by sheaves of drawings. "Where?"

The Artist laughs and gently wraps a large hand around her arm. Marje feels her skin turn to gooseflesh. "I mean let me draw you. Your face is lovely, and I have a commission for a Saint Barbara that I should finish before leaving the Low Countries."

She had thought the hand a precursor to other, less genteel intimacies (and she is not quite certain how she feels about that prospect) but instead he is steering her to the door. She passes a line drawing of the Garden of Eden which is like a window into another world, into an innocence Marje cannot afford. "I . . . you will draw me with my clothes on?"

Again that smile. Is it sad? "It is a bust—a head and shoulders. You may wear what you choose, so long as the line of your graceful neck is not obscured."

"I thought you were going to tell me a story."

"I shall, I promise. And show you a great marvel—I have not forgotten. But I will save them until you come back to sit for me. Perhaps we could begin tomorrow morning?"

"Oh, but my lady will . . ."

"I will speak to her. Fear not, pretty Marje. I can be most persuasive."

The door shuts behind her. After a moment, she realizes that the corridor is cold, and she is shivering.

"Here. Now turn this way. I will soon give you something to look at."

Marje sits, her head at a slightly uncomfortable angle. She is astonished to discover herself with the morning off. Her mistress had not seemed happy about it, but clearly the Artist was not exaggerating his powers of persuasion. "Can I blink my eyes, Sir?"

"As often as you need to. Later I will let you move a little from time to time so you do not get too sore. Once I have made my first sketch, it will be easy to set your pose again." Satisfied, he takes his hand away from her chin— Marje is surprised to discover how hard and rough his fingers are; can drawing alone cause it?—and straightens. He goes to one of his folios and pulls out another picture, which he props up on a chair before her. At first, blocked by his body, she cannot see it. After he has arranged it to his satisfaction, the Artist steps away.

"Great God!" she says, then immediately regrets her blasphemy. The image before her looks something like a pig, but covered in intricate armor and with a great spike growing upwards from its muzzle. "What is it? A demon?"

"No demon, but one of God's living creatures. It is called 'Rhinocerus,' which is Latin for 'nosehorn.' He is huge, this fellow—bigger than a bull, I am told."

"You have not seen one? But did you not . . . ?"

"I drew the picture, yes. But it was made from another artist's drawing—and the creature he drew was not even alive, but stuffed with straw and standing in the Pope's garden of wonders. No one in Europe, I think, has ever seen this monster alive, although some have said he is the model for the fabled unicorn. Our Rhinocerus is a very rare creature, you see, and lives only at the farthest ends of the world. This one came from a land called Cambodia, somewhere near Cathay."

"I should be terrified to meet him." Marje finds she is shivering again. The Artist is standing behind her, his fingers delicately touching the nape of her neck as he pulls up her hair and knots it atop her head. "There. Now I can see the line cleanly. Yes, you might indeed be afraid if you met this fellow, young Marje. But you might be glad of it all the same. I promised you a tale, did I not?"

"About a girl, you said. Like me."

"Ah, yes. About a fair maiden. And a monster."

"A monster? Is that . . . that Nosehorn in this tale?"

She is still looking at the picture, intrigued by the complexity of the beast's scales, but even more by the almost mournful expression in its small eyes. By now she knows the Artist's voice well enough to hear him smiling as he speaks.

"The Nosehorn is indeed part of this tale. But you should never decide too soon which is the monster. Some of God's fairest creations bear foul seemings. And vice versa, of course." She hears him rustling his paper, then the near-silent scraping of his pencil. "Yes, there is both Maiden and Monster in this tale . . ."

∞   ∞   ∞

Her name is Red Flower—in full it is Delicate-Red-Flower-the-Color-of-Blood, but since her childhood only the priests who read the lists of blessings have used that name. Her father Jayavarman is a king, but not *the* king: the Universal Monarch, as all know, has been promised for generations but is still awaited. In the interim, her father has been content to eat well, enjoy his hunting and his elephants, and intercede daily with the *nak ta*—the ancestors—on his people's behalf, all in the comfortable belief that the Universal Monarch will probably not arrive during his lifetime.

In fact, it is his own lack of ambition that has made Red Flower's father a powerful man. Jayavarman knows that although he has no thought of declaring himself the *devaraja,* or god-king, others are not so modest. As the power of one of the other kings—for the land has many—rises, Jayavarman lends his own prestige (and, in a pinch, his war elephants) to one of the upstart's stronger rivals. When the proud one has been brought low, Red Flower's father withdraws his support from the victor, lest that one, too, should begin to harbor dreams of universal kingship. Jayavarman then returns to his round of feasting and hunting, and waits to see which other tall bamboo may next seek to steal the sun from its neighbors. By this practice his kingdom of Angkor, which nestles south of the Kulen hills, has maintained its independence, and even an eminence which outstrips many of its more aggressive rivals.

But Red Flower cares little about her plump, patient father's machinations. She is not yet fourteen, and by tradition isolated from the true workings of power. As a virgin and Jayavarman's youngest daughter, her purpose (as her father and his counsellors see it) is to remain a pure and sealed repository for the royal blood. As her sisters were in their turn, Red Flower will be a gift to some young man Jayavarman favors, or whose own blood— and the family it represents—offers a connection which favors his careful strategies.

Red Flower, though, does not feel like a vessel. She is a young woman (just), and this night she feels herself as wild and unsettled as one of her father's hawks newly unhooded.

In truth, her sire's intricate and continuous strategies are somewhat to blame for her unrest. There are strangers outside the palace tonight, a ragtag army camped around the walls. They are fewer than Jayavarman's own troop, badly armored, carrying no weapons more advanced than scythes and daggers, and they own no elephants at all, but there is something in their eyes which make even the king's most hardened veterans uneasy. The sentries along the wall do not allow their spears to dip, and they watch the strangers' campfires carefully, as though looking into sacred flames for some sign from the gods.

The leader of this tattered band is a young man named Kaundinya who has proclaimed himself king of a small region beyond the hills, and who has come to Red Flower's father hoping for support in a dispute with another chieftain. Red Flower understands little of what is under discussion, since she is not permitted to listen to the men's conversation, but she has seen her father's eyes during the three days of the visitors' stay, and knows that he is troubled. No one thinks he will lend his aid (neither of the two quarreling parties is powerful enough to cause Jayavarman to support the other). But nevertheless, others besides Red Flower can see that something is causing the king unrest.

Red Flower is unsettled for quite different reasons. As excited as any of her slaves by gossip and novelty, she has twice slipped the clutches of her aged nurse to steal a look at the visitors. The first time, she turned up her nose at the peasant garb the strangers wear, as affronted by their raggedness as her maids had been. The second time, she saw Kaundinya himself.

He is barely twenty years old, this bandit chief, but as both Red Flower and her father have recognized (to different effect, however) there is something in his eyes, something cold and hard and knowing, that belies his age. He carries himself like a warrior, but more importantly, he carries himself like a true king, the flash of his eyes telling all who watch that if they have not yet had cause to bow down before him, they soon will. And he is handsome, too. On a man slightly less stern, his fine features and flowing black hair would be almost womanishly beautiful.

And while she peered out at him from behind a curtain, Kaundinya turned and saw Red Flower, and this is what she cannot forget. The heat of his gaze was like Siva's lightning leaping between Mount Mo-Tam and the sky. For a moment, she felt sure that his eyes, like a demon's, had caught at her soul and would draw it from her body. Then her old nurse caught her and yanked her away, swatting at her ineffectually with swollen-jointed hands. All the way back to the women's wing the nurse shrilly criticized her wickedness and immodesty, but Red Flower, thinking of Kaundinya's stern mouth and impatient eyes, did not hear her.

And now the evening has fallen and the palace is quiet. The old woman is curled on a mat beside the bed, wheezing in her sleep and wrinkling her nose at some dream-effrontery. A warm wind rattles the bamboo and carries the smell of cardamom leaves through the palace like music. The monsoon season has ended, the moon and the jungle flowers alike are blooming, all the night is alive, alive. The king's youngest daughter practically trembles with sweet discontent.

She pads quietly past her snoring nurse and out into the corridor. It is only a few steps to the door that leads to the vast palace gardens. Red Flower wishes to feel the moon on her skin and the wind in her hair. As she makes her way down into the darkened garden, she does not see the shadow-form that follows her, and does not hear it either, for it moves as silently as death.

∞ ∞ ∞

"And there I must stop." The Artist stands and stretches his back.

"But . . . but what happened? Was that the horned monster that followed her?"

"I have not finished, I have merely halted for the day. Your mistress is expecting you to go back to work, Marje. I will continue the story when you return to me tomorrow."

She hesitates, unwilling to let go of the morning's novelty, of her happiness at being admired and spoken to as an equal. "May I see what you have drawn?"

"No." His voice is perhaps harsher than he had wished. When he speaks again it is in softer tones. "I will show you when I am finished, not before. Go along, you.

Let an old man rest his fingers and his tongue." He does not look old. The gray morning light streams through the window behind him, gleaming at the edges of his curly hair. He seems very tall.

Marje curtseys and leaves him, pulling the door closed behind her as quietly as she can. All day, as she sweeps out the house's dusty corners and hauls water from the well, she will think of the smell of spice trees and of a young man with cold, confident eyes.

∞   ∞   ∞

Even on deck, wrapped in a heavy hooded cloak against the unseasonal squall, Father Joao is painfully aware of the dark silent box in the hold. A present from King John to the newly elected Pope, it would be a valuable cargo simply as a significator of the deep, almost familial relationship between the Portugese throne and the Holy See. But as a reminder of the wealth that Portugal can bring back to Mother Church from the New World and elsewhere (and as such to prompt him toward favoring Portugal's expanding interests) its worth is incalculable. In Anno Domini 1492, all of the world seems in reach of Christendom's ships, and it is a world whose spoils the Pope will divide. The bishop who is the king's ambassador (and Father Joao's superior), who will present the pontiff with this splendid gift, is delighted with the honor bestowed upon him.

Thus, Father Joao is a soldier in a good cause, and with no greater responsibility than to make sure the Wonder arrives in good condition. Why then is he so unhappy?

It was the months spent with his family, he knows,

after being so long abroad. Mother Church offers balm against the fear of age and death; seeing his parents so changed since he had last visited them, so feeble, was merely painful and did not remotely trouble his faith. But the spectacle of his brother Ruy as happy father, his laughing, tumbling brood about him, was for some reason more difficult to stomach. Father Joao has disputed with himself about this. His younger brother has children, and someday will have grandchildren to be the warmth of his old age, but Joao has dedicated his own life and chastity to the service of the Lord Jesus Christ, the greatest and most sacred of callings. Surely the brotherhood of his fellow priests is family enough?

But most insidious of all the things which cause him doubt, something which still troubles him after a week at sea, despite all his prayers and sleepless nights searching for God's peace, even despite the lashes of his own self-hatred, is the beauty of his brother's wife, Maria.

The mere witnessing of such a creature troubled chastity, but to live in her company for weeks was an almost impossible trial. Maria was dark-eyed and slender of waist despite the roundness of her limbs. She had thick black curly hair which (mocking all pins and ribbons) constantly worked itself free to hang luxuriously down her back and sway as she walked, hiding and accentuating at the same moment, like the veils of Salome.

Joao is no stranger to temptation. In his travels he has seen nearly every sort of woman God has made, young and old, dark-skinned and light. But all of them, even the greatest beauties, have been merely shadows against the light of his belief. Joao has always reminded himself that he observed only the outer garments of life, that it was the souls within that mattered. Seeing after those souls is his sacred task, and his virginity has been a kind of armor, warding off the demands of the flesh. He has always managed to comfort himself with this thought.

But living in the same house with Ruy and his young wife was different. To see Maria's slim fingers toying with his brother's beard, stroking that face so much like his own, or to watch her clutch one of their children against her sloping hip, forced Joao to wonder what possible value there could be in chastity.

At first her earthiness repelled him, and he welcomed that repulsion. A glimpse of her bare feet or the cleavage of her full breasts, and his own corrupted urge to stare at such things, made him rage inwardly. She was a woman, the repository of sin, the Devil's tool. She and each of her kind were at best happy destroyers of a man's innocence, at worst deadly traps that yawned, waiting to draw God's elect down into darkness.

But Joao lived with Ruy and Maria for too long, and began to lose his comprehension of evil. For his brother's wife was not a wanton, not a temptress or whore. She was a wife and mother, an honorable, pious woman raising her children in the faith, good to her husband, kind to his aging parents. If she found pleasure in the flesh God had given her, if she enjoyed her man's arms around her, or the sun on her ankles as she prepared her family's dinner in the tiny courtyard, how was that a sin?

With this question, Joao's armor had begun to come apart. If enjoyment of the body were not sinful, then how could denial of the body somehow be blessed? Could it be so much worse in God's eyes, his brother Ruy's life? If there were no sin in having a beautiful and loving wife to share your bed, in having children and a hearth, then why had Joao himself renounced these things? And if God made mankind fruitful, then commanded his most faithful servants not to partake of that fruitfulness, and in fact to despise it as a hindrance to holiness, then what kind of wise and loving God was He?

Father Joao has not slept well since leaving Lisbon, the ceaseless movement of the ocean mirroring his own unquiet soul. Everything seems in doubt here, everything seems suspended, the sea a place neither of God or the Devil, but forever between the two. Even the sailors, who with their dangerous lives might seem most in need of God's protection, mistrust priests.

In the night, in his tiny cabin, Joao can hear the ropes that bind the crate stretching and squeaking, as though something inside it stirs restlessly.

His superior, the bishop, has been no help, and Joao's few attempts to seek the man's counsel have yielded only incomprehending homilies. Unlike Father Joao, he is long past the age when the fleshly sins are the most tempting. If his soul is in danger, Joao thinks with some irritation, it is from Pride: the bishop is puffed like a sleeping owl with the honor of his position—liaison between king and pope, bringer of a mighty gift, securer of the Church's blessing on Portugal's conquests across the heathen world.

If the bishop is the ambassador, Father Joao wonders, then what is he? An insomniac priest. A celibate tortured by his own flesh. A man who will accompany a great gift, but only as far as Italy's shores before he turns to go home again. Now the rain is thumping on the deck overhead, and he can no longer hear noises in the hold. His head hurts, he is cold beneath his thin blanket, and he is tired of thinking.

He is a only a porter bearing a box of dead Wonder, Joao decides with a kind of cold satisfaction—a Wonder of which he himself is not even to be vouchsafed a glimpse.

∞   ∞   ∞

Marje has been looking at the Nosehorn so long that even when the Artist commands her to close her eyes, she sees it still, printed against the darkness of her eyelids. She knows she will dream of it for months, the powerful body, the tiny, almost-hidden eyes, the thrust of horn lifting from its snout.

"You said you would tell me more about the girl. The flower girl."

"So I shall. Let me only light another candle. There is less light today. I am like one of those savage peoples who worship the sky, always turning in search of the sun."

"Will it be finished soon?"

"Tale or picture?"

"Both." She needs to know. Yesterday and today have been a magical time, but she remembers magic from other stories, and knows it does not last. She is sad her time at the center of the world is passing, but underneath everything she is a realistic girl. If it is to end today, she can make her peace, but she needs to know.

"I do not think I will finish either this morning, unless I keep you long enough to make your mistress forget I am a guest and lose her temper. So we will have more work tomorrow. Now be quiet, Marje. I am drawing your mouth."

∞   ∞   ∞

As she steps into the circle of moss-covered stones at the garden's center, something moves in the darkness beneath the trees. Red Flower turns her face away from the moon.

"Who is there?" Her voice is a low whisper. She is the king's daughter, but tonight she feels like a trespasser, even within her own gardens.

There is a tiny rumble of thunder in the distance. The monsoon is ended, but the skies are still unsettled. He steps out of the trees, naked to the waist, moonlight gleaming on his muscle-knotted arms. "I am. And who is there? Ah. It's the old dragon's daughter."

She feels her breath catch in her throat. She is alone, in the dark. There is danger here. But there is also something in Kaundinya's gaze that keeps her fixed to the spot as he approaches. "You should not be here," she says at last.

"What is your name? You came to spy on me the other day, didn't you?"

"I am . . ." She still finds it hard to speak. "I am Red Flower. My father will kill you if you do not go away."

"Perhaps. Perhaps not. Your father is afraid of me."

Her strange lethargy is at last dispelled by anger. "That is a lie! He is afraid of no one! He is a great king, not a bandit like you with your ragged men!"

Kaundinya laughs, genuinely amused, and Red Flower is suddenly unsure again. "Your father is a king, little girl, but he will never be Ultimate Monarch, never the *devaraja*. I will be, though, and he knows it. He is no fool. He sees what is inside me."

"You are mad." She takes a few steps back. "My father will destroy you."

"He would have done it when he first met me if he dared. But I have come to him in peace and am a guest in his house and he cannot touch me. Still, he will not give me his support. He thinks to send me away with empty hands while he considers how he might ruin me before my power grows too great."

The stranger abruptly strides forward and catches her arm, pulling her close until she can smell the betel nut on his breath. His eyes, mirroring the moon, seem very bright. "But perhaps I will not go away with empty hands after all. It seems the gods have brought you to me, alone and unguarded. I have learned to trust the gods—it is they who have promised me that I shall be king over all of Kambuja-desa."

Red Flower struggles, but he is very strong and she is only a slender young girl. Before she can call for her father's soldiers, he covers her mouth with his own and pinions her with his strong arms. His deep, sharp smell surrounds her and she feels herself weakening. The moon seems to disappear, as though it has fallen into shadow. It is a little like drowning, this surrender. Kaundinya frees one hand to hold her face, then slides that hand down her neck, sending shivers through her like ripples across a pond. Then his hand moves again, and, as his other hand gathers up her sari, it pushes roughly between her legs. Red Flower gasps and kicks, smashing her heel down on his bare foot.

Laughing and cursing at the same time, he loosens his grip. She pulls free and runs across the garden, but she has gone only a few steps before he leaps into pursuit.

She should scream, but for some reason she cannot. The blind fear of the hunted is upon her, and all she can do is run like a deer, run like a rabbit, hunting for a dark hole and escape. He has done something to her with his touch and his cold eyes. A spell has enwrapped her.

She finds a gate in the encircling garden wall. Beyond is the temple, and on a hill above it the great dark shadow of the Sivalingam, the holy pillar reaching toward heaven. Past that is only jungle on one side, on the other open country and the watchfires of Kaundinya's army. Red Flower races toward the hill sacred to Siva, Lord of Lightnings.

The pillar is a finger pointing toward the moon. Thunder growls quietly in the distance. She stumbles and falls to her knees, then begins crawling uphill, silently weeping. There is a hissing in the grass behind her, then a hand curls in her hair and yanks her back. She tumbles and lies at Kaundinya's feet, staring up. His eyes are wild, his mouth twisted with fury, but his voice, when it comes, is terrifyingly calm.

"You are the first of your father's possessions that I will take and use."

∞   ∞   ∞

"But you cannot stop there! That is terrible! What happened to the girl?"

The Artist is putting away his drawing materials, but without his usual care. He seems almost angry. Marje is afraid she has offended him in some way.

"I will finish the tale tomorrow. There is only a little more work needed on the drawing, but I am tired now."

She gets up, tugging the sleeves of her dress back over her shoulders. He opens the door and stands beside it, as though impatient for her to leave.

"I will not sleep tonight for worrying about the flower girl," she says, trying to make him smile. He closes his eyes for a moment, as though he too is thinking about Red Flower. "I will miss you, Marje," he says when she is outside. Then he shuts the door.

∞   ∞   ∞

The ship is storm-tossed, bobbing on the water like a wooden cup. In his cabin, Joao glares into the darkness. Somewhere below, ropes creak like the damned distantly at play.

The thought of the box and its forbidden contents torments him. Coward, doubter, near-eunuch, false priest—with these names he also tortures himself. In the blackness before his eyes he sees visions of Maria, smiling, clothes undone, warm and rounded and hateful. Would she touch him with the heedless fondness with which she rubs his brother's back, kisses Ruy's neck and ear? Could she understand that at this awful moment Joao would give his immortal soul for just such animal comfort? What would she think of him? What would any of those whose souls are in his care think of him?

He drags himself from the bed and stands on trembling legs, swaying as the ship sways. Far above, thunder fills the sky like the voices of God and Satan contesting. Joao pulls his cassock over his undershirt and fumbles for his flints. When the candle springs alight, the walls and roof of his small sanctuary press closer than he had remembered, threatening to squeeze him breathless.

Father Joao lurches toward the cargo hold; his head is full of voices. As he climbs down a slippery ladder, he loses his footing and nearly falls. He waves his free arm for balance and the candle goes out. For a moment he struggles just to maintain his grip, wavering in empty darkness with unknown depths beneath him. At last he rights himself, but now he is without light. Somewhere above, the storm proclaims its power, mocking human enterprise. A part of him wonders what he is doing up, what he is doing in this of all places. Surely, that quiet voice says, he should at least go back to light his candle again. But that gentle voice is only one of many. Joao reaches down with his foot, finds the next rung, and continues his descent.

Even in utter blackness he knows his way. Every day of the voyage he has passed back and forth through this great empty space, like exiled Jonah. His hands encounter familiar things, his ears are full of the quiet complaining of the fettered crate. He knows his way.

He feels its presence even before his fingers touch it, and stops, blind and half-crazed. For a moment he is tempted to go down on one knee, but God can see even in darkness, and some last vestige of devout fear holds him back. Instead he lays his ear against the rough wood and listens, as a father might listen to the child growing in his wife's belly. Something is inside. It is still and dead, but somehow in Father Joao's mind it is full of terrible life.

He pulls at the box, desperate to open it, knowing even without sight that he is bloodying his fingers, but it is too well-constructed. He falls back at last, sobbing. The crate mocks him with its impenetrability. He lowers himself to the floor of the hold and crawls, searching for something that will serve where flesh has failed. Each time he strikes his head on an unseen impediment the muffled thunder seems to grow louder, as though something huge and secret is laughing at him.

At last he finds an iron rod, then feels his way back to the waiting box. He finds a crack beneath the lid and pushes the bar in, then throws his weight on it, pulling downward. It gives, but only slightly. Mouthing a prayer whose words even he does not know, Joao heaves at the bar again, struggling until more tears come to his eyes. Then, with a screeching of nails ripped from their holes, the lid lifts away and Joao falls to the floor.

The ship's hold suddenly fills with an odor he has never smelled, a strong scent of dry musk and mysterious spices. He staggers upright and leans over the box, drinking in the exhalation of pure Wonder. Slowly, half-reverent and half-terrified, he lowers his hands into the box.

A cloud of dense-packed straw is already rising from its confinement, crackling beneath his fingers, which feel acute as eyes. What waits for him? Punishment for his doubts? Or a shrouded Nothing, a final blow to shatter all faith?

For a moment he does not understand what he is feeling. It is so smooth and cold that for several heartbeats he is not certain he is touching anything at all. Then, as his hands slide down its gradually widening length, he knows it for what it is. A horn.

Swifter and swifter his fingers move, digging through the straw, following the horn's curve down to the wide rough brow, the glass-hard eyes, the ears. The Wonder inside the box has but a single horn. The thing beneath Joao's fingers is dead, but there is no doubt that it once lived. It is real. Real! Father Joao hears a noise in the empty hold, and realizes that he himself is making it. He is laughing.

God does not need to smite doubters, not when He can instead show them their folly with a loving jest. The Lord has proved to faithless Joao that divine love is no mere myth, and that He does not merely honor chastity, He defends it. All through this long nightmare voyage, Joao has been the unwitting guardian of Virtue's greatest protector.

Down on his knees now in the blind darkness, but with his head full of light, the priest gives thanks over and over.

∞ ∞ ∞

Kaundinya stands above her in the moon-thrown shadow of the pillar. He holds the delicate fabric of her sari in his hands. Already it has begun to part between his strong fingers.

Red Flower cannot awaken from this dream. The warm night is shelter no longer. Even the faint rumble of thunder has vanished, as though the gods themselves have turned their backs on her. She closes her eyes as one of Kaundinya's hands cups her face. As his mouth descends on hers, he lowers his knee between her legs, spreading her. For a long moment, nothing happens. She hears the bandit youth take a long and surprisingly unsteady breath.

Red Flower opens her eyes. The pillar, the nearby temple, all seem oddly flat, as though they have been painted on cloth. At the base of the hill, only a few paces from where she sits tumbled on the grass, a huge pale form has appeared. Kaundinya's eyes are opened wide in superstitious dread. He lets go of Red Flower's sari and lifts himself from her.

"Lord Siva," he says, and throws himself prostrate before the vast white beast. The rough skin of its back seems to give off as much light as the moon itself, and it turns its wide head to regard him, horn lowered like a spear, like the threat of lightning. Kaundinya speaks into the dirt. "Lord Siva, I am your slave."

Red Flower stares at the beast, then at her attacker, who is caught up in something like a slow fit, his muscles rippling and trembling, his face contorted. The nosehorn snorts once, then turns and lumbers away toward the distant trees, strangely silent. Red Flower cannot move. She cannot even shiver. The world has grown tracklessly large, and she is but a small thing.

At last Kaundinya stands. His fine features are childish with shock, as though something large has picked him up by the neck and shaken him.

"The Lord of all the Gods has spoken to me," he whispers. He does not look at Red Flower, but at the place where the beast has vanished into the jungle. "I am not to dishonor you, but to marry you. I will be the *devaraja*, and you will be my queen. This place, Angkor, will be the heart of my kingdom. Siva has told me this."

He extends a hand. Red Flower stares at it. He is offering to help her up. She struggles to her feet without assistance, holding the torn part of her gown together. Suddenly she is cold.

"You know your father will give you to me," he calls

after her as she stumbles back toward the palace. "He recognizes what I am, what I will be. It is the only solution. He will see that."

She does not want to hear him, does not want to think about what he is saying. But she does, of course. She is not sure what has happened tonight, but she knows that he is speaking the truth.

∞   ∞   ∞

Marje is silent for a long time after the Artist has finished. The grayness of the day outside the north-facing window is suddenly dreary.

"And is that it? She had to marry him?"

The Artist is concentrating deeply, squinting at the drawing board. He does not reply immediately. "At least it was an honorable marriage," he says at last. "That is something better than rape, is it not?"

"But what happened to her afterward?"

"I am not entirely sure. It is only a story, after all. But I imagine she bore the bandit king many sons, so that when he died his line lived on. The man who told me the tale said that there were kings in that place for seven hundred years. The rhinocerus you see in that drawing was the last of a long line of sacred beasts, a symbol to the royal family. But the kings of Cambodia have left Angkor now, so perhaps it no longer means anything to them. In any case, they gave it to the king of Portugal, and Portugal gave its stuffed body to the Pope after it died." The Artist shakes his head. "I am sorry I could not see it when it breathed and walked God's earth."

Marje stares at the picture of the Nosehorn, wondering at its strange journey. What would it think, this jungle titan whose ancestor was a heathen god, to find itself propped on a chair in Antwerp? The Artist stirs. "You may move now, Marje. I am finished."

She thinks she hears something of her own unhappiness in his voice. What does it mean? She gets up slowly, untwisting sore muscles, and walks to his side. She must lean against him to see the drawing properly, and feels his small, swift movement, almost a twitch, as she presses against his arm.

"Oh. It's . . . it's beautiful."

"As you are beautiful," he says softly. The picture is Marje, but also not Marje. The girl before her has her eyes closed and wears a look of battered innocence. The long line of her neck is lovely but fragile.

"Saint Barbara was taken onto a mountain by her father and killed," the Artist says, gently tracing the neck with his finger. "Perhaps he was jealous of the love she had found in Jesus. She is the martyr who protects us from sudden death, and from lightning."

"Your gift is from God, Master Dürer." Marje is more than a little overwhelmed. "So are we finished now?"

She is still leaning against his arm, staring at the picture, her breasts touching his shoulder. When he does not reply, she glances up. The Artist is looking at her closely. From this close she can see the lines that web his face, but also the depth of his eyes, the bright, tragic eyes of a much younger man. "We must be. I have finished the drawing, and told you the tale." His voice is carefully flat, but something moves beneath it, a kind of yearning.

For a moment she hesitates, and feels herself tilting as though out of balance in a high place. Then, uncomfortable with his regard, her eyes stray to the portrait of the Nosehorn, watching from its place on the chair, small eyes solemn beneath the rending horn. She takes a breath.

"Yes," she finally says, "you have and you have. And now there are many things I must do. Mistress will be very anxious at how I have let my work go. She will think I am trying to rise above my station."

The Artist reaches up and briefly squeezes her hand, then lifts himself from his chair and leads her toward the door.

"When I have made my print, I will send you a copy, pretty Marje."

"I would like that very much."

"I have enjoyed our time together. I wish there could be more."

She drops him a curtsey, and for a moment allows herself to smile. "God gives us but one life, Sir. We must preserve what He gives us and make of it what we can." He nods, returning her smile, though his is more reserved, more pained.

"Very true. You are a wise girl."

The Artist shuts the door behind her.

DAVE WOLVERTON

WE BLAZED

Peter: **Dave Wolverton** is the author of several novels, including a *Stars Wars* bestseller. He has also written much short fiction. He lives in Oregon with his family, and his résumé—properly checkered—includes a job as a pie maker. I don't know why that should delight and fascinate me so much, but it does.

Janet: Dave is one of the few people I know who owns—and has actually read—the Mormon book I ghostwrote in one of my hungrier years. He is also one of the few people who doesn't think I'm crazy for living in Las Vegas. Dave is a fine, often "literary" writer, with a fundamental belief in dotting i's and crossing t's, no matter what his subject matter. Those who know him best as a *Star Wars* author would be well-advised to dig deeper. It was his other novels and his short fiction which first caught my attention.

We Blazed

KAITLYN PROMISED TO LOVE ME FOREVER, AND whether that was ten thousand years ago, or a hundred thousand, or more, I didn't know.

One morning three years past I had wakened and begun hunting for her in this strange land, a land where banana plantations were carved precariously from the sodden forest, a land where the chatter of green parrots and peeping of frogs and whirring of insects filled the jungle. Strangely, there were no monkeys; it was as if God had discarded them.

I walked the muddy roads, often passing caravans of men of questionable descent—small men with enormous black mustaches, men too dark to be European, too stocky to be African. They walked barefoot and wore baggy cotton outfits called *tahns,* dyed in solid reds and yellows, yet always the men's attire was so stained by the road as to have faded to an uncertain gray. Their breath smelled of anise and curry, ginger, red pepper and spices too obscure to be named.

As for the women—well, they ran when they saw my skin, translucent and gleaming like pearl. It was an unnatural whiteness, and, like my height, it marked me as someone unique. The immortal.

Sometimes I'd walk into a village, a collection of huts made of mud and sticks, and the women would run, shouting "N'carn! N'carn!" They would grab their small daughters and flee, afraid that I would rape four-year-old girls. The men would draw short, curved daggers from their belts and try to herd me, drive me from the village.

Sometimes they'd cut me and watch disbelieving as the wounds closed. The first time it happened, when a young father tried to gut me, I'd been frightened, and the dagger had hurt terribly in my belly, an invasive cold chunk of metal. I'd thought it would kill me, so I'd pulled the dagger from my attacker's hand and concentrated on giving him as good as I got, slicing him from navel to sternum, then twisting the blade into his heart. The blood had poured over my fists, and the smelly little man coughed and slumped forward, his wrists limp over my shoulders, like a drunkard who'd passed out while dancing in my arms.

I'd thought it would feel good to repay him for his hospitality, and if I'd died then, I'd have felt justified. But immediately after the attack I looked down as my own wounds painfully began to close. The cries of the dead man's children, the wailing of his wife, followed me from the village that day, and haunted me for many months to come.

I never took vengeance on one of them again.

For a long time, I hid from the people. But outside their huts at night, I'd sit in the darkness and listen, until I learned some of their language.

I knew my name, Alexander Dane, though my friends, when I still had friends, used to just call me Dane. But I did not know *what* I was. Sometimes I imagined I could sense vague roots to these people's words. They called me N'carn, and I imagined I was the *incarnate* or the *reincarnated,* some being they had known before, reawakening into this age. But if that were the case, why did they fear me?

I could not be killed. If I did not eat, I felt pangs of hunger but did not starve. Could I be a ghost?

Once I found an ancient city that might have been New York. Dark men there were mining the junkyards, where they'd hit veins of aluminum mingled with other metals. I saw crumpled Coke cans, flattened and fused by age, interspersed with ancient bricks and liquid RAM casings and Barbie dolls. But the miners there were digging at two hundred feet.

How many years had passed? A million? I had no memory of any interval between some vague date near 2023 and the time that I woke to begin searching for Kaitlyn. The earth had warmed, and that could have happened in only a few centuries, but some mornings the sun seemed to rise redder and colder than I remembered. How many millions of years would it take for the sun to grow cold? Had it been that long, or was I imagining things?

Did it matter? Kaitlyn promised to love me forever. If ten thousand years had passed, or a million, it should not have mattered.

Or could it be that these differences in the world were not really exterior to me? Could the difference really only be in the way this new body perceived things? On nights when the myriad stars threatened to set the heavens afire, or on days when the wildflowers in the meadow smelled too alive or that the perfect blue summer sky was not white enough on the horizon, I imagined that perhaps I was only dreaming, or that I was living someone else's dream of Earth.

In the spring I found the river that would lead to Kaitlyn—a muddy, churning flow that carved its serpentine way through broad flatlands. The natives called it the Ki'tack River, but it could have been the Congo or Mississippi, and I would not have been able to tell.

I only knew that such a mighty dark river would have to lead to her.

When Kaitlyn and I were young, we'd sung together in a band called Throat Kulture. Our first big hit had been called "River of Darkness," and as I saw the Ki'tack, the chorus began playing in my head:

(Me) "There's a place, we're all going to . . ."
(Kaitlyn) "River of Darkness,"
(Me) "And I'll be waiting, there for you.
        You can't escape, a love so true"
(Kaitlyn) "River of Darkness"
(Me) "Yes, I'll be waiting, there for you. . . ."

So I followed the straight road that paralleled the river. Along the muddy track, I'd often find crossroads leading to small villages. One never knew how far back into the jungle such villages might be—twenty yards, or twenty miles. And I could not tell who might live in the villages. There were no signs in the sense that we use. The art of writing words had been forgotten by these people.

But there *were* signs, of a sort, to show who would be in each village. At the crossroads, villagers would pile mud, which over the decades would bake in the sun, and in this mud would be many small cubbyholes. A cubbyhole might contain a parrot feather tied to a twig, telling the traveler that in this village lived a man named Parrot Feather married to a woman named Twig. I had no idea what name Kaitlyn would use, so I personally checked almost every village.

One hot afternoon, I stepped off the road to let a small caravan pass. The sun had dried the road to dust over the past several weeks, and the elephants in the caravan were churning the dust as they walked. One reached down with its trunk and threw dust onto its head to ward off the stinging flies—much to the dismay of its mahout, who began cursing the elephant and beating its ears with a stick.

As I stepped from the road, I noticed an unpromising crossroad that led to a small village. The village road was covered with short grass, attesting that it was seldom used. The village would be far away, I suspected. I glanced at the cubbyholes with their pieces of obsidian, dried beetles, and salamanders carved from wood. The village marker was situated under a fig tree, its leaves dusty and denuded from the passing elephants, but on the far side of the tree, away from the road, were a few sweet figs. My stomach was tight from hunger, so I pulled down a fig, brushed the dust from it, and began to take lunch, when I noticed something strange.

On the bottom of the village marker, near the back, was an ancient seashell—a snail shell that might have been the yellow of dawn at one time. I'd been traveling upstream for a year, and I was a thousand miles from the ocean. It was unlikely that anyone would have been named Yellow Seashell so far inland. I knew it was hers. Kaitlyn loved seashells, and her favorite color was yellow.

I stepped under the trees and found that the buzzing of stinging flies was louder there. For a long time I followed the ancient trail through a boggy track, and once I stopped while a pair of wild water buffaloes lowered their black heads and stared at me, as if to charge. Sometimes I heard alligators croaking in distant pools, but other than that, there was little sign of life in the deep woods.

As I hiked throughout the afternoon, storm clouds swept overhead, bringing the first rain in days. After five miles, when I came out of the jungle, I found the road following the broad river, its waters almost black under dark skies. A rooster crowing and the grunts of pigs alerted me when I neared the village—that and the fact that the road was heavily trampled here.

But just before I reached the village, I found something that disturbed me. Beside the road, lying in the mud, was an ancient statue carved of granite.

It wasn't a big statue—perhaps only four feet tall. But it caught my attention because it was a statue of me, my face twisted in a grimace, squatting, naked, holding over my head a huge twisted horn, as if I were in the act of impaling someone with it.

I went to the statue, grunted as I hefted it upright. The left side of the face was covered in black mud and rotted leaves, but I felt sure that it was me. My face had never been twisted so savagely in rage, but everything else—the size, the musculature—all was mine except for one thing: the figure had balls but no penis.

The statue was old. Stone had flaked off the face, as

if it had been lying here for millennia. At the feet of the statue were three rotting eels among the leaves, a gift left for some dark god.

I went into the village.

A circle of perhaps twelve huts squatted beside the riverbank. Since it was raining, everyone was inside. A small herd of black-and-white pigs rooted beside the smoking remains of a cooking fire. A pole above the fire held the carcass of a giant blue catfish, four feet long, waiting to be cooked. A family of red chickens nervously stood in the lee of a hut, pecking for grain by the villagers' grinding bowls, waiting for the last drops of rain to fall.

One of the huts was much larger than the rest—perhaps sixty feet in diameter. I knew that this must be the headman's hut; it was enormous. Smoke poured from the smoke hole at its top, and from inside I could hear singing.

There were no electric guitars or keyboards in this world. Some musicians struck up a tune on conga drums, panpipes and hand harps. A woman began singing in the nasal local dialect. It was Kaitlyn.

My heart began beating hard, and my mouth felt dry. I wondered if Kaitlyn would look the same, or if she would be wearing another body. Had she and I somehow been reborn, to meet in this new world? That is how I felt, reborn. But aside from the unnatural luster of my skin, the way I glowed like starlight on water in the darkness, I looked the same.

I recalled when I'd first met Kaitlyn singing in a little club in Soho, a willowy eighteen-year-old woman going on fifty, with long blond tresses.

She'd been a slave to designer drugs like Ecstasy, VooDew, and Scythe, an idealist who couldn't handle a fucked-up world, so she fucked herself up whenever she could. But that girl could wail.

She strutted across stage to the dizzying pyrotechnics of an AI-mastered light show, a hologram of a red phoenix tattooed to her forehead, and you could feel the blaze from her, a thrill like electroshock.

We'd shared the quest for fame. For awhile it seemed we'd made it. But when the road wore us down, Kaitlyn quit blazing and started wearing greens and blues. We moved to the 'burbs, bought a house with a big backyard. Then I woke up here.

I walked into the headman's hut. It had a dark corridor with walls made of tapestries that smelled like hemp, painted in bright batik patterns of ivory and emerald.

At the end of the hall was a large open room, with a couple dozen people sitting round a fire. Firelight flickered yellow on their faces, and I smelled the local bread cooking beside the fire, bread made with several kinds of grain, along with dried garbanzo beans, and flavored with cumin and other spices.

In the shadows at the far side of the room, several men and women were playing pipes and drums. Naked children danced around the fire while Kaitlyn wailed for them.

She stood between me and the fire, with her back to me, swaying gently, crooning in the local gibberish. The children gazed up at her, dark eyes shining with adoration.

Kaitlyn looked much the same, long wheat-blond hair curling down over her thin hips, bones protruding slightly through her forest-green *tahn*. Only her skin was different—shining and opalescent, like mine. As if light had been captured in her pores and were leaking through.

The villagers watched her sing with rapt attention, and none noticed me until I was right behind her, then one woman gasped and pointed at me.

I didn't know quite what to say, so I walked up behind Kaitlyn and whispered in her ear, "Hey, babe, it's me, Dane," then kissed her temple above the eye.

Kaitlyn turned and stared at me half a second in disbelief, then slapped my face.

Around the room, men drew daggers while women grabbed their daughters and hid. The room filled with shouts and whirling bodies. Kaitlyn twisted from my arms and tried to cross the room, calling "Abim! Abim!" It was the masculine form of the word, "Water," and only the feminine form was ever used when speaking about water, so I knew she was calling a man. In her haste, Kaitlyn tripped over a small boy and fell into the lap of a woman who played the harp.

But from the darkened corners, a man bellowed and charged. I saw at once that he was large—skin of dark brown, black hair cascading over his shoulders. Unlike others, he did not wear a *tahn*. Instead he wore short pants of white cotton, a vest of cream-colored silk that exhibited the rippling muscles of his arms and chest. I knew at once that he was rich, for he wore sandals of thick leather in a style that only the richest people affected.

He lunged into the light, and I gasped. He was at once the most handsome and powerful man I've ever seen—a face with strong lines, gray eyes glimmering like dark ice. And as he rushed at me, he pulled a scimitar from a sheath at his side, whirling it over his head.

He stopped between me and Kaitlyn, and I heard women weeping and shouting "N'carn!" The dark men at my back were growling and had pulled their knives, began circling me, yet they all stayed away more than an arm's length, as if afraid I would charge them.

There were nine of them, and one man kept dancing in close, as if wanting to be the first to score. He kept shouting in his local dialect, "Kill it! Kill it!"

But Abim shouted, "No, you cannot kill him! Stay back!"

The little man danced in with his knife, a gleaming blade shaped like a horn. I didn't want to fight him, but I also knew that if he scored on me, it would hurt like hell.

He lunged and struck a shallow gash on my calf. There was a time when I'd thought that as a star, I might need to know some self-defense just to hold "my people" off. I remembered enough from my tae kwon do classes to kick him in the face. Blood spurted from it, and he staggered backward, little worse for the encounter.

"It is me you want!" Abim shouted at me dangerously. "I am the one who desecrated your altar! It was *I* who made the women quit leaving sacrifices! Your fight is with me!"

I'm sure he thought he was being noble as hell, but I frankly didn't give a damn who'd desecrated my altar. Still, his shouting made the other men stop, as if willing to let me and Abim battle it out. They seemed relieved, as if believing that once I'd ripped off Abim's head, I might somehow be appeased enough to let them alone.

The problem was, I didn't really want to fight. I'm just a rocker with a colonial-style house in the Jersey suburbs.

I asked Kaitlyn in English, "What the hell is going on here?"

She stared at me, uncomprehending. "He's come for me!" she shouted in the native dialect. Abim's eyes widened.

"No!" Abim seemed unwilling to admit that I'd want Kaitlyn. "It is a sacrifice he wants—a virgin! One of us must give him a daughter!"

"Samat!" I shouted at him like a trader in the marketplace. *"K'tarma Kaitlyn!"* No, I want Kaitlyn, and I pointed at her.

Abim glanced down at Kaitlyn, still sprawled on the floor behind him. She gazed up at him lovingly, imploringly, and Abim charged me and swung his sword.

His scimitar arced gracefully, and as the fire flickered on the blade, it glinted yellow like the sunrise. It hit my neck, and I felt the smallest jolt as blade cleaved through bone, then I was tumbling backward, my head slamming down then bouncing on the dirt floor with a mind-numbing thud.

My head rolled to a man's dirty bare foot, landed in a platter of bread, and I was looking up. I tried to blink crumbs from my eyes, and the man above me looked down and screamed in horror, kicked at my face.

I could not die then, no matter what they did to me.

For the next several moments, I was kicked across that floor by one man, then another, all of them too terrified to stop.

I shouted for mercy, but since I had no lungs, no

words came from my mouth. Once I saw Abim hacking the arms from my headless torso, but mostly I saw only darkness, the spinning room, the callused brown toes kicking at me.

At last my head stopped rolling across the floor, and Abim peered down at me, asking "Are you dead yet, demon?"

I said nothing, was afraid to move my lips or blink.

"No, he's not dead," Kaitlyn said. And she rushed near me. She huddled at Abim's side touching his shoulder hesitantly, reassuringly.

Two little girls with dark hair came to Kaitlyn. They were both old enough that they wore clothes. The youngest was probably six, the older ten. They clutched at the forest-green cotton leggings of Kaitlyn's *tahn*. "Mother, mother?" they cried in terror.

Kaitlyn held them tenderly and whispered, "Hush, my little orchids." And as I saw the girls look up at her with their angelic faces, a sense of regret washed through me. Their hair was a muted brunette—Abim's dark black mingled with Kaitlyn's blond. But the girls' dark eyes shone like obsidian, nothing of Kaitlyn in them.

Kaitlyn had sometimes said she wanted children, but I'd never taken her seriously. At first, when we were new as a group, just out on the road, I'd pointed out that a lot of Throat Kulture's popularity was based on her looks. She looked really blazing, and it wouldn't do to have her belly hanging out over her pants. So we'd waited.

Later, when we moved to the 'burbs, she sometimes talked softly about "doing the family thing," but so far, I hadn't been able to give up my dreams of going back on tour.

But seeing her, there with the girls, Kaitlyn looked so natural as a mother, so at peace, that I felt as if I had done her wrong.

"How can the demon not be dead?" Abim asked Kaitlyn, squatting over me. He held his sword tightly, gripping its black hilt with both hands.

"A new body will sprout from its head, in time. You cannot kill such a creature." Kaitlyn whispered at his back. She spoke with obvious authority, for like me, her skin shone with her immortality.

"And what if I hack the head in two?" Abim asked.

"The demon will grow back—in a week, a month. You cannot kill it."

"N'carn," Abim intoned his name for me reverently, watching me with wide, superstitious eyes.

"Yes, the unicorn," Kaitlyn whispered. Her eyes went unfocused, reflective, as if she were looking deep into her past. "I remember him. . . ."

My heart leapt. Yes, it's me, Dane, I wanted to say. If she remembered me, I thought, then she would remember that she'd loved me, that she'd promised always to love me. But as quickly as the moment of reflection had begun, it ended, and she looked away, as if I were only a stranger she'd heard of long ago.

Abim grunted, satisfied for the moment that I could not harm him. "It is my fault he is here," he apologized to the others. "I threw down the altar. Perhaps if we give him a sacrifice, he will leave. A virgin. He likes virgins?"

Kaitlyn's nostrils flared wide with fear. "Yes, yes, it likes virgins. . . ."

A vague memory stirred in me of a time when I'd first been dating Kaitlyn. She hadn't joined the band yet, had in fact only come to listen to us play in the basement of a friend's bar. He'd let us practice there mornings, as long as we gigged his place once a week.

Our lead guitarist, Scott Walsh, was jamming just for Kaitlyn, thrashing on stage, as if he had ten million fans in the basement. He could really crank that ax, almost as good as me, but I couldn't play lead and sing lead at the same time, so I stuck to the base. Anyway, Walsh always felt that I was competing with him for the ladies, so he told Kaitlyn that we'd have to quit practice early because I had a date.

Kaitlyn had smiled at me a little, and said, "Oh, he's gonna thrill one of his fans?"

And Walsh had laughed, "Only if she's a virgin. Dane likes his fans nice and tight."

I let the comment slide, and a few months later, while he was out riding his Harley, Walsh was so stoned that he hit a semi and got his head siphoned through the grill. But six years later, after we'd been married for four of those years, Kaitlyn and I made love on the sofa one night, and afterward Kaitlyn surprised me by asking, "What did Walsh mean when he said you only liked virgins?"

Her voice held accusation, as if she'd secretly believed over the years that Walsh and I had had some kind of contest, popping virgins. I said, "Man, I don't ball my people," and it was true. After I met Kaitlyn, I'd never thought twice about another woman, but she knew that I wasn't being totally honest. I'd sampled my share of sweet meat.

"Who will we sacrifice?" Abim asked. "Arrota? N'kot?" he named some girls.

"They're too young," Kaitlyn said. "Besides, what mother would let that monster have them? How can we decide to give another mother's daughter to such a creature?" and Abim looked back mournfully at his own daughters.

"W'karra?" he said. The oldest of Kaitlyn's two little girls trembled—she could not have been more than ten—and she clung to Kaitlyn's leg.

The little girl looked up at her mother and father dutifully, as if willing to give her life if they asked.

"But how will the monster rape her, without a body?" Abim wondered aloud. His brows knit together in concentration, and he glanced at me.

"No!" I mouthed the word, trying to tell him that I did not want the child.

Abim's eyes grew wide, frightened. "Look, it talks!" he shouted excitedly, and he urged Kaitlyn and the others closer. "It does not want a virgin!"

"Kaitlyn," I mouthed. "I want Kaitlyn!" But Abim seemed not to understand. In truth, I believe he knew what I was saying, but he did not want to admit it to me, at least not in front of Kaitlyn.

"I do not understand you, demon," he said. And he took my head, turned it over on the dirt floor so that my face was toward the floor.

He sat down with his people to hold a counsel. "What should we do with this demon?" Abim asked.

"Kill it! Kill it!" they all said. "Get rid of it!"

"But how?" Abim asked. "My wife is immortal, like it is. She says it cannot be killed. Given time, a new body will grow from the head!"

"Burn it!" someone said.

"No," Kaitlyn answered. "You cannot kill the demon with fire. Even if you cook it whole, it will grow back, when the fire cools."

"Bury it then!" someone else said. "Dig a deep hole, and bury it under rocks."

"And what then?" Kaitlyn asked. "The body will grow back, and it will dig its way up from the grave."

"Feed it to the alligators," someone suggested, but his voice faltered when Kaitlyn's expression showed that this, too, would not work.

"I know what to do," Abim said at last. "I will keep the head nailed to a post, and each day, when a new body is growing, I will prune it off again."

There was mumbling approval from the others within the hall, and I feared they would indeed take me then, keep me nailed to a post forever.

But someone said, "And what if jackals come into the village at night and drag the head away? What then? The demon will simply come back and take vengeance on us all!"

That news seemed to sober them, until at last Abim said. "Then I will cook him in a fire that never cools."

"And where is that, my love?" Kaitlyn asked.

"Northwest of here—a three-day run—in the pool of fire at Flaming Mountain."

"The volcano?" Kaitlyn asked. "Even that might not kill him, I fear. In time, even volcanoes cool."

"But that will be ten thousand years from now," Abim said. "And even if it does cool, what then? The demon will be buried deep under rocks. How will it claw its way out?"

"Would it work?" Kaitlyn asked, a thrill of hope in her voice. There were grunting murmurs of assent from the wild men who crowded around my head.

It was the best plan they could devise. So Abim fetched a hemp sack that had once held oats, and he shoved my head in, blocking out all light. While his people prepared food for his journey, Abim dropped my head outside the hut.

I heard Kaitlyn whimpering, talking to him tenderly, asking him to return soon. Never had Kaitlyn spoken to me with such desperate yearning. She told him that she loved him, that she would be waiting for him and would not sleep until he slept beside her.

I heard Abim kissing her passionately while his daughters cried in the background, full of concern.

A pig found the sack I was in, came and began grunting, sniffing at its contents. It nudged me over, and Abim shouted to startle the pig. The pig squealed and ran off. Abim swung the sack over his back, and in moments we were bouncing along the road as Abim ran through the jungle.

I began growing again in the sack. I did not grow quickly, as I did when someone merely cut me. Instead I felt it first as a tingling, a little nub at the base of my neck where the tailbone began to poke through my scabby neck wound. In a few hours, the healing began to quicken, a powerful burning sensation in four quadrants as hands and feet began to take form.

By nightfall, I could move my stubby little fingers, and wiggle my toes. Almost I could maneuver around in the sack, but my head vastly outweighed my body.

So it was that Abim must have noticed the new shape of the sack, for just after sunset when he stopped to make camp, he pulled me out of the bag, looked at my new torso.

He laid me on the ground. I tried to twist over and crawl off, but Abim merely turned his head aside in disgust and sliced off the new growth of body. When he finished, he pulled it away—the torso of an infant—and hurled it into the tall reeds outside camp.

Abim set my head on a fallen log, barkless and bleached white with age, and he stared at me as if afraid to look away while he ate a brief dinner of jerky and spiced bread.

"I do not hate you, demon," Abim muttered darkly, and I watched him, a man as handsome and muscular as any I've ever seen, and I thought about him rutting with Kaitlyn, the woman who'd promised to love me forever. At that moment, though he did not hate me, I hated him.

"I would not cut off your body, if it would not grow back," he apologized, as if suggesting that by force of will I could stop regenerating myself. He tore at his jerky with strong, even teeth, and said softly, "I would feed you if I could, but now you have no belly to fill."

He stared at me, and I mouthed words begging him to let me leave, to let me walk away and never return. Whatever Kaitlyn had once felt for me, it was over, promises aside. I wondered again if I were a ghost on some eternal quest for the woman I loved. If I were, would my spirit now rest?

Abim watched my lips move, but became frustrated. "I cannot tell what you are trying to say!" he shouted. He went on the far side of the fire, threw himself on the ground.

I lay watching him. Abim tried to sleep, but he fretted and kept rolling over, eyeing me.

I heard the snarling and chuckling of hyenas in the brush, tearing at an infant's body.

At last Abim fell asleep, and a new body began to emerge and take shape on me. Testing, I reached out with tiny hands, kicked with infant's feet.

I managed to fall off the log without waking Abim, and I began crawling to him. My small lungs would not let me talk, not with my large esophagus and voice box, but I hoped that if I got close enough, I would be able to whisper to him, plead with him to let me go.

I worked at reaching him for a long hour, till a silver fingernail of moon rose, gauzy through the high, sheer clouds. I was only halfway across the camp.

Abim woke, howled in dismay when he saw that I'd been struggling toward him. "What did you think to do, demon?" he accused. "Would you have bitten out my throat!"

He charged me, and, in one vicious swipe, pared away my body, then hurled my head back into his bloody sack, and began loping through the tall grass.

Once, I heard a lion roar in the darkness, and Abim called to it softly, "Hey, my brother, I do not want to be eaten this night. Go away." The lion did not attack. A while later I heard the occasional croak of an alligator, the plop of frogs leaping into deep water. Abim was jogging beside the river, in the darkness.

Abim talked to me incessantly for the next two days. He apologized for what he felt he must do. Five times he pruned away that which grew on me, then hid me in his rucksack.

My presence unnerved him. He could not rest. When he managed to sleep fitfully for a moment, he would waken afterward, complaining that in spirit I had come to him in his dreams. What he believed I said, what troubling commentary I may have given him, I will never know. But I'm sure I will haunt his dreams across the years to come.

I had time to think during those travels. I'd believed that the people of this land referred to me as the *Incarnate* when they called me N'carn. But Kaitlyn had referred to me as the unicorn.

It was a word only she could have known in this land, for it was no longer in these people's vocabulary. Kaitlyn was the only other immortal I'd met. She was far older than the others. She must have given me that title, I realized.

So, some things began to make sense. When I saw Kaitlyn with her daughters, that felt right all the way down to my marrow. Kaitlyn loved children, had wanted them for years.

And her belief that I had specifically tried to seduce virgins—I could see where such memories might come from.

But the statue in the village, the penisless statue of

me holding that strange horn, striking someone with that horn, that unicorn's horn? I couldn't understand that.

And I reasoned that Kaitlyn might have sculpted that statue in ages past. She'd admitted that she remembered me. But where would she have gotten such an image as that shown on the statue? What could I have done that would make her dim memories of me into something so monstrous? And why would she call me "the unicorn"?

I wished desperately to talk to Abim, to question the man. On the morning of the final day, while I still had an infant body, I managed to plead that he would let me speak.

But Abim hacked off my torso, and whispered fiercely, "I know what you want, demon! You came for Kaitlyn. You cannot have her, and I will not listen to you beg!" He shoved me in the sack for the last time.

Later that day, he brought me out into the mountain air. The scent of the sky was sweet with jungle, malodorous with the bite of sulfur. Abim stood on the lip of a volcano, and showed me the pools of burning lava below. Plumes of smoke rose from the ground, and chunks of black rock floated at the edge of the lava, like ice in some fuming drink.

"Here, demon"—Abim shouted, laughing maniacally—"this is where you will stay, stay for eternity! Kaitlyn is mine now!" His hands were shaking, and Abim sobbed. He turned me to face him. His own face was dirty from jungle pollens and dust so that his tears made clean rivers down his cheeks.

I mouthed the words, "Mercy. Have mercy on me." Abim watched my mouth move, his face frozen in horror.

"I cannot have mercy!" Abim said. "Kaitlyn will

always be mine! You are immortal, like her. But this thing, too, you must know: Kaitlyn has loved me forever. She loved me in the beginning of the world, and I do not die like other men. I stopped counting after ten thousand years of life, and that was many, many thousands of years ago. Her love for me has made me immortal, too. So if you come back again, ever—you must contend with me!"

Abim's lips were trembling as he made his threats. Perhaps he feared that in some distant future, it would be me throwing *his* head into a volcano. But I doubted it. I do not really believe he feared death as much as he feared separation from Kaitlyn, the woman he loved.

In that final moment, I decided that I liked the man. The things he was forced to do in order to get rid of me were wounding his soul, which suggested that he was a compassionate man. And he loved Kaitlyn and her daughters, was willing to do anything for them.

And Kaitlyn loved him, more, I realized, than she'd ever loved me.

I hoped they would be happy once I was gone, and if I'd had a voice, I'd have told Abim so.

At last, he took me by the hair and cocked his muscular arm, then hurled me as far as he could. For a moment I lofted over the flowing lava. I looked out above the bowl of the volcano, at skies so blue they hurt my eyes, and I felt the hot thermal winds rising up off the lava.

I was not afraid. I am immortal. And I mouthed the words to Abim, "I forgive. . . ."

All too soon I dropped into the pool of fire. Every inch of skin became a searing pain. I tried to close my eyes, protect myself. I wished to die with all my soul.

Nothing helped, and I seemed to burn for an eternity.

I opened my eyes, cleared them from fog. There was a hot pain at the base of my neck where my neural jacks met the interface to an artificial intelligence owned by a small corporation called Heavenly Host.

I was reclining in a comfortably darkened room in a plush leather chair, the low humming of compressors the only sound. In front of me sat the Heavenly Host AI in a vast glass cryochamber, the brown filaments of its neural net floating like the groping roots of some strange plant in the clear blue gel of liquid memory.

A technician stood at my side, studying my face. "How did it go, Mr. Dane? Did you find out what you wanted?"

I had to let my head clear for a moment. More than three years of memories were jamming in my head. My thoughts had never felt so tangled.

I remembered slowly. I'd come here to Heavenly Host, bringing a memory crystal that Kaitlyn had given me last year on our wedding anniversary. This was one of those places that sold immortality to the dead. By downloading your thoughts and dreams and memories, you could create your own universe in virtual reality, your own heaven, and live there for what seemed like forever.

On our last anniversary, Kaitlyn had given me her download on a gray Mitsubishi memory crystal in a box with black velvet lining, and said, "Now, if I die, you and I can still live together forever. I'll always love you."

I'd thought even then that it was a strange gift. Hell, Kaitlyn is only twenty seven, hardly old enough to be obsessing about death.

"How long was I in there?" I asked, nodding toward the AI, still waiting for my head to clear.

The technician cleared his throat. "Realtime? Less than point-oh-four seconds. Every hundred years is equal to one second, realtime."

I thought about that. It had taken about fifteen minutes from the time that we'd plugged in Kaitlyn's memory crystal to the time that we got my own consciousness downloaded and on-line. I hadn't had a complete download. Instead, I'd asked to go in "cold," not knowing how I'd come to be there. I'd wanted to view Kaitlyn's heaven objectively.

But during that fifteen minutes that it took to do my partial download, Kaitlyn had lived in her VR heaven for ninety thousand years.

The technician shook his head. "I can see by your frown that you didn't get what you wanted. It happens that way sometimes. They're all living at light speed in there"—he nodded vaguely toward the AI, the Heavenly Host—"even more than we're living at light speed out here. They forget things a little slower than we do, but they do forget. It helps give them the illusion, over time, that they really are living forever. Even if they understand at first how they got there, the memory fades. But sometimes things get lost, changed from what we expected, or hoped."

I considered what he said. I don't think that the VR world that Kaitlyn's subconscious created was her idea of heaven. She'd once told me she believed that global warming would turn most of the world into a jungle in the far future, and she expected mankind to breed out racial differences until we were all dark, one uniform color. I think her mind must have played tricks on her, creating the VR world she'd expected rather than one she wanted to inhabit for eternity.

Then again, perhaps her world wasn't far from her ideal.

"No, no, it wasn't a total loss," I tried to reassure the technician. I looked up at the fellow. He was no one to me, just a nerdy, hatchet-faced guy who was charging me a lot of money. But he'd heard of Throat Kulture, said we blazed, and I felt I owed him some explanation.

"Kaitlyn slashed her wrists last night," I said. There was a hollowness in my chest. I didn't want to divulge such private information, but he'd learn about it in the tabloids tomorrow anyway.

"Ah, hell," the tech swore softly. "She okay?"

"Yeah, yeah," I said. "She'll make it fine, but I been thinking, and I couldn't figure it, you know? We've got everything—money, fame, a nice house." I just recalled that we'd been on tour for the last six months, and the band was doing better than ever. That was a memory I hadn't taken into the Heavenly Host with me. "So I just couldn't figure it. But now, I've got some clues."

"Good," he said, a verbal slap on the back, a gesture he was too intimidated to give.

I let him unplug the neural jack at the base of my neck, then got up to go.

"You want me to turn your wife's program off?" the tech asked, gesturing to the AI.

I looked at the mass of neural netting in its blue gel, thought for a moment. It cost a shitload of money to run that program for an hour.

"No," I said, "let it run for the night, give her a couple million years. She's happy in there." And she hadn't been happy in a long time. I'd realized last night, after I first found her bleeding in a tub where the warm water had gone crimson, that she had to have been thinking about this for months. That's why she'd given me the memory crystal for our wedding anniversary.

I took the people tube home, cramped among the unwashed bodies of street punks who stared at me in awe and the clean aloof business class on their commute home from the city. I seldom used public transit, but right now I needed the comfort of warm bodies around me.

And as the tube lurched through its starts and stops, I thought about what I'd learned.

I'd believed that Kaitlyn and I were living our dreams, but after seeing her VR heaven, I realized now that we'd only been living *my* dreams. She wanted something else from life.

I thought about Abim, the man she'd created to be her perfect lover. It stung me that she would make something like him, when she could as easily have re-created me. I thought about the children she wanted, the tours she would throw away.

I wondered at how, in the Heavenly Host, her image of me had become so warped, so distorted over time. Her people had made sacrifices to keep me away, I realized in horror.

And I wondered why she called me the "unicorn." I did not have to look far.

When I got home, I had the house turn the lights on to their brightest, so that all shadows fled from the house. Everything was pristine and glistening white inside.

And I just stood for a moment in the doorway and

looked at the far wall in shock. On the wall just inside our doorway is an old picture of me and Kaitlyn and Walsh, back when Throat Kulture had just formed. It's flanked by some platinum records, with "River of Darkness" on the right.

I hadn't really noticed it in years, but in the picture, I saw that strange pose, the one I had in the statue. Only in the picture I'm holding my guitar upside down and making a jabbing motion, as if to impale my fans. My face is twisted in a grimace. Three really blazing women are spotlighted on the floor at my feet, groping for me on stage, and I realize that there is something sexual, almost pornographic, in my gesture, something I hadn't seen before. At the time, I'm sure that I'd made that gesture innocently, just part of the stage show. But as I looked closely, it was as if my guitar were a giant dildo, and I was jabbing the women, balling them all.

I wet my lips, my heart hammering, and looked up closely at the picture. I reached up and touched it with a forefinger that is almost all callous after years of playing, fingers that can touch but seldom feel. And on the soundboard to that old white guitar, an instrument I'd discarded years ago, I found the faded manufacturer's logo: a blue unicorn.

I went to the fridge to get a beer to settle my nerves, and I wondered how I could get Kaitlyn to love me forever, to dream about me forever, to let her know how desperately I loved her.

Then I called my agent on the vidphone to tell her that Kaitlyn and I were canceling our tours, that from now on we might only release recordings—if we didn't retire completely.

I put on a clean shirt for my visit to the hospital. Before I left the house, I stood for a long minute by the front door under the brilliant lights, listened to the silence.

I stilled my breathing and I thought, this is how the house would sound if Kaitlyn were dead. Empty. Hollow.

Then I breathed again and thought of the sweet dark-eyed daughters of Kaitlyn's dreams. I struggled to imagine what this house would sound like in some future year, when the cheering of crowds at our stage shows had faded from memory.

Sometimes when I compose, I can close my eyes and hear a song in my head before it is ever played. Now, as I listened, I could hear the sound of my breathing multiplied so it became the breathing of several people, a whispering that gradually grew loud enough to fill the void of these rooms. Almost as I stood at the door, I could hear a tumult echoing from the future, the clattering of footsteps tumbling, the giggling of girls laughing with delight as they raced toward me through the living room. A sweet longing came over me as I imagined how Kaitlyn and I would give flesh to these dreams, give flesh to children like unwritten songs waiting to be played on our guitars.

CONTRIBUTORS

Peter S. Beagle was born in New York City in 1939. He has been a professional free-lance writer since graduating from the University of Pittsburgh in 1959. His novels include *A Fine and Private Place*, *The Last Unicorn*, *The Folk of the Air*, *The Innkeeper's Song*, and the illustrated novella *Unicorn Sonata*. When *The Folk of the Air* came out, Don Thompson wrote in the *Denver Post*, "Peter S. Beagle is by no means the most prolific fantasy writer in the business; he's merely the best." His short fiction has appeared in such varied places as *Seventeen*, *Ladies Home Journal*, and *New Worlds of Fantasy*, and his fiction to 1977 was collected in the book *The Fantasy Worlds of Peter S. Beagle*. More recently, he wrote a series of novellas in the world of *The Innkeeper's Song*, which were collected in *Giant Bones*, and a number of his other short stories were collected in *The Rhinoceros Who Quoted Nietzche and Other Stories*.

His film work includes screenplays for Ralph Bakshi's animated film *The Lord of the Rings*, *The Last Unicorn*, *Dove*, and an episode of *Star Trek: The Next Generation*. He has also written a stage adaptation of *The Last Unicorn*, and the libretto of an opera, *The Midnight Angel*.

Peter currently lives in Davis, California, with his wife, the Indian writer Padma Hejmadi.

Kevin J. Anderson and **Rebecca Moesta** have managed to stay married even after writing eighteen books together, including all fourteen volumes of the bestselling

Young Jedi Knights series. Rebecca has also written three solo Junior Jedi books. Kevin's other work includes numerous *Star Wars* and *X-Files* novels, high-tech thrillers written with Doug Beason, and hard science fiction. He has been nominated for several major awards, and is in the *Guinness Book of World Records* for the largest single-author book signing in history. His current project is a prequel trilogy to *Dune*, written with Frank Herbert's son Brian.

Janet Berliner's works include the award winning Madagascar Manifesto series (co-authored with George Guthridge), and the critically acclaimed *Rite of the Dragon*. Her work is most often referred to as socio-political horror or magic realism. She is also the creator and co-editor of *David Copperfield's Tales of the Impossible* and its sequel volume *Beyond Imagination*, as well as *Desire Burn: Women's Stories from the Dark Side of Passion*. Currently, she is co-editing an anthology of mother-daughter fiction with Joyce Carol Oates, and working on several novels, including *Dance of the Python*, the tribal African sequel to *Rite of the Dragon*.

Janet was the 1998 President of the Horror Writers Association and is a member of the Council of the National Writers Association. She lives and works in Las Vegas, Nevada, where reality can be said to be a figment of your imagination.

Charles de Lint is a full-time writer and musician who presently makes his home in Ottawa, Canada, with his wife MaryAnn Harris, an artist and musician. His most recent books are *Someplace to Be Flying* (1997) and a reprint of his classic novel, *Greenmantle* (1998). In January 1999, he will publish *Moonlight and Vines*, a third collection of Newford stories. For more information about his work, visit his website at http://www.cyberus.ca/~cdl.

Karen Joy Fowler was born in Bloomington, Illinois. She now lives in Davis, California, with her husband and two children. Her novel, *Sarah Canary*, won the Commonwealth Book Award for best first novel by a Californian. It has been compared to E.L. Doctorow's *Ragtime*. The *New York Times Book Review* said of it, ". . . Ms. Fowler's prose is beautifully simple and evocative, and the narrative conception itself is a *tour de force*." She has also published *Artificial Things*, a collection of short stories. She has written many short stories which have been published in all manner of magazines and anthologies.

Fowler's most recent books are the feminist baseball novel *The Sweetheart Season*, and the collection *Black Glass*.

In 1982, **George Guthridge** accepted a teaching position in a Siberian-Yupik Eskimo village on a stormswept island in the Bering Sea, in a school so troubled it was under threat of closure. Two years later his students made educational history by winning two national academic championships in one year—a feat that earned him the description as "Alaska's Jaime [*Stand and Deliver*] Escalante" and resulted in his being named one of seventy-eight top educators in the nation. Essays on his teaching techniques have been included in such books as *Super Learning*.

As a writer, he has authored or coauthored six novels, including the acclaimed series *The Madagascar Manifesto* (with Janet Berliner), the third of which, *Children of the Dusk*, won the 1997 Bram Stoker Award for Year's Best Horror Novel. "Mirror of Lop Nor"–one of sixty stories he has sold—was a finalist for the Nebula Award; he also was a finalist for the Nebula and for the Hugo Award for earlier fiction.

George teaches English and Eskimo education at the University of Alaska Fairbanks, Bristol Bay. He enjoys watching opera and videos, being outdoors, and traveling in Thailand with his wife, Noi. "Lop Nor," meant as a story about forced separations, was written while they were waiting for her immigration clearance.

Novelist and public radio host **Ellen Kushner** grew up in Cleveland, Ohio, and attended Bryn Mawr and Barnard Colleges. After graduating from Columbia University, she found a job in publishing at Ace Books as fantasy editor, and then went on to edit fiction at Pocket Books/Simon & Schuster. When she quit her publishing job to write, she supported herself in New York City freelancing as a book-reviewer, copywriter, literary scout, and artist's representative. In her spare time she sang in choirs and folk coffeehouses.

In 1987, Ellen Kushner moved to Boston and began a career in public radio at WGBH-FM, doing live programs of classical, folk, and world music, and hosting and producing innovative national programming for PRI, including The International Music Series, and The Door is Opened: a Jewish High Holidays Meditation.

Since April 1996, Ellen Kushner has been best known to national public radio audiences as the host of Sound & Spirit, a weekly program from PRI that explores the myth and music, traditions and beliefs that make up the human experience around the world and through the ages. Some people call it "Joseph Campbell meets Ellen's record collection." Sound & Spirit is currently heard on over 100 stations nationwide (http://www.wgbh.org/pri/spirit).

Ellen Kushner's second novel, *Thomas The Rhymer*, winner of the 1991 World Fantasy Award, as well as the Mythopoeic Award, is a fantasy based on British folklore and balladry. Her first novel was *Swordspoint: A Melodrama of Manners*, now hailed as the progenitor of the "MannerPunk" genre of fantasy. Her short fiction often appears in *The Year's Best Fantasy And Horror* (ed. Datlow & Windling) and in the "Punk Elf" *Bordertown* series (ed. Windling). Her short story, "The Fall of the Kings," written with Delia Sherman, was a 1997 nominee for the World Fantasy Award.

With Don Keller and Delia Sherman, she is the editor of *The Horns of Elfland: Stories of Music & Magic* (1997).

Michael Marano was born in 1964, the youngest of nine children. His interest in horror is, therefore, self-evident. His first novel, *Dawn Song*, a continuation of the themes explored in "Winter Requiem," is one of the most acclaimed books of 1998, and has received praise from authors as diverse as William Peter Blatty (*The Exorcist*) and Fred Chappell (*Farewell, I'm Bound to Leave You*).

Marano began studying alchemy and Kabbalah while pursuing a degree in Medieval history at Boston University. After an abortive (and mercifully brief) stab at academia, he held a number of positions, including college writing instructor, apartment building manager, rare book dealer, and Punk Rock DJ.

From 1990 to the present, as "Mad Professor Mike," Marano reviews Horror/SF and Fantasy movies on the nationally syndicated Public Radio program Movie Magazine; his Punk/Heavy Metal style of criticism has been described as "combining the best of *Cahiers du Cinéma* with the spirit of pro-wrestling." In this capacity, Mr. Marano has seen and critiqued no fewer than 400 movies and is now unsuited for almost any other form of employment. Marano currently reports for *Sci-Fi Universe Magazine* and does part-time commentary for the World Fantasy Award nominated publication, *DarkEcho*.

He loves his wife, Nancy Nenno, more than anything else in the world.

Elizabeth Ann Scarborough is the author of twenty-two books and numerous short stories. A Vietnam-veteran nurse, she won the 1989 Nebula award for best novel for *The Healer's War*, a fictionalized account of her experiences in Vietnam. Her most recent books are *The Godmother's Web* and *The Lady in the Loch*. She and her four cats lives in the town on which Port Chetzemoka is modeled. "Port Chet" is teeming with urban deer, coyotes, coons, and the occasional cougar, but alas, no unicorns.

Robert Sheckley was born in New York and raised in New Jersey. After serving with the U.S. Army in Korea, he attended New York University. He began selling stories soon after his graduation, and produced many short stories, which are represented in such collections as *Untouched by Human Hands* and *Pilgrimage to Earth*.

Sheckley's first novel, *Immortality, Inc.*, was made into the movie *Freejack*. His short story, "The Seventh Victim," was the basis for the movie and novel, *The Tenth Victim*. His complete short stories in five volumes were published by Pulphouse Publishing. He has written many novels in the science fiction and fantasy genres. In 1994, he completed three novels with Roger Zelazny—*Bring Me the Head of Prince Charming*, *If at Faust You Don't Succeed*, and *A Farce to be Reckoned With*.

Recently, Sheckley turned in a novelization in the *Babylon 5* series; his most-recent novel is *Godshome*. He lives in Portland, Oregon, with his wife, the journalist Gail Dana.

Dave Smeds, a Nebula Award finalist, lives in Santa Rosa, California, with his wife, Connie, and children, Lerina and Elliott. He is the author of six books, including the high fantasy novel *The Sorcery Within*, and has sold over one hundred pieces of short fiction. The latter have appeared in such anthologies as *In the Field of Fire*, *Full Spectrum 4*, *David Copperfield's Tales of the Impossible*, *Return to Avalon*, *The Shimmering Door*, *Sirens and Other Daemon Lovers*, *Marion Zimmer Bradley's Fantasy Worlds*, *Prom Night*, and *Warriors of Blood and Dream*; and in such magazines as *Asimov's Science Fiction*, *The Magazine of Fantasy & Science Fiction*, *Realms of Fantasy*, *Inside Karate*, and *Pulphouse*.

After its initial appearance in the hardcover version of *Peter S. Beagle's Immortal Unicorn*, his novelette "Survivor" reached the preliminary Nebula Award ballot and was reprinted in *Best New Horror 7*.

Dave's work, called "stylistically innovative, symbolically daring examples of craftsmanship at the highest level" by the *New York Times Book Review*, has seen print in over a dozen countries.

Before turning to writing, Dave made his living as a graphic artist and typesetter. He holds a third degree black belt in Goju-ryu karate and teaches classes in that art.

Somtow Papinian Sucharitkul (S.P. Somtow) was born in Bangkok and grew up in Europe. He was educated at Eton College and at Cambridge, where he obtained his B.A.

and M.A., receiving honors in English and music. He has published more than twenty-five adult and children's novels and much short fiction. He made his conducting debut with the Holland Symphony Orchestra at age nineteen, has since conducted, among others, the Cambridge Symphony Orchestra, and has been a director of the Bangkok Opera Society. He writes and directs movies, among them a gothic-punk adaptation of *A Midsummer Night's Dream* starring Timothy Bottoms.

Recently, Somtow handed in the long-awaited sequel to *Vampire Junction*, *Vanitas*, to his publishers. His semi-autobiographical *Jasmine Nights*, published in 1994 by the British literary publishing house Hamish Hamilton, will be made into a fourteen-million-dollar motion picture, filmed entirely in Thailand, by AFFS. It has just been published in the U.S., and has received astonishing praise on both sides of the Atlantic.

Somtow's forthcoming writing projects include a new literary novel, a short story collection from Gollancz, *The Pavilion of Frozen Women*; and a fourth young adult novel, *The Vampire's Beautiful Daughter*.

Melanie Tem's novels are *Prodigal* (recipient of the Bram Stoker Award for Superior Achievement, First Novel), *Blood Moon*, *Wilding*, *Revenant*, *Desmodus*, *The Tides*, *Black River*, and, in collaboration with Nancy Holder, *Making Love* and *Witch-Light*.

Several dozen of her short stories have appeared in anthologies and magazines. She has published numerous nonfiction articles.

Tem also was awarded the 1991 British fantasy award, the Icarus for Best Newcomer.

A former social worker, she lives in Denver with her

husband, writer and editor Steve Rasnic Tem. They have four children and two granddaughters.

Tad Williams lives with his wife Deborah, their son Connor, and three astoundingly useless cats in the San Francisco Bay Area, although they still return to London every now and then when sunshine and actual retail service get to be too overwhelming.

Tad is currently working on *Otherland* (a four volume novel) and other projects for film and television. His books are published in twenty or so languages, and on many of the known continents. Tad is busily researching the laws of publishing and copyright for various unknown continents as well.

Dave Wolverton began working as a "prize-writer" in college during the 1980s, and quickly won several literary awards. He first hit the bestseller lists in science fiction with his first novel *On My Way To Paradise*, which won the Philip K. Dick Memorial Special Award as one of the best SF novels of 1989.

His novels *Serpent Catch* and *Path of the Hero* also received high acclaim. *Star Wars: The Courtship of Princess Leia* placed high on the *New York Times* and *London Times* bestseller lists, and was soon followed by the highly successful, *The Golden Queen* (1994). Dave's novel, *Beyond the Gate*, was released in hardcover in the summer of 1995.

Dave has also published short fiction in magazines such as *Asimov's* and *Tomorrow*, and in numerous anthologies.

In 1992, Dave became the Coordinating Judge for the Writers of the Future contest. Among other things, he edits their anthology and teaches at their workshops. He has been a prison guard, missionary, business manager, farmer, a technical writer and editor, and a pie maker. He currently lives in Utah with his wife and children.